"How many girls have y[...]

Ritz slanted a long-lashe[...]

"Not enough. Do you w[...] asked.

"No!" All of a sudden, Ritz was staring again at his wide, sensual mouth and wondering what it would feel like on hers.

"Are you sure about that?" He twisted the key and punched on the radio. His fingers tapped on the dash to the salsa beat. "How about we get out and dance?"

"Here?"

His hand brushed her cheek. Electricity sparked through her. She shook her head and he laughed. The shade of the live oaks seemed to wrap them in darkness as they sat there. Beyond his chiseled profile the world was bright, the grasses high and brown, the sky cobalt-blue. And yet being in the darkness with him held more mystery and appeal than anything.

Reaching across her lap, Roque took her hand in his, startling her. When he kissed her fingers, one by one, unfolding them, she burned and ached all over.

"Come on, Ritz, let's enjoy being outlaws together," he whispered in a velvet, low tone that was as fascinatingly beautiful as the rest of him.

The two girls were riding bareback. Ritz's sturdy, sun-

ANN MAJOR

Marry a Man who will Dance

ISBN 1-55166-956-0

MARRY A MAN WHO WILL DANCE

Copyright © 2002 by Ann Major.

Visit us at www.mirabooks.com

Printed in U.S.A.

I dedicate this book to my beloved mother, Ann Major, whose only advice on the subject of marriage was "Marry a man who will dance."

Acknowledgments

We make plans. Then real life happens. So it was with this book. I had a vision. Then I wrote something entirely different. During desperate creative moments when I struggled to see my way clear, several people held my hand.

First, I must thank my editor, Tara Gavin, for all that she always does and does so well. All of my books are better because of her. Next, I must thank my husband, Ted, for his infinite patience. My agent, Karen Solem, was extremely helpful. I would like to thank Dianne Moggy and Joan Marlow Golan, as well.

Kay Telle and Cathy Mahon helped me with the horse research by lending me books and letting me visit their horse barns and cherished horses. Dick and Ann Jones are always helpful when it comes to ranching. Geri Rice helped with the completed manuscript and Lydia Suris with the Spanish.

Prologue

Beside the fire, as the wood burns black,
A laughing dancer in veils of light,
Whose dance transforms the darkness to gold

—Adu Abd Allan ben Abi-I-Khisal

Prologue

Houston, Texas
April, 2001

The Harley roared and bucked and writhed under his muscular thighs as wildly as a fresh border whore. And since he was half-Mexican and half-Anglo, and oversexed to boot, Roque Moya was just the man to know.

Not that anyone in Texas called him Moya. Here he was Blackstone, a name he hated, a name most people hated. But not nearly as much as they feared it. His father had seen to that.

The stripes that divided the interstate lanes blurred into a fluid white line flying beneath his wheels. His thickly lashed eyes flashed on the speedometer. One hundred and ten.

He was in too big of a hurry to slow down.

Only when he passed the world famous R.D. Meyer Heart Institute on the outskirts of Houston a few miles later, and the traffic began to thicken, did he use his left foot to gear down.

Fury knotted his gut.

Don't think about her!

Cities. It was cities he hated. They always seemed like filthy jails. Even up here in *el norte,* on this side of the border where they were supposed to be safer, cleaner, and more respectable, they were still prisons.

Especially this city which happened to be where his once rich daddy had made himself so notorious by manipulating juries he despised with his well-told lies.

She lived here. She'd married another man and *hidden* from him here.

His black leather glove gripped the throttle with a vengeance. Thoughts of *her* up ahead in addition to the soaring speed of his bike gave him an adrenaline rush.

He had a funeral to get to. And he was late. A funeral he was very much looking forward to.

Her husband's.

Ritz.

He thought of Ritz at the damnedest times. Thought of what she'd done…and what she hadn't. Thought of her glorious yellow hair blowing in the wind, thought of her blue eyes, how they could change from blue to violet when she got hot for him. She didn't think she was sexy, but she was.

He had to know why she'd crawled into his bed two months ago, why she'd been so eager to sleep with him, her warm, silky body aquiver. She'd been a perfect fit, better than before.

And yet…she'd kept secrets that night.

If it had been half as good for her as it had for him, why had she gone home to her husband?

Since that night, he'd done some research.

Were all the sordid stories Josh had spread about her true?

Border saint? Or border tramp? Or something in between? Someone far more complex? She wasn't a girl anymore. She was a woman.

And a widow now.

Time to find out who she really was.

He'd waited a hell of a long time for his turn.

Thumpty-thump. His big wheels hit cracked pavement. Big piles of dirt, earth-moving equipment, and cranes littered either side of the interstate. Houston seemed to be falling apart. In the shimmering heat beneath a white soupy sky, the downtown skyscrapers undulated like strippers to the frenzied tempo of his bike. On either side of the freeway, office buildings, signs, restaurants, strip shopping centers, malls and huge parking lots whipped by.

Progress? Were they going to pave the whole damn world? For a second or two he felt like Mad Max roaring to his doom on a crotch-rocket across some crazed, futuristic landscape.

He should have noticed the lanes narrowing, the traffic beginning to hem him in. But he was flying past the blinking yellow lights on the orange barrels and all those little white signs that warned the freeway was under construction before he really saw them.

His mind was on Ritz and the telephone call he had received six hours ago on the ranch.

"…dead!"

"But I thought.…"

"Caught us by surprise, too, Roque. Nobody thought he'd go this fast!"

"How?"

"In his sleep…painlessly."

"How's *she*…taking.…"

"…too devastated…to even call *me!* Frankly I'm worried.… And she's sick. A stomach virus or something."

For no reason at all that news had gotten him edgy. "How sick?"

"Threw up everywhere. Been at it a week."

After all she'd been through, nursing a dying man, her formerly rich, famous husband…. His old nemesis, Josh.

So…she'd loved Josh after all. The realization hit him hard.

Ten thousand taillights blazed blood-red. As if on cue, six lanes of vehicles slammed on their brakes all at once.

An eighteen wheeler's trailer loomed ahead like a solid wall of silver.

"Híjole," he whispered, easing off the gas, gearing down, braking so fast, his bike went into a skid.

G-forces hurled his powerful, leather-clad body straight at the mirrored trailer. To avoid slamming into it, he put his bike on its side. Sparks flew off his crash bar across asphalt.

Hanging on and hunkering low, a jagged rock sliced his cheek as he hurtled under the eighteen-wheeler. A second later he shot out the other side across two congested lanes of stalled traffic.

An exhaust pipe blistered his stubbly jaw with a wave of hot fumes. A strip of black leather flapped loose from his shoulder.

But he was alive.

"You, son of a bitch!" a man yelled at him.

Gears ground. Brakes slammed again as Roque skidded to a halt just short of the guardrail.

Only when he was stopped did Roque notice the hole in his black jacket and see the blood oozing from his chest.

He was alive. And so was she. All of a sudden he felt a hell of a lot better.

Sudden longing wrenched his being. He saw violet eyes and golden hair spread all over his pillow.

She was free again and so was he.

He lifted the silver St. Jude medal he'd worn around his neck for good luck and kissed it.

Then he began to shake.

"Shit."

He rolled the throttle and made his rice burner roar.

Where the hell was *her* house in River Oaks?

Ritz Keller Evans was to the manor born. She was a real lady. Elegant. A princess.

At least she was supposed to be.

She patted her stomach uneasily.

Today she'd certainly dressed the part she was pretending to play—that of Josh's wealthy, grieving widow.

She wore a black sheath. No jewels. Not even her gold wedding band. That she'd slipped off her finger, maybe a little too eagerly to be buried along with Josh in his coffin.

Her honey-blond hair was swept back. Her skin was so pale and her expression so reserved, few people dared to intrude upon her grief. Very few of the mourners spoke to her. Her own mother and father had refused to come.

Ritz was a Keller, of the legendary Triple K Ranch of south Texas, the last of the big-time, fairy-tale, ranch princesses. And since Texas is founded on the lie that a kingdom of a million acres, thousands of cows and a lot of oil wells should make any girl happy, the headlines about her fascinated a lot of people.

What if they knew the truth? That she was estranged from her family? That she'd slept with her old boyfriend, Roque, the virile cowboy she'd spent years avoiding. Not just any cowboy, but Roque Moya Blackstone, son of odious Benny Blackstone, whom Roque had gotten disbarred. Roque himself was a self-serving, multimillionaire developer of the impoverished *colonias* she sometimes visited as a nurse. Not so long ago she'd even gotten him fined for building inadequate houses without utilities.

Even if he was Blackstone's son, being half-Mexican, how could he prey on poor Mexican immigrants?

Better question: knowing who and what he was—how could she have crept into his bed and used him as a stud? *Had she hoped lightning would strike her twice?*

Josh's funeral had her second-guessing herself. She was broke. She hadn't known what to do with herself when Josh had lost everything and their marriage failed.

Now all she wanted was *this* baby.

Until Josh's business had failed and he'd left her, everybody had thought she led a charmed life. Then he'd taken her back, only to die fast. Naturally everybody was curious. Naturally she was photographed, written about, gossiped about

She'd believed in love and marriage and children.

In babies.

How strange that Josh, whom she'd known from childhood, the son of a rancher, should have ended up the richest dot.com king in Houston, only to lose everything as swiftly as he'd made it. Still, for five years they'd lived in this castle in River Oaks, Houston's most reputed posh enclave for its millionaires and billionaires, especially those who have a flair for high drama or scandal.

Unconsciously she pressed against her thickening waistline. Just as quickly, her slim fingers fluttered away before Mother Evans or any of Josh's friends could see.

Nobody could know. Not her estranged family. Not Josh's. Not Jet, her long-time girlfriend, nor Jet's saintly father, Irish Taylor.

Nobody.

Especially not the baby's real father.

Not until Josh was properly buried and all his friends and family had gone home; not until Ritz was a long way from Texas and the gossips who watched her every move, would she breathe easily.

This time she had to carry her baby full term. That would be her atonement. What else did she owe *him?*

She was equally determined there would be no nasty rumors or newspaper smears, no counting up of months, no wondering how Josh could have gotten her pregnant in his condition.

Ritz had known she was pregnant even before there had been any symptoms or visible signs. One day she had awakened in this house of death and broken dreams, and opened her window. The sweet peas that climbed her trellis had glowed brighter and smelled sweeter. She had breathed in their fresh fragrance and felt queasy, and she had known.

She'd whispered the name, "Roque," and touched her stomach.

Then she'd shivered and snapped the window shut, realizing he was the last person she could ever tell and the last person she could ever desire.

Fear of *him* made her heart flutter when a very tall, dark masculine figure opened her front door. But it was only Irish Taylor, her father's brilliant foreman. His craggy face was kind as he nodded at her.

Before the baby, Ritz would have said she wished she'd never met Roque Moya Blackstone. Roque, biker, cowboy, horseman, womanizer. Roque, who was way too sexy whether he covered his black hair with a red bandanna and rode his bike or whether he wore his Stetson and sat astride a prized stallion.

Daddy had always said he was the reason her life had gone wrong. She had learned a long time ago, that nothing was as simple or as black and white as Daddy had said.

Sometimes Ritz wondered what would have happened if she hadn't seen him dance by firelight on that long-ago summer night. If some shiftless cowboy hadn't left the Blackstone Ranch gate open the next afternoon. What if the Kellers and the Blackstones hadn't been feuding? And what if Jet hadn't given into temptation and locked Ritz inside "the forbidden kingdom?"

What if Jet hadn't seen Roque naked and stolen his clothes? What if Ritz hadn't been so curious? What if Roque hadn't been so stormily virile and turned-on all the time?

What if he hadn't stolen Ritz's mare, Buttercup?

What if he hadn't put his hands around her waist and lifted her up beside him, whispering in that sexy, velvet voice of his, "Do you want to fly?"

But he had done all those things…and more.

She'd only been fourteen.

Too young to fall in love.

Then he had to go and pretend to get hurt saving her and winning her heart. She'd given him her treasured St. Jude medal, and of course, he'd refused to give it back, and ever since, she'd been caught in the tangle of his dark spell.

Yes, looking back, Ritz could pinpoint the exact moment her life took its fatal turn. It had been the night she'd watched Roque Blackstone dance like a savage half-naked on that beach. The driftwood had burned like fire and gold, and she'd felt something alien and thrilling; she'd come alive and been changed…forever.

And a woman is prone to look back, especially at her husband's funeral—when she's made huge mistakes, especially man mistakes, that seem to grow and compound and haunt, mistakes that keep on rebreaking her heart until she loses all hope of peace of mind and has no faith that she can ever get her life right—at least where men are concerned.

But now she had his baby to think of and plan for.

Just because she made bad choices, did that mean that her entire life was ruined? That she couldn't be a good mother? That she couldn't start over? Somewhere far away from Texas and the scandals of her marriage and the grandeur of the Keller name?

One thing she knew—her heart was broken in so many pieces; it would take her a lifetime to pick them all up. She was through with men and marriage and wealth and fame.

Most of all, she was through with Roque Blackstone, the man who had shattered her as a girl and had the power to shatter her again.

If she could just get through the funeral, she would finally be free to make her own choices.

Until then she had to pretend.

Her lavish ballroom with its elaborate commode, twin fauteuils, and nineteenth century bronzes was so redolent with the cloying sweetness of white roses, Ritz almost gagged. Tables of crab, shrimp, and salmon were piled high. Unthinkingly her hand kept caressing her stomach protectively.

The organist was playing "Amazing Grace." The newspaper obituary had been long and impressive. Everything about the grand River Oaks funeral, even his young widow in black, about whom so much had been written, was just as the deceased had planned it—solemn, stately, regal, in a word—perfect.

As outwardly perfect as the sham that had passed for his life.

His mother, queen for the day in her rustling black silk and showy diamonds, was a whirlwind of decorum and efficiency mincing from room to room in that tippy-toed gait that made Ritz want to scream. Mother Evans's smile was even more fixed and pompous than Josh's had been in his coffin, and she greeted everyone, except Ritz, with moist eyes and a soft, saccharine voice. From time to time she even brushed a nonexistent tear from her well-powdered, parchment cheek.

No wonder Josh had been unable to love Ritz or make her feel as Roque had. But there was no going back, no changing Josh…or his mother. Or herself.

Plump old Socorro knew the truth and sympathized. But then she had always had a soft spot for Roque.

Poor Socorro. Usually, she spent her days ironing upstairs where she could smoke and hide out and watch her *telenovelas*. Today Mother Evans had Socorro racing in and out of the kitchen with heavily laden trays.

The good reverend could not seem to stop with the Bible verses, either.

Therefore I tell you, do not be anxious about your life… Look at the birds of the air…consider the lilies of the field.

One more verse and Ritz was afraid she'd pop out of her black sheath.

Grief? Nerves? Guilt? Terror?

All of the above.

But it was her fear of *Roque* that turned her fingers into claws around her china coffee cup and made her head drum.

What if he did come?

Not much longer…and this day that Josh had so painstakingly planned would be over. Ritz had tried to talk him into a simple ceremony, but he'd selected his favorite Armani suit, saying he wanted his embalmed body to rest in state in the grand salon of their mansion for the whole day before the funeral.

So, all of yesterday, legions of Houston dignitaries had trooped by his polished casket to tell Ritz how wonderful he looked and how exhausted she appeared, poor dear. She'd stood there, enduring hugs and murmured condolences, feeling sicker and sicker, until Josh's owlish, gray face in the casket had started to spin, and she'd fainted.

The dead roses along with the aroma of smoked salmon were really getting to her. So, she moved out of the dining room. Oh, how she longed to breathe fresh air—to never ever come back inside this ostentatious house that she couldn't afford on six acres in Houston's posh heart.

"She's shameless...all that bleached yellow hair," pronounced her busybody neighbor, Mrs. Beasley to Mother Evans as Ritz glided past them.

The scarlet poppy on Mrs. B's big black hat swished back and forth like a conductor's wand.

Mother Evans fixed Ritz with a chilly smile.

"I live next door." The old lady's voice lowered to a whisper, assured that everybody including Mother Evans would stop talking and listen. "The things that have gone on in this house since he married *her*—"

Ritz stared at a vase of roses on the fabulous commode by Riesener that Josh had found in Paris.

"—all those young boys—"

When? Oh when would it ever be over?

One minute Mrs. Beasley was queen of her gossipy little clique.

"—never loved your poor boy—"

But I thought I did.

"—high school sweethearts—"

Socorro let out a muffled cry. The front door slammed open, and a gust of hot, humid air swirled inside along with the tall, lean man clad in black leather.

Noses high in the air, everybody turned to gape at the biker with the windburned face, who stood framed in the rectangular white glare.

Only when he knew he had their attention did he shut the door, and so quietly, his gentleness was hostile. Like a magnet, he pulled every well-bred woman's gaze into his bad-boy orbit.

"Roque...."

A green wave of nausea hit Ritz. Her heart began to

pound like a rabbit's. She didn't know whether to freeze or run.

It wasn't him—

Who else had high cheekbones that looked like they'd been hacked with blades? Who else would show up at a funeral with a red bandanna tied like a skullcap over his head to hold back blue-black hair that was way too long? Who else would sport a silver stud at his earlobe...in River Oaks...on such a sacred day?

Her head buzzed.

Or show so little respect to a man of Josh's stature as to wear a black leather jacket with a four-inch rip at the shoulder?

Roque's black-lashed, green eyes drilled Ritz. The frank sexuality in them turned her insides to water as they had that first night when he'd danced so wildly before that leaping fire.

She fought to look anywhere but at him.

Impossible.

She winced and had to hold herself in check when she saw that there was blood on his cheek and that he was limping a little.

A dozen voices interrupted Mrs. B.

"What's Blackstone doing here?" Irish, Ritz's father's foreman, demanded almost savagely.

Roque's green eyes never left her.

Ritz felt as if electric currents vibrated in the air around her.

When she stiffened, the lines under his eyes tightened imperceptibly.

His skin was so brown. Everybody else was so white.

"Excuse me," she whispered to no one in particular, desperate to get away from him and everybody else's prying eyes.

A waiter held up a platter of lobster and pink salmon

on a bed of parsley and offered to make her a plate. The fishy odor made her throat go dry. Hot little salty drops popped out on her forehead.

She couldn't breathe. ''No…please…just…take it… back to the kitchen…anywhere…''

She fought the urge to be sick and then bent double.

The last thing she saw was Roque. His swarthy, piratical face went white and his green eyes brightened with fierce concern. Then he rushed to help her.

''No…no….''

Tight spasms sent the contents of her stomach roiling up her throat.

The shock of his warm fingers at her waist made her forget everything else.

''Don't touch me!''

''You okay?'' he rasped.

Her cup and saucer smashed to the floor.

She tried to stand up and spin free of him, but his hand locked on her arm like a vise.

She expected his nastiest, most mocking smile.

The tenderness in his rough voice took her breath away as he dabbed at her mouth with his bandanna. His black hair fell in wild disarray around his shoulders.

''Are you going to have a baby?'' His voice was raw; his glittering eyes stark and naked.

No. No. Just say *no.*

But she couldn't. All the lies she should have shouted died in her throat.

''So it's mine.'' Again, his eyes met hers squarely, honestly.

''No. Of course not.'' She fought to loosen herself from his bruising grip.

''You owe me the truth—this time!''

Still, she could only stand there, mute, agonized.

Finally, she pushed against his chest, but the more she

fought, the more like steel his hands and arms and huge body became. She kicked at him and lost her balance, the leather sole of her shoe sliding on the polished floor.

Her hand hit the parquet floor before he could catch her. A sliver of china slashed her arm. Blood pooled.

Somebody screamed.

A woman.

Surely not her.

Then why was everybody staring at her? And why was Roque's brown face spinning like a carved god's in the midst of Josh's shocked friends?

"I've got you now," he said gently. "You've cut yourself."

Livid red dribbled from her arm onto his brown hand and then to the white china chips. He lifted her to her feet.

Jet and Irish, dark figures in black, raced through the fascinated throng of mourners.

"—darling! Your coffee cup—" Somehow Mother Evans and Irish deftly pushed Roque aside.

"—shattered it!" Jet said.

"Your arm! Oh, dear!" Mother Evans began to fuss. "And you were sick again... Your dress!"

"I don't think it's broken," Irish said, examining her arm, and although he was a cowboy, he would be the one to know.

Jet took over. "Socorro, get me a towel."

And still, Mrs. Beasley couldn't stop.

"—Josh was a gardener, grew all his own roses. She cut every one for the funeral, and then forgot to put them in water and let them wither—"

"—too bad she couldn't be faithful—"

"—big money—"

"—*hers*. Keller money, you know—"

"—thought they cut her off—"

Through it all, Roque stared at her. Only at her.

"—all that messy yellow hair. She doesn't look like a border saint to me—"

"—there's too many of them—"

"—shouldn't help them—"

"—overrunning us—"

"—her work at the *colonias* was just her excuse to get away from Josh so she could sleep with all those other men—"

Roque's aquiline features hardened.

Her own nerves clamored as if every cell in her being was tuned to him. Only to him.

She was pregnant…with his child…again. And he knew it.

He wasn't a powerless boy from Mexico, the despised son of his evil rich white father anymore.

Jet had the towel around Ritz's arm now and was squeezing. "It's just a scratch. You'll be fine in a minute."

"Thank you," Ritz whispered brokenly. "I—I think I need to go upstairs and lie down."

"—didn't shed a single tear at the wake," came the unstoppable Mrs. Beasley.

"I did, too!" Ritz whispered. "When I was chopping onions…for Mother Evans's caviar."

Just then Roque's dark, masculine eyebrow flicked upward in sardonic mockery.

"Shh," Jet said.

"I promised Josh I would cry. That's why I chopped…."

"It doesn't matter," Jet said, pulling her gently away from the others.

"No…not that way…" she pleaded when Roque stepped in front of them.

But it was already too late.

"I'll take it from here," Roque said, blocking their path.

His jaw was square, his fierce eyes dark emerald. The cu
on his cheek blazed.

Everybody held his breath, but anyone who expected a
scene was disappointed. Jet stepped meekly aside. And
Ritz let herself be led by Roque Blackstone upstairs to her
bedroom.

Not even Irish attempted to rescue her.

The minute they were in her room Roque closed the
door, his eyes zeroing in on the pile of slashed strips of
black fabric scattered messily all over the floor and then
on her open suitcases spread across her bed.

Ritz went white. Why hadn't she thought? She should
have directed him to any other room. But she'd been too
upset to think.

Roque knelt and lifted a scrap of black wool and then
another of silk and waggled them beneath her nose. "What
the hell is going on?"

"Nothing." She took a breath. "While you amuse yourself, I'll go brush my teeth."

Next he leaned across her bed to finger a lacy bra and
a pair of sheer panties that spilled out of her suitcase.
"Nothing? Taking a trip?"

Her cheeks heated. "Give those to me!" When she tried
to snatch her panties from him, he held on, stretching the
elastic.

"Nice panties," he said. "Fit for a princess." He let
them go with a snap.

"I—I…went to the closet to hunt for a black dress…to
wear today," she began in a rush, wadding her panties,
throwing them at her suitcase.

"Really?" he drawled even as he absorbed every detail
about her, every nuance of expression—reading her.

She turned her back on him and headed to the bathroom
to brush her teeth. She wasn't about to tell him she'd been
like a crazy woman last night. That suddenly she'd been

snipping, first her best black silk, then her favorite black wool jersey, not that she could have worn anything that hot today.

She'd cut and torn—until she had piles of tiny squares that she couldn't cut any smaller. Even then she'd started shredding the remnants.

Hours later, Jet, who was a fancy lawyer now, had found her in the middle of the bed, yanking at the tangles of black threads like a madwoman.

"What are you doing?"

"I can't cry and I'm supposed to wear black. Only I cut up my best black dresses," Ritz had said. "Even my slinkiest black nightgown."

"Well, you wouldn't want to wear a slinky nightgown to a funeral."

Ritz had started laughing and hadn't been able to stop.

When Ritz came out of the bathroom, Roque's face was hard. Every muscle in his body was like a coiled spring. No, Ritz couldn't tell him any of that.

Suddenly she burst out laughing just as she had last night with Jet.

"Get a grip," he said quietly, rushing toward her. "It's a good thing you're packed."

"I don't understand."

"You're pregnant with my child."

"No...."

"A very simple test will prove me right."

"You wouldn't...."

His hard eyes lingered on her belly. "I would do anything to protect my unborn child this time—*even marry you.*"

"I...I'm never ever getting married again."

"Oh, yes, you are. Very soon. To me, *querida.*"

"No!" Blood pounded in her head. This couldn't be happening!

"Why, are you doing this... You...you...don't love me...."

"You couldn't get pregnant by your fancy husband, could you?" he whispered, his low voice dangerously smooth. "Or by any of your other lovers? You needed a stud. Someone you knew for sure could get you pregnant—even if I am a Mexican."

She began backing away from him toward her bed.

"You slept around on him, didn't you?"

Her stiff steps were awkward, but she didn't deny what he accused her of.

"Didn't you?" he demanded in a harsher tone. "I was nothing to you. Then you went back to him so you could pass my kid off as his."

"No...."

"How many others did you sleep with...before you crawled into my bed?"

"That's not what happened and you know it."

He grabbed her, crushing her arms as he pulled her into a tight embrace. "Don't lie to me—ever again."

Her breathing was rapid and uneven.

"You still think you're the *princesa* and I'm the Mexican lowlife."

She couldn't look up at him, not even when his hand lifted her chin and she felt him stripping her with his eyes.

"You used me as a stud— Well, *querida,* this Mexican stallion comes with a stud fee. And that fee is marriage...to me."

"But you don't want this baby. You just want the ranch."

He drew a long contemptuous breath. "Do you ever think about that little grave with all the buttercups on top of it?"

She whitened.

"You're not killing another baby of mine."

His voice was so sharp and hate-filled; his words cut her like blows.

She gasped. "You're crazy."

"Yes, I am," he murmured, drawing in a harsh breath as he pulled her closer. "Kiss me and we'll seal this crazy deal."

"What?"

"We're going to be married. Man and wife. And all that that means."

"I—I just want to be myself. Me. For once. Not somebody's wife. Never yours!"

"You should have thought about that before you used me to get pregnant."

She mistrusted the look in his eyes and the hardness in his voice. But before she could twist free, he crushed her body into his. Even as she fought him, his lips covered hers.

There was domination as well as the desire to punish in his devouring kiss. Always before he'd been so gentle, so infinitely tender.

And yet, even as his mouth ravaged hers, underneath this assault, surely this brutal stranger was Roque. Roque whose bronzed body was made of molten flesh. Roque, who was so fantastic and tender in bed. Roque, who always made love to her for hours. Roque, who turned her into a wanton. Roque, who made her forget why their love could never be whenever he so much as touched her.

The last time they'd made love, he'd kissed every inch of her skin from the hollow beneath her throat to the tips of her toes.

On a shudder she nestled closer to him, opening her lips to his endlessly, inviting his tongue. When she arched, his body tensed. He groaned. In the next breath, he ripped his mouth from hers.

Always, always he made her want and ache and need.

She sighed, starved for more, so much more, and yet hating herself because she felt that way.

"Marriage is the only way I know how to stop you," he said hoarsely, warningly, as if he despised both her and despised himself.

"You can't be serious...about this. About...us."

His fathomless eyes bored into hers. "Are you going downstairs to tell them our happy news?"

When she hesitated, his gravelly tone grew ever more bitter with sarcasm. "Or do you want me to do it?"

Nobody could peel their eyes off the white marble staircase. But like any audience when the stars go offstage, Josh's mourners were getting restless.

"—simply awful...her up there...all this time...with *him*—"

"—today of all days—"

"I really need to pick Chispa up at the groomer's before he closes. If I leave her there too long she always potties on the front seat."

"We can't just go...not without telling *her* goodbye. How would that look?"

"As if *she* cares about that?"

The idle chatter caused a mad rushing in one person's ears.

Then a door clicked open upstairs, and two tall, black-clad bodies appeared on the white marble landing beneath the glittering Murano chandelier and stood there for a long moment, waiting.

The voices and laughter died abruptly and a brittle hush settled over the house. Everybody, especially the observer, was impatient for the final curtain of Ritz's little farce.

Something was dreadfully wrong.

Blackstone's dark hand gripped Ritz's as he dragged her forward to the railing. Her yellow hair had come loose and spilled like butter over her shoulders. Her stricken eyes glowed like dying purple stars in a porcelain doll's face. She was so white. He was so dark.

She was the perfect tragic queen.

Beautiful. Spellbinding.

Even if she was heartbroken, Roque made her come alive. She seemed ablaze.

Had the horny bastard screwed her up there in the bedroom? Did he think the Triple K was already his?

Blackstone. The name alone made the observer's flesh crawl. But a practiced smile masked the wild hatred as well as the other dark emotions that flare so easily in the damaged soul.

Without further preamble, Blackstone said, "We're getting married."

When a look of terror flashed across Ritz's face and she tried to free herself, Blackstone yanked her closer.

His triumphant eyes roamed, meeting the observer's ever so briefly, causing as always that involuntary little shudder of fear before the rage took over.

Had he seen what was there?

No. Ritz wasn't the only one who could pretend.

The smile, the perfect facade was in place.

Nobody suspected. Not Ritz. Not Moya.

Nobody would—until the killings started again.

Then it would be too late.

Book 1

O body swayed to music, O brightening glance,
How can we know the dancer from the dance?

—William Butler Yeats

1

*South Texas
Border ranch lands
1990*

"Do you want to see a naked boy?" Jet whispered, her giggles sly and excited, her breath hot and tickly against Ritz's ear.

Ritz shivered when she remembered the boy, not a boy really, a man, dancing by his campfire on the beach last night. He'd sensed her there in the darkness. He'd moved away from the fire, held out his hand. Her blood had beat like a savage's. She'd wanted to dance, too. But she'd run. Not that she was about to admit last night to Jet.

"First the sheriff's puma! Now a naked boy!" Ritz said offhandedly. "Mother's always saying you're a born troublemaker."

"Oh, she is, is she? But, I'm fun, and you're boring. It didn't take much to talk you into sneaking off to see the puma!"

"There'll be hell to pay when I get home, though!"

The two girls were riding bareback. Ritz's skinny, sunburned legs dangling lazily in front of Jet's more shapely denim-clad limbs as Buttercup clopped along.

Ritz forced herself to think about cats instead of the boy last night, so she wasn't really listening. Pumas, to be exact. Very large pumas that followed the rivers up from Mexico just to eat little girls in Texas. Especially now, 'cause the Mexicans down in the Yucatán were burning off their crops.

Or at least that's what she thought Sheriff Johnson had said.

And ever since they'd left the courthouse in Carita, Ritz's eyes had been fixed on the fence lines on either side of the ranch road the Kellers were forced to share with the Blackstones. Particularly, she watched the Blackstone's ten-foot-high electric game fence. The grass over there was so much higher—high enough for a big cat to crouch in.

As usual, she'd forgotten her hat, a mistake Jet, who was careful of her pale skin and more fragile beauty, never made. If Mother would be mad they'd sneaked off—she'd really be in a rage that Ritz was sunburned.

It was a six-mile ride into town. So, it was a six-mile ride back. Which meant—they'd been in the sun way too long. And since they were nearly home, facing Mother was a growing worry. Not that Mother would punish, but she'd tell Daddy.

So every so often, Ritz forgot about cats for a second or two and licked her blistered lips, but that only made them sting worse.

"I said I know where there's a *cute* naked boy!"

This time Jet's lascivious challenge penetrated.

Did she know about last night?

"You wanna see him or not?"

Ritz burst into nervous giggles. Then she hid her face in case Jet might suspect.

"Not just any boy," Jet persisted.

"Who?"

"Promise you won't tell your mother—"

"Do I ever—"

"Roque Blackstone."

"Oh, God!" Ritz clamped a hand over her mouth. *She knew.* Somehow she managed to make her tone innocent. "Imagine! Just like the puma—Roque Blackstone is up from Mexico!"

Jet lowered her voice. "And his thingy is almost as big as Cameron's."

"No! No way! You're kidding!" Surely she would have noticed that last night.

Cameron was Ritz's daddy's bad-tempered blood bay stallion, the very same horse that had tried to kick her brother, Steve, and four cowboys to death two days ago.

"Well, you'll just have to sneak into the forbidden kingdom and see for yourself...little girl, same as I did. Then you'll know for sure."

More giggles. More pretended innocence. "You didn't sneak over there!"

"Did, too!"

"When?"

"Yesterday afternoon. The day before that, too. He swims there every afternoon...at five."

"Wow! That's just like you...to sneak over there and watch him every day. What if he saw you—"

Ritz remembered the firelight flashing on that strong bronzed arm he'd held out to her before she'd run.

"I was sorta hoping he would."

Jealousy stabbed Ritz's heart. Not that she knew why she felt pain.

They were nearly to the forbidden Blackstone gate. At least it had been forbidden ever since Uncle Buster had lost all his money and shot himself right in front of the funeral home out of consideration for Aunt Pam. Less than a month later his widow had repaid his consideration by marrying Benny Blackstone, the man who had driven him to suicide in the first place.

It was Ritz's lifetime ambition to end the feud between her father and Benny Blackstone and become another legendary Keller lady and have her portrait hang in the family gallery beside her ancestors for the next hundred years.

Only Ritz wasn't thinking about the dumb feud or her saintly Uncle Buster or even her own grand ambition.

She was thinking about the magical boy last night and about Cameron's gigantic *thingy*. Not that the cowboys had called it that. They had a dirtier word, a word Ritz had memorized on the spot. Not that she dared repeat it—ever.

It had taken three trainers and Steve to lead the muscular stallion into the breeding room, and his thingy had nearly dragged the ground. The moment he'd seen the mare in full heat, the aroused stallion had gone wild, kicking and screaming. First off, he'd bitten a hunk out of the mare's shoulder. Then he'd wheeled loose from the trainers, rearing, nearly kicking the stall door to pieces in his rage. He'd even taken a run at Irish, the foreman, Jet's daddy.

When Cameron had mated, the noise in the stall had nearly deafened Ritz. All that male energy and fury and power. All that charged, animal excitement. The stallion had reared and bitten and plunged. Ritz had put her hands on her ears and clamped her knees around the rafter. Eyes wide-open, she'd watched him knock the mare down and mount her. Maybe Ritz would have still been there, shocked as all get-out but excited, too, if Daddy hadn't come in and yelled up at her to get.

The beautiful boy last night hadn't seemed nearly so cruel.

"If...if *he's*... I—I mean if *it's* as big as Cameron's...does it make him mad like it does Cameron... I mean when he sees a girl?''

Both girls got real quiet for a moment as they remembered the blood streaming from the mare's shoulder after the crazed brute had finished with her.

''If Roque had seen you, what would he have done to you?'' Ritz whispered.

The boy last night hadn't fit with the facts that went with him. Roque was Benny Blackstone's oldest son, the bad son everybody said Benny didn't like too much. He'd flunked school last year. His mother was a Mexican, a real Mexican, who lived down in Mexico. She was a Spanish teacher and Benny's second ex-wife. She didn't let Roque come to Texas much. Only sometimes in the summer. His father only invited Roque because Caleb loved him so much.

Roque was supposed to be sulky and hateful whenever he did come. His own father hated him. Everybody said it was because he'd nearly gotten Caleb killed that first visit when he raced with the bulls.

Caleb, the younger, golden brother, was everybody's favorite, especially his father's. Caleb's mother had been Benny's favorite wife, too.

Roque was bad with girls. So bad he got sent home early last summer for something he did with Natasha Thomas in the back seat of her car. Natasha was four years older than he was, and she worked in a bar. Worse—she was Chainsaw Hernandez's girl. Chainsaw was in prison on a drug charge.

''Remember Natasha?'' Ritz added, her stomach quivering as she remembered that wild, haunting Spanish music and Roque's deliberately provocative, sensual dance. He'd known she was there and had tried to lure her into the amber glow of firelight. ''What do you think Roque would've done to you—if he'd seen you?''

Jet smiled so eagerly Ritz wanted to strike her. "He's *so* huge."

"Well, it…it must be awfully heavy. How does he stuff it into his jeans? How does he even walk?"

"If you go see, you'll know for yourself how he stuffs it in, now won't you? But don't let him catch you, or he might stuff…"

Ritz cupped her fingers over her mouth. "You're lying. He's not anywhere near *that* big. You're just boy crazy."

"You will be, too, when you grow up."

If you only knew…

Jet was fifteen. She had curly black hair, blue eyes, and creamy pale skin. Maybe she wasn't boy crazy. Maybe it was like Jet said—boys were just crazy about her.

Who could blame them? She had flair and an exciting personality.

"A flair for trouble," Mother said.

Ritz felt a fresh surge of jealousy along with a secret wish to be just like her friend.

Jet was developed. She had big breasts and a tiny waist and looked way better than any of those skinny models in the magazines. All the other girls at school were still as flat as pancakes—like Ritz. Most of them wore braces, same as Ritz, too. And glasses. Ritz hated her awful wire-rimmed glasses.

"Guess what else?" Jet whispered. "Yesterday I stole his clothes! I watched him run home naked, too!"

It was still early June. Even so, the afternoon was swelteringly hot. Both girls were so sweaty, they smelled worse than Buttercup.

"I'd rather see Roque Blackstone naked than see that old captured puma," Jet said.

That was saying a lot, but Ritz understood. Still, the cat in its chain-link cage under the live oak tree behind the courthouse had really been something. Maybe not worth plodding twelve endless miles in pea soup humidity under a hot sun. Maybe not worth getting yourself burned purple so your nose would peel off and Mother would get really mad and tell Daddy—but mighty exciting, nevertheless.

The cat had tricked Ritz into coming up real close. Its eyes had been slitted as if he were dozing. When Ritz had crept too near his chain-link cage, Jet had poked him with a stick. He'd lunged so hard he'd flipped his cage over on top of Ritz. She'd screamed and he'd snarled and yowled.

Ritz had clutched her silver St. Jude medal and yelped out a quick prayer. Sheriff Johnson had dropped his half-eaten doughnut in the scuffle to pull her away before the cat could claw her. But she wasn't ever going to forget those pointy gold ears pricking forward after he settled down on his haunches or those big beady eyes tracking her and staring straight through her.

"Does he eat people?" Jet had wanted to know.

Jet wasn't usually as interested in the natural world as Ritz, but the cat had been impressive, even to Jet.

"Only skinny little girls…like your four-eyed friend here…or a fat, lazy horse, or a brat fool enough to poke him with a stick…." The sheriff's laughter boomed when Buttercup whinnied. Ritz gulped the last of her cola and hid behind Jet.

Sheriff Johnson was a stocky man with heavy jowls and a permanently red, large, pie-flat face. Mother said he could mess up a uniform faster than any law officer she'd ever seen but he shared his doughnuts. Once he'd let Ritz wear his badge for a whole day.

Suddenly Johnson said, "Don't you worry none. He only eats little girls…only when he can't get a deer."

Jet heaved a deep, relieved sigh, for the ranch was well stocked with deer. But Ritz had felt sorry for the deer.

"So, what's he doing here?" Jet had asked. "How'd you catch him?"

Johnson had shoved his Stetson back and mopped his red brow. There were dark sweat stains under his sleeves. "If it's hot here, it's hell down in Mexico. Those damn Mexicans have been burning off their crops down in the Yucatán, and the fires got out of control, so now all the animals are on the move. Pumas follow the rivers, you know."

"What about creeks?" Ritz asked in a trembling tone, pushing her glasses up her perspiring purple nose.

Keller Creek traced a meandering, north-south path through the Triple K when there was water in it.

"Same thing as a river. Cats come out when the sun's going down. They crouch low in tall grasses to stalk their prey."

"Do they really eat horses?"

"Sure they do." He leaned down so his jowly face and bulging brown eyes were level with theirs. "Cats are killers. They eat anything that moves. They'll jump you from a tree. Had a horse a cougar jumped once. No man ever spread his legs across that mare's back again."

Static buzzed on his walkie-talkie. Grabbing it, he barked, "You girls better get. You've got that long ride and I've got work to do. Cattle rustlers. You be careful going home, you hear? Don't you get yourselves gobbled up by a cat, you hear!"

Ritz had been watching the sun sink ever lower, wiping the sweat off her lenses, and on the lookout for cats ever since. Every time Buttercup pricked her ears back or snorted, Ritz imagined pointy ears in the high brown grasses. Every time they passed a hole animals had dug to burrow under Benny Blackstone's high electric game fence, she wondered if a puma could slink under it.

The caged puma and the cool safety of the air-conditioned courthouse were nearly six miles behind them now. So were the frosty colas out of the courthouse soda pop machine. If Ritz didn't get a drink real soon, her tongue was going to swell and her throat was going to close.

It was really, really hot, hotter than it usually was even in the dead of summer. The grasses that had been fresh and green and sweet smelling in May were already seared brown around the edges. The last of the red and yellow wildflowers were wilted and dusty, and the air smelled a little smoky.

Ritz squinted up at the cloudless sky. A blindingly bright sun broiled them from above while the black asphalt steamed them from below. Their sleeveless, cotton blouses and cutoffs were so wet; they stuck to their bodies like glue. On Jet, the effect was so sexy, the sheriff's young deputy had eagerly rushed off to buy her a cola. Ritz had thrust out her flat chest and stared at him hopefully, but in the end she'd had to dig in her pockets and plunk in her own quarters.

Ritz's sunburn made her feel feverish. Her temple throbbed. She was almost glad Jet had mentioned Roque. At least, thinking about his thingy had distracted her from being so scared of cats.

"He must've been something running home naked...."

Roque was so dark and handsome and fierce. Even before she'd snuck up on him last night, she hadn't been able to keep her eyes off him. Not that she got to see him much. There was the dumb old feud. He was a Blackstone, and she was a Keller. Their families avoided each other.

Last summer though, she'd seen him once at the hardware store in town buying fencing. She'd stared at him, and he'd taken off his aviator glasses and stared back so intently, she'd grabbed a pair of pliers as if she was interested in them. Only she hadn't been able to pretend. It was like he smelled her fascination. That single glance before he shoved his glasses back in place had set her heart racing.

It had been weird, the way she hadn't even looked at those pliers. Just at him. Her hands had begun to shake, and she'd dropped the pliers with a clatter. He'd dashed over, as silently as a cat, and she'd stared at his weird silver-toed boots.

Then Daddy had yelled at her and she'd run. Roque had laughed and thrown the pliers into the pile of stuff the Blackstones were buying.

"His father beats him," Jet said out of the blue.

"How come?" Ritz asked, remembering the way Roque had swayed, bronzed and shirtless, before the fire.

"He's crazy. First time he came, the cowboys were working cattle, and he jumped in the pens with the bulls. He set off a string of firecrackers and nearly got himself trampled. Then Caleb jumped in, too. Only he fell. Even though Roque dived under a bull to save him, his daddy beat Roque and would've killed him if Pablo hadn't stopped him. He's got scars…everywhere."

Ritz shivered, remembering the purple marks on his back. Just thinking about Roque getting beatings after saving his brother made Ritz feel sorry for him.

To their right, on Keller land, a patch of dense brush was thick with mesquite and live oak. Ahead, she could see their tall white, ranch house with its welcoming shady verandas shimmering in the heat waves. Soon they would be past the Blackstone gate and on their own private road.

On the left, a caliche road meandered from the Blackstone gate across open pasture vanishing into the distant trees.

Ritz shuddered. The gate gave her nightmares. Used to, it had never been locked. Used to, Blackstone Ranch had made up two divisions of the Triple K. Used to, Uncle

Buster had been alive and married to Aunt Pam, and Ritz's cousins, Kate and Carol had lived there.

Benny Blackstone had married Aunt Pam just a month after Uncle Buster had died. Bad things had happened behind the gate ever since.

When the gate rattled, Buttercup's forelegs skewered to the right.

"It's just a silly old gate, girl," Ritz said even as she grabbed the mare's neck and clung.

In Ritz's nightmares the ten-foot high electric fence that separated the Triple K and Blackstone Ranch had been cut, and the gate was swinging back and forth. Always she was running down the caliche road to find her cousins. Always, she ended up in Campo Santo, the ancient Keller cemetery, standing over two open graves.

Sometimes she'd wake up screaming. Then she'd remember Kate and Carol lived up in San Antonio now with Grandma Keller because Benny Blackstone didn't want them. He only wanted Aunt Pam, who was beautiful and famous. He only wanted his own boys, even Roque, the bad one he beat.

All of a sudden the lopsided shadow of the Blackstone's massive gate slanted across the road, swallowing them whole as it did in her nightmare.

Ritz made a strangling sound. Clutching the reins and knotting fingers into Buttercup's mane, she urged the mare faster.

Wings whooshed above them. Jet clenched Ritz's waist tighter and then pointed toward the gate. "What's that?"

Shadows of black wings swept low along the grassy shoulder beside the game fence.

Buttercup pinned her ears back and jerked her head.

"Easy. Easy," Ritz said as the big black bird made a crash landing on a thick gray stone post.

"It's just a buzzard. That's all," she said to Jet.

"Not that dirty old buzzard, silly!" Jet pointed at a bit of gold glitter beside the fence post. "That! It looks like…a…lock…."

Then the wind played in the tops of oaks and rustled the brown grasses so that the bit of gold vanished.

Jet was about to jump down and run see what it was, when another wild gust of wind swung the gate away from the posts.

"Why, it's open," Ritz breathed.

Like in my nightmares.

The metal gate banged back into the loose chain hanging down from a stone pillar with a thud that made the chain rattle and the buzzard take off.

Not one for loud sounds, Buttercup snorted and shot forward. When she started bucking, the girls tumbled backward onto sizzling asphalt.

Jet screeched and sprang to her feet. "Ritz, watch out!"

Dark forelegs crashed dangerously near Ritz's head. Then the gate swung eerily and Buttercup wheeled away.

Ritz clapped her hands to get Buttercup's attention before the gate slammed and really spooked her.

"Come here, girl…."

Buttercup's nose was in the air, and her staring eyes that were ringed with black, rolled. Then the mare bolted straight for the gate. Dark mane flying, tail arched high and snapping like a flag, she went off at an angle. She was through the gate, galloping down the caliche road, stirring up puffs of white dust as she dashed toward the woods that concealed the pond and the forbidden Blackstone Ranch Headquarters.

"We'll never get her back now," Ritz said gloomily after she disappeared into the trees.

"Oh, yes, *you* will."

"*Me?*"

"You want to get the ranches back together, don't you?

Hey!'' She glanced at her wristwatch. ''It's five o'clock. Your horse just ran straight for the pond where Roque skinny-dips.''

Ritz felt a pang of pure misery mix with wild fear as she watched the dust settle on the caliche road while Jet knelt down to search for the bit of gold she'd seen. Ritz's gaze wandered from the road back to the ugly yellow signs Benny Blackstone's cowboys had posted on his game fence.

Every time her daddy drove by them, the yellow signs made him madder than spit. He said they mocked him and her—and everything Keller.

No trespassing.

Posted.

Keep Out.

Jet jumped up from the ground, dusting off an open, bronze, hasp lock. ''It's the lock! And a key, too! We can ride inside now…anytime we want to.''

''I don't want to. Not ever. Daddy would…''

''Daddy doesn't have to know. What are you so afraid of anyway?'' Jet said. ''You used to get to play there, didn't you?''

''Every Sunday,'' Ritz admitted.

''After church with your rich cousins.''

''Carol and Kate. We fished for guppies.''

''Right before Daddy and I moved here,'' Jet added, that odd, jealous note creeping into her voice.

''They're not rich anymore, though,'' Ritz said softly, to mollify her.

Jet shrugged. ''I used to be rich, too. Daddy was famous—''

She was always bragging like that. Maybe because like a lot of people, she felt put down by the Keller name and ranch.

''You told me.'' *Lots of times.*

"We lived in a great big house—bigger and newer than yours."

"Where?"

Jet rushed on. "My mother kept our mansion perfect, too. Not dusty like yours."

"I don't live in a mansion!"

Jet was always talking about her perfect mother. But if she was so perfect, where was she?

"So—how come you came here?"

Jet stared at the sky. "Are you going to get your dumb horse or not?"

Jet didn't talk much about her father or the double-wide mobile home they shared now. Irish was nice, nicer than her own father, but if you saw Irish and Jet together, they never laughed or talked or even looked at each other much.

Jet was her best friend, but Ritz had only been inside her trailer once…to see why Jet hadn't come to school. The living room had been dark and messy with beer cans and dirty dishes and trash everywhere. Irish had come to the door in a dirty T-shirt and stared down at Ritz. Usually he was neat and polite. Not that day. He'd simply said that Jet was sick and for her to go home.

When Ritz had told her mother, she'd taken the Taylors homemade soup and offered to clean the place for him. But Irish had kept the screen door closed and refused.

Jet stared at the gate and then down the caliche road. "You'd better get Buttercup."

"I'm not going in there!"

"Roque's brown all over…even down there. And his thingy is big and thick and long! And…and when he saw me, it stuck out."

Ritz blushed as she remembered his tall, male body undulating to that wild, Spanish tempo. "He's disgusting."

Jet laughed. "He's hot."

Ritz turned her back to her friend. What would she do if Buttercup didn't come back?

At least it felt cooler standing in the shade of the gate. The prevailing southeasterly wind from the bay played across the grasses. Ritz's damp blouse ballooned with air and little tendrils of her yellow hair blew against her brow and throat.

She was working hard not to think about last night or Cameron or what Roque's tanned, aroused body might look like when a burst of dark fire flew out of the distant trees.

Buttercup tossed her black mane and galloped straight at her.

Ritz sighed in relief. "I won't have to go in there after all."

"Maybe she saw *his* big thingy!"

"Would you shut up?"

When Buttercup got near the gate, Ritz held out her hand and called her name. A hinge groaned. Then the gate swung back and forth, causing the mare to snort and dance skittishly.

"Hold the gate, Jet, while I go get her."

The wind shifted and a cooling breeze struck Ritz as she ran onto Blackstone land. Buttercup raced off, hoofs thundering, her black tail high and pluming out. Finally she stopped a hundred yards away and watched Ritz, eyes wary, ears pointed. Then she lowered her head to the grass.

"Why do you even bother calling her?" Jet taunted as she slung a leg over the gate to watch. "She never comes to you."

Ritz forgot her friend and concentrated on coaxing the mare closer. Only when she finally got the reins and turned to yell in triumph, Jet was gone.

When she raced over to the gate, it was closed and

locked. In a panic, Ritz tugged at the lock and rattled the gate. Then Buttercup pinned her ears back.

A tiny pulse pounded in Ritz's throat. The horse needed water. Oats. There was no telling what the Blackstones might do to her mare if they found her.

Ritz was trapped inside the forbidden kingdom.

If his wide brown shoulders and lean torso had her in to a dither last night, what would happen if she came face-to-face with naked Roque Blackstone?

2

It had been a hellish hour. Ritz had pranced back and forth in front of the gate astride Buttercup, torn between abandoning the mare and staying with her. All her grand dreams of ending the feud were as nothing.

Oh, why couldn't Mother or Ramón drive by and rescue her?

Ritz was hot and tired and thirsty. So was Buttercup.

Maybe just maybe, Ritz could get out of this trap if she rode all the way down to the beach.

Maybe. The beach was five miles away. Probably another fence would cut her off before she got there.

A red sun hung low in a rosy horizon. With a frown, she pushed her glasses up her nose and studied the caliche road and the oak mott atop the ancient dunes. Tangles of thick, thorny brush—mesquite, huisache and oak and prickly pear trailed down the sides of the dunes. Her gaze wandered over the greenery twisting across the flat pasture following the course of Keller Creek.

Surely Roque wouldn't still be naked at that pond on the other side of those trees. Not that she'd risk going that far. She'd only go as far as the oak mott, to the edge of the creek, in the hopes that it might still be running even this late in the year.

She nudged Buttercup. Even if it was dry, at least she and Buttercup could rest and cool off in the shade.

As they made their way toward the trees, she couldn't help remembering less anxious outings when she'd come here with her cousins and Uncle Buster, who had always said this was the prettiest pasture on the Triple K Ranch.

Blackstone Ranch now.

Oh, how she'd loved Uncle Buster. He'd been a lot like her daddy except way more fun.

A yowl from the brush pierced the silence. A little brown rabbit sprang up underfoot. Buttercup reared. Clenching her legs tight and seizing fistfuls of black mane, Ritz held on as the rabbit made a wild dash for it.

Letting out a war whoop, Ritz and Buttercup raced after it.

Crazed with fear, the rabbit dived into a hole.

Buttercup circled, pawing and snorting.

Then Ritz remembered where she was and glanced nervously toward the oak mott.

No sign of a cat…. Nor a tall, dark naked man-boy.

Pressing her calves tighter, she and Buttercup were soon inside the shade of the oak trees. The creek was no more than a narrow trickle of water spilling over rocks and sand and damp brown leaves. Four yellow birds fluttered in the sand near a clump of Spanish dagger, chirping.

The banks were stony, littered with sticks, and thorny with yellow-berried *Granjeno,* which made for dangerous riding, so Ritz dismounted Buttercup, because she was too precious to her to risk a leg injury.

Quietly, so as not to startle the birds, Ritz grounded the mare. The birds fluttered to the high green branches that arched above like a natural cathedral. Buttercup sunk her muzzle and guzzled sloppily from a little pool. Ritz knelt on the bank, dabbing cool water onto her red face and sunburned arms. She kept thinking about Roque Blackstone and wondering how she'd ever get out.

When she'd cooled off a bit, she just sat there, mesmerized by the guppies flashing in the dark waters. Wishing she had jars to catch them with, she forgot she was trapped in the forbidden kingdom with a naked boy.

Scooping up a handful of water and two guppies, she smiled as they wriggled their tails spraying wet pearls of sunlight. Releasing them, she saw Buttercup a good ways downstream nibbling mesquite beans.

Buttercup was not to be trusted, so Ritz got up to go after her. Then she spied a darling black spider curled up in a white flower. When she peeled back the petals, the spider curled up as small as a pill bug.

"Don't be afraid, little spider."

Little legs tickled her ankle. When she brushed at the bug, she saw an amber colored army of ants racing along a miniature highway in the tall brown grasses. Every ant returning to the mound carried a leaf bigger than it was. She fell to her knees to watch them. Every ant coming out of the mound bumped into every ant carrying a leaf.

"Why?" she wondered aloud, spellbound. "Do you have a secret language?"

For a long time, she was aware of nothing but the ants. Then a large animal sneezed. She jumped to her feet.

"Buttercup?"

The yellow birds weren't singing anymore. The last of the red-gold sunlight flickered in the twisted, wind-skewered branches. An owl went, "whoo, whoo, whoo."

Where was Buttercup?

Ritz ran in the direction where she'd last seen her. When she stopped to get her breath, she was in a part of the oak mott she'd never been in before. Shrouded eerily with mistletoe, the trees were like dancers frozen in some dark spell.

The owl hooted again.

Sometimes witches took the shape of owls and changed little girls into birds...at least, in one of Ritz's favorite fairy tales. Ritz shivered.

The trees, the creek—all that had seemed so familiar and wondrous were suddenly strange and terrifying. She was all alone. Without the wind to rattle the palmetto fronds and stir the brown leaves that littered the ground, it was too quiet.

She stared up into the branches looking for cats. Then she remembered the No Trespassing signs, and a pulsebeat pounded in her temple.

This was Blackstone land. Why hadn't she climbed the gate and run home? She had to get home—fast—really fast, before something really bad happened. She would have to end the feud some other day when she was bigger and braver.

"Buttercup? Where are you—"

There was no answering snicker. The sun went behind a cloud and the glade darkened. Branches moaned in the wind. Leaves rained down and scuttled at her feet.

Then a twig crackled behind her.

Sobbing with fury and terror, she whirled. Sunlight and shadows played across the grass. Alert, triangular, gold ears above the waving brown tips pointed straight at her.

A cat!

Her heart slammed against her rib cage.

Another gust of wind sent more leaves flying. The grass waved. The big ears disappeared.

Oh, my God! Where was he? Her eyes glued to the spot where those ears had been, she pushed her glasses up. Then she stealthily tiptoed backward, moving robotically, one careful little half step at a time because she knew she wasn't supposed to run. Not from a cat—they liked to chase things.

To a big cat, she'd be no more than a mouse was to Molly, Mother's gray Persian that was forever catching birds…just to play with them and kill them. A big cat would bite her neck, crunch her bones, toss her around like a rag doll, paralyze her and then drag her off to some tree or hole—

Last year she'd seen a dead little filly over near the beach house that a cat had gotten. There'd been nothing left but bones and strips of hide and a few strands of black mane and tail blowing in the wind.

She conjured this image so vividly, she forgot not to run. With a panicky yell, Ritz twisted and sprinted full out toward the sunny pasture and pond.

Her sneakers flew across fallen branches, logs and rocks, splashing sloppily through the mud and water. When her foot got stuck between two rocks in the slippery ooze, a rattler hissed from the bank. At the sight of those brown coils, she yanked at her ankle with the frenzy of a coyote chewing its leg off to get out of a trap.

Then she was free, sobbing but running wildly. Thorns scratched her legs. Cutoffs weren't right for such dense brush. Cowboys wore leather leggings and jackets and gauntlet-type gloves.

Her right toe hit a rock wrong, and she pitched forward, hitting the ground so hard, it knocked the breath out of her. Her bleeding palms burned from skidding across gravel and sticker burrs, but she was too stunned and too terrified by what she saw beyond the trees to even whimper.

There *he* was!

Not naked!

Worse!

Bold as brass, Roque Blackstone stared straight at her, unzipped his fly and shook his big thingy out.

Just like last night, she covered her eyes with her fingers and crouched as still as a mouse and prayed, hoping *he* hadn't heard her, hoping *he* hadn't really seen her.

Finally her terrible curiosity got the best of her and she peeked through her slitted fingers.

"Oh, my God!"

His skin was as brown as mahogany. He had it pointed at her now and was deliberately spraying a rock not five feet in front of her with a stream of yellow pee.

Adrenaline. Sweat. Sheer terror.

Slowly, when nothing happened, her dreadful curiosity took the ascendancy of her common sense.

She squinted and tried not to see *that* part of his anatomy. Only somehow that was all she saw. It was big and long and purple-pink. It stuck straight out. At her!

Don't look at it!

She couldn't seem to stop.

Like last night, he had the same chiseled face of a prince out of one of her favorite storybooks. Just the sight of his wind-whipped black hair, along with his awe-inspiring muscular chest, his broad shoulders, and his lean, brown, rangy body sent funny little darts zinging through her stomach. And she hadn't even looked...not really *down there*. At least not on purpose.

But she had because, truth to tell, she was as fascinated by him as Jet was. Maybe more so.

He shook it after he finished, and then *it* got hung up in his jeans and he couldn't zip his fly. She forgot all modesty and observed his deft brown fingers that yanked up and down at the zipper. Suddenly he stopped fiddling with his zipper and stared straight at her.

Hot color scorched her cheeks. Not that she closed her eyes or even blinked. But her glasses fogged. She took them off and wiped them with the grubby tail of her shirt. Then she shoved them onto her nose.

He was big, way bigger than her brother, Steve, but not nearly as big as Cameron. Which was such a relief she hugged herself. Still, he was wild and bad, and it showed somehow on his face. It was like he was a prince under a witch's spell, or maybe he was a pirate who had walked out of a legend into real life. Or maybe somehow she'd plopped herself inside a storybook and was about to be a princess or a maiden and have a big adventure.

He was a Blackstone. The bad Blackstone brother, who did bad things to girls. He was old—eighteen or so. He'd even flunked a year.

Holding her breath, Ritz slithered backward, away from him, keeping to her awkward crouch until the trees completely hid her and she could run for home. Then she ran, just like she'd run last night. Even as she felt some weird pull not to.

No sooner had Roque finished unsnarling the blue-white threads from his zipper than a horse snickered in the distance, somewhere off to the south. The sound brought a strange peace to him, especially this evening.

He loved horses. A lot more than he loved people. They connected him somehow to a larger, truer, and very ancient world.

His dark fury returned. Why couldn't people just leave him the hell alone? Caleb? His father? Most of all, his father!

Something stirred in the thick foliage of the oak mott. A branch bent gently. Shadows danced.

Dios, he'd forgotten about *her.* Was she hiding in the *mogotes* (thick patches) and *cejas* (thickets) like before? Like last night?

Yesterday she'd stolen his clothes and laughed when

he'd run. Then she'd snuck up on him when he'd lit a fire on the beach and danced. Sucking in a fierce breath, Roque jerked his dick inside his pants and zipped his fly.

Had she seen him? Shyness made him flush.

If she had seen him, he hoped it hadn't turned her off. He wanted to kiss her, to see how far she'd go. Maybe she'd have some pot or booze. She was the kind who would. He wanted to forget about his father. He had to forget.

The air was cool and breezy after the long, hot afternoon. The glassy pond with the ducks and willows and the taller oaks along the southern bank was a place Roque often came to sit and watch the grass blow and the clouds sail in the utter silence and stillness. Not that it was all that pretty really with the water so low and so much muddy shoreline exposed. But it had a wild, lovely aspect that had grown on him.

Sometimes he sunbathed on a rock. Sometimes he walked in the woods or swam in the raw. Sometimes he just felt homesick for his mother and his sisters who spoiled him, for all his boisterous Moya aunts and uncles and cousins, for Mexico, its art, its music, its people, its passion. Not that he really belonged down there, either.

He had a gringo father, who'd divorced his mother and broken her heart. *Mamacita* never let him forget it, either. Neither did his uncles. Still…nobody up here knew how to cook like his mother. Nobody made him *tamales Yucatán* or did anything special for him. Nobody except Caleb.

Sometimes Roque just daydreamed. About horses sometimes. About girls mostly. About white girls when he was up here.

Not tonight.

Not when his father had just beat the shit out of him at the corral.

For nothing.

Not for nothing. 'Cause he was a Mexican. 'Cause he was scared he'd hurt his precious Caleb.

As if he'd ever hurt Caleb.

The only reason Roque had started coming to Texas a few years back was that when Caleb had found out he had an older brother, he'd begged to meet him. Their father couldn't deny Caleb anything.

Roque had felt so angry and out of place on that first visit, he hadn't known what to do with himself. One afternoon when Pablo and his men had been working cattle, Roque had gotten so bored, he'd set off a string of firecrackers and thrown them into the pen. When the livestock stampeded, he'd dived into the pen with them. What a thrill that had been—whooping and yelling and running with those bulls while their hooves pounded the earth. He hadn't cared whether he'd lived or died. Then Caleb's thin, fearful cry had rent the air.

Through a blur of horn and red flank, he'd watched Caleb's bright head bob and then disappear. Roque had grabbed onto the biggest bull's horns and hung while the beast pushed through the others. Miraculously Roque had reached Caleb before he was trampled. All Caleb suffered was a broken wrist and a bad case of hero worship, but to this day, their father still believed Roque had deliberately stampeded the bulls because he was so jealous of Caleb that he wanted to kill him.

All of a sudden Roque wanted to be as bad as his father always told everybody he was. He wanted to screw and drink and get wasted with a pretty, wild girl—to forget, to go dead on the inside, to lose the hate, or at least some of its edge…just for a little while. He was too Mexican to ever fit in up here.

Where the hell was she?

Suddenly the hair on the back of Roque Moya's neck

stood on end. Good, he wasn't wrong about her. He stared at the woods and felt her eyes on his fly. He was about to call her bluff and go after her when he heard flying footsteps and shouts right behind him.

"Roque—"

His father? Roque felt a surge of panic and despised himself. His daddy's eyes had gone colder than a rattler's right before he'd lifted that chain a while ago. Roque leaned down, his hand closing around a rock. If his father so much as raised a hand to him ever again…

Whirling, staring over his shoulder, he caught a whiff of cow dung and fresh grass. Then he saw that familiar, beloved, bright head bobbing against the pink sky.

Caleb. His slim, lithe form dashed through the waist-high grasses toward him. Caleb, who followed him everywhere.

Fury mingled with jealousy. Then his heart swelled with love. Damn, you Caleb! Damn you for being so smart and sweet…and brave…and perfect. For being the easy kind of kid fathers were proud of. He made straight A's. He liked books. He could read better than most college kids, which was galling to Roque, who practiced reading secretly every night.

Roque was good at math like his Moya uncles, who were engineers, but math bored him. He preferred liberal arts. Not that he did well in them. Whenever he tried to read, words got all mixed up on the page. Spelling was even harder, but at night before they went to bed, Caleb often tried to teach him. If alone, Roque would struggle over the words for hours.

When Caleb saw him look his way, his warm white grin spread from ear to ear the way it always did. Involuntarily Roque smiled back. Caleb, not the money his rich daddy bribed *Mamacita* with, was the only reason Roque ever came to Texas.

Roque dropped the rock and stared from his little brother to the green line of oaks where he knew she was waiting for him. Since last night he'd hoped she was a real *puta* in heat. Not that he'd ever had a *puta*. Still, he told himself he hoped she wanted a bellyful as much as she'd wanted an eyeful.

Gringas. He hoped his macho *tíos* were right when they said that *gringas* were even hornier than most men. Even the pretty, young ones. His uncles were always telling him that a real man screwed every pretty girl he could. Once, anyway. This girl had black curls and big boobs and the whitest, softest skin he'd ever seen on any girl, even a *guera.*

He had to ditch Caleb—and fast.

With seeming casualness, Roque began unbuttoning his loose white shirt. When Caleb was within earshot, Roque said, "Didn't I tell you not to follow me unless I invited you along?"

"Can I..."

"Daddy said I wasn't supposed to go near you! So—no!"

The sparkle went out of Caleb's face and he looked down. "It's a free country," he said sullenly, kicking rocks. "Since when do you care what Daddy says?"

"Since this!"

Roque peeled his bloodstained cotton shirt off, and Caleb winced at the blood-crusted wounds crisscrossing Roque's already scarred brown back.

His little brother loved him...so much. In his own way, every bit as much as *Mamacita* did.

Caleb—the favorite son. The perfect son. The white white son.

"Why don't you ever just tell him you're sorry, Roque, so he'll stop?" Caleb demanded in a soft, worried voice.

"'Cause I'm not. 'Cause I hate him for always thinking I want to hurt you."

Caleb gasped. "You're dumb. If—"

"Don't say that!"

"So dumb, your dumb zipper's half open! If you hadn't mouthed off, I could've explained and your back wouldn't look like hamburger meat."

Roque fumbled with his fly until he got the zipper up.

His father had grown angrier at each stroke. Caleb was the one who had run forward and risked the chain himself by grabbing their father's hand. Not the cowboys. Not even Pablo, the ranch manager... Pablo, his friend. They'd just stood there, their boots planted in the thick dirt, their black heads hung low, some of them snickering nervously.

"I told you to get lost. I came here to be by myself so I can think."

"I won't say anything. Think away." Caleb circled him, his green eyes almost popping out of his freckled face as he edged closer to get a better look at his brother's bloody back.

Roque wadded his shirt into a ball and pitched it angrily into the pond. Nothing was working out. He glanced toward the trees. No sign of the brazen girl, who had stolen his clothes yesterday.

Caleb squatted down and rocked back on his heels. "He beat you even worse than last time...."

"I said scram."

"You didn't have to smart off."

"Git—Daddy's pet."

Caleb, who was fourteen, rubbed his glistening eyes in shame. Then he shook his head proudly making his blond bangs fly.

Suddenly hoofbeats rumbled. Both boys swiveled when the strange, sorrel horse shot out of the forest, interrupting their standoff. The mare stopped when she heard them, her chest heaving. Her ears were pointed straight at them.

"That's the Keller girl's horse," Caleb said.

La princesa. Roque had seen her once or twice. She was very white, plain, and ever so haughty.

"Not anymore. Be quiet and watch this." Roque whistled to the mare.

Her *friend* must've ridden over. He'd steal her horse to pay her back for stealing his clothes.

The mare tore a mouthful of grass out of the ground. Watching him, she began to munch warily.

In long graceful strides, Roque moved through the grass toward her.

"What are you going to do?"

"Get lost, kid. You'll only get in my way." He paused. "If Daddy catches you with me, he'll beat me. Is that what you want?"

Caleb went so white every freckle stood out. His thin shoulders sagged. Roque was stunned when his own dark heart twisted with remorse.

"Get," he said.

"Who wants to catch a dumb old horse anyway," Caleb said.

Roque really felt chagrined when Caleb turned his back on him and started walking home.

"Caleb…"

Roque forced himself to let it go. "I'm a real jerk, kid," he muttered to himself. "Just like Daddy! The sooner you get that, the better for all three of us. When I go home this time, I'll stay there. I'll forget I ever had a *gringo* brother. I will! If it's the last thing I ever do, I will!"

Catching her horse soon distracted him from his guilt trip. It wasn't long before Roque had the reins and was stroking the mare's dark nose with the flat of his hand.

She was leaning her head into his every touch, nuzzling his open palm.

"Friends?" he whispered when he mounted her.

A dazzling white smile crept across Roque's lean, tanned face. He made a clicking noise. "Where's your sexy mistress, girl?"

If only *she* would be as easy to seduce as her horse.

Ritz was running down the caliche road when she heard the violent thunder of hooves thudding behind her.

She turned. Roque Blackstone was galloping Buttercup straight for her, stirring up thick clouds of white dust. His hair streamed like wet black ink back from his dark face. His wet shirt was plastered against his lean body. His eyes flamed a savage, incandescent green.

With a yell, she tried to run faster. Just when she thought he'd surely trample her or grab her up by the hair and scalp her, the furious pounding stopped. Then Ritz was enveloped in dust so thick, she had to put her hands up over her tear-filled eyes as she began to cough.

Buttercup snorted and stomped the earth.

When she could breathe again, Ritz sprinted for the gate.

"Whoa, girl! Whoa!" yelped a harsh, male voice. "You can't outrun me or my horse."

She stopped. "*My* horse!"

"Yours?" He laughed, the soft, velvety sound jeering her. "Who the hell are you?" His green eyes raked her skinny body.

He was looking at her, his eyes burning, challenging her the way all those other boys challenged Jet.

Oh, if only I were as gutsy as Jet—

Roque Moya had a peculiar effect on her. Last night she'd felt all grown up and on fire. Suddenly she felt strange, almost gutsy. Almost pretty.

"Ritz Keller! That's who!" she snapped, pushing her glasses up her nose.

"You really think you're somebody, don't you? A real *princesa?*"

Up close his eyes were so fierce, she felt consumed by their unholy fire. "I'm not scared of you, Roque Blackstone!"

Liar.

"So, you know who I am?"

She almost stopped breathing when he smiled. Jet would have smiled back and said something clever.

"You're a Blackstone—the worst of a bad bunch. You flunked…"

His face twisted. "If you don't like us, what the hell are you doing on Blackstone land, *Meeez* Know-it-all Keller? Where's your pretty friend?"

"Jet?"

"Are you like her? Did you come to watch a *meens* swim naked and steal *heez* clothes?"

"Man?" she corrected, tilting her nose in the air.

He flushed.

Sassily she put her hands on her hips. "You're no man."

"Like you're some expert—"

"You're just a stupid, mean boy nobody likes. Not even your father!"

"You don't know what you're talking about."

"Last year he sent you home…to Mexico 'cause…'cause…"

Roque swore violently under his breath, first in Spanish and then in English. "'Cause a bad girl told my father she liked me…too much—Four Eyes."

"Well, I don't like you." Ritz stuck out her tongue.

He laughed. "Most girls do. That gets boring after a while."

"You are too conceited to believe."

Another quick burst of his male laughter made her heart skitter.

"I'm not boy-crazy…not like Jet."

"Jet." He purred. "So, that's her name. She is pretty, your boy-crazy friend. Older. She follows me."

The red sky burned green.

"She's only a year and a half older!"

"More than that," he said, peeling clothes from her skinny frame with his indecently bright, emerald eyes. "You're a baby. She's a woman. Last night she…"

"Are you going to give me my horse or not?"

He shook his head. "She's mine now."

He pranced back and forth. "And you're on Blackstone land."

A red sun slanted a kaleidoscope of rays behind him, giving him the devil's own halo while keeping that pretty face of his in the dark. She had to squint to make out his well-shaped, glossy, black head and that hair that was so long it whipped against his hard, dark jawline and tangled with the ends of the scarlet bandanna he wore at his neck.

With the sun at his back, he was mostly a black figure. Still, she got an eyeful of sleek, brown torso under that wet shirt that seemed made of nothing but ripply muscle. Indeed, even up close, every part of him seemed made of muscle, too—his squared-off shoulders…his arms…his lean waist and…his legs. He looked better by sunlight than by firelight.

Black jeans clung to those powerful legs. Jet said boys who wore jeans that tight were too nasty for nice girls to talk to. And here she was—Ritz Keller, fourteen years old, talking to just such a boy.

She'd watched him dance, seen his thingy. Catching a scared, little breath, she remembered he wasn't nearly as big as Cameron. And he wasn't as mean, either, no matter what people said about him.

"Like what you see, squirt?" he whispered.

"You're a nasty boy."

"I just like girls. And girls like your friend, Jet, like me back."

If you only knew.

Buttercup snorted and blew, moving skittishly to one side, thereby changing the angle of the sun, so that Ritz could finally see the conceited brute's face, or at least three-quarters of it.

Up close he looked bad and wild like the rock stars on Jet's posters that hung all over her bedroom walls. But he was way more handsome. His blatantly masculine face seemed hacked from hot, sun-baked stone. A sheen of perspiration set him aglow and made him seem like a god come to life. He had a high brow, an aquiline nose, and a wide, sexy mouth. Thick, spiky black lashes shaded green eyes so bright and feral, they literally knocked the breath out of her.

For a long moment, she couldn't move or breathe a word.

He went equally still.

Nervously she pushed her glasses up. For a long second their gazes remained fixed.

"You're bad," she said.

"Stupid, too?" he mocked, using those eyes of his to twist her around his little finger.

Ritz stiffened.

"What are you doing here?" he repeated.

She didn't dare look at him again. "I-I'm here...to get...to get...t-that horse, *my* horse, Buttercup!"

"*My* Buttercup now." His voice deepened and roughened, bringing those little shivers again.

"You have to give her back!"

"Make me, squirt."

Her hands balled into fists. When she lunged, Buttercup trotted off.

"W-who is she, Roque?" another boy cried out from the tall grasses as he ran toward her.

Ritz whirled so fast, the blond kid nearly fell.

"You!" Roque said. "Caleb, I told you to git."

Caleb held up his hands. His smile was so engaging, Ritz smiled back, which only made his older brother's scowl darken.

It wasn't hard to see why Caleb was more popular than Roque. He was just a boy not much older than she. He had blond hair, green eyes, and sandy eyebrows and lashes. His freckled nose was almost as red and blistered as hers.

He was nice cute; not nasty cute like Roque. Not intimidating cute, either.

"Don't forget," Roque jeered. "He's a hated Blackstone, too."

"I'm Ritz Keller, that's who, and if you and your brother will give me my horse…"

"You're trespassing!" the younger boy whispered to Ritz, grinning at his brother to win his approval.

"Well, Caleb, somebody left your gate open and Buttercup ran inside. I had to come after her. Your big brother here is riding a horse with a Triple K brand. In other words, he's a horse thief."

"If she's yours, why'd she run from you?" Roque demanded.

"Do you know anything? Anything at all about horses?" she demanded, tilting her head as imperiously as a queen.

"I caught yours, didn't I?"

"Just give her back."

"If I do that—then you'll ride away. I want to know more about your pretty friend."

"Well, she doesn't like bullies or horse rustlers...or stupid..."

"You have a saying up here in Gringolandia, Señorita Smartie Pants. Finders. Keepers."

"She said you're ugly naked!"

"Híjole!" He pulled back a little on the reins and leaned down.

"So, you came to see for yourself!"

"You're disgusting!"

"Then why the blush?"

She looked down, but she felt his eyes on her face and got hotter.

"Go home, little girl, before you get into real trouble. Tell your friend she can swim in our pond...anytime." His lilting purr sent a hot shiver through her. "Tell her, I'll be waiting for her tomorrow."

"I'm not going without Buttercup."

"All right." Holding the reins, Roque sprang lithely off Buttercup, landing so close beside her, she jumped back. Then he slapped Buttercup on the rump and sent her trotting off.

"We're going to let Buttercup decide," he said, "who she wants, you...or me."

"No—"

"Because you know she'll choose me," he jeered.

"You're very sure of yourself," she said.

"Sí. It's one of my failings."

She felt her jaw go slack. Her heart raced. She thrust out her chin anyway. "A Keller's way is better than a Blackstone's any day."

He grinned. "You're going to be hell on wheels when you grow up," he murmured. "A while ago you asked me if I knew anything about horses. What if I told you I had a way with horses, same as I do with little girls? Big girls, too?"

It was getting dark. In the queer half-light, with his intense aristocratic features, he was absolutely stunning—tall, muscular, graceful even. Not awkward like the other boys she knew. She remembered him dancing and how she'd longed to dance, too.

"You can't beat me…'cause I'm a Keller."

"Little Killer Keller," he purred. "I can beat you any day."

"Wanna bet?"

3

A warm gust of air stirred Ritz's golden curls and ruffled Buttercup's tail. Sighing in exasperation, Ritz scowled at her mare.

"So, we'll let Buttercup decide who she wants?" Roque repeated.

She put her hands on her hips. "I don't have to play your silly game. This stubborn, mulish, black-tailed idiot is mine."

"Careful how you talk to her, or she won't choose you."

Ritz tossed her head and would've spun away, but he grabbed her arm.

"Ouch. You're hurting me."

"Okay. Okay." Instantly the long brown fingers loosened. His dark face was grim. "So, you don't have to play my game or prove anything. Maybe I just want to teach you something."

"You left marks." She rubbed her elbow.

The long shadows made his face darker, crueler. But when he fixed his bold green eyes on her, his expression softened. "Okay. I'm sorry. I don't ever like hurting anybody, especially not somebody smaller or…a girl. I have two big sisters.''

''Down in Mexico?''

Instead of answering, he blurted, ''I'm not a bully! Not like my father!''

His hot gaze and the pain in his voice stripped her soul and demanded intimacies she didn't understand and wasn't ready to share. His wild eyes slid from her face to the red place above her elbow. ''I could show you marks!'' He began unfastening his shirt, but when she shrank from him, misreading his intent, he sucked in a hard breath.

''*Híjole!*'' His brilliant eyes devoured her flat chest and then her skinny, sunburned legs as he cursed low in Spanish.

She blanched at his rough language.

''*Tú hablas….*'' he whispered when he realized he was scaring her even more.

She nodded and then stared at his scarred boots and at her own pigeon-toed feet. ''*Por supuesto.*''

''*Lo siento,*'' he muttered in apology.

Spanish was the working language on the Triple K. She was a Keller. Everybody spoke Spanish. Everybody except Jet. But Jet was a natural at music and was learning it fast. She had a gift for imitating sounds, same as she had a gift for boys. Ritz wished she had Jet's gifts. But other than being a Keller, she was plain and ordinary—as Roque had just so cruelly pointed out.

He gave her skinny body another of those insolent sideways glances that sent her heart rushing in stilted, painful beats.

''Quit looking at me,'' he whispered in a raw tone, ''with those big blue eyes that eat me alive. And…and I didn't meant to scare you…or hurt your feelings.''

''You just can't help yourself.''

''What are you—thirteen…to my eighteen?''

"Fourteen!"

"You're too damn young to be hanging around me."

"So, give me my horse and I'll…"

"You're skinny and not even pretty."

Tears pricked. "You said that already!"

"And you've got spots."

"Freckles!" Ritz shouted. "What's wrong with freckles?"

"Same thing that's wrong with your last name and all that metal in your mouth. I don't like them."

Just when she was feeling weird and sad and hurt, his low tone gentled. "You've got pretty hair, though. Mexicans have a thing for yellow hair. At least I do even though I don't see colors like other people. Yours is really something. Who knows…in another year or two…maybe you'll be even prettier than your friend. You've got something…she doesn't. I'm not sure what it is exactly." His voice had gone smooth.

She felt a strange, powerful pull to move toward him. "I don't care what you think! Just give me my horse!" But she put her hand over her lips to hide the beginnings of a smile.

"Your horse?" he began in a teasing vein that made her blush again. "We'll see whose horse she is. We'll both call her. We'll see who she chooses. I'll even let you go first, *guera*," he offered magnanimously, eyeing her yellow hair.

Guera was slang in Mexico for blonde.

When she shook her head, causing her hair to bounce on her shoulders, he laughed. "Scaredy-cat. Go on. Call her. If she comes. She's yours."

"It's a trick!" Ritz muttered, catching a breath and then cupping her hands to the sides of her mouth and calling out, "Buttercup!"

Munching grass, Buttercup didn't even raise her head or

prick her ears. When Ritz called her again, the obstinate beast chewed lazily.

"I need an apple," Ritz said.

"Give?" her foe taunted.

"Buttercup!" Ritz cried, her voice tinged with desperation.

"That's no way to coax a pretty lady," Roque said smugly, directing his brilliant gaze to the mare. He swaggered toward the beast, his brown hands outstretched.

Buttercup jerked her head out of the grass and flicked her nose out at him. She snorted, her nostrils flaring. Her black tail lifted and seemed to float in the wind like an inky banner.

When he had her full attention, he splayed his long fingers open like claws.

Ritz sprang in front of Roque and called again. "Buttercup! Come here, sweetheart!"

"Cheater," he purred. He stood so close she could feel the heat of his breath against her neck.

The sun was gone. The tall grasses and big sky were aflame, the horizons ringed in pink.

"Buttercup," Ritz pleaded, truly scared now.

Buttercup nibbled, her nose low to the ground. Roque strutted toward the horse, squared his body to hers and stared directly at her.

The mare bolted.

"My turn," Roque said jauntily.

"You made her run away just when I was trying to call her."

"I can make her come back, too."

"I hate you!"

"You sure about that?" He laughed and began clucking to Buttercup.

The mare stopped running. Roque squared his shoulders

and stared fixedly at her again. Again, Buttercup ran from him.

"She doesn't want you, either."

"She'll change her mind after I court her a little. All the girls, big and little, want Roque Moya. Just you watch."

"You are disgusting."

"Your sexy friend doesn't think so. Maybe some-day…when you grow up and I court you, you'll change your mind, too."

Was he flirting with her?

No way.

But if he was, it was a heady game to play with a bad wild boy like him, a Blackstone.

"Watch me, Four Eyes," he said softly. "She'll come to me."

And the mare did. In less than twenty minutes. He didn't even have to call her. Buttercup just stopped running and started watching everything he did as if hypnotized. Soon the mare's head dropped, and she walked slowly toward him, licking and chewing. Only she didn't have any grass in her mouth. Roque kept his body at a forty-five degree angle to the horse, avoiding eye contact as she approached.

Sensing some baffling, silent chemistry between Roque and her horse, Ritz held her breath. Furious as she was, she felt a strange thrill when Buttercup walked up to the fiend and held her nose less than an inch from his broad shoulder.

Ritz wanted to shout, "She's mine! Mine!"

But what he'd done was so fantastic, she didn't want to break the spell.

When Roque turned and walked away from Ritz, But-tercup followed. They walked in a circle before returning. Finally Roque faced the horse and lifted his hand, stroking

Buttercup between the eyes. Then he stared at Ritz and grinned.

Ritz was stunned.

"He can talk to horses." Caleb's eyes shone.

Ritz had forgotten Caleb was even there. "How?"

"Not in words, but Roque says horses talk just the same. He's going to teach me their language."

"Their language?"

"*Horse.* He read about it in a book and taught it to himself, and he can hardly read."

It was obvious the younger Blackstone was much in awe of his older brother. Even though she didn't want to admit it, he wasn't stupid like people said he was. He was smart and different—special.

"I can, too, read!" Roque blurted, stung.

"I want to learn *horse,* too!" The words just popped out of her mouth.

"Do you want to start now?"

She scowled at Roque when he flung himself to the ground and began yanking his scuffed black boots off. He pulled off his socks, too, and wiggled his long, naked toes.

Why was watching him do the most ordinary things so fascinating? The keen sweetness of hay being cut somewhere made her heart ache. Or was it just him, balling his dirty socks and stuffing them into his boots that made her feel so strange?

If Ritz had thought more about boys before last night and this afternoon than she'd ever admit, she felt possessed now. Roque's dark sensual male beauty made her long to be older and prettier—desirable.

"There's sticker burrs," she said lamely when he finally stood up.

"So?"

She tried not to look at his gorgeous black head when he turned. But his bold green eyes claimed her somehow, holding her with that same, mysterious force she hadn't understood last night.

"I'm not going to walk," he said. "I'm going to fly. Do you want to learn to fly, *princesa?*"

He extended his brown hand just as he had last night, inviting her to put hers inside it. She stared at those long, tapered fingers and then at the purple-black grasses that curled away from them in endless waves. With a shiver, she shook her head.

"Scaredy-cat." He laughed. As she gasped, he sprang up on Buttercup's back, urging the mare forward with his toes into a springing trot.

"Get off her," she whispered.

"I won, remember."

Soon he had Buttercup cantering round and round in a perfect circle. They were so beautiful, Roque with his black hair and Buttercup with her black mane streaming in the wind as they danced in that sea of tall grasses.

Even before Roque stood up and went dangerously faster, Ritz was trembling with a mixture of fright and wonder.

"Don't," she pleaded silently.

But he stretched both his arms out like wings.

"No...no..." Even as she begged, her heart thrummed, and her spirit sang along with those thudding hoofs.

"Yes," she breathed. "Yes."

Roque's wickedness and wildness made him seem like a god, who was connected by spirit and blood to the mare he rode, connected to the endless sea of purple grasses, to the darkening sky itself, to the whole universe—connected even to her. She'd felt the same thing last night, only now her feelings were stronger.

Buttercup galloped so fast, Roque did indeed seem to fly. When Caleb spread his own arms like wings and ran after his brother, she did the same thing. The three of them soared on their make-believe wings, running round and round, both flying and dancing.

Caleb and she ran after him until they collapsed in laughter, breathing hard. Ritz put her hand over her heart as the galloping horse and the bad Blackstone boy flew away. She began to laugh, forgetting all sense of ownership when Roque turned, and she realized he was galloping back to her.

"He's magical," she whispered. "He's like a centaur."

Buttercup slowed and Roque sat down again and smiled down. A stillness descended upon her when he came close and held out his hand to his brother.

"Do you want to fly?"

Caleb shook his head.

"I do!" she cried in an eager voice that did not belong to her.

Roque gave her a long look. Then he leaned down. This time when he extended his hand toward her, she grabbed it.

Sweet heat flicked through her veins like summer lightning. Oh, what had gotten into her? Was it his wildness? His badness?

Caleb shrieked with joy and ran up to them. Kneeling, he cupped his dirt-encrusted hands. As bravely as Jet, Ritz put her foot in his fingers and sprang up in front of Roque. His warm hands circled her waist, burning her skin through her thin blouse.

When he urged Buttercup into a trot, she forgot all about hating him.

Never had cantering been such a glorious experience. It was like dancing. A chemistry flowed between the three of them. They weren't just a boy and a girl and a horse. They belonged to an ancient world and a primitive time that was truer than anything modern, a paradisiacal time before man had been expelled from the kingdom of nature.

He stood up and then helped her to stand, too. When she teetered, crying out to him, he steadied her until she got her balance. Soon she was holding her arms out just as he had. Slowly his thrilling hands at her waist fell away. Then he extended his arms behind hers, and they were flying together, racing in that endless magical pasture, the thudding rhythmic hooves singing in her blood.

For a few brief moments there was no high game fence, no feud. It was just Roque and her and the magic between them. Then a black pickup sped toward them on the caliche road, belching angry white fantails of dust.

For a few brief moments longer, horse and riders were free, and the range was as wild and open as their hearts. Ritz's hair blew against Roque's dark face, so that she felt herself part of him as well as part of the sky.

Then the truck braked. Benny Blackstone hopped out, shaking his fists and cursing when he saw Caleb running toward the galloping riders with his arms outstretched. Not that Ritz really heard Ben.

Buttercup's hoofs were thudding, and she felt too wonderful. Even when Roque turned Buttercup, so that they seemed to charge the truck and Caleb, she was only vaguely aware of his father.

Everything seemed to happen in slow motion. Ben leaned inside the cab and pull his Winchester off the gun rack behind the driver's seat.

"Caleb—" Ben shouted. "Sunny—"

Caleb stopped, but Buttercup kept galloping at him, Benny raised the rifle to his chest.

Caleb yelled when his father aimed at Roque, "No! Daddy! No!"

Roque let out an Indian war whoop and charged faster. The Winchester cracked. And still Roque charged.

Almost carelessly Benny ejected the empty shell and raised the rifle again. The gun popped a second time, bouncing rocks in front of Buttercup. The mare reeled. With a scream, Ritz tumbled backward into Roque.

He grabbed her, rocking precariously, grabbing wildly at the air. Buttercup reared.

"Dios," he muttered as her forelegs came down with a thud.

Ritz's heart was pounding when he slipped. Still, holding her, he shielded her somehow. His body struck the rocks first. She fell on top of him, crushing him against the ground. Something inside her knee popped. When she tried to stand up, she couldn't.

Mad with fear, Buttercup circled them frantically, got too near and stepped on Roque's arm.

The bone snapped, but Roque didn't utter a sound. He lay in a broken heap like a doll thrown down by an angry child, his dark face as white as bone.

"Sunny!" Benny shouted. "Are you crazy? He was trying to kill you! How many times do I have to tell you to stay away from him?"

Caleb ran to Roque. "You shot him—deliberately! There's…there's blood on the dark grass." Caleb drew back a hand, wet with the stuff, and began to cry.

Ritz knelt over Roque and choked on a sob. "Roque! He's not moving."

Through her sobs Ritz heard Caleb's muted pleadings. His father stalked toward them, his Winchester lowered now, his expression grim.

"Move, kids." Benny sank to his knees and examined Roque. When he was done, he stroked Roque's black hair for a long moment. "He'll be all right." His voice was strange, hoarse. "Take more than a fall to kill a devil like him. Broken arm. Let's hope it'll teach him a lesson. He shouldn't have charged me. Run get a blanket, Sunny."

When Caleb loped off, Benny fiddled with his radio, shaking it and cursing. In a few minutes Caleb was leaping back through the tall grasses with the blanket. His father took it and threw it over Roque.

"You'd better git," he said to Ritz.

"My knee—"

"Damn. I can't get anybody on the radio. I'm going to have to call the ambulance from the house. Can you stay here with him until I get back? I'll phone your parents and tell them what's happened. If he comes to, don't let him move—"

Her eyes widened. "You can't call my daddy! When you come back...if you'll just put me on Buttercup and leave the gate open...."

He shook his head. "I'm liable for you. You stay here. Roque's just crazy enough to hurt himself if he comes to alone and is disoriented in the dark."

She looked at Roque's crumpled body and then at the black sky. Then she rubbed her burning eyes and nodded. "Daddy's going to be so mad."

Benny stood up. "Come on, Sunny."

"I want to stay with Roque, too!"

"This wouldn't have happened, if you'd stay away from him."

Benny Blackstone seized Caleb by his collar and pulled him, his boots scuffling across the rocks, all the way to the truck. They roared away in geysers of white dust.

Ritz swallowed a hard lump in her throat. Roque lay so still. He was very white, and his hair spilled like rich black chocolate across the rocks and grass.

"Roque?" Leaning closer, she caught his scent, which was musky, and clean, all male. "Roque!" she yelled.

When he didn't answer, she brushed a lock of his hair from his brow and gasped. His beautiful face was swollen and out of shape.

"Oh! No!" She pressed her hand to his temple. When

her finger came away sticky, she didn't dare shake him. "Roque! Please... Please wake up!"

High above them, the evening star twinkled like a lonely sentinel in an opalescent, purple sky. Then a gray owl swished low over their heads toward the oak mott, melting into the dense shadows of the brush. A chorus of night bugs began to sing.

His pulse! That's what she was supposed to check for!

At the thought of laying even a single fingertip on that dark throat, she sucked in a quick breath. With an eye on his still, white face, she lowered her hand and ran it along his warm skin all the way to the base of his throat.

Finally, when her fingers were still, she felt a flutter. She pressed harder, and the pressure of his heart's slow, steady thudding, made her own heart leap.

"Don't die," she whispered. "Please...please..."

She lifted her St. Jude medal and said a fervent prayer to the saint. And then she looked up at the new stars and the moon and prayed to God, too.

Hardly knowing that her fingers unfastened the silver chain, she removed the medal. She caught her breath. Aunt Pam had given her Uncle Buster's medal at his funeral. Ritz had promised to treasure it always.

With a heavy sigh, Ritz fastened the medal around Roque's dark neck.

"Save him," she murmured. "Please, Uncle Buster and St. Jude, and you, too, God."

Roque's eyes remained tightly closed.

After that, time passed in slow motion. Ritz rubbed her neck, and felt all alone and scared as she thought of the puma and those pointy ears she'd seen earlier.

When a pack of coyotes began to yip off to the north, she began to shake as hard as a rabbit or whatever little animal they were terrorizing. The sky and brush blackened ominously.

Aloud Ritz said, "Roque, I'll stay out here all night long—in the dark, no matter how scared I get, if you just, please...please...don't die.... I'll even take back every mean thing I said. You're not nasty...or...or pure sin...just 'cause you wear tight jeans. I'm sorry I watched you pee. It was fun flying with you. The most fun I ever had in my whole life...until you charged—"

Clasping his lifeless hand, she bent closer, so that she could broadcast straight into her powerful medal.

"You won Buttercup—fair and square. You can have her, too...if you'll only wake up. And...and...you're not stupid, even if you flunked a grade. Nobody but a rare, genuine genius could talk *horse*...could learn it from a book...when you can hardly read. And...and it wasn't Jet last night.... It was me! I watched you dance, so don't you dare die."

Horror mingled with delight when he stirred and she felt his gaze.

"You're just scared there won't be anybody to teach you horse if I die," jeered a thready voice that made her heart leap.

4

Its wings spread wide, a hawk circled low over Roque. Talons curling, the bird hurled itself at the highest branch of a tall live oak, stilling the roar of the cicadas' night chorus. In that brief silence, the dark field felt warm. Then the humid wind licked his skin, bringing with it the sweet, familiar smells of grass and salt and sea, and the cicadas began to sing again.

Not that Roque noticed any of those things on a conscious level. The hot little daggers of pain that spiked up his arm were so fierce they dulled his awareness of all else. He couldn't move his arm or feel his fingers.

The hollow beneath his right eye felt stretched and itchy. His temple throbbed. Half of him was numb; the other half burned. He wanted to twist and writhe and howl like a wolf at the bright sliver of moon hanging straight over him. But the ragged whisper he uttered cost him so dearly, he bit his lips.

"Roque? Did you say something?"

Had he? He tried to speak again.

He heard *her* gasp, felt her fingertips on his mouth. Then pain blurred everything into nightmare again. He was in the wire mesh round pen. Caleb was begging him to teach him to ride, and since their father was gone for the day he'd said yes. But suddenly his father, who'd looked shorter and squattier than usual in baggy jeans and custom-made boots and yet unreasonably terrifying, was stomping toward him, yelling and swearing nonsense that he was trying to kill Caleb again.

Pausing to grab a chain off the nail outside the tack room, he'd pushed Pablo and two cowboys out of his way.

"Nobody had better interfere with me—y'all hear!" When the cowboys lowered their heads, Benny raised the chain. "You trying to kill Sunny on that damn horse, you stupid Mexican son of a bitch!"

Mexican. The way his father said it, had made Roque writhe.

"I begged him to teach me, Daddy," Caleb said.

"Every summer he comes, you want to race bulls or something else crazy!"

"No, Daddy—"

He slammed the chain down on Roque's back.

Roque screamed. Caleb jumped as if he'd been hit. The next blow cut Roque's thighs and sent him sprawling face-down into wood shavings. He hit the ground so hard he swallowed dust laced with horse dung.

As he spit and choked, Caleb hurled himself at his father's knees.

"You idiot!" Benny yelled at Roque. "You won't stop until you kill my good son—you, who never should have been born!"

Again the chain zinged, this time gouging out a hunk of flesh. Roque rolled into a ball, grabbed his knees.

"Say you won't disobey...."

"You're not my father!"

"Say you're sorry!"

"Go to hell."

"He wouldn't hurt me, Daddy!" Caleb shouted. "He's not stupid. He was teaching me *horse* and...and to ride."

When Benny raised the chain again, Caleb let go of his father's leg and threw himself on top of Roque. "He's sorry, Daddy."

Caleb's thin body was hot, and he was crying as he circled Roque's neck with his arms. "If you hurt him, I'll.... I-I'll run away to Mexico! I'll be a Mexican, too!"

"Get off me, kid!" Roque whispered. "I don't want you to hate him...or love me."

"But I do...love you."

Her soft voice cut through Roque's anguish and pain. *Her* gentle fingers trailed his throat, soothed. He strangled a curse.

Dios. Pain stabbed him again.

"I'll even give you Buttercup!" the girl said.

Chinga!

She was holding something and praying to St. Jude. Roque wasn't religious. Still, he'd been brought up Catholic.

He hung on every syllable of the girl's prayer and went still when she fastened her St. Jude medal around his neck. When her voice died, her hand skimmed along his throat and jawline. She lifted her medal and kissed it.

So, it had been her last night. *Her.* He'd wanted to hold this girl close and dance near the fire, to dance. Suddenly he wanted to feel those lips on his skin.

"So, you're just scared there won't be anybody to teach you *horse* if I die. I—I could teach you to kiss too," he whispered.

She dropped the medal and jumped back.

Híjole!

He stole a peek. Big glasses. Smudged clothes. She wasn't much to look at—at least, not yet. Better to keep his eyes closed. But she sure as hell had a pretty voice, especially when she prayed. Those low, husky tones shouldn't belong to a bratty little girl with wires in her mouth. That voice went with a real woman.

Dios. She was just a kid. Younger than Caleb.

Her fingers came back, cautiously gliding along his skin as she prayed again, her comforting words and warm breath falling against his earlobe.

Uno. Dos. Tres... He never made it to ten. The pressure against his fly was too extreme.

Pervert. She was a kid. Fourteen. Not even pretty.

When her gaze drifted down his body, he broke into a sweat. Then he slitted his good eye wider. Even though he was partially color blind, his vision at night was extraordinary. Like a cat, he could see shapes and figures that were invisible to anyone with normal eyesight.

Like now. Every freckle on her pert, slightly upturned nose stood out. Her tears glistened like diamonds. More than a hundred yards away, he saw Buttercup grooming herself.

A sliver of moon in a vast black sky peppered with stars enveloped them. Cicadas were buzzing louder than ever. In the moonlight her ugly glasses glimmered on her thin, unsmiling face. If only she'd been pretty like her friend with the big boobs.

It was hard to imagine her ever growing a figure or ever being beautiful. But she'd spied on him last night and today she'd stood up to him. She'd flown with him. He'd had fun with her before he'd fallen and hit his head. With her he didn't feel homesick.

Nobody here, except for Caleb, ever made him feel as if he belonged.

But she did. Maybe she was a Keller, but she was an innocent, shy and sweet. As sweet as *Mamacita* when he'd had the mumps.

Chinga!

She was sweeter than Ana and Carmela, his sisters, when they were in good moods and hovered over him.

I can't like you, girl! You're the high and mighty Keller princess!

"Don't die." She squeezed his hand.

"I'm just a Mexican," he growled. "You couldn't care less whether I live or die."

She ripped her silky fingers that had his groin in an uproar from his throat.

"Be…be careful," she said in *that* supersweet voice. "I think your arm…. It's all funny and twisted."

"It's broken. What's it to you?"

She shoved her ugly wire-rimmed glasses up her nose. "Nothing. I'm only waiting for your father to come back. He's sending an ambulance."

"So, how come you didn't take your horse and run when you could, little girl?"

"'Cause…'cause my knee got hurt."

"Aren't you scared of being out here all alone in the dark? You ran last night…."

She hesitated and then shook her head. "I didn't want to run. I wanted to dance."

"You're all alone with me," he whispered, "in the dark. I could make you kiss me."

She was slower to answer. "I'd stomp on your broken arm if you did."

He laughed. Then he puckered his mouth and leaned toward her. "Last chance to get your kissing lesson from the best kisser in Mexico."

"No…" Holding her knee, she scooted a few inches away from him.

He lay beside her, silent, wondering what to say to make her come back, but he couldn't think of anything. All too soon he heard his daddy's pickup roaring along the caliche road even before he saw his lights. Finally it stopped. The headlights went out.

Flashlights bobbed. Dogs yapped. Benny Blackstone shouted above their frenzied barks. Then an ambulance screamed on a distant ranch road.

"Over here," Ritz called.

His father waved his flashlight.

Suddenly everything dimmed—their voices, her plain, skinny face—even the barking dogs racing toward him.

"I don't feel too good," he whispered right before he began to shake. "Kiss me." When she still hesitated, he said. "If I die, you'll never get to—"

She put her arms around him and kissed his cheek really fast. "You're gonna be okay."

"I came to this pond hating life here, hating— I... I..." He stopped himself before he blurted something really stupid. On a different track, he said, "I don't want you scared of me. And...and.... Hey, there's a key to the gate in my left pocket. Get it. Take your old horse."

"Where is she?"

"Over there." He pointed. "I don't want her. I never did. I was just teasing you because I wanted to meet your sexy friend."

"Jet?" Her voice quavered.

"You're okay...for a skinny kid."

"But you wish I was Jet?"

"I'll decide later...when you're older. You might be pretty. Not that it would matter. You're a Keller, so you'll have to hate me."

"So, you think I...I might be pretty someday?"

He stared at her face as if it were very difficult to imagine her pretty. "We'll have to wait and see about that, now won't we?"

The fierce hope that shone in her eyes cut him somehow. He closed his eyes to shut her out.

To his surprise he felt her lips, soft and warm and yet fervent somehow hesitantly graze his.

He kept his eyes closed long after the kiss was over, savoring the taste of her innocence. All this from a girl who'd been scared to dance.

He had to forget her.

Somehow he knew he never would.

"Did that boy put his hands in your pants and feel you up?"

"Daddy!" Ritz squealed, her fingers closing around the key Roque had given her. "How could you think that?"

Irish was sitting behind her in the back seat.

Mortified, she covered her eyes. It was an old habit, something she'd done as a child when she'd felt shy and needed to shut out someone or something that was suddenly too much.

"I know his type," her father said.

"Easy, Art," Irish mumbled behind her.

Irish had come along to check her knee. He said it was a ruptured ACL, and he'd stabilized it with an old knee brace he'd brought along.

"But you don't know *him*," Ritz said.

Her father grunted.

"Have you ever spoken to him—even once?"

"He wants to kill his own brother. Last year they caught him half-naked in the back seat of Natasha's car with his hands down her pants."

"Jet said Natasha had her hands in his—"

"What would you—a fourteen-year-old girl—know about trash like that?"

Irish kicked the back of the seat and then said, "Sorry."

Art slammed the fist holding his cigarette against the dash and shot sparks everywhere. Ritz had to brush at her clothing frantically.

"You planning to be his next slut, girl?"

"Don't talk to her like that," Irish admonished.

"Well, are you?" Art thundered. "Did you know he's been seen riding around with Chainsaw Hernandez, that no-good ex-con?"

You don't know everything, Daddy!

The rebellious thought crystallized into one of those life-changing epiphanies. Her father was used to giving commands, used to being the last authority on every subject.

"Talk to me." When she didn't, her father fumed. "What's gotten into you?"

Roque Moya, that's what!

He'd made her braver somehow, and even though she was in more trouble than she'd ever been in before—she wasn't as scared.

The truck hurled itself down the rutted ranch road like a stampeding bull. For once Ritz was glad her daddy was smoking. The acrid fumes gave her an excuse to cough and sputter and wave her hands. Her eyes teared. Her throat burned.

"You're just fourteen. I guess that makes you prime for the pickin' for a low-down Mexican cur like Moya."

Ritz didn't dare defend him out loud again, so she coughed and waved her hands.

Her father, who was usually so careful never to smoke around her, took another long drag. Irish opened his window.

Smoke spewed out of her father's flaring nostrils and spiraled up from the cigarette's tip. Another coughing spasm had Ritz leaning forward and clenching the dash. Through tears she made out the blur of red ambulance lights.

"Roque…"

"You're to stay away from that boy—you hear me, girl?"

"Yes, Daddy." Her voice sounded so weird and small and unreal.

"You should see yourself! Staring after those lights like a boy-crazy fool! He's no damned good, I tell you! And if you mess around with him, he'll bring you down to his level! You're not to think about him—ever."

Her father yanked the steering wheel to the left. When the truck rumbled over a cattle guard, she whirled around to see if the lights were still there, but Irish's broad frame blocked her view. By the time she moved, the black night had swallowed the lights whole.

Ritz placed a hand over her heart. "What if he dies?"

Her daddy's cigarette flamed brighter than an infected boil. "You should be worrying about your mother. She's frantic about you. Ever since you threw the kitchen rugs on the porch without even shaking them and ran off, she's been driving the roads and calling everybody."

"Did Jet put you up to this?" Irish asked softly.

"No!"

Art squashed out his cigarette. Then he rolled down his window. He sighed heavily and pulled another cigarette out of his pocket.

"Boss—"

"Don't nag, Irish!" But Art didn't light it. They were nearly home, and Mother didn't like him smoking because of his high blood pressure.

Ritz glanced his way. In the flying darkness, all she could make out was his white hair and his rigid black shape. She hoped his neck wasn't that awful bright red—his fighting color, as Mother and Irish called it.

At six feet four, her daddy towered over every man on the ranch except Irish. Her father's eyes were the same violet shade as Ritz's. Only his were hard and piercing and had an indomitable quality while hers were soft and vulnerable. His yellow hair had turned white the day Buster had died. Not that he looked old. No, on him it was distinguished.

If you'd been casting a movie, he would have been pure, vintage, cowboy hero. A man of his word, if the boss said a horse was sound, it was. Once he'd run into a burning building to save Ritz's puny foal, Buttercup. Despite his good qualities, he was feared. Nobody wanted him as an enemy.

The narrow ranch road was bumpy. But her daddy knew it like the back of his hand. Hardly glancing at the black-top, he swerved from side to side to avoid the potholes and rough patches.

Instead of the tension between them lessening, it thickened, the closer they got to home and to Mother.

Ritz rolled down her window and set her rigid chin against the edge. Not that breathing in the fresh, stinging wildness of the night air helped.

She felt like a prisoner.

"So you think I…I might be pretty some day?"

She clasped her arms around her waist and hugged herself shyly.

Would you care?

I didn't ask him that! I didn't!

"We'll have to wait and see, now won't we?" The memory of his body swaying to the music last night lit her up inside. If he ever asked her to dance again, she would.

Funny, how the night bugs sounded just the same on Keller land as they had when she'd been with Roque.

Only with *him* she'd felt wild and free and so alive.

She clenched her hands in her lap. "I just wish I could float out this window into the black night sky."

"If you're gonna say stupid stuff like that, just be quiet."

"How come I have to hate him just because he's a Blackstone?"

"Did you get yourself a crush on that boy, girl?"

She pushed her glasses up her nose. "How come I have to hate him?"

"Because I hate his father, and you're my daughter."

"But, Daddy, you started this silly old feud! Not me!"

Irish coughed.

"Silly!" Art hit the brakes hard. For a long moment her father stared straight ahead. He gripped the steering wheel, his shoulders tightening.

"You weren't with me at the funeral home when I identified Buster—were you, girl? I won't forget that day—ever. My big brother's brains all over that buttery beige leather seat of Pamela's brand-new Cadillac."

Behind her, Irish groaned. Ritz whirled. His craggy face was so stricken, she turned back without saying anything. She wasn't sure how or where exactly Irish had known Buster, but her daddy had told her they'd been good friends when they were young, which was the main reason he'd hired Irish.

"I'll see that on my dying day," her father muttered. "Buster was so smart. He wanted to be a doctor. Did you know that? From the time he was little, he was always taking care of sick animals just like you do. If they died, he'd cut them up to try to understand what killed them. He even went to medical school for three years. Did you know that, girl?"

Irish slammed the windows behind him shut again. All of a sudden, she felt as if she wasn't Daddy's only prisoner in the pickup. Irish heaved a furious breath.

The back seat had to be tight for someone his size. He kept shifting his weight, kicking her seat.

Not that Art paid him any attention. "Then Daddy got sick and said Buster had to forget medicine and come home and be a rancher…that I was too young to take over. Buster held things together until I grew up. I owe Buster everything. When he reapplied to medical school, they said he was too old and there wasn't space. He would have been one fine doctor. That's all he ever wanted to be.''

"Oh, God—" Irish's gravelly voice died on a breath.

"Sorry, Irish," her father muttered.

Ritz squeezed herself tightly as Art hit the accelerator. "Uncle Buster's death wasn't Roque's fault."

"You're not listening. Your father never said it was," Irish said.

Nobody said another word. Not even when the truck rattled over the last cattle guard and her father swerved onto the driveway that led to the clapboard sprawl of rambling additions that was their home.

Maybe the old three-story house had been the ranch's headquarters for more than a hundred years. Maybe it was a historical landmark. But to Ritz, it was simply home. For the first time ever she dreaded going inside.

The screen door opened, and her mother ran out onto the porch and then froze in the yellow light at the top of the steps.

Her daddy turned off the ignition. "You're not to worry her with talk about that boy—you hear me? She's been through enough today."

"He was hurt. I had to stay with him."

"I won't ask you what you were doing over there in the first place."

Remembering Irish, Ritz couldn't say Jet had locked her inside.

"You're to stay away from those people from now on. Until I say different, you're grounded! Every step I take, you take. Your mother says this isn't the first time you've run off with Jet without doing your chores. Watch yourself! You don't know as much as you think you do."

"Well, maybe you don't, either, Daddy."

He slammed his fists against the steering wheel. "You never used to act like this."

"You can't just lock me up." Her hand closed over the gate key she'd removed from Roque's pocket.

When they didn't get out of the truck her mother flew down the steps. Her daddy got out and flung his door shut. Ritz and Irish hopped out, too.

"Art, you're that awful shade of red! Ritz, you look like a boiled lobster!"

Ritz and her father glared at each other.

"Irish, what's going on?"

Irish headed silently toward his own truck.

"It's late, Fiona," her daddy said.

"Ritz! Where's your hat? I've told you and told you…"

Instead of running up the porch stairs, Ritz lingered by her mother's prize roses. The yellow porch light made them look sickly. Blood-red petals splattered the clay earth.

"Ritz! Are you coming inside?" Her mother stood at the door, holding it open until Ritz climbed the stairs.

She went to bed without eating. The next morning her parents had a long talk about her. Two days later the tabloids ran pictures of Benny along with photos of Blanca Moya showing off Roque's back and broken arm. She accused her ex-husband of abuse.

Every morning her parents talked about the trashy Blackstones. As Ritz listened to her father's unfair judgments and speculations about Roque through the kitchen door, her fears and distrust mounted.

Because her parents resented her sullen attitude, they supervised her closely. Thus, it was several weeks before Ritz could sneak away. First chance she got, she galloped Buttercup to the Blackstone pond a little before five.

But Roque wasn't there. She sat on a wide flat stone on the bank. Never before had the pond seemed so bleak and wild. The patchy grass was brown and so thin rocks and dirt showed through. Even the prickly pear and reeds along the bank seemed stunted.

For seven days straight, she returned to sit on that rock at the pond's edge. Clasping her knees to her thin chest, she always stared up at the vast sky until she got too hot and had to seek shade.

On the eighth, she found Caleb sitting on her big, flat rock, skimming stones, making ducks fly up and circle. Every time they landed again, he threw another rock.

She tiptoed up behind him, picked a warm stone from his pile, tossed it carelessly, and it sank at the water's edge.

"You're not very good." Caleb laughed, pleased. Then he notched his pointed chin so that it was higher than hers.

"Better than you!" she said, growing competitive.

His smoldering green eyes jeered her. Just for a second they reminded her a little of his handsome brother's, and her stomach turned over.

Very carefully she selected a rock that was as flat and thin and yet as round as a quarter.

"Get your own," Caleb said, cupping his hands around his pile like a miser hoarding gold.

With a deft flick of her wrist, she sent the rock hopping all the way across the pond to the opposite shore. "Eight skips!"

Caleb pitched a stone that sank near her first one in the muddy soup near the bank.

"See! I am too better!" she cried.

"Who cares?" Caleb threw all his rocks into the water at once. "He's gone!" Caleb sprang to his feet and jammed his hands into his pockets. "He won't be back, either. I hate you!"

His voice was harsh and trembly, and his eyes were red. She hoped fiercely that he wouldn't cry because then the tears that pricked at her own eyes would fall, too.

"He won't be back! Not ever." Caleb stared at her. "Because of you!"

"Me?"

"His mother, Blanca, came to the hospital with Roque's uncles. She took one look at Roque's black eye and started shouting at Daddy. When she saw Roque's back, she freaked. Next thing, she starts calling lawyers and reporters. The only reason she ever shut up was 'cause Daddy paid her off. She dropped all charges and hauled Roque off to Mexico. Right before he left, Roque asked me to come here and tell you goodbye."

"He did?"

"I didn't want to, only he got mad and forced me to swear I'd come every day until…" Caleb frowned. "Only you never came, so I stopped for a while. You weren't really his friend. You're just a Keller."

"I was grounded, stupid. I—I came the first chance I got."

Their gazes locked.

"I think the feud is stupid," she said. "But my daddy doesn't care what I think! If he finds out I saw you today, he'll ground me forever."

"My daddy thinks Roque's mean and jealous and that he wants to kill me," was all Caleb could think to say. "But he's not. He's nice."

They both threw a few rocks that went flying across the pond.

"Thanks…for coming to tell me today, Caleb."

He grinned sheepishly.

She paused, uncertain, too. "Well, it's getting late. I'd better go."

"If you gotta go—" But his grin broadened a little. "Roque liked it here. He liked this pond. He liked me. He was going to teach me *caballo,* too. *Caballo* is Spanish for *horse*.…"

"I—I used to play here with my cousins," she said. "All the time."

"My daddy says I have to forget Roque," Caleb said.

"Mine, too!"

"But I won't. He's my brother."

"Well, he's nothing to me," she lied, staring up at a cloud until her neck started hurting. "I-I'd better go."

"You said that already."

Still, she lingered, digging her toe into the dirt.

Here, not so long ago, the wind had ruffled her hair, and Roque's hands had circled her waist. He'd held her while Buttercup's hooves had thudded as wildly as her own heartbeats.

"Do you...do you think Roque will forget us?" Ritz whispered.

"He said he would. He said I wasn't his brother anymore. And if he won't remember his own brother, why would he remember a dumb girl who broke his arm?"

"He charged your daddy! Not me—"

"He won't remember you...."

"He'd remember Jet I bet."

"Who wouldn't?" Caleb lowered his eyes. "She's really something."

"And I'm not?"

"I didn't say that. Forget Roque." He hesitated. "Could you come over some time... I mean...just to see me? Nobody would ever have to know. We could ride together, maybe get that book Roque had and try to teach ourselves *caballo*—"

"It wouldn't be the same without Roque—"

Book 2

"... The moment one knows how, one begins to die a little. Living is a form of not being sure, of not knowing what next or how... One leaps in the dark!"

—Agnes de Mille, Dance Choreographer

5

"Mr. Daniels, please don't throw us out—" Ritz begged. "Please! I can explain—"

The high school principal shook his head and frowned. "You leave me no choice." He opened her older brother Steve's silver flask and lifted it to his nose.

Josh's eyes blazed with jealousy every time they fell on Ritz. If anything, Jet was even angrier than Steve, whose face contorted every time Ritz looked at him.

"If only you'd let me explain why I did it," she said to Mr. Daniels.

Working his bulbous nose back and forth like a giant, earless rabbit, Mr. Daniels inhaled. "Vodka!" he spat. "Just as I thought. Kids—get out of my dance!"

Josh, Jet and Steve ran for the doors, but Ritz stood paralyzed. Even when Mr. Daniels pointed toward the doors and said, "Move it, princess!" her legs wouldn't budge.

The school gym throbbed with rock music. Not that anybody was dancing. All her classmates were watching the humiliating scene under the red Exit sign. Her face burned.

"But I didn't do anything wrong."

Placing his hands squarely on her shoulders, Mr. Daniels pushed her toward the door.

"I thought we were going steady," Josh muttered when she stepped outside.

"That doesn't mean you own me," Ritz replied as she began to shiver in the chill night air.

"You shouldn't have danced with Caleb Blackstone," Steve said.

"I want to see all of you in my office—first thing Monday. Understand?" Mr. Daniels ordered. "All four of you! With your parents!"

"But Steve didn't mean anything," Ritz said. "And neither did I." Carefully she avoided Jet's gaze. "Please don't throw us out of the dance! We weren't drink... dwink...drinking...either."

Why was her tongue so thick it stuck to the roof of her mouth? Why was Mr. Daniels' big nose spinning?

"First thing Monday!" he repeated.

"But I'm in community college now," Jet retorted.

"So am I," Steve said.

"Fine. But if you two ever want to attend a school function again with Ritz, be here."

The principal turned his back on them. When the gym doors clicked behind him, Steve almost fell headfirst down the stairs. Weaving, he grabbed the railing. Then he headed for the parking lot.

Ritz put a hand on Josh's sleeve. "I can explain—"

He stared at her hand until she removed it. When Ritz turned to Jet, she stuck her chin in the air and raced after the boys.

"Where the hell is he?" Steve yelled to no one in particular. "Where's that damn red sports car?"

Her brother's wide face was flushed, his eyes bloodshot. Suddenly Ritz felt sick at her stomach. "Did you put vodka in my cola, Steve?"

"What if I did?" he growled. "Where's Blackstone?"

"Just forget about him, why don't you?" Ritz pleaded.

"You been seeing him behind my back?" Josh demanded.

"Sunny's a friend."

"Oh, so now it's Sunny." Josh glared.

"Forget about Caleb. You won't even try to understand. Steve, just calm down. We're in enough trouble already. When Mr. Daniels tells Daddy they kicked us out of the school dance because you got in a fight—"

"Me?" He fell against a car and then righted himself as he stumbled through the dark parking lot toward the van. "You danced—"

"Shut up—both of you," Josh said. "Let's just get rolling and get home."

"Home?" Steve unlocked the van and punched the door locks so everybody could get in. "Hell! We're gonna find that son of a bitch if it's the last thing we do."

Jet laughed. She cast a sly, dark look at Ritz and patted Steve on the shoulder. "Get 'im, cowboy."

When everybody but Ritz laughed as they piled inside, Ritz felt sicker. What should she do? She didn't want to make her friends and brother any madder. But she was too afraid to stay at the gym all by herself and call her daddy to come pick her up. Because then she'd have to tell him she'd danced with Caleb. She was Daddy's perfect little girl.

Numbly she climbed into the back seat. Jet slammed the van door. With frozen fingers, Ritz fastened her seat belt. "Can't we just go home?" she whispered.

"Those dumb bastards had no right to kick us out!" Steve grumbled. "No right to give Caleb a head start. Especially not in that souped-up car. I'm gonna catch the runt and finish what he started!''

"No," Ritz said.

"Yes, little sister." Steve punched the steering wheel with the flats of his palms. "It's all your fault, Ritz, for dancing with a Blackstone!"

Jet's hands were clenched in her lap. Her face was twisted away from Ritz. "Why did he have to ask you to dance anyway? What was that all about?"

"We were friends. Since the last time his brother was here. Friends. We wanted to end the feud. I'm sorry, y'all!" Ritz cried. "Okay?"

"Not okay, Little Miss Perfect! Okay?" Steve revved the engine, burning rubber as he careened out of the parking lot. "Ramón told me you ride with that son of a bitch sometimes."

"Slow down! Let me out!" Ritz screamed as the van speeded up.

"He didn't do anything!"

"You led him on!"

"Why don't you both just shut up," Jet muttered.

Bright yellow eyes gleamed in terror from the center stripe.

Steve swerved.

The van jounced into a pothole and skidded. Laughing, Jet inserted a CD and turned up the volume, flooding the interior with a thudding blare of static and beat that matched Steve's wired mood.

The highway overpass flicked past.

"Slow down, Steve! Please!" Ritz begged.

The traffic thinned, but Ritz's eyes remained glued to the speedometer.

"Steve, that sign said forty. You're doing eighty! You're going to kill us—"

"And there's not a damn thing you can do about it, Little Miss Perfect!"

Mexican Christmas music blared from the cheap tinny speakers of the speeding pickup. Not that the driver was really listening to it. He was too busy trying to catch Caleb in the sports car up ahead. He leaned forward, gripping the wheel, trying to see through the blur of darkness.

Christmas—the loneliest time of year for those who live with ghosts.

Maybe it was the familiar music. Memories of *his wife* seemed to swirl around him like smoke.

Her brown eyes filling with revulsion every time she looked at him. "I married you because you were somebody."

Her wedding ring lying abandoned on the coffee table beside the undecorated Christmas tree in his big, deserted house.

Her side of the garage dark and empty.

Once she'd adored him.

Adore.

His eyes burned. Sometimes he felt as if he lived in his pickup. He was always in a rage driving somewhere.

His callused hand shook when he reached for a cigarette pack from among the litter of tapes, magazines, and tools in the passenger seat.

He lit it, smoke trailing from his mouth and nostrils as he forced himself to concentrate on the bobbing red lights up ahead. The gossips all said that cute sporty car his rich lawyer daddy had given Caleb would be the end of him.

When Caleb's taillights vanished for a second, the man's heavy boot slammed down on the accelerator. The big pickup rolled beneath him, jouncing heavily over every rough spot.

If he caught him, would he have the nerve to do what was necessary?

When a fleeting cloud passed across the moon and snuffed out the cruel glimmer of the winding stretch of road, the driver squashed his cigarette and hurled it out the window.

Where were those damn headlights? The road was suddenly as black as pitch.

His stomach felt queasy from the rough ride, but he slammed his right boot to the floor.

What the hell was he doing? Who the hell did he think he was—God? How could he be God—when there was no God?

He'd learned that the day he'd been sacrificed in a court of law, when jackal lawyers had used the American legal system to tear him apart.

He stared at the strip of flying road, at the clouds and the stars and felt his madness and yet his smallness in the universe.

He hadn't always felt so small. Once he'd had immense, unshakable confidence. Once he'd been a god, a giver of life instead of a taker. There hadn't been any doubting voices in his head then. He'd simply known what was right.

Benny Blackstone had taught him there was no right and wrong; there was simply a verdict—guilty.

Caleb was only sixteen years old, a cowboy prince if ever there was one.

Too young to die.

Caleb wasn't even responsible....

The driver's fists knotted on the wheel as he remembered long white legs, the two figures writhing on that narrow cot at the beach house.

The moon came out, and the red taillights winked again. The closer he got, the more conscious he was of his

fears and pangs of conscience. His heart sped up. He began
to shake and sweat.

Yellow center streaks raced under his wheels. Yanking
his Stetson lower, he lit another cigarette. In between drags
his long fingers fisted and flexed. He was going so fast,
the scrub oak on either side of the road swam together.

He felt the truck sail off the road. A tire lifted into the
air. He took his foot off the gas and waited.

Tires hit, spinning and screaming on pavement. He
fought for control.

Damn the kid. Damn the kid to hell.

Furious, he caught him again and flashed his brights. He
hung on the brat's bumper for a minute or two, nudged it
even. Just to show him.

Weaving, the kid sped up.

Banks of black clouds swept across the moon, heading
north. A sure sign that tomorrow it would get colder.

The drive had eased off three car lengths when the kid
hit Dead Man's Curve too fast and lost it.

Twin cones of white bounced across the tops of the high
grasses and fence posts. For a second or two the sports car
seemed to surf the plumes of dirt and gravel that frothed
beneath him like a wave. Then the little car catapulted off
the shoulder.

The man hit the brakes and fishtailed. By the time he
stopped the pickup, steam and smoke were spewing from
the mangled sports car. A tiny flame flickered under the
car.

With its windshield gone and its roof sheered off, the
car looked like a squashed tin can. But the horn was blaring, and the radio was still playing "Jingle Bells."

Above the wreckage, stars floated around the moon in
the milky haze of the chilly, dark night. The man sucked
in a harsh breath. The kid was slumped like a broken pup-
pet under the steering wheel.

His tanned face was ashen. There was blood in his long, wavy blond hair and cuts across his brow. A smudge of black darkened his high cheekbone.

The man had lain awake nights longing for this, wanting to cause it. So how could he feel torn as he stared at the dead Blackstone boy?

Then the kid's long lashes fluttered. A startled pair of green eyes drilled him and a muffled gasp escaped those bone-white, trembling lips.

The man forgot his hate and stretched a hand toward the kid's cheek. Then the smell of gasoline hit him. Too late, he saw dark liquid gushing toward his boots.

Bright flames licked the front of the car. As more gasoline gushed toward him, he stared at the boy, an oddly protective tenderness filling him. There was nothing, he, who had fought death so many times, could do even if he'd wanted to.

He was running, faster than he'd ever run when the tornadic whoof of flame, glass, and metal engulfed him. The blast lifted him and pitched him facedown onto the highway. Pain splintered up from his knee. Lava heat singed his hair. Fenders and hubcaps shot past him. Ribbons of flame curled upward into the night.

Burning steel rained onto the road just as headlights lit the high grasses again.

Another vehicle was taking Dead Man's Curve way too fast.

The man was barely crawling by the time he reached the shoulder. Then his boot hit a piece of hot metal that burned all the way through his heel. Pain arced up his leg.

Black sky and stars whirled. Then the stars collided in a white explosion that obliterated everything.

Blackstone's kid was dead.

"Welcome to hell, Benny boy," he whispered, laughing and yet not knowing that he laughed.

He hadn't laughed in years.

The wind brushed his cheek, and a lone owl hooted. He thought of *his wife*. He saw her wedding band on the table. He remembered Caleb and wiped at his eyes, so his tears wouldn't fall.

Steve pounded the dash. "So, where's my fuzz buster, y'all!"

Jet laughed. "Under your boots, cowboy!"

A second or two later, Josh had the radar detector attached to his visor and plugged into the cigarette-lighter socket.

Steve laughed. "Happy, Little Miss Perfect?"

"You're going over a hundred.... How much vodka—"

"You ain't seen nothin', honey."

"What's that? Up ahead?"

Ritz blinked at the eerie orange glow on the other side of Dead Man's Curve. Her head was really beginning to spin. Maybe it was just the speed.

Then the van was hurtling into the sharp curve, its back wheels sliding off the asphalt onto rocks, losing traction. Seconds later, the front tires blew. Then the back tires exploded. The van tilted onto its side.

Everybody started screaming when it rolled.

"We're going to die!" Ritz whispered.

She heard Roque's voice. *Do you want to fly?*

Ritz's mind was playing tricks on her. Was she dead already?

She was fourteen again, watching Roque dance on the beach. Then she was standing on Buttercup, bare toes curling into her dark hide, her thin arms outstretched, her long hair blowing against Roque's face. Again, she was a part of Buttercup, a part of Roque, too, and a part of the sky. And again, it was as if she'd always known Roque and always would.

Then he was gone. She remembered the hours she'd spent primping in front of her mirror every summer, wondering if this were the summer he'd come, wondering if she was too skinny or pretty enough.

But he hadn't come.

Now it wouldn't matter if he did.

He would hold out his hand and ask another girl to dance.

The naked branches of a mesquite tree loomed.

I'll never see Roque again!

The van exploded.

Everything went black.

She wasn't dead.

But something was very wrong. Black and orange shapes swirled woozily around her. Her head hurt. So did her legs.

Ritz blinked. A pulse beat like a tattoo on the left side of her head. Her lips were dry. She couldn't make sense of anything.

What was that red blooming against the inky night sky? Why were the stars in the wrong place?

The air was oily, and her skin felt like ice.

She rubbed her arms. Somebody had turned the heater off in the van, and she was shaking and burning up, too. Her neck felt stretched and strained.

Then she realized, she was hanging upside down in her brother's overturned van, her long blond hair sweeping its ceiling.

When she twisted, her legs cramped, and her head ached even more. The thick strap had rolled and cut into her neck and thighs like a knife.

Not a strap. Her seat belt.

She was strung-up like a slab of meat in L.D. Dobbs's butcher shop.

She remembered the yellow strip in the middle of black rushing. Rushing.

She had cried out…

They'd taken the turn, and then…

What then? What was it that she couldn't remember?

Her teeth began to chatter. She felt confused and disoriented. All she knew was that she had to get out of the van.

In a panic, she began to struggle to undo her seat belt, but her fingers wouldn't work properly.

Then Jet moaned, her voice echoing weakly as if she were a long way away.

Jagged nightmarish flashes hit Ritz in fits and starts that made no sense.

The spindly Christmas tree soaring to the gym's rafters.

Caleb, tall and golden with his shy, movie star grin that reminded her more of his brother's every day, his voice croaking when he asked her to dance.

Her busybody big brother Steve gulping down his cola, squashing the cup and pitching it to the floor and then crushing the soggy paper to pulp with his boot heel.

The music fading. An expectant hush filling the gym as Caleb Blackstone led Ritz Keller to the dance floor.

Steve charging Caleb's big inlaid turquoise belt buckle.

Take your hands off my sister, you son of a bitch!

The chaperones surrounding the grappling boys on the floor.

Steve's mouth bleeding, his fists pounding Caleb.

Kids yelling and swearing, jeering, egging them on.

Everything going quiet and tense when Mr. Daniels yelled, "Boys!"

The night air reeked of gasoline.

Ritz was hanging upside down again in the van.

How? Why?

She squinted. Something was burning on the other side of the road like a gigantic, poisonous flower spitting flame.

"Jet, are you okay?"

"I think so," came a groggy whisper from somewhere behind her.

"Where are the guys? Steve?"

"I don't know," Jet whimpered. "Oh, Ritz, there's something black and sticky on my blouse. My...my shoulder..."

There were tears and terror in her normally, cocky voice.

"Is everybody else okay?"

"I—I don't know."

Why had Ritz said yes to Caleb? Why had she ever thought she could end the feud by making friends with Caleb?

Not my fault.

Steve's fault...for going crazy and driving too fast.

"You have to get me out! We have to find them! Hurry! My belt! It's jammed!"

"Ritz.... Ritz...."

Steve's voice.

She saw his shadowy figure on the ground by the road.

"Steve?"

He didn't answer.

She had to get out of the van—fast.

"Jet...please..." Ritz pressed at the buckle frantically. Then she remembered. Jet was mad at her, too, and jealous because Caleb had asked her to dance.

Suddenly the buckle snapped loose, and she crashed onto the ceiling. For a long moment she just lay there, her face mashed into the roof. Then she rolled over and got on her knees and crawled toward a broken window.

Beyond the jagged shards, she saw Steve's outstretched body silhouetted in the amber-red glow. She inched across the asphalt and rocks into the sticker burrs.

"Ritz, I can't move anything except my head." Steve sounded lost and scared, the way he had when they'd been kids playing hide-and-seek and he hadn't known where she was.

"Don't try to move," she whispered.

"I...I can't feel my toes." He began to whimper.

"Oh, my God."

She forced herself to calm down. "Yes, you can."

Steve stared up at her, his blue eyes big and bright. "No..."

Hovering over his pale face, she smoothed his blond hair from his high forehead and began to pray.

Behind her she heard a footstep.

"Jet? Josh?"

Ritz turned.

No one was there.

Black clouds scudded high above the sea of flame. A hellish moon and a burning car lit the world.

When she turned back to Steve, she *felt* an uncanny presence behind her.

"Who's there?" she whispered, turning around.

No answer.

"Can I help?" came a deep, slow voice right behind her.

Again she turned. A tall man with a shock of dark, wavy brown hair, his long legs spread widely apart, towered over her.

Her eyes widened. "Irish? Where did you come from? I didn't hear you drive up."

Silently Irish knelt beside Steve.

She said, "He can't feel his toes."

Again he was slow to answer. It was as if some invisible, almost impenetrable wall separated them.

"I know." As if he knew just what to do, Irish's long, supple fingers began to massage Steve's neck.

"I didn't think you were supposed to move him," she began.

"Take off his shoes," he ordered crisply, not stopping his work with Steve's neck for another minute. Finally he sighed in satisfaction, and his large hands stilled. "Better?" he demanded of Steve.

Steve took a deep breath. "I...I can breathe."

"Can you feel your toes?"

"My God! Yes! They're starting to tingle. They're burning. They...they feel like they're on fire. Like ants biting me everywhere. They hurt! Oh, God— Make the pain go away."

Jet and Josh ambled toward them. In the glare of headlights sweeping them, they looked young, white-faced and very frightened. Jet's black hair was wet and stringy, and she was biting her nails.

Brakes squealed. Doors opened and slammed.

"Call 9-1-1. Get the paramedics here—fast," Irish ordered. To Steve, he said, "Son, wiggle your toes."

"I can move them...a little," Steve whispered in wonder. "How did you—"

"Put your hands under here," drawled Irish.

Ritz slid her hands into Steve's blond hair. Slowly Irish eased her fingers into the correct position and removed his own.

"What?"

"All you've gotta do is hold his neck like that till you get to the hospital. Don't let anybody move him."

"But— Where are you going?" Ritz whispered.

"To check on the others. Just hold his neck. Understand?"

"I can't.... I don't know how."

"You'll be just fine."

"Don't leave me," Ritz whispered.

He smiled. She looked down at Steve. When she looked up again, Irish was examining Josh.

Later Chainsaw Hernandez, who chanced to drive by, told her it took the paramedics thirty minutes to get there. But she had no sense of time as she huddled over her injured brother, her fingers cramping because she couldn't move; no sense of anything as more and more cars stopped, and their occupants got out to help.

Sirens screamed. The police arrived and took over, and still Ritz knelt beside her brother and cradled Steve's neck in her fingers even though her shoulders, back, and hands felt stiff and ached.

Firefighters raced in with hoses, blasting water everywhere.

"Steve, it won't be much longer. They'll brace your neck. They'll take you to the hospital. Everything is going to be all right."

Then she heard Jet's voice, thick and stark and old, utterly different than it had ever sounded before, behind her.

"Caleb's car's on fire. His body's inside it! We killed him, Ritz! We killed him!" Jet was shaking. She seemed dazed.

"I'm so sorry I danced—"

"You don't understand—"

Jet sank down beside Ritz. Her eyes were glazed. Jet grabbed her and held on, sobbing brokenly. "I killed him." Then she turned and stared at her father.

6

"I want to talk to that snotty little bitch you call a daughter! Ritz killed my boy, Caleb, and she's going to pay."

Ritz shuddered. Her heart pumped wildly. She hadn't been this close to Benny Blackstone since the day Roque had charged him and Benny had fired his Winchester.

Not that he sounded quite as arrogant as he usually did. Beneath his anger, she sensed terror and a grief even more paralyzing than her own.

She opened her eyes, expecting to find him about to pounce on her, but she was all alone in a lime-green room, her wrists tied with white bandages to a stretcher that had raised aluminum rails.

When Benny wasn't there, she gulped in a huge sigh of a relief. Then she realized he was right outside in the hall, pacing back and forth while her father spoke in a hard voice that was so low she couldn't distinguish individual words.

"Not my fault," she whispered, splaying her fingers in a helpless gesture.

Then Sheriff Johnson interceded kindly. For such a big man, he had a gentle voice. "You've been through hell. Why don't you go on home, Benny?"

"I'm gonna sue the county. I'm gonna sue you too, Keller, same as I sued your wimp of a brother."

Bodies slammed hard against a wall.

The sheriff's voice, gentle no longer, boomed. "Go home, both of you—unless you want to share a jail cell!"

"Not my fault!" Ritz whispered, her voice growing shrill with tears. Why didn't they believe her?

Suddenly she was crying and shouting and tugging at the sheets, and she couldn't seem to stop. Until Dr. Wanner and a stern-faced, fat nurse, whose big bloodshot blue eyes stared through her like she was a murderess, came in and popped her with a needle that stung and then made her sleepy.

After that the lights in the E.R. were so bright, Ritz couldn't stay awake. Next Dr. Wanner's close-set kindly brown eyes peered down at her as he pressed an icy stethoscope to her chest.

Normally he was six feet tall. All of a sudden, like a creature out of *Alice in Wonderland,* he sprouted to twelve feet, give or take and inch, and his beaky nose grew as long as Pinocchio's. His soft voice roughened and began to come and go, as if someone was tweaking his volume knob. His blue-eyed nurse bloated and floated above him and Ritz's stretcher.

Or was she just woozy…seeing and hearing things? Half the time Ritz didn't know who she was, where she was, or what had happened. And when she did know, the reality was so terrible it brought back her hysteria.

"I want my mother! I want to go home!"

"*Shh.*"

A gloved hand poked her toes, pried her eyes open and shone lights into them.

"I—I want my mother…."

Nurse Blue Eyes held her down.

"—squeeze my hand—"

"Are you on hard drugs—"

"Not my fault..."

Then Dr. Wanner came in again. Only this time he tip-toed and was as small as a mouse while his syringe was huge.

"Mother... I want my mother. Where's Steve?"

Vaguely Ritz remembered the ambulance ride, the attendants not much older than she was, all of them scared to death, afraid Steve would be paralyzed, treating him like he was made of crystal even as they tied down and braced his neck so tight he'd mumbled incoherently about pain.

"Why me?" Steve had wept.

Why Caleb?

Voices in the ambulance.

"—unstable neck—"

"—an MVA rollover down on Dead Man's—"

Steve hadn't been a human being to them. He'd been a patient with a mask covering his face and plastic bags of fluid attached to his arms that made strange gurgling sounds. Instead of answering her questions, they'd stared at her hard and told her to stay calm.

Ritz's mind played tricks on her. Thoughts dissolved. New thoughts burst in showers of stars.

Caleb... Caleb...

Sometimes she was riding Buttercup through the surf or across a pasture and Caleb was on Long John. Nobody except Jet was supposed to know that Sunny and she had been friends ever since Roque went away for good.

Nobody was supposed to know that they met at the pond or at the old Keller graveyard or even at her daddy's beach house and went riding on long hot summer afternoons.

Instead of ether, Ritz smelled leather and horsehair and grass and wet, salty, sea air. Leather reins cut her fingers as she raced Sunny along the beach. Long John was a fine black Friesian stallion with a gentle temperament but friskier than Buttercup, so Caleb always won hands down.

"Roque would really beat you if he were here," Caleb said once, his eyes gleaming.

She remembered Roque's long, lean body, his strong, tanned hands clasping her waist when they'd flown.

"Do you ever hear from him?"

"He'll write…someday. Spelling, writing, reading…those things are hard for him—"

"So, the answer is no."

"Race you to the beach house!" Caleb had retorted.

The dream always changed here.

Suddenly the wind was blowing, and she saw two figures, a boy and a girl in the beach house. Innocently exploring each other with their hands. Going too far. Experimenting. Then they were naked and writhing.

The disturbing vision dissolved. Ritz was running from the house in tears.

She thought of Caleb standing under the Christmas tree in the school gym, folding her hand into his as he winked down at her.

"Why can't we be friends?" he'd asked. "Why can't we dance together? Just once? Declare ourselves? Forget what happened in the beach house. It's wrong for me to have to hate you just because you're a Keller."

Then Steve and Josh were there, drunk, their blunt fists flying.

Next orange flames licked an inky-black sky.

Caleb floated away every time the door opened, and she would catch snatches of hushed, worried, adult conversations.

"—daughter okay—"

"—mainly just want to observe her—"

"—son in critical condition—"

"—fracture to cervical spine—"

"—MRI—"

"—c-4 fracture—"

"—said he couldn't feel his toes—"

"—Irish Taylor—"

"Mother—I want my mother!"

7

Ritz woke up screaming.

"Ritzy, honey what's wrong?"

She opened her eyes to sunshine splashing across green walls. Wrinkling her nose at the antiseptic, hospital smells, she fingered the plastic bracelet on her right wrist. Slowly she read her name and some little black numbers that made no sense.

"Ritz—you were whimpering—"

Her mother's voice. At last!

"I—I don't know." She rubbed her brow. "I—I had the most terrible dream...."

An IV was attached to her left arm. Her long yellow hair was tied into a ponytail. Somebody had stripped her and dressed her in a blue hospital gown.

Absently she fingered the flimsy material. It felt so alien. Her mouth hurt. When she ran the tip of her tongue along the edge of her teeth, her tongue burned. Had she bitten it?

"Ritzy?"

At the childhood nickname Ritz's throat caught. She swallowed on a hard lump and opened her eyes wider.

Her pretty dark mother hovered above her. Beyond her

slim form, her father slouched over bright red poinsettias centered in a sunny window. His broad back was to them; he stood as far from her as he could and still remain in the room.

"Daddy…"

He stiffened at her voice.

Ritz's heart twisted as she stared at his rigid, broad back.

"What's so interesting out there in the parking lot?"

At her question his neck turned that dangerous shade of mottled red. Ritz clutched her sheets tighter. Drawing them to her chin, she almost ducked under them and hid the way she used to when she'd been a little girl. He jerked a cord, and the blinds slammed to the windowsill so fast he had to grab the poinsettias.

"Don't be mad, Daddy."

When his neck darkened to an even more ominous shade, Ritz curled her fingers into her sheets and squeezed really hard.

"How come you can make me feel so small and afraid without even looking at me?"

He slammed the poinsettia plant down and raised the blinds again.

"I wish you'd come over here, Daddy—"

And put your arms around me. Or at least touch my hand…or maybe kiss my cheek the way you used to when I was little and scared. And I am scared, Daddy. Please, won't you please tell me everything is going to be all right?

I've tried so hard to be your favorite little princess. Don't you remember how you used to come to my room and tell me bedtime stories about the monsters in the brush that can eat ten cowboys wearing spurs in one bite?

I used to shiver and shake and hang on every word. Steve always wiggled and interrupted and made your face turn red. I tried to be good—your perfect little princess.

But, it's so hard to be perfect.

"How's Buttercup?" Buttercup was settled and expecting her foal before too long.

Her father shrugged.

The red poinsettias were tied with a crisp, white satin bow.

"Daddy—hmm…who are those pretty flowers from?"

He flinched. "They're from your mother, damn it."

"Your name's on the card, too, Art," Fiona said softly.

He reeled, and for a split second, under his cold, critical eye, Ritz's blood turned to ice. "I didn't write it."

"I'm supposed to be perfect…to do what you say—always—Daddy?"

"If you'd behaved sensibly, if you and Steve hadn't gotten into my vodka, none of this would have happened."

"Art! Not now!"

Her mother's soft, reproaching tone startled Ritz. Rarely did her sweet mother intercede on her behalf with her father. Fun loving Fiona Keller had married her older rancher husband too young. Although he was too strict to suit her, she revered him the way some women do God.

"Say something, Daddy," Ritz pleaded as she struggled to sit up straighter in her hospital bed.

He didn't turn around.

"Did you and Mother have a fight…because of me?"

"This is a whole helluva lot more important than a fight between your mother and me, girl! Caleb Blackstone is dead 'cause a bunch of you kids got drunk and crazy at the dance and then played around in cars!"

At her mother's soft gasp, Ritz began to tremble.

"I—I wasn't drunk…."

Her mother began to fuss, straightening the bedsheets, smoothing Ritz's ponytail.

Ritz caught her hands and gently pushed them away. "How's Steve?"

"Fine," came her mother's gentle, too-soothing voice.

There was a long, electric silence. Her mother went white. Her mouth thinned. The lines between her dark brows were carved so deep she actually looked all of her forty years.

"Fine?" Her father ground out the word. "Steve's got ten pounds of weight pulling his neck back like a turkey stretched out on the block. He's in some contraption that swivels on a metal frame, so that the nurses can flip him every thirty minutes."

His brown hand grabbed the cord and then threw it so violently, the blind fell again, snapping against the window-pane on the way down. This time he jumped aside and let the poinsettias crash to the floor. He grabbed the broken pot. Dirt spilling out, he flung the tangle of red flowers back on the ledge.

"Your brother's fine, all right. He's got amnesia. Brain-damaged probably."

"Art, why don't you go outside—"

"And do what?"

"Relax."

He whirled. "Don't either of you tell me what to do!"

Her father's face was purple. "The whole damn county knows. Benny Blackstone slapped me with a lawsuit this morning. He intends to steal my half of the Triple K the same way he stole Buster's half."

"Art, don't—"

Usually when her father was in the mood to rant, he stayed outside and worked horses, loaded feed, or cleaned guns.

But he had to be here—caged in a hospital with them, his wife and children.

"Caleb asked me to dance. That's all, Daddy. Caleb's a friend. I wanted to dance."

"There's nothing wrong with dancing," Fiona whispered.

"Right," he thundered. "We can't argue that point, can we?"

It was an old, deeply charged argument. Her mother loved parties; he loved working cattle out in the open. He was fierce. She was soft and gentle.

"Haven't I told you kids never to play with cars and to stay away from that Blackstone bunch?"

"I'm all grown up, Daddy. I can choose my own friends."

"Like hell! Look what happened!"

She bit her lip.

He wouldn't look at her.

"But, Daddy—"

"You'll be going home this afternoon, dear," her mother whispered. "It's not good for you to worry about anything. You've had a shock."

"Stop it! Both of you! A friend of mine is dead— He is! And…and…you said his daddy is suing…"

Again she smelled the stench of gasoline. She twisted her face away from them.

Caleb would never ride Long John again. He'd never ask her or anybody to dance again…and all because…because she'd danced with him. No. That wasn't why. His death was an accident.

Ritz's IV made a gurgling sound when she hugged herself tightly.

A lady slammed a door outside and shouted down the hall that she couldn't take green pills because anything green made her break out in hives. She wanted her little pink pills.… She had to have pink pills.

"Oh, God!" Ritz put her hands over her eyes and began to cry. "We wanted to end the feud. That's all."

Her father said, "The sheriff wants to talk to you."

"The sheriff?"

The blind slapped the windowpane again. When she looked up, her father was stomping out of the room.

She felt her mother's soft, hesitant hand lift her bangs. "He doesn't know what to do with himself. And you, dear, you really do have to talk to the sheriff. Like you said, you're not a little girl anymore. It won't be easy. But I'll be here in case you get rattled."

Something in her low voice made Ritz understand how different everything was now. She looked into her mother's blurred, frightened face and then up at the broken pot and the bedraggled poinsettias.

"I'm so sorry, Mother."

Fiona nodded.

"But saying I'm sorry won't change anything, will it? I—I used to want your love...and...and Daddy's respect."

"You have them."

Ritz stared past her mother. "I wish I could be your perfect little girl again."

"Always," her mother whispered.

"I used to look at all those pictures in the gallery. Especially those of my great-grandmothers. I wanted my picture to hang there. I wanted my children to think I was great."

"They will."

Hard knuckles rapped on the door.

Sheriff Johnson stuck his jowly face inside. He was carrying a battered white box and brushing crumbs off his shirt.

"Y'all got room for some doughnuts?"

"No, thank you," Ritz said.

"Do you feel up to a few questions?" He smiled, but his eyes remained grave.

Ritz caught a glimpse of her chalk-white face in the

mirror above the sink. "I—I think I will have a doughnut, Sheriff—"

Squaring her shoulders, Ritz sat up a little higher and munched the sugary doughnut while her mother gripped her hand.

"I want the truth, the whole truth about what happened the other night—"

She squeezed her mother's fingers. How could you explain a crazy accident?

Caleb was dead.

Nothing would ever be the same.

8

Cuernavaca, Mexico

Roque Moya scowled as he sat astride his Harley on crowded *Avenida Morelos*. Throwing his head back, he sucked in a stew of black exhaust fumes that burned his throat and probably ate the last of his brain cells.

Mexico. His homeland throbbed with people and life. His country was as powerful as a violent beast, and as passionate as a possessive lover—and impossible to ignore. And like his country, he was part beast and part poet, too. Unfortunately he was just beginning to realize that being a Mexican wasn't all of him. No matter how often *Mamacita* or his sisters, Carmela or Ana, said it was. He had a dual citizenship.

Wraparound mirrored sunglasses, slashed jeans and his black leather jacket screamed—bad-ass biker. His filthy mood more than matched his image. The only thing that didn't fit was the silver St. Jude medal dangling from his neck.

The December weather was unseasonably warm. His face felt raw and gritty from the long ride from Puebla.

He was burning up in his jacket; indeed, he was so hot, his T-shirt felt glued to his back and armpits.

He needed a shower, clean clothes and cologne. Not that he was anxious for the light to change even though he was only a few blocks from the turnoff to his mother's home. He had a confession to make to his passionate, jealous, obsessive *Mamacita.*

Spanish polka blared from the car radio behind him, and he tapped his leather boot to the beat.

When the greasy smell of tacos and *papas fritas* wafted from an open-air restaurant, Roque's stomach growled. He hadn't eaten since he'd gotten his grades at the university in Puebla. Since Caleb's phone call right afterward.

Estúpido. Why hadn't he dropped out in time? And why hadn't he told *Mamacita* he had made plans with Caleb for New Year's?

Mamacita always made such a fuss when he came home. It was Christmas break. She was through with her classes, too. She would have cooked all his favorite foods for the party she was giving tonight in honor of his home-coming—her special mole, enchiladas, guacamole, *carne asada* and *Tacos Yucatán.*

His mouth watered as he thought of roaring up to her portico. Their colonial mansion would be lit with red pepper Christmas lights. She would be watching for him from the roof. Like a girl, she would come running down the spiral staircase, her high heels clicking like a Spanish dancer's. Then she would laugh and kiss him before he could swing his leg over his bike.

"I've got to tell her about the *F*'s first thing. And then about my plans to see Caleb over New Year's."

His gut knotted. She was a teacher. Grades were every-thing to her. How many nights had she'd slaved to teach him to read?

Four *F*'s. He could see her black eyes growing huge and blazing with love and disappointment.

''At least I know what I don't want to do with my life—''

His gaze shifted to the sidewalk littered with cellophane candy wrappers, paper cups, empty plastic cola bottles, papaya and avocado peels. A poor Native woman squatted in the middle of the garbage. Her wrinkled brown breast was exposed as she nursed the baby wrapped in her shawl, her arms extended to anybody that passed.

Mexico—land of incredible wealth—incredible oil, gas, gold. Some of the world's richest men were Mexicans.

Mexico—land of excruciating poverty, land of high walls behind which the rich lived because they were so afraid of their poor.

Suddenly the smell of tacos and diesel nauseated him.

When the light changed, nobody in Roque's lane moved. Horns blared. The driver behind him stuck out a beefy, tattooed arm and shot foul hand signs. Roque rolled his throttle and jumped, gunning his bike.

Finally the old school bus in front of him roared to life. Gears downshifting, the green beast belched diesel from a rusty exhaust pipe straight into Roque's face before it rumbled forward. The *avenida,* indeed the whole city of Cuernavaca that had once been such a garden city, was already choked with diesel fumes. *Mamacita* was always complaining about what the pollution did to her flowers.

Híjole!

He was sick of straddling an eggbeater. The highway from Puebla had been under construction. Twice cops had stopped him. Cops—hell—*bandidos.* Four thugs strutting around his bike in khaki uniforms and black boots. When they'd patted black holsters, he'd dropped his *tíos'* names and pulled out his wallet.

Roque needed a drink, not a squabble with his mother.

Then he caught sight of the Native woman on her make-shift throne of garbage again.

When the traffic began to move, he swerved across two lanes, pushed his bike onto the sidewalk, went inside the restaurant and ordered three tacos. He wolfed down one, and then thrust the other tacos into the beggar woman's outstretched hands. Up close she didn't look any older than he was.

She nodded. He jumped on his bike and leaped out into the traffic, switching lanes, whipping past cars and buses like a madman.

"You're in a helluva rush, Moya—to be going no-where."

Until his failure this semester, he'd been sure his future lay in Mexico with his uncles, *los ingenieros.*

Now his future held nothing.

He was going too fast to make the turn to his mother's, so he rolled the throttle, leaned forward and just hung on.

The bar was too dimly lit to read the book in his back-pack, so Roque didn't take out Caleb's Christmas present.

Four empty beer bottles were the only centerpieces at the sticky, corner table where Roque sat. His long legs were sprawled in front of him; in his right hand he held an icy bottle against his powerful chest. Maybe he'd picked the wrong bar to find courage and relax. The beers made him edgier, and he dreaded his mother even more.

Smoking and nursing their beers, a dozen men seethed at small round tables beside him. The place had a danger-ous atmosphere. It wouldn't be smart to lower his sun-glasses and chance meeting a stranger's eye.

The only entertainment was the slim brunette in a white slip dress behind the bar. Her bee-stung lips were glossy red; her eyes were inked blacker than Cleopatra's. Batting long, false eyelashes, she'd leaned over him so far when she'd brought him his *cervezas,* he'd been afraid her breasts might pop out of the thin, white silk.

The only woman in this dive, she damn sure knew how to make the most of it.

She was familiar somehow. Not that he could place her.

He had his eye on the little blue rose she'd tattooed above her right breast when she smiled. She was licking her lips with a lot of wet tongue when he heard a roar from the next table. Suddenly a fat brown hand yanked a chair out from under Roque's table, toppling his four empties. The bottles rolled, smashing on the tiled floor.

Roque lifted his beer bottle lazily in a mock salute. *"Cuidado, hombre!"*

With a threatening flourish, the man whirled the chair around and sat in it backward, his thick legs spread-eagled. The stench of body odor and garlic and rotten breath was so foul, Roque covered his nose.

"So, you like our women, *gringo?*" the man's hoarse voice growled in heavily accented English.

The girl went white. The men at the next table roared with laughter.

"Buenas noches, amigo," Roque said in soft, smooth Spanish even though he was bristling with fury.

"I asked you a *pregunta, gringo.*"

"That is a difficult question, *señor.* What if I say, *sí,* I like your women?" He waved to the girl at the bar. "What if I say, I like *her* very much?"

"Mi Rosita?"

Rosita. The name rang a bell. Suddenly the brunette's smile attached itself to a bittersweet memory. *Mamacita's* gardener had had a little girl named Rosita. She used to dig in the rose beds with a rusty spade that had a broken handle while her father pruned. Rosita. She'd been a year or so younger than Roque. Roque had given her a new spade. After his gift, she'd followed him everywhere just like Caleb always had until her father had run off to find work in *el norte*.

"Rosita. I used to know a Rosita."

The man's gold tooth spit fire. "*My* woman." He hit the table with his open palm. "You talk too much about *my* woman. I theenk we have a *problema, gringo*."

Roque twirled his beer bottle easily between his palms even as he felt the muscles in his jaw tighten. "What if I say, no, no, I don't like your women, *señor?*"

"Then you insult her!" The man rose so abruptly the table crashed to the floor. "And me, too!"

"There's just no way to make some people happy."

"You make *chiste?* Well, joke not funny!" Before Roque could defend himself, the squat, heavily built stranger slammed a fist into his jaw.

Roque reeled backward. Through a fog of pain, he heard the girl screaming. The brute had his hands around Roque's waist now as he wrestled him onto the floor. Face-to-face, the man was one of the ugliest men Roque had ever seen. Scars crisscrossed his flat, misshapen nose.

The man's arm shot around Roque's shoulder, vising his neck in a hammerlock. As his attacker began to squeeze, the girl threw herself on top of the giant's back and began to pull his greasy hair and collar. He began to choke, spittle dribbling out of his mouth. Then she reached around his face and dug a long red fingernail into his eye. When the ogre screamed and rolled backward from Roque, broken glass crunched.

"Ugh!" The ogre yelled as blood spurted.

"Run!" Rosita ordered.

Dazed, Roque blinked up at her. The broken shards reflected what light there was in a dazzle of amber brilliance. When the jackals from the next table inched toward him, Roque grabbed the longest shard of glass he could find and sprang at them.

Bent on escape, Roque, hurled chairs aside and stumbled toward the door. He was almost outside when the girl flung herself at him and clung.

"Piérdete, chica," he snarled. "Scram!"

"But you like me, *sí?"* Her voice fell piteously. "You remember your little Rosita, no? *Tu amigita* from the *jardín?"*

She sounded young and vulnerable.

"Dios." That darling girl child had become…what too many poor women in Mexico…

"You gave me a *regalito*. A little spade."

Like the darling little girl he remembered, she curled her arms around his neck. When still he hesitated, she said, "Pepe will kill me."

Without a word, Roque lifted her into his arms. She laid her head against his chest and hung on as he raced through the tables toward the rectangular flare that cut a hole in the far wall.

When they were outside on the street by his bike, Roque handed her his helmet. "Where do you want me to drop you?"

"I want to go with you."

"Sorry. I've got to be somewhere—" He shoved his sleeve back to check his watch. *"Dios!"* *Mamacita's* little welcoming party was probably in full swing by the swimming pool. *Tío* Marco and *Tío* Eduardo would be sprawled in a corner waiting to pounce on him with their latest off-color jokes. The courtyard and house would be bulging with cousins, aunts and uncles.

La familia Moya would all be there, to welcome him home. No way could he get *Mamacita* alone and confess he wasn't ever going to be an *ingeniero* like his Moya uncles. Or that this year…because he missed Caleb so much, he had to go see him.

Now this girl in her cheap white dress—Rosita, with the overly made-up eyes had her own uses for him.

Roque swore under his breath. "I'm late, *chica*."

"You don't look happy about going wherever you think you have to go, *gringo*."

"I'm Mexican…just like you, damn it."

"Not just like me. You have a rich *gringo* daddy. I remember his pictures in your room."

"Those pictures are gone."

Her expression was dreamy. "I wish I could be a rich *gringa* and live in *el norte*."

His mouth twisted. "That's because you don't know what you're talking about."

"They're rich and blond. They have lots of pretty clothes. That's enough to know." She smiled up at him in triumph.

"*El norte* is not like on TV."

"But better than here, *no?*"

When he had no answer, she shrugged. "You go see your family in *el norte* this Christmas, no?"

"New Year's. I have a half brother near Carita, Texas—"

"Where do you cross?"

"Reynosa."

"I have a cousin there. And a father in Houston." She smiled. "You're rich. You think Rosita's pretty, no? We could have fun—"

"Not interested—"

"You're Mexican, *no?* A man? I know a room that's cheap. It's not far."

Pop. Pop. Pop.

Sharp cracks of gunfire ricocheted off the stone walls outside.

Even though Roque's eyes opened instantly, they refused to focus, just as his brain refused to think.

He blinked. The room was dark, filled with lumpy, unfamiliar shapes, and he was alone.

Men were running and shouting outside in the alley. When more gunfire erupted, Roque hit the floor. Crawling to the window, he lifted the shade.

More pops. A red flower flashed against a black sky, raining red sparkle. Breathing a sigh of relief, he pushed his hair out of his eyes and began to rub them.

More pops, followed by a white explosion this time.

Fireworks. Every church bell in town began to chime, each gong sounding so loud they resonated in his pounding temples.

Machismo. Was every male in Mexico cursed with the disease? Did even the bell pullers have to pull at their ropes until their shoulders screamed because of this ancient unspoken competition each had with every other man?

A roach skittered across the windowsill right in front of his nose, and Roque jumped back. His gaze followed the roach up a dingy wall with peeling paint. He turned. The bed was still made. He was fully dressed.

Where was Rosita?

His eyes scanned the bed, the small, scarred desk, the single chair upon which dangled his backpack and her white, silk dress.

No Rosita.

Water splashed in the bathroom. When she began to sing ''Guadalajara'' off-key in the shower, his headache throbbed, and his eyes began to burn.

Five beers. Had he slept with a—

His stomach turned. Maybe he should get the hell out of here before—

He grabbed his backpack and dug into his pocket for his keys.

No keys, just his leather wallet. He flipped it open and breathed a sigh of relief.

His keys jingled teasingly behind him.

"Looking for me?" came a throaty voice from the bathroom door behind him.

He saw her in the mirror over the little desk. She was stepping toward him, wearing nothing other than a white towel wrapped around her head. The overdone eye makeup was gone. Her young face was scrubbed clean; her brown, slender body open to his gaze.

He went still. His heart thudded.

When she shook his keys again, he jumped.

Languidly she stretched a hand toward him, his keys dangling from her red-tipped fingers.

Lithe as a cat, yet careful not to touch her, he grabbed them.

"What are you so afraid of?" she purred.

Her pert breasts stuck straight out. Unlike the rest of his male friends at the university at Puebla, he was unaccustomed to the easily proffered nakedness of whores.

Her dark, velvety skin gleamed in the rosy light. Rosita was young, shapely. Smiling at him, she lifted her hands and slowly unwound her turban, letting her black, wet hair spill all over her shoulders.

An incandescent smile lit her impish face. She was so beautiful. So eager and young. Except for her eyes. They were way too old for a girl.

Even so, instinctively he reacted to her wild, erotic beauty. His stomach knotted. In an instant he was hard and hot enough to make his *tíos* proud.

"Roque—" she urged.

He stared at her rose tattoo.

"Get dressed."

"But—"

"If I wanted to have sex with you, I would have stripped you naked and taken you."

Her smile died. When she just stood there, willing him

to take her, his anger and sexual desire tangled. More fireworks lit the sky. On the verge of an explosion himself, he leaned down, grabbed her towel and threw it at her.

"Cover yourself before I pitch you out on the street naked!"

"Take her," shouted a demon in his mind. "You're supposed to be a man. A Mexican. She's a whore. This is Mexico. You can brag to the *tíos,* too."

"If you have a problem, I can help," she said softly, rubbing a hand up his arm. "I can make you feel like a man. I swear." Her fingers glided across his chest and began to play with his St. Jude medal.

On a shudder he ripped her hand away.

"I have a baby to feed," she whispered. "A little girl…"

Again he saw the Native woman on the sidewalk.

"How old are you?"

She beamed at him. "Nineteen."

"The same age as my little brother."

With a scowl Roque pulled his wallet out of his back pocket. She wrapped the towel around herself. Not that it mattered much. The image of her naked body was imprinted on his unwilling mind. He wanted to touch the velvet, honey-brown skin, to run his hands through the black silk of her hair, to stroke her breasts, to bury himself to the hilt inside her.

"Some cops held me up on the highway. Took most of my money—" His hands shook so badly he dropped the wallet.

Bills scattered everywhere. She fell to her knees, grabbing for them.

"Food for your baby," he muttered.

"Babies." She patted her stomach.

"*Claro!*" he said angrily.

Mexico. *His* country.

She stuffed the pesos between her breasts. "I save this money to go to *el norte* to find my father. He's in Houston."

Feeling sick, Roque ripped his backpack off the chair and bolted.

Roque roared up to the back alley that led to his mother's house and cut the motor. Then he grabbed the handlebars. Dodging three chickens, potholes and plastic sacks of garbage, he pushed the Harley through a row of tightly parked cars.

He was halfway to the house when the shiny toe of his boot sent a cola can clattering across the rocks into Señora Molina's house. Her two terriers sprang to attention, howling down at him from her roof.

"*Cállate.* You'll wake the dead."

The terriers spun like dervishes, barking even louder.

"*Cállate, perritos.* It's just me." This time he spoke with such affection that the pair lowered their heads, perked their ears at him and began wagging their tails.

Then Roque pushed the bike past a familiar blue Town Car and then did a double-take when he read *Tío* Eduardo's bumper stickers. *Dios.* Wasn't that *Tío* Marco's big old white Pontiac station wagon right by the gate?

Híjole! Were they all waiting up? *Mamacita* must have been frantic with worry when he hadn't showed. They never stayed over.

The bike was heavy. By the time he reached her tall iron gates, he was out of breath and his arms ached.

Using his spare key, he opened the gate and let himself inside. The house with its grilled windows was quiet and dark. There were so many cars jammed inside the courtyard, there was no room for his bike.

Híjole.

What the hell was going on? Why was everybody still

here? He reached in his pocket and pulled out his pack of cigarettes. Leaning back against the stucco wall, he lit a cigarette.

"Stay cool." He inhaled, threw his dark head back, and blew smoke rings skyward, but when he glanced at the cars, he got queasy all over again. He threw his cigarette down, squashed it out and spun around, striding toward the ornately carved front door, which he opened slowly. Even that soft rush of air, however faint, stirred the gossamer curtains. Instantly his nerves grew as taut as guitar strings.

Holding his breath, he scanned the high arches and heavy beams running across the high ceiling. The house that was so familiar seemed eerie in the dark.

He was moving swiftly across the family room when he nearly tripped. He stopped so abruptly, his stomach went into a spasm. A bare foot, its toes spread awkwardly as if with rigor mortis, stuck straight out from under the coffee table.

A body! He saw the second tangle of arms and legs wound up in sheets sprawled on the floor. A massacre.

Híjole! More bodies littered the foldout couches and chairs. They were everywhere. Suddenly the Saltillo tiles seemed to quake under his boots.

Then *Tío* Eduardo let out a loud snort from his spot on the floor. Roque, who had been holding his breath, jumped.

Not dead bodies. Just the Moyas. They were asleep like the enchanted inhabitants in their castle in Carmela's favorite fairy tale, *Sleeping Beauty.*

Sharing a sheet with her mother, Raquel Moya, his plump, younger cousin lay on a mountain of pillows on the terrazzo floor. His two uncles were facedown on the throw rugs. Their wives slept beside them on the couches.

Roque grew increasingly bewildered as he wandered through the house and found cousins and friends asleep in every room on the lower floor. He had to tiptoe over half a dozen relatives to reach the stairs. These he ascended hoping to find his mother, who suffered from insomnia and was often awake at all hours.

No such luck. Still dressed, she was fast asleep on top of her bed beside his two sisters, who were also dressed in their street clothes. On the bedside table beside his mother lay the latest copy of *¡Alarma!* Mexico's and his mother's favorite blood-soaked tabloid. The cover featured lurid shots of massacred drug dealers and the latest young rape victims from Juarez.

In the shadowy bedroom, *Mamacita* didn't look a day older than plump, honey-colored Carmela or stick-thin, pale Ana. She was slim and lithe in the melon-colored, hand-woven cotton dress he'd given her for her thirty-eighth birthday last summer. Silver jewelry she'd picked out in Taxco for him to buy her last Christmas blazed at her throat and wrists.

"*Mamacita*, you're as beautiful as a girl."

"For you, *mi precioso*. I dress this way only when you come."

Her long curly hair was tied back in a pink scarf. Another gift from him that she'd picked out herself.

"I like things so much more, I truly treasure them, *mi precioso*, if they are gifts from you. But having you home for Christmas is the real gift, *mi hijo*."

So many memories. So many harsh new realities.

He shut the door and escaped to his own room. He was about to sling his backpack on top his bed, when the sheets rustled, and a little boy moaned.

"Don't get me.... Don't get me...."

Roque dashed to the window and opened the curtains. A bar of moonlight slanted across a pale, angelic face framed with glossy black curls.

Juanito, his much spoiled nephew, who worshiped him,

but in the most irksome ways, was buried up to his chin in Roque's bed. The little rascal, who reminded him of Caleb at the same age, had probably been up here messing in stuff he knew he was supposed to leave alone.

Sure enough, not an inch from the brat's face, the sharp tip of a Bowie knife glinted beside a pile of arrowheads. The kid must've taken the knife to bed with him. The damn blade was pointed straight at the sleeping boy's eyes.

"Brat—you know you're not supposed to mess with my knife and arrowhead collection," Roque whispered. But he smiled with both concern and affection as he slipped the knife into his back pocket.

Video games were strewn all over the floor.

Roque sank down on the mattress. "You were up in my room hiding out, weren't you? Playing games by yourself." He wound a black curl around his finger. "You should have been downstairs with the others. But…you're a kid after my own heart, and we both know it."

His sisters' bedrooms were rented out to the foreign language students *Mamacita* fed and housed to earn more money. So, there was nowhere he could sleep. If he showered, he'd wake Juanito for sure. The last thing he needed was to wake everybody else in the house.

Roque was wondering what to do when the white shimmer of the swimming pool outside caught his eye. At least the chaise longues were empty. Careful not to disturb Juanito, Roque stole a blanket off the foot of the bed and a towel out of a drawer. Quietly he slipped back down the stairs and out of the house.

The grounds were a mess. Paper cups and plates and napkins blew across the lawn. A dozen cups and plates bobbed in the pool. His party must have been a blowout. Usually *Mamacita* picked up as soon as a party ended.

Roque went to the pool bar and sloshed tequila into a paper cup and downed it with a swallow. Then he grazed from a bowl of stale chips and black guacamole until it was gone.

Yanking off his clothes, he dived into the water.

It was so cold, he popped to the surface shivering and gasping. To warm up he swam fast down to the shallow end, his arms splashing geysers out of the pool.

"*Mira!* Looky! Looky!" a voice piped from his upstairs window. "Roque's naked!" Juanito swung a shutter open and was pointing gleefully.

All the lights of his mother's house came on, and the mansion glowed like a gigantic jack-o'-lantern. However, a strange lantern for red-hot Christmas pepper lights dotted the roofline.

The big old house with its stone arches and pool had seen better days. Still, especially lit up, it was impressive in the dark. It had been a colonial ruin that dated back to Cortez and a local landmark. Fifty years ago, his grandfather had bought it for a summer home and restored it. Since then, the Moyas' mines had failed, and the Moyas had lost most of what was left of their fortune in the devaluations of the early eighties. The big house had become a perpetual challenge for his mother to maintain.

The shadowy figure of a woman slid the patio door open. *Mamacita*, her black hair flowing down her shoulders, scampered toward him barefoot. She slowed, walking heedlessly through the party litter.

Her beautiful face was gray and frozen, the makeup around her eyes smudged. Usually, when he was anywhere near, her black eyes lit up with love, and she threw herself into his arms.

Not tonight.

Without taking his eyes off her, he climbed out of the pool and grabbed a towel.

Still, she didn't speak.

He dried off and wrapped it around himself. When he

moved toward her, he felt like he was stepping into a nightmare. Nothing in this familiar landscape, not even her, seemed real.

His uncles came outside, too. Then his aunts and cousins. Like his mother, they were silent and still. Which was strange. Usually they were so loud. Staying on the patio they clumped together and locked their arms around each other.

Roque loped into his mother's arms. "I-I'm sorry I'm late. I came out here because I—I didn't want to wake you."

"Roque, *mi vida, mi precioso.* I wanted so much to be pretty for you tonight. My dress, the pretty dress you gave me—remember?"

"Last summer—"

"I fell asleep in it, so now it's all wrinkled."

"I'm sorry, *Mamá.* I should have called."

"Oh, my darling, it doesn't matter—"

"What's wrong?"

She hurled herself against his broad, wet chest.

"What's going on?"

She touched his face with the back of her hand. Still, she didn't answer.

"Will somebody tell me what's going on?" he yelled over her curly black head even as he pressed her closer.

The Moyas clung to each other fearfully.

"It's...it's your brother," *Mamacita* whispered at last.

"Caleb? Did he call? He's such a pest. He wrote me, you know, like he always does and invited me up for Christmas again.... Don't worry. I won't leave you. Not on Christmas... Maybe just for New Year's..."

She reached up and sealed his lips with a fingertip. For the first time, he saw that her eyes were red and wet and that her bottom lip was trembling.

Dios. His teeth began to chatter.

"I love you so much."

Suddenly he knew. Still, he said, "Not Caleb— *Por favor,* not Caleb—"

She cupped his face in her long fingers and spoke again, her throaty whisper replaced by a monotone. "Oh, my darling—"

He felt helpless, his body draining. Then he began to shake.

"I'm so sorry," she said.

Over and over, she repeated those words like a mantra.

His vision blurred. His arms fell away, and he slowly sank down upon the lawn, falling back on the wet cool grass and paper cups like someone in a state of shock.

His mother's face above him whirled and then seemed to grow smaller against a background of black and stars. Her lips moved. Was she speaking? He couldn't hear her.

Racing footsteps. The Moyas circled him protectively. They were all talking loudly. *Tía* Lucia was on her knees praying. They loved him as only a close, Mexican family like the Moyas loved one of their own. And yet never had he felt more alienated.

He wasn't one of them.

He had a *gringo* daddy. Hard as he'd tried he couldn't ever forget it. Not even here. And now Caleb—

Closing his eyes, involuntarily Roque clutched the St. Jude medal at his throat.

Just let me be.

9

Roque stirred his black coffee and then lifted it to his lips, but when he sipped, he couldn't taste anything. Not that he gave a damn. He was exhausted, and he felt frozen and dead inside. He couldn't imagine ever caring about anything again.

Beside his saucer lay a thick dog-eared copy of *Crime and Punishment*. On top of the novel, Caleb's favorite, Roque had stacked the plastic box that contained the taped version of the novel as well as a brand-new tape recorder. All were Christmas gifts from Caleb. They had arrived when Roque was still in Puebla.

He wadded up the red wrapping paper and pitched it at his garbage can.

"I sent you nothing, *hermanito!* Nothing! You wrote me. All the time you wrote me. You worshiped me. You believed in me.... You poor little fool. Why? Why? I threw all your letters away. All but the last one."

Roque had stayed up most of the night reading that letter, rereading it. Then he'd listened to the first tape of the novel, mouthing every word incoherently, struggling repeatedly until he got them right. After his batteries had gone dead, he'd sat in the dark, clutching the book against his chest.

There wasn't a God. No God would allow an angel like Caleb to die.

From the window Roque could see his uncles and cousins sweeping the trash into orderly piles beneath a brilliant, blue sky. His sisters were arguing—Carmela would be arguing that she did all the work. In reality it was Ana, his quiet sister, who did everything.

It should be raining. He clenched his fist, dug his nails into his palms, wanting to hurt. Something should hurt…his heart maybe. His little brother was dead, and he was up here in his bedroom waiting listlessly for the father he hated to return his call.

Suddenly he grabbed his backpack and unzipped it. He turned it upside down, so that its contents spilled onto the red tiles—an engineering text, letters from home, and another book Caleb had sent.

Kneeling he lifted it and read the title aloud. *"Dreams of My Russian Summers."*

He flipped it open to the first page where Caleb had jotted one of his quick, eager messages.

"You're going to love this one, too, maybe even more than *Crime and Punishment*. Oh, Roque—the poor horses…" Further down, Caleb had finished with, "We'll be in London Christmas, but I'm so glad you're coming for New Year's. Gosh, I miss you. I want you to meet Long John so much. And my girl! You'll never believe— You have to meet her, too. Only you'd better not steal her—"

Instead of working math problems and studying for his finals, Roque had stayed up late, struggling to read Caleb's book. The images of the wounded calvary horses racing around wildly with sabers stuck in their bellies had gripped him.

Caleb always knew just what books would appeal to him.

"Since you can't read fast like me, you can't waste your time on bad books. I'll scout 'em out and make sure to choose the good ones."

Shouts from the courtyard interrupted his thoughts. Roque slammed the book shut and threw it beside the other one on the windowsill.

"Roque! Come down here, so we can cheer you up," Carmela yelled.

If only you could.

"Roque? Where are you? Where are you?" they chanted.

Locked in my room. Hiding from all of you.

"I know somebody pretty who has a crush on you—"

Blanca's high heels clicked *tapity-tap, tapity-tap* outside the door again. Her voice was artificially sweet when she called out to him. "*Hijo! ¿Mi Amor? ¿Dónde estas?* Don't you hear? They want you!"

His jaw muscles bunched, but he didn't answer her.

"Be that way," she whispered, hurt, possessive as always, so fierce was her love for her only son.

Her high heels tapped louder and louder, the farther away she got. Then her door at the end of the hall slammed. She'd been banging doors all morning—ever since he'd called his father.

As usual his father had been too busy to talk.

"*He's in a meeting. Who should I say called?*" his secretary had asked politely.

"*His son.*"

"*His son is dead.*" The soft voice had stayed carefully neutral. "*Who is this?*"

"*Roque.*"

"*Oh?*"

Roque had hung up fast. An hour, maybe more, had

passed. He dropped a second sugar cube into his coffee mug. When he brought it to his lips, again he could taste nothing. He felt nothing. Not even his incomprehensible anger that was always with him. There was just this huge void, this nothingness.

He placed his mug on the windowsill and stared at the sky. The big sky made him think of his father's endless pastures, of those waving grasses stretching to a far horizon.

He saw Caleb running through the high grasses.

For two years Roque had tried never to think of that ranch or his father. Never to think of Caleb. Or that skinny Keller girl with the freckles and glasses...and wild, defiant spirit.

Was she pretty now?

He shut his eyes, believing himself indifferent to the answer only to be startled by a vision. He saw her, standing before him on a sorrel horse, her arms spread like wings. Caleb, his arms outstretched, flew behind them.

Suddenly the memory of that little girl's golden hair whipping his throat like strands of loose silk moved through him like electricity.

Sweat drenched him as he sank to his knees in tears. He wiped his eyes. When he stood up, he felt nothing.

He was dead again. Dead like Caleb. Until last night, Roque had believed death and dying were for other people.

"Roque?" *Tío* Eduardo shouted, his yell loud enough to rouse the entire *colonia.* "We need some music down here—"

"Leave me alone," he yelled back.

Clickity, clickity click. Taps from the shadowy corner distracted Roque.

Roque's gaze flicked first to his guitar and then to Juanito, who sat bolt upright in the shadowy corner, his pale face aglow before the computer as if he were mesmerized by the purple boy hopping around on his computer screen. Juanito's hands were flying back and forth, shoving and clicking joy sticks with a vengeance.

Chartreuse zombies and neon-yellow dragons and red wizards chased the purple boy, who zipped like lightning through tunnels in a hellish, mazelike cave.

"Juanito," he lashed. "Get the hell out of here—"

Juanito's eyes remained in glazed, pinball mode. "You said hell. I'm going to tell."

"Get out!"

Chin jutting, Juanito risked a glance at him to assess whether or not he really had to mind.

"You heard me—out!"

The purple boy exploded in yellow stars. "You made me die...."

Die? The word hit a nerve. "Don't even say that—"

Only when Roque sprang at him, did the boy sprint toward the door, shrieking. "Help! Anybody! *Tía! Tía* Blanca! Roque said hell—"

"Roque?" his mother called. "Is that true, *mi precioso?*"

Juanito stuck out his tongue and licked the tip of his nose. Then he crossed his eyes and skipped lightly out into the hall.

Roque banged his door shut and shot the bolt. Alone at last, he slid the folded manila envelope that contained his failing grades out of his leather jacket. Then the phone rang, and his hand fisted, crumpling the envelope. He rushed out into the hall.

Mamacita got to it first. He covered her hand on the receiver with his. "Why don't you let me...just talk to him without you...just this once."

"This is my house." She tilted her chin in the air. "I can have a rational conversation with the father of my own

son, can't I?'' She let it ring two more times before she
lifted the receiver.

"Answer it!"

"*Bueno,*" she began almost innocently. Then her lower
lip bloomed petulantly. "Roque? He's right here! Of
course, I told him! What kind of *idiota* do you take me
for—"

"Just hand me the phone, so we can avoid the usual—"

She began to shout into the receiver. "You cheated on
me! When I was pregnant! I wish I had run over you in
that car!"

"Rampage," Roque whispered.

Blanca stomped back and forth, her black curls hanging
over the mouthpiece as she spit out sentences. "*Te odio!*
I hate you. I hate you! *Cabrón!*"

"*Mamá!*" Roque seized the phone.

"This is all your fault," she screamed at her son. "Because of you, I am a *divorciada*. A woman of no respect."

"*Mamá!* Caleb is dead—remember?"

She threw her hands in the air and flounced into her
bathroom and banged the door so hard, the house shuddered.

His father began to speak at the exact moment she
turned her shower on full blast. "Your bitch of a mother
tried to run me over in my own Cadillac! Has she ever
told you that?"

When his mother began to scream and pound and slap
the stucco walls with her open hands and fists, Roque
could hear nothing.

Roque ran into his room with the cordless and shut the
door.

"*Hola,*" he whispered.

"After Blanca's usual crazy explosion, you know damn
well, it's me—your father. You may be half-Mexican and

as crazed with jealousy as she is, but you're half-American too, damn it. Speak English.''

"Hello." Roque wrapped his tongue around the word and made it as thickly accented as possible.

"Caleb's dead. Do you hear me, you bastard? My good son is dead. And I know you're glad."

Pain—grief, and yes, jealousy, and rage knifed Roque. Instead of offering his father consolation, he stared at his motorcycle.

"Sí. Te oigo."

"Speak English, damn you."

"You came to Mexico to learn Spanish, so you could manipulate juries. You used my mother for that purpose, *verdad?* If she was jealous, you gave her reason, no?"

"Is that what Blanca says? Your mother is a moody and insanely jealous bitch."

"I wish to hell she'd never married you! I wish I *was* a bastard."

There was a long silence. "So the hell do I."

Roque gripped the phone.

His father sighed. "Caleb was murdered. Ritz Keller killed him. He was in love with her."

"I don't believe—"

"He wrote about it. If it's the last thing I ever do, I intend to get revenge."

"Ritz and Caleb?"

Benny changed the subject abruptly. "If it were up to me, I'd never lay eyes on you again. But it won't look good…if you don't come back—at least for the funeral."

"When?"

"Two days from now." His father hesitated. "But we'll wait for you—if that's too soon for you to get here. I know how impossible your mother is."

"Don't start—"

Roque stared down at the courtyard. His cousin Manuel

was playing his guitar and crooning Christmas carols. His mother had stopped screaming. Her shower was still running. Which meant she was only weeping now.

"I'll be there."

Silence. Then the phone went dead.

After a long moment Roque carried the phone down the hall. When he'd replaced it, he knocked gently on the bathroom door.

"*Mamacita?*"

"What does that lying, cheating bastard want this time?"

"I have to go, *Mamacita.*"

She flung open the door, her beautiful face, swollen and red, and glazed with wet tears. "He slept with my maids. He almost killed you the last time."

"Don't cry. You were so pretty last night. Your makeup's a mess."

"It's Christmas. My turn to have you."

"My little brother... Caleb... Last night you understood."

"You're my son. Mine."

He shrugged.

She threw herself at him and clung. "He leaves me for maids. I scare him in a parking lot, so he divorces me. He marries another woman. He has this son, this perfect son— by her, the saint. I've sacrificed everything for you."

"I love you too, *Mamá.*"

Gently he untangled her arms from his neck.

"You can't go. I won't let you."

He stared at her. When he cupped her cheek, she jerked free of him and slammed the door in his face.

Enraged at both his parents, he strode down the hall and grabbed his backpack. He threw Caleb's gifts and a few clothes inside. Then he stomped down the stairs.

All the Moyas were ringed around his bike to tell him goodbye.

All but his mother.

From the grilled window she yelled down to him. "It's dangerous to drive the highways in Mexico at night. Don't you dare drive at night."

"I'll call you when I get to Texas, *Mamá*."

"How can you leave me all alone at Christmas?"

"You're not all by yourself—"

"Nobody counts except you."

Tío Eduardo patted Roque on the shoulder. "We'll take care of her."

Roque jumped on his bike and revved it. Señora Molina's roof dogs went on red alert, barking maniacally.

He was buckling his helmet when *Mamacita* and his sisters ran down the spiral staircase and threw their arms around him. He removed his helmet again and kissed their wet cheeks.

"Take care of her," he said to his sisters.

"You're never coming back," *Mamacita* wept. "You're just like your father—running out on me when I need you the most!"

"Blanca—" *Tío* Eduardo pulled her into his arms. "Be fair."

"What do you know about it?" She pushed free and slammed back into the house.

Their faces dark, the Moyas nodded at him to go.

Before he was halfway down the alley, he heard his mother screaming and pounding the shower tiles again. He thought he would hear them all the way to the border, but at the end of the alley, a slight figure in a black shawl with a baby in a *rebozo* jumped him.

He swerved the bike and hit a garbage can. A cloud of flies swept upward from the can like curls of smoke. The girl drew her shawl aside to reveal her pretty, brown face.

"Rosita?" he growled, righting his bike.

She blushed and held up a baby wrapped in a pink blanket. "Elena. She's asleep. Your maid told me about your *gringo* brother. She says you're going to Reynosa."

The hope in her eager voice made him tense. When she hesitated, the air between them grew brittle.

"Take us with you, Roque. Please."

"No."

"Por favor."

He ripped his helmet off and shook his head.

"I'll never get across once I have the baby. What can I give my children here?"

"Look, my brother—"

"No…no…" She refused to listen and kept holding the baby for him to look at, repeating her request. "I will find my father in Houston." Then she thrust her hand into her rebozo and withdrew handfuls of pesos. "I have enough money for the *coyote*. To get us across. I have a cousin in Reynosa."

"No. It's too dangerous."

"If I go back to the bar, where I work—Pepe, the man who fought you, he will kill me. Because of you. What will happen to my babies then? With no mother? In Mexico."

"I can't be late to my brother's funeral—"

Roque roared to the border with Rosita clinging to him, pressing Elena against his back, her skirts whipping his legs.

But it wasn't Rosita who made him late. A mile short of the bridge the shaft of the clutch disk seized and killed the motor of his bike. He had to push the bike to a shop with Rosita trailing behind carrying Elena and a plastic bag with all her belongings. A young mechanic agreed to help him tear the bike down.

"How long before it'll run?"

"*Mañana.*"

To Rosita, Roque said, "You tell your *coyote* and cousin to pick you up at the shop."

"I've caused you enough trouble."

"I want to meet them."

The *coyote* or *pollero* (chicken-wrangler) as some less than respectful people called such a man rumbled up in a broken-down, blue van stuffed with a dusty group of tightly packed, sweat-stained *pollos* or chickens.

The *coyote* was thin. He had jumpy black eyes and slicked back hair. He wore aviator glasses and a silky gold shirt.

He took off his glasses and shot Rosita a lewd grin. "Hey." For a long moment his eyes ran up and down her figure while he fingered the black mustache that drooped past the corners of his wide mouth.

"Your wife?" he demanded of Roque in a surly tone.

"I'm single and...and alone...except for the baby," Rosita said quickly.

The *coyote's* grin widened.

Negotiations were fierce. The *coyote* demanded all Rosita's money.

Roque pulled Rosita aside. "Don't trust him."

"But my cousin. He knows him."

The *coyote* said, "Make up your mind. I'm in a hurry."

When he turned his back and stomped toward the van, Rosita ran after him and tearfully handed him the money before climbing into the crowded van.

Roque wrote his father's ranch phone number on a scrap of paper and handed it to her. "Just in case...you don't find your father...." When he patted Elena and kissed her on the brow, she cooed for him.

"*Dios. Qué preciosa.*" His voice was gentle.

Rosita beamed at him, hugged him tightly and then got into the van with the baby.

The next day a terrorist scare caused such a long line at the bridge, he wished he'd crossed at Matamoros. A friend from college, Porfirio, had a home there. He could have spent the night at Porfirio's hacienda, had a beer maybe or hunted rattlers. He could have forgotten about *Mamacita* and Caleb and quit worrying about Rosita and Elena and those men in the van for a little while.

He never crossed the border without feeling like he was betraying his mother. Today hundreds of trucks, tourist buses, as well as private vehicles were stalled. To add to the confusion fifty pigs were on the rampage. They'd gotten loose when a border guard forgot to lock a trailer gate after checking it for contraband.

The pigs squealed in panic as they ran from the men who chased them. Their pink bodies dashed around the honking trucks and hollering drivers, around his bike. Even as Roque began to clap and laugh and cheer for the pigs, he thought about his mother.

You're never coming back!

He'd sworn to her over and over he was all-Mexican. But those four *F*'s meant he didn't have a clue about what he'd do with the rest of his life.

He'd been born to two people who had always been at war with each other his whole life. With Caleb dead, he felt more torn apart than ever.

Finally the last pig was captured, and the buses and trucks and Chevys and Dodge Rams with their oversize wheels and hood ornaments began moving sluggishly past ill-built, decaying cinder-block buildings where cheap souvenirs were sold. Then he was inching forward onto the bridge. Bored, he chunked pesos at the upended plastic milk bottles tied to long sticks that beggars held up against the chain-link fence that lined the walkway.

Mexico.

Then he was across.

Stars and stripes snapped in a brisk wind. Instead of stampeding pigs, there was a profound, immediate sense of order.

El norte. McAllen, Texas. The United States. Disneylandia.

Did anybody in the whole world believe the American Dream more fiercely than poor Mexicans?

Roque scowled at the straight billboards and clean sidewalks and streets without potholes.

Ritz.

And my girl. I want you to meet her, too. You'll never believe who—

Ritz? Was she really Caleb's girl? Was she pretty? Did she still like to ride?

Had she killed Caleb?

The line of cars stopped. He shoved back his visor and angrily lit a cigarette. He was only half done smoking it when the green light flashed, startling him.

He lurched forward and only avoided ramming a souped-up low-rider with a loud muffler by swerving and pulling alongside.

Loud young voices cursed him. *"Chinga tú—"*

Four *chollos* or punks, their faces savage, leaned out of their old Chrysler and shot him the finger. They had green and pink hair and heavy silver chains around their necks.

Roque smiled. When they gunned their engine and insulted his mother, he flicked his cigarette inside their car.

The driver yelped and swerved sharply. The rest of them scrambled for the cigarette.

Roque was flying when he heard a crash behind him.

In his rearview mirror he saw border guards running toward a purple Chrysler with steam pouring out of the hood.

Roque rolled his throttle and sped north.

10

The speedometer read twenty-five.

"Oh, dear, Buttercup..." Ritz tapped the brake repeatedly until she got the big truck back down to twenty.

Keeping her left hand on the wheel, she slung her right arm over the back of her seat and twisted around to make sure the horse trailer and her pregnant mare were all right.

When she looked back at the road, buzzards were black slivers soaring and gliding high on warm currents in a blue sky streaked with wispy winter clouds. Not that it was cold. The norther that had blasted through the brush country the morning after the wreck had come and gone.

The day was so warm and humid Ritz wore only a light, black, cotton sweater and jeans. Her windows were down. The scent of grass and manure and brush country perfumed the wind that blew her golden curls about her face. Every time she hit a bump or pothole, her stomach clutched, and she turned around to check on Buttercup.

Buttercup was due to foal soon. Ritz was spending most of her time with the horse because Buttercup seemed like her only friend. But this morning the mare had been dull-eyed and rolling around in her stall, a sign of colic. The water in her stall had been dirty. In guilt-stricken panic,

Ritz had refilled the buckets with fresh water and then walked her for half an hour. When Buttercup seemed a little better, she'd loaded her into the trailer, hoping driving around would distract her from the pain, and she'd improve. So, for the past hour Ritz had driven the back ranch roads because this method had worked in the past.

Nearly a year ago, Long John had broken out of his hot-wired pasture and had gotten into a pasture with Buttercup. Sunny was going to be so excited if they got a good foal.

Caleb.... A sob caught in her throat. She wrenched her hand to her lips as his loss hit her again.

Her brother, Steve was the one with partial amnesia. Why couldn't she remember for more than five seconds—Caleb was dead? And everybody in five counties blamed her—even her own parents.

Due to a family member being delayed, Sunny's funeral had been put off a day. Thus, he was being buried this afternoon at Campo Santo, the ranch cemetery, neutral territory between the Keller and Blackstone Ranches. Except Benny Blackstone had had the sheriff issue a threat that no Keller better set foot in the cemetery between two and four.

Ritz frowned. A solid wall of horns and burnished red flanks blocked the road up ahead. At least a dozen of her father's prized Santa Gertrudis cattle meandered along the shoulder and down the middle of the road. Oh, dear. Sometimes bands of illegals passing through cut fences and left gates open.

Then she saw the fence posts on the Keller side of the road had been torched. An enormous swath of grass was scorched.

The words, Ritz, Killer Keller, had been branded into the shoulder of the road.

It's Your Turn To Die.

She hit the brakes too fast.

"*¡Cuidado!*" Socorro screamed when she was thrown against her seat belt. "Buttercup—"

"Oh no."

Ritz cut her engine, and the cows mooed at her in greeting.

"Honk at them," Socorro said, anxious to distract her. "Oh, I don't like this. Pablo told me..." Staring at the burned patch, she clamped a hand over her mouth.

Pablo was Blackstone Ranch's plant manager. Maybe the Kellers and the Blackstones were feuding. Not so with Pablo and Socorro, the Kellers's housekeeper. The pair had long been lovers. As a result, there were all sorts of shared secrets between the warring households.

"Pablo told you what?"

Socorro flushed and lowered her eyes.

"Ben Blackstone's telling everybody I murdered Caleb—"

"Nobody believes him."

"My teachers do." Ritz drew a quick breath. "When I went to school to get my history textbook, Mr. Hensley and Mr. Daniels were very cold. Then Mrs. Cosby wouldn't help me find stuff at the convenience store when I asked her to. Mr. Muñoz at the filling station won't speak to me, either."

"Pablo, he say Señor Benny is mad with grief."

Ritz shivered. Her mother kept telling her people were upset, but they would realize it was an accident, that she mustn't dwell on the wreck, that she had to put it behind her and go on.

Jet, who'd been jealous when Caleb had asked Ritz to dance, avoided her. Josh hadn't come to the hospital to see her. He hadn't called since she'd gotten out, either.

The accident had shaken Ritz's world to its foundations.

Her own father was the most condemning of all. For the first time in her life, she felt all alone and lost.

More than anything, she wanted to go to Caleb's funeral. He'd been her friend. Her secret friend. They'd shared books and their dreams. In trying to end the feud, they'd only made it worse.

Somehow she had to find a way to place a rose on Sunny's casket and tell him she was sorry.

Again, she turned around and stared at Buttercup. The mare's large eyes were open and alert as she watched the cows.

Ritz opened her door and got out and rushed back to the trailer. Climbing up on a rung, she peered in at Buttercup.

The mare stared gravely back at her. Sorrel ears twitched, and Ritz thought she heard a faint cry.

"What was that?"

Buttercup's ears stayed on the alert.

"Why...it almost sounded like a baby."

Ritz listened for a long time before climbing back into the truck, but the cry was not repeated.

Flashing red lights blinked from the center of the highway. Roque was soaring, speeding dangerously fast. He'd thought he was done with border hassles and with the heavy burden of Rosita and her problems.

The red lights and the orange glow of sodium lamps that lit up the huge border-patrol checkpoint south of Carita, Texas, made him worry about her all over again.

Where the hell was she? He didn't like thinking about how scared and big-eyed she'd looked crammed in that dark van with all those men.

"Damn."

He eased his boot off on the gas. He'd been flying in the dark, reveling in the cool night air.

Nothing better to a biker than a good, smooth, bandit-free road. He liked the nothingness of the big ranches on either side of the wide highway, too. He'd liked being free of Rosita and Elena, too. Liked it so much, he'd even stopped at a roadside park and sat on a picnic table staring at the stars and listening to the silence.

He braked just short of the huge shed. Dozens of green and white border-patrol vehicles were parked everywhere. What chance did Rosita and her baby have against all these armed, uniformed men in dark green?

Off to his right a pitiful bunch of starved-looking illegals in cheap jeans and dirty shirts sat crammed into a Dodge Ram.

The unwanted, the unwashed. Like Rosita and Elena. Like those *pollos* in the battered van.

Like me.

Roque's body tensed when a tall officer with a big belly and a big gun stepped up to his bike.

"You an American citizen?"

Roque yanked his passport out of his jacket. "American. Mexican. Take your pick."

The officer tapped a page with a thick fist. "Double citizenship? American father?"

Roque curled his lip.

"Blackstone? Home for the funeral?"

Home? Roque nodded.

"You can go, son."

He shouldn't have looked over at the Dodge Ram again.

One of the prisoners wore aviator glasses and a dirty gold shirt. His hair was slicked back. He was tweaking his black mustache as he stared at Roque through the bars.

Rosita? Where was Rosita?

The officer frowned. "You know him?"

"Never saw him before in my life."

"He's a *coyote*. One of the worst. Sometimes he works with drug smugglers. Hell. Why am I telling you this?"

Roque gritted his teeth. Alarm for Rosita shot through him.

"We found baby bottles and diapers and a scrap of pink blanket—"

Rosita. *Dios.*

When Roque gunned his bike, the officer backed out of his way.

Pamela Blackstone's bedroom was bathed in golden light. Golden light for a golden girl.

There was a soft knock at her bedroom door.

"Come in."

"Phone for you, *señora.*"

Pamela removed a diamond ear clip and lifted the pink phone by her bed against her ear. However, she was careful not to mess her perfectly styled blond hair.

"Pamela—"

Her husband's deep voice cut to her heart. Not that he spoke with the slightest trace of emotion. He never did, so she was careful to conceal her feelings from him, too.

"Hello." Her single word of greeting was flat and uninflected.

"Is everything ready?"

She pressed her lips together. "Just as you ordered."

"I finished in court early. We won. A hundred million. I'm at the airport."

He hung up without even saying goodbye. She held the phone against her ear for a long moment. Then she realized she had to hurry. It would take his jet less than an hour to make the private strip on Blackstone Ranch.

The radio was blaring. The news was all about that miserable group of undocumented aliens found in terrible straits in a remote part of Blackstone Ranch that bordered on Keller land. The rumors were there had been some sort of sordid gang rape. The men had scattered. The woman and her baby were missing.

Just what Benny needed—his ranch in the papers, more bad publicity. The press never mentioned that these horrible people shot their cattle, cut their fences, and murdered each other. Then there were the drug runners. Even Pamela carried a loaded pistol in her car.

Quickly she glided across the room and switched the radio to a soothing classical program. After all, she didn't have much time to make sure everything was perfect for Ben.

She went to the mirror and gazed at the slim, blond figure in black cashmere and diamonds with the critical eye of a stylish woman who was much admired for her beauty and taste. She lifted her slim delicate chin, so the angle was more flattering. When she'd been younger she'd been a model. Her face had graced hundreds of magazine covers.

Never had she looked more beautiful. She was glad.

One glance at the huge diamond on her left hand was enough to make her blush. She remembered the day Benny had slipped the ring onto her finger. He'd wanted to embarrass her, to brand her with his dazzling chunk of ice…to show her he owned her….

People warned her he was the devil.

And yet all Benny had to do was call her, and she felt like a girl. Buster, the saint everybody had loved, had never made her feel so…so…what….

So raw. So gritty. So real. So alive.

Not that Benny cared how she felt. She was a trophy, something he'd won in one of his battles. She meant no more to him than his plane, or his cars, or this ranch. Maybe less.

Theirs was a marriage of convenience. He was a clever

lawyer. The cleverest son of a bitch lawyer in Texas he constantly bragged. The Kellers said he'd used the law to manipulate an illiterate jury to strip Buster of his last cent, which had driven him to suicide. Then Benny had bought her like a slave on the auction block.

She rolled the diamond to the back of her hand, flushing as she remembered those days right after Buster's funeral when she'd thought she might starve. Buster, the saint, had not provided for her.

Benny had. He'd even married her, hadn't he?

She padded across the thick carpet and went down to the kitchen to speak to the caterers. Half an hour later she was gliding through her living room, smiling as she touched vases of flowers and arranged the framed pictures of Caleb as well as those of Benny surrounded by celebrities.

There was even a portrait of Caleb's mother. But not a single picture of Roque. Nor was there one of her—at least not of her alone. In the two in which Pamela was present, she was barely visible behind Benny.

People would be coming soon. But not before Benny. He'd made a point of telling her to instruct her friends to give her the morning alone—to grieve. How he'd laughed after he'd said that.

The real reason he wanted her alone was more selfish.

She was blushing when she heard unexpected thunder in her driveway. She eyed her diamond wristwatch. It was still too early for Benny, but her heart knocked anyway when loud, booted feet sprang up her porch steps two at a time and a heavy fist began to pound. Susana came running into the room just as a black boot kicked the door open.

"Roque!"

Holding a heavy bundle of foul-smelling rags in his arms, her stepson towered over her. He was so much taller than Pamela remembered. At twenty he no longer seemed a boy. His perfectly honed body was sleek and powerful. He had blue-black hair. His startling widow's peak, that was like Benny's, reminded her that that this young, dazzling god in Ray-Bans really was Benny's despised son.

"Roque?" Pamela whispered, feeling unsure.

Suddenly she gasped. The bundle of rags was a pitiful brown girl whose coarse black hair fell in wild snarls all over his shoulders. Her arms dangled lifelessly.

"Is she dead?"

"No. Pablo just found her."

Pamela felt a little dazed. "Are those bruises on her face?"

He nodded.

"I'm too jet-lagged to think." For some reason she focused on the leaves and little twigs in the woman's impossible hair.

"I—I just got in from London. I was planning Christmas at the Savoy when Caleb…"

Everything was catching up with Pamela. Suddenly she felt so tired and worried, she didn't know how to deal with Roque and this thin, battered girl.

"She's illegal?" Pam whispered. "Is she even conscious?"

"The weird thing is she's somebody I know from Cuernavaca. Her father used to work…"

"I can't deal with this."

"I gave her a ride to the border. Then I gave her Pablo's phone number if she got into trouble. Some of the men she was with called him when they abandoned her to a gang of thieves."

"Thieves on this ranch? Again?"

"Pablo's out looking for them."

"What about her?"

"She drank bad water out of one of our stock tanks too.

She's vomiting and has diarrhea. She was wandering around half out of her mind looking for her baby.''

"Elena," the girl whispered wearily.

"She stinks!"

"You would, too, if you'd been robbed and raped."

"I don't want to hear—"

When the poor girl moaned again, Pamela focused on the stains marring the girl's soiled skirt.

"Diarrhea? You can't bring her in here—"

"Blood. She aborted her baby, too—"

"We've got to call the border patrol—"

"No— She needs food, water, and medical attention. We've got to bathe her and pull the thorns out of her feet. She hid her daughter…somewhere on the ranch."

"She has another…child?"

"We've got to find her baby daughter before she dies."

"This can't be happening. Thieves…this girl. We've already postponed the funeral because you— Thieves? We've got the governor coming—"

Roque's arms tightened convulsively around the thin girl in rags. "I told Pablo to get as many men as he could out to the southern pastures to look for her baby and the thieves who nearly killed her."

"But that's near the cemetery. Benny will kill me…if he finds out about this. Why do these people keep coming up here? This is our ranch. They're nothing but trouble."

"If you hand this girl over to the Border Patrol while she's sick or before we find the baby, and she or that baby dies, I'll go to the press and paint this in the worst possible light."

Pamela swallowed. "All right. But she can't stay on Blackstone land. Benny can't know about her."

Confused and more than a little frightened by the bizarre chain of events—his four *F*'s, Caleb's death and now Rosita, Roque stuck to the shadows of Caleb's room.

Rosita was nothing to him. Nothing. And yet...

"If you hadn't given her a ride, she wouldn't be here," Chainsaw Hernandez, who was keeping her in his trailer, had reminded him.

Slowly the old snapshots of Caleb as well as pictures of Roque and him together tacked all over the wall drew his attention.

Smiling grimly, Roque studied those images that froze split seconds of their past. If only...

He crossed his arms to ward off the chill that convulsed him. There were no pictures of him in the rest of the house, no reminders that he'd ever existed. Only Caleb had cared.

Yanking off his sunglasses, Roque leaned closer to check out two recent snapshots of Caleb. Gently he touched the yellow hair and then ran his finger over the crazily happy grin. His little brother had grown so tall and so handsome.

In another photograph Caleb held one his father's precious Winchesters. In still another, he sat erect and broadshouldered astride a big black stallion. Roque removed the tacks and pocketed both photographs inside his black leather jacket.

Pacing restlessly, he stared at Caleb's treasures in the bookshelves. Thoughts of Rosita hit him. Through broken sobs, she'd clung to him and blurted out every horrible thing that had happened to her.

"I lost my baby...babies.... They raped me."

He'd stroked her hair.

"Find Elena."

Not so easy on a ranch of half a million acres.

In frustration, Roque tore a battered teddy bear off the highest shelf. Caleb used to drag this bedraggled, old thing around everywhere.

Wumpo? Yes. Wumpo was its name. This particular

bear was Caleb's oldest, dearest stuffed animal. His fur was matted from being mauled by a loving toddler. His left eye was missing.

Roque looked up at the other teddy bears and old Star Wars toys lining the bookshelves. Then he studied the jumble of the pictures of himself that Caleb had tacked to his wall. There was one of a skinny girl riding a horse in an arena. A bright halo of lights crowned her head.

The bookcases were jammed with horse books. In one corner of the room sat Caleb's first horse, a Fisher-Price, plastic pony on wheels. Roque remembered everybody telling him Caleb had put Wumpo on the plastic pony and pulled it behind him when he could barely toddle.

Blinking back hot wetness, Roque was squeezing Wumpo hard when his gaze drifted to the mirror. Deadly green eyes drilled him. Streaked with purple shadow, his face looked so wild and dark, he recoiled.

"You weren't ever a real brother. The only reason Caleb liked you, you selfish bastard, is because you were his history."

Roque ran a tense hand over Caleb's scarred desk and neatly stacked diaries. Clutching Wumpo under one arm, Roque sank into the chair and thumbed through the top volume. A picture of Caleb at the beach with a pretty blond fluttered onto his leg.

He was riveted by the slim girl in the soft, pink dress. Her skin was creamy; she had a mass of long yellow curls tied up in a pink, gingham ribbon. At least he thought it was pink. Her wide tremulous mouth somehow gave a man, at least a man with too much Moya blood dirty thoughts.

Ritz.

No more thick glasses or braces. She was slim and tall. Her features were fine, her skin lightly tanned. Her smile was bright; her violet eyes large and trusting as she gazed up at Caleb.

And that mouth. Why did it have to be so incredibly sexy?

For an instant Roque's heart filled with bitter jealousy. Had Caleb kissed that mouth? Had he had her?

He caught himself.

"Bitch, did you kill my brother?"

He wadded her picture up. But his hand shook as he slowly began to read from his brother's diary.

We ride together. Nearly every day. We go to her beach house 'cause it's her secret place. I take my books there and she brings hers. Sometimes we trade. We're going to end this feud. We are. We've got a crazy idea to...

When the door opened, and a cool draft whispered against his hot cheek, he slammed the diary shut. For a second or two, he almost expected Caleb to whip inside, grab the diary, and either hug him or fuss at him for destroying the treasured photograph.

"You're jealous...'cause Ritz's so pretty now...'cause she's all mine—"

Roque's senses reeled. Furious, he looked up at his stepmother, realizing again that Caleb would never walk through that door again.

Because of Ritz.

Pamela, his beautiful, blond stepmother, glided toward him. She had to be in her forties. Not that she looked it. When she smiled, he relaxed a little.

Her beauty was so different from Ritz's and from Rosita's, too. He'd always thought his stepmother was sophisticated, worldly, glamorous, and as cold as ice. For the first time he saw that her eyes were even more haunted than Rosita's. He thought of Ritz's open smile and her treacherous, shining eyes and then of Rosita's terror.

Ritz embraced life with immense enthusiasm. Rosita had risked her life for the American dream.

What did Pamela care about? She'd been a Keller. The Kellers said his father had bought her.

"Do you have a suit?" Pamela said in her husky voice.

Roque stood up, pitched Wumpo onto the bed. Then with an air of indifference, he fingered the bottom edge of an older snapshot of Caleb on the tall black stallion tacked to the wall. "Long John?"

"You're not supposed to be in here. Nobody is. Benny—"

"The kid must've learned to ride since I saw him last," Roque said. "He's sure a natural."

"He wanted to do everything you—" She broke off. "If Benny catches you—" Her gaze dropped. "He's…he's very upset." She went still. "He's even threatened to shoot Long John so nobody else can ever ride him."

"He what?" Roque shot out of his chair so fast, it flipped over.

"Do you have a proper suit?" she repeated.

Roque stared at his stepmother blankly, still trying to absorb what she'd just said about his father's intentions toward Caleb's horse. "What?"

"A suit? Something appropriate to wear to his funeral?"

"Oh, right. Appearances. Shooting a valuable horse Caleb loved is nothing. The governor's coming. Black leather won't do."

"I was thinking about Caleb. You're here for him, not the governor."

"What about you? Why are you here? Why did you marry my father?"

When she didn't answer, he laughed harshly. "For his money?"

"Please—"

"What do you have to do to earn it? Does he beat you for kicks, too?"

She blushed. "I have a man down the hall...in your bedroom. He brought everything you'll need. Everything he had in stock that we thought could possibly fit you. I have a barber, too."

He started to argue. Then he caught another glimpse of the wild biker in the mirror. Long ebony hair. Black leather. If Caleb was anywhere around, he wanted to do right by him—if just this once.

Instead of swearing at her, he murmured a soft thank you.

When his father's jet buzzed the house, Roque jammed his Ray Bans back on.

"Benny!" She ran to the window. Her beautiful face lit up like a girl's as the jet dropped behind the mesquite and huisache.

Then she turned. "It really would be best...for both of us...if Benny didn't catch us here in Caleb's room. And whatever you do, don't tell him about that poor girl at Chainsaw's, either."

Benny Blackstone strode through the door and banged it shut behind him. The sight of Roque's bike was enough to make him furious.

Benny pitched his thick briefcase brimming with research on mold against the wall.

"I own it. I can break it." Wasn't that what he always said?

Always he radiated impatience—and power, raw, unadulterated power. Nobody knew that underneath his bantam rooster facade he was running as scared as the next guy, maybe even more so.

He'd just won a judgment for a hundred million!

He'd won!

But his victory felt hollow. Caleb was dead. Roque was home.

Better than losing, though.

As a kid, Benny had been a runt and poor to boot. Every bully on the block had chased and beaten him. He'd made up his mind early that when he was grown, he'd be tall and handsome and big and strong. Then he'd be the bully.

But he hadn't grown tall or handsome. He wasn't well hung, either. Not that he allowed himself to dwell on any of his deficiencies because doing so drove him so crazy. His rapier sharp mind was his sex organ, his weapon—his everything. With his brain he raped; he pillaged. And he enjoyed the hell out of it!

His features were dark and bluntly squared, his hair blue-black. His green eyes blazed when he was excited. He had a striking widow's peak and high forehead. His enemies said if you were casting the devil in a movie, he'd be perfect for the part.

He laughed at their insults. He wanted them scared. Then they wouldn't see how scared he felt. Like today. Sunny was dead. And all he could do was give the kid a funeral fit for a king.

Yes, people had been scared of him ever since his first big case when he'd taken on the revered Dr. R. D. Meyer, Houston's world famous heart surgeon, and won. People had thought Meyer had walked on water back then. Now who was he? Where was he for that matter? Benny had destroyed him. Since Meyer, he had only to threaten lawsuits. When the opposition heard his name, they usually settled. He eviscerated the rare defendants who had the balls to stand up to him.

He loved doing it because every time he did it, he was a runt kid again, only this time his fists were up and he was hammering the bullies. Only the legal system, at least in Texas, was way better than fists.

Benny loved the money, the power. Women flocked to him even if he wasn't big where it counted. Even the high and mighty Pamela Keller was his.

Today, for the funeral he'd chosen a dark suit, a starched white shirt, gold cuff links, and a black striped silk tie. He didn't give a damn that he looked like a fat cat, big-city lawyer instead of a rancher.

When he heard the swish of Pamela's silk slip beneath her wool dress, Benny strode across the living room that was too quiet without Sunny. Carefully he avoided looking at the silver-framed pictures of the one son who had once delighted him so much. Even knowing they were there made him feel frightened and lost, like a child who couldn't find his way home in the dark.

He had eyes for his wife alone. She looked like an icy queen in black; but today as never before her beauty in this temple of death drew him like a magnet. He wanted to run across the room into her arms.

She froze.

He told himself he didn't care that she didn't care. She was his. The fact that she didn't care for him, wouldn't ever care for him, only fired his eagerness to have her.

"The house looks perfect. You look perfect," he said.

She didn't speak, but a shock went through him when he crossed the room and took her cool hand and led her to their bedroom.

"Draw the curtains," he commanded as he locked the door. "Turn off the light. I want you."

The ritual was familiar to both of them.

Like a queen, she was always so icily cold and formal with him in public.

She played by different rules in the dark.

He moved forward and grabbed her, knowing she would let him, knowing she wanted this as much as he did.

He yanked his zipper down. "Suck me."

She gasped.

"Do it. Now. Crawl."

He heard her sliding across the carpet toward him on her knees. She'd barely begun tonguing him when he had to have her underneath him. He had to be inside her. He had to strip and dominate her. He had to show her who was king of Texas.

His arms circled her. Quickly he lifted her skirt and ripped her panty hose down her thighs.

I own it. I can break it.

Then they were on the floor. Her arms, gentle and soft but urgent, oh, so damned urgent, came around him.

He was inside her, battering, plunging like a bull.

She was crying out, coming even before he did. She was still whimpering when he exploded. Then she came again, more violently than before, holding onto him, rocking, shaking, weeping.

She started to get up as she always did. They never spoke or touched afterward. But he clutched her arm like a frightened little boy holding onto his mother in the dark. Only his mother had never held him.

Don't think about her.

He felt so lost today. So strange.

The house was so still.

Cupping Pamela's icy face in his warm hands, he kissed her on the lips for the first time.

She tasted so sweet, so incredibly sweet. Then he remembered she was a Keller. She'd given birth to Kellers.

When his eyes began to burn he tried to push her away.

"Oh, God, no," he sobbed.

But she held him, stroking his hair, until he quieted.

"I'm sorry," she whispered. "So sorry about Caleb."

The tenderness in her voice surprised him so much he nearly got choked up all over again. He didn't trust himself to speak for a long time.

"Roque's here," she said.

"It's about time. To hell with him. Be downstairs in five minutes," he said. "The governor called me while I was in the air—"

Benny went into the bathroom and splashed water on his face. When he came out, she was still on the floor where he'd left her.

"Get up," he said, almost hating her because he'd cried.

Her damn first husband had been a living legend. Buster Keller, the saintly bastard, had adored her. Worshiped her. She'd been madly in love with him, too.

Benny knew there was no way he could ever compete.

"She married you for your money," his enemies jeered.

"So the hell what? She's mine now."

"But for how long? Till somebody richer—"

"I can possess her anytime I want."

That had to be enough.

She was so beautiful, so stylish. She was everything he wasn't.

Resenting the hell out of his growing dependency on her, especially today, Benny strode past her, out the door and then down the hall. He was in the living room when Sheriff Johnson pulled up in a swirl of dust beside Roque's motorcycle.

Benny had tried unsuccessfully to call the sheriff from his plane. Glad of this diversion from his wife, Benny stormed out onto the porch and flung himself down the stairs. "What the hell are you doing here, Johnson?"

Johnson's jowly face hardened as he studied Benny and then the vast brown pastures that stretched on all sides of them.

Benny attacked as if to a crazed drumroll. "You should be bringing Sunny's killer to justice. Steve Keller was driving drunk, and he killed him. His sister put him up to it."

The sheriff's face went blank. "Caleb was drinking, too. Caleb's car was already on fire before Keller rolled his van."

"Do you local yocals have peas for brains or what?"

"The girl claims Caleb and she were good friends. He asked her to dance. Her brother punched him. They got in a fight. Kid's stuff! The principal confiscated a flask of Stoli and told them to leave."

"Daniels and those incompetent bastards loosed that Keller bunch on my boy, knowing they were drunk and steamed up."

A tall, lithe figure loped around the corner of the house. *Roque.*

He was handsome as the devil, too. At the sight of him, the kid flushed angrily and avoided his eyes. He didn't smile or say hello.

That jealous bitch, Blanca, had made Roque hate him. The kid was as sick and jealous as she was, and Benny loathed him as he'd never loathed anybody. Why was he alive when Sunny...

"Where the hell have you been?"

Roque green eyes flared with sullen indignation.

"Like I said," the sheriff continued, "Ritz Keller claims your son was her friend, and that she loved him very much."

"Kellers don't love Blackstones," Benny thundered.

"Then why did you marry Pamela?" Roque whispered.

"Go to hell. Caleb was murdered, and that Keller girl has to pay."

Benny finished with a stream of curses.

The sheriff glared at him as he opened his car door. "I

wouldn't go around making idle threats. Feelings around here are running mighty high."

"You tell me that—when I'm the one with the dead kid—my one and only good son."

Roque went white.

The sheriff lowered his eyes.

Benny banged a fist onto the hood of the sheriff's car. "What the hell are you going to do about it—Sheriff?"

11

Benny clenched Pamela's hand. His glazed eyes looked anywhere but at the shiny bronze casket beneath the massive floral spray of white roses that seemed to float above the awful sea of artificial green grass.

The kings and queens of Texas were seated under the oaks and palms circling the gravesite. Funny, for once he didn't give a damn.

Benny's gaze narrowed suspiciously on Pablo and the Spanish-speaking cowboys standing at attention behind the coffin in their best blue work shirts and jeans.

Where the hell was Roque? His son—the Mexican.

If Roque were in the casket, maybe then he could bear to look at it. Benny was pulling his sunglasses out of his pocket and putting them on, so no one would notice his glistening eyes when a shocked murmur went through the crowd.

People stood up behind him, whispering excitedly. Father Moore stopped reading the Bible.

Benny's jaw fell when his gaze was drawn to the tall young man with blue-black hair and the stark widow's peak too much like his own.

Roque was too damn stunning in a custom-made black suit as he led Sunny's huge black stallion to the casket.

"What the hell...?"

Pamela shook him. "Remember where you are...who's here."

Pushing her aside, swiping at his streaming eyes, Benny erupted out of his chair. "You low-down Mexican bastard...you have no right...."

Roque stood between Sunny's casket and Sunny's magnificent black stallion.

Not only had Roque saddled Long John; he'd jammed Sunny's brand-new custom made boots backward into the silver studded stirrups.

Sunny's horse... His empty black boots with those blood-red embroidered roses....

Sunny had spun wildly around and around, almost dancing, in front of the store mirror the day Benny had bought them for him in San Antonio. The kid had stomped around in them day and night for a week. Hell, he'd even slept in them.

The empty boots and that riderless stallion made Benny know that Sunny was never coming back.

"Somebody shoot that animal! No! I'll shoot it myself!" Benny grabbed for his shoulder holster, but it wasn't there.

So many threats had been made against his life, he'd gotten a handgun permit.

"Sit down, Benny. Please," Pamela pleaded. "The governor..."

"Just get me a gun."

When nobody moved, he began to burn like a man tied to a stake with his bowels ripped out. Mad with grief and rage and feelings of impotence even worse than those of his childhood, he lunged at the tall, dark boy with that bitter, insolent mouth.

"How dare you just stand there...alive...gloating? Murderer! You're not my son!"

A shock went through the crowd. Even the governor was staring at him.

I own it. I can break it.

Benny lunged, seizing Roque by the tie, trying to strangle him as he attacked that beautiful face with his fists. The kid was too stunned to fight back, and Benny might have killed him, if Pablo and the other cowboys hadn't dragged him off.

His face purple, Roque scrambled slowly to his feet, yanking his tie loose, gasping for breath. His eyes wild, he wiped his bloody lip with the back of his hand, smearing a red streak across his high cheekbones.

"You were stealing his show!" Benny screamed. "This is his funeral! Sunny's last show on this earth! He's important! He's everything! You're nothing! Nothing— He was so smart. You can't even read!"

Pamela's soft voice finally penetrated the black fog that gripped Benny. "Roque's your son, too!"

"The hell I am," came the boy's hard, low voice as he spun around and seized Long John's reins from Pablo. With raw violence, he pulled first one embroidered boot and then the other out of the stirrups and flung them at Benny's face. Then he swung himself into the saddle.

"Get off that horse!" Benny yelled.

The kid went rigid. The glittering anger in his eyes terrified Benny.

A born rider, the hellish boy looked glorious on that prancing, black devil. Clicking his tongue against his white teeth, Roque shot Benny a nasty, triumphant smile before galloping away into shin-high grasses and dense brush.

"You're not my son," Benny yelled. "If it's the last thing I ever do, I'll see you dead!"

* * *

A single tear flowed down Ritz's cheek. Shakily she lowered her binoculars, unable to watch the solemn group massed around Caleb's coffin. She'd snuck as close to Campo Santo as she dared. Not that the serene cemetery with its olive trees and palm trees and oleander brought her any peace.

Birds chirped, and she could hear the soft whisper of deer in the brush. The same breeze that stirred the grasses and trees caressed her yellow curls that she'd tied back at her nape with a pink ribbon. Great puffs of white sailed overhead, causing sunlight to come and go upon the white, wooden crosses and tombstones.

Her breath caught on a sob. How could Caleb's funeral day be so beautiful?

Then she lifted the binoculars again and got a real shock. Looking stunning and too male, Roque Moya was leading Long John up to the casket. In the next second his handsome brown face went blotchy with panic and he was staring straight at her.

She dropped the binoculars and sank behind a tree. Soon curiosity bested her, and she refocused on his dark, narrow face and wide, bitter mouth. The angles of his untamed face were as precise and masculine as ever—sharp, high cheekbones and too much jaw.

He was so tall and dark and fierce she could hardly look at him and breathe. Blushing, she sank to her knees once more. When she looked again, his green eyes burned so brightly, she was sure he was crying.

Tears sprang to her eyes. Caleb had said he'd come home, and she hadn't believed it.

When she looked again, Roque was sprawled on the ground, his face bloody. Pablo and his cowboys had Benny in a bear grip. When Roque struggled to stand, weaving unsteadily, she realized he'd been hurt. Then he was in the saddle, whipping the reins, flying toward her.

Her hand on the binoculars wobbled and she was staring at a man, who, incredibly, was staring at her through the scope of his deer rifle.

"Oh, God...."

A bullet zinged past her and she screamed.

Roque didn't even feel his father's knuckles crunch into his jawbone. It was as if he were in a dream or was a ghost like Caleb. Even when he saw the blood on his father's hands and tasted copper, even when he galloped hard for the brush, none of it seemed real.

Only when Roque reached the dense oak and sycamore, did he come to his senses and pull back on the reins. When his father shouted to him to come back, he clicked his teeth and set off for the pond. Once there, Roque dismounted and unsaddled the black stallion Caleb had loved. Long John had a sweet temper, a lovely Friesian face, enormous, sensitive black eyes, and a powerful body.

"Nobody's going to hurt you," Roque soothed.

Roque couldn't move or breathe in his new clothes, so he unknotted his tie and unbuttoned the starched shirt to the middle of his chest. Folding the jacket and tie, he placed them on top of the heavy saddle.

Then he went up to Long John and rubbed noses with the stallion.

"You were Caleb's," he whispered. "I'm Caleb's big brother. So, I'm your friend."

Long John stood still and silent as Roque brushed his fine, sensitive muzzle.

Roque slipped a hand in his trouser pocket and pulled out the picture of Caleb on Long John. When Roque looked up across the waving grasses toward the horizon he saw Caleb, his golden hair flying as he'd leapt through the tall brown grasses on that long ago afternoon.

Roque sighed. Placing his arms around Long John's powerful neck, he just held him. Slowly he placed his right hand on his own heart and his left palm above Long John's heart, so he could feel them beating together.

If the sun was warm on his skin, it was even hotter on Long John's black coat. A bird with a yellow head and tail landed in the grass a few feet from the stallion and pecked at the ground. The shadows deepened, and Roque found solace in the beautiful day and the stallion's stolid, comforting presence.

Some slight rustle came from the brush. Startled, Long John perked his ears back. His black eyes widened and rolled. Something glinted from the trees. Roque heard a bullet. Next he saw a flash of pink.

"Who's there?"

Roque sprinted toward the trees, his strides long and leaping. He nearly stumbled over an empty plastic water jug and a dirty diaper.

Pebbles flew from his boots and trickled down the hard-packed path as he flung himself up the ancient sand dunes that were overgrown with high grasses and mesquite.

Soon he was sloshing knee-deep through the muddy stream that fed the pond. Heedless of the cold water and the thorny bushes, he kept on. There were more water jugs along the trail as well as old shoes and plastic sacks.

When he stopped to catch his breath, gnats and flies buzzed above another diaper. A big black horsefly landed on his shoulder and bit greedily.

"Ouch!" Roque sucked in a deep breath. The mesquite and dry grasses smelled clean and sharp. Then the breeze stirred the leaves overhead and sent the plastic sacks rasping among the dead leaves on the trail. A covey of quail, their six brown heads bobbing, their wings half spread, scuttled down the path with their chicks.

Then the imperial parade vanished, and the woods went still. The trail was worn smooth by hundreds of footprints. It had to be the regular north-south route across Blackstone Ranch that Pablo had told him the undocumented aliens followed to bypass the highway checkpoint.

He couldn't be far from where Pablo had found Rosita.

He began to walk purposefully in the direction he'd been running. He hadn't gone a hundred yards, when he saw something pink fluttering on a mesquite branch. He grabbed what turned out to be a gingham ribbon and wound it around a brown finger.

Whose was it?

A quarter of a mile down the path, a soft, feminine voice floated toward him.

''Oh…oh… Oh, dear, dear—''

The velvet sound slid through him like a caress. He knew *that* voice. It went with a skinny girl with freckles and glasses. It went with pretty yellow hair and a sassy mouth.

''Ritz?''

A baby mewed softly.

Roque's eyes widened.

''Don't be scared,'' Ritz crooned. ''I've got you now. Goodness' sakes. What's a little girl like you doing out here all by yourself?''

Silently, so as not to startle them, Roque crept forward until he was so close, he nearly stumbled into the slim, golden girl in a pink, gingham shirt and skintight jeans. She was crooning over a baby in a torn pink blanket.

¡Dios! She wasn't skinny anymore. Hell no! She had the cutest, most perfect butt he'd maybe ever seen.

He knew that blanket. *Elena.* How the hell—

''It's okay, little sweetheart—''

Ritz was kneeling on the ground, rocking back and forth from her knees, her golden head bent low over the wriggling bundle in her arms.

"Ritz—"

She whirled, her blue eyes huge with fear. When he strode toward her, she drew Elena even closer.

"Touching," he said, stopping a mere foot from her, he spread his boots wide in the deep sand. "Afraid, *princesa?*"

Her brows snapped together. "Not of you. Somebody just shot at me."

"I wonder why?" He crossed his arms over his powerful chest, assuming the stance of a conqueror.

She notched her chin upward.

"You think I'm the devil incarnate, no?"

"Your own father would agree."

"Did you kill my brother?"

Her face blanched. "No!"

"Is Caleb lying in that coffin burned to a crisp because of you?"

She bent her head.

"Look at me, damn it!"

"It was an accident. I'm so sorry. Now somebody wants me dead, too."

His heart thudded. The pain in her choked voice and the tears on her cheek stopped him cold. He knew what it was like to be falsely accused.

She was pretty. So damn pretty. It bothered him that she was pale as a sheet and cringing from him, too. He felt her pain as if it were his own. And he'd heard the gun.

He forced a nasty smile. "What were you to my brother? His whore? Is that why your brother chased my brother?"

"We were friends. Friends. Why won't anybody believe me?" She flushed. "Oh, just leave me alone!"

He felt the heat rising in his cheeks before she lowered her head over the baby, murmuring to her in a low, tortured tone as she scooted backward away from him.

Guilt washed him. "Her name's Elena," he said, his tone oddly gentle. "It's a miracle you found her."

Her hand froze on the baby's head. "Elena?"

"Her mother's a girl from my city—Rosita. I—I gave them a ride to the border…. Then the guide and the other men she was traveling with left her—" His voice broke. Why was he telling her this? "I'd given her Pablo's number." He didn't want to go into the rape or all the embarrassing things he'd done for her or felt for her afterward, so he stopped. "She was…hurt…badly. The men got scared. They ran. But somebody broke into a cabin and called Pablo. Thank God he did. Pablo found her. For now, she's with a fairly strange buddy of mine."

"How do I know *you're* not lying?"

He squared his jaw. "I wish to hell I was. I wish to hell I'd never gotten involved…." He stared at the baby's wild black thatch of hair and at her scrawny, wriggling arms. "Because of me, they nearly died. But now Rosita sees me as some sort of hero." He sighed wearily. "Like I said, it's a miracle you found her baby before coyotes or…"

"Oh, God… You're right. Or a puma," Ritz breathed, forgetting her fear of him in her alarm for the baby.

Elena made a fist and let out a cry. Then she began to suckle at the pink gingham above Ritz's breast soaking the cotton through to her nipple.

His gaze fell to that aroused pink berry. Blushing, Ritz let out an embarrassed gasp that made his own color rise.

"She's hungry," Ritz murmured, turning even redder when he couldn't quit staring.

He nodded, mute. Then he sank down on his knees. "She's got to be starving."

"Daddy would call the Border Patrol."

"No, Rosita needs a doctor. She's not strong enough to travel. She can't go back to Mexico, either." Why the hell did he feel so responsible for Rosita? Frowning, he lapsed into an uncomfortable silence. "I could hold her for you—"

"What kind of mother would leave—"

"A very sick and scared mother. I won't hurt Elena. I want to take her to Rosita. You've got to trust me."

"But you're a Blackstone—"

"Caleb trusted you...and you trusted him," Roque said. "Why can't we—"

"It's not the same...with you."

He felt the color drain from his face. "Because I'm a Mexican?"

"That's not it." Her gaze fell unwillingly to his lips.

Why was there this pull between them? He'd felt it even before he'd seen her when he'd danced on the beach like an idiot.

"I'll just take her to her mother," he said quietly.

Stubbornly shaking her head, Ritz stood up. The sudden movement jarred the baby into suckling fitfully at her breast again.

"Oh, dear." Ritz jerked her face to the side but not before they both blushed again.

"I'm not giving her to you," she said quietly.

"Then will you at least go with me and see Rosita?"

She tilted her chin back, her gaze on his cut lip. "I saw what your father did to you at the funeral."

"I—I wish you hadn't."

"It made me feel sorry for you."

"I don't want your pity."

"That's not what I meant. My father hasn't been very understanding, either." Her voice was small and lost. "It's like he hates me, and he'll never forgive me."

Their eyes met. Before he could jump back, she moved

forward and gently touched his swollen lip with her trembling finger.

How softly she pressed his wound. When she pulled her hand away, red blood glazed her fingertip.

"Oh, dear," she whispered. "I—I…shouldn't have…"

"I shouldn't be with you, either."

"If I go with you to meet Elena's mother…to see if you are telling the truth… That doesn't mean anything. Understand?"

"So you'll go?"

"If I do—it doesn't mean I like you…or trust you…. It's just that I can't hand Elena over to you or anybody else…except her mother…if she's a good mother. I'm not leaving her on Blackstone land unless I'm sure she'll be okay."

"So you'll go?" he repeated.

"I shouldn't go anywhere with you."

"'Cause I'm a Blackstone and your sworn enemy." He grinned. "You sure about that?"

"Don't look at me like that!"

"But you're cute," he whispered.

"Don't say things like that, either!"

His answer was a soft, sexy chuckle.

"I said don't look at me like that—"

"What if I can't help myself? You're cute and bossy— like the women in my family. You'd fit right in. Not that I'm proposing…"

Much to his surprise, she smiled at that.

Elena's hands fisted. Her face purpled as she began to kick. Her mouth puckered. Her forehead crinkled. She gasped for breath and then burst out with a fierce cry of outrage.

"There. There," Roque whispered so gently that when he held out his arms, Ritz forgot not to trust him.

His brown hands slipped under the baby's tiny thrusting

arms so naturally, she let him have her. He drew Elena up to his face and kissed her runny nose.

"What big tears! You're going to *Mamá, preciosa.* Right now. You're not going to starve. No, you're not."

The fierce wrinkle between Elena's forked black eyebrows smoothed. Her button-black eyes brightened. Her tiny mouth curved.

"At least one female around here trusts me."

"She's too young to know better."

"She trusts her instincts."

When the baby cooed flirtatiously, Ritz felt an odd pang of jealousy.

"Coming?" Roque demanded.

12

Cupping Elena's small black head against his chest with his hand, Roque had vanished into the trees. The prickly pear and sticker burrs in the mesquite were so thick, Ritz had to pick her way through the tall burned grasses.

"Roque! Wait!"

No answer.

"Where are you? I—I should never have trusted you with the baby!"

When she sprinted to catch up, a thorn stabbed her ankle.

"Ouch!"

"Roque!" she yelled, fuming as she knelt to pull out the thorn.

She stood up again and frowned at the sagging fence that skirted the edges of the path. The landscape had taken on a bleak, shaggy aspect. Barbed wire strands were either loose or nonexistent or trampled into the dirt. Two skinny gray cows stared at her from beneath a scraggly mesquite. Trash—clumps of plastic bags, dozens of beer cans, tampons and old mufflers—littered the ground.

She jumped when she heard footsteps crunching thick

brush just ahead. Then Roque reappeared, the sleeping baby cradled against his broad chest. "You okay?"

"I couldn't keep up." She rubbed at her ankle. "Where are we going anyway?"

"Chainsaw Hernandez's."

"That…that awful ex-con with the tattoos and the stripper girlfriend?"

"He's got a law degree."

"And where did he get it? Prison?"

"He outsmarted my father out of five hundred prime acres, too."

"Blackmail probably. Daddy says Hernandez doesn't work and that he lives off women. He says he harbors illegals."

"Chainsaw works…just not at a job. He's a sculptor. *Princesa*, not many people get to live a fairy tale life like you do."

"You can't take Elena there."

"He's got a big heart. She'll be safe…with her mother. Nobody but a fool messes with Chainsaw. This isn't Blackstone land. You can come see her anytime you want."

Elena began to squirm. "Come on. She's hungry. She needs her mother," he said.

Before she could argue, Roque resumed his long-legged gait, and Ritz had to run to keep up. As soon as they broke through the trees, and she saw Chainsaw's squalid, spray-painted trailer with its surveillance camera mounted above the front door, she was more alarmed than ever.

Ritz sighed. If the trailer was depressing, its surroundings were worse. Old washing machines, dryers, and a stack of tires littered a bare, dirt yard. Two rusting cars had been laid to rest on concrete blocks beside a rotten fence.

"See, he's a sculptor." Roque pointed toward a ramshackle shed filled with animal carvings and chainsaws.

All Ritz saw was the Bengal tiger pacing back and forth in a chain-link cage beside the shed, eyeing her hungrily.

With a little cry, Ritz grabbed Roque just as the trailer door banged, and a beefy man with a permanent scowl stuck his wooly brown head outside. His huge potbelly had an intricate tiger tattoo on it.

In one fist, he gripped a foam cup. In the other, he held a cocked pistol pointed straight at her.

"Yo—Roque!"

"Don't shoot!" she screamed. "That's the second time a man's pointed a gun at me today."

Chainsaw leered at her contemptuously. "If you'd told me you was bringing a lady, I would have dressed up."

Lowering his pistol, he wiggled his hips in such a way as to hitch up his low-slung, camouflage shorts.

He turned back to Roque. "Hot damn. You found the baby."

"No, I did," Ritz said.

"Rosita will be so happy. The doctor just left. She won't stop talking about you. She's scared out of her mind that *la Migra* is going to come and take her away. You can't let that happen."

"What the hell can I do about it?"

"I told you what—"

"And I told you where to go."

Chainsaw scowled. "Then you and me—we've got a problem because she's damn sure not my responsibility!"

"Later."

Roque climbed the stairs and disappeared through the sagging door.

Ritz froze. Her throat closing with fear when she heard their raised voices from inside the trailer.

"You've gotta do it, Moya! So they don't have to go back."

Roque shoved the door back open. His smoldering black eyes moved over her as if the argument was her fault. "You coming?"

A deer scampered by. When the Bengal tiger roared and leaped against the chain link, Ritz sprang up the stairs.

"Yes!" Ritz squeaked, grabbing onto Roque's sleeve again and following them into a foul warren cluttered with dirty dishes and clothes. The small room stank of stale beer and moldy food. Twice she stumbled into contorted sculptures of pumas and tigers.

Chainsaw shambled down a short, narrow hall, past paneled walls plastered with snapshots of a bone-thin platinum blonde with bowling ball breasts, who wore sparkly red pasties and a matching G-string. Natasha...

Chainsaw opened the door at the end of the hall and turned on a light. The tiny bedroom was immaculate. So was the thin, dark girl with the gleaming, black braids wound round her head, who lay in bed.

Rosita looked like a child playing dress-up in her mother's oversize, fluffy pink robe. She smiled wanly until she saw Roque and Elena. Then her soft eyes brightened.

"Elena! Roque!" She spoke rapidly to them in hushed, pleading Spanish. Roque's hurried retorts sounded like angry bursts of gunfire. As soon as he placed the little girl in her eager mother's arms, Elena began making ravenous sounds as she suckled at the heavy brown breast.

Roque flushed.

"She'll be fine," Chainsaw said. "The doctor wants to check her again in a week. She's supposed to eat and drink. Hell, I don't think she understood a word he said, but she's damn near eaten everything in the house."

"That's on me."

"This whole thing is on you, like I told you. You brought her to the border. You—"

"Shut the hell up."

"She can stay two days—max. Then she's all yours. And another thing. The baby stinks worse than a javelina—same as Rosita did when you brought her. You ain't going nowhere until that little gal finishes nursing and you give her a bath same as you did Rosita."

"You bathed Rosita?" Ritz whispered.

Roque's lips thinned. He turned bright red.

"Then I'll bathe the baby," Ritz said.

Long John twisted his massive neck to watch Roque as he sank to his knees beside the flowers piled high on Caleb's grave. Roque picked up a black, stuffed horse with a red bow around its neck.

The evening air held such a keen edge of sweetness it almost hurt Ritz's lungs. Or maybe it was watching Roque's strong brown fingers absently sift through strands of that mane that shredded her heart.

His broad shoulders slumped. His dark face was so remote and lost. Ritz almost felt his pain seeping like tears from those sensitive fingers into that stuffed animal.

Ritz's gaze drifted past the magnificent sprays of roses to the rows of white crosses. She didn't know what to say. Maybe there was nothing to say in the face of such bottomless sorrow.

Finally Roque pitched the horse down and looked up at her. "I want to know about your friendship with Caleb."

"Why?"

"I want to know my brother."

"You should have answered his letters."

"I was a real bastard."

She bit her lip and looked up through the trees where bright, blue sky shone through what was left of the leaves.

"He loved me," Roque said quietly. "No matter what I did...or didn't do. But I wasn't here for him. You were. Despite the feud. You were. You've got to talk to me. I won't go back to Mexico until we talk."

"What about your father?"

"To hell with him!"

"But he hates me! Maybe he hired that man who tried to shoot me. You're supposed to hate me, too! He wants everybody to believe I killed... What would he do to you if he knew you were with me right now?"

Roque seized her arm and slowly pulled her closer. "Forget him! I'm through with the bastard. He can't make me hate you. What if nobody's to blame? Not you? Not me? Not even God?"

When she struggled to free herself, he pulled her against his chest. "Caleb's just dead. That's all. People die. You're innocent of all blame except...except for maybe love...and courage...exceptional courage to love somebody forbidden."

"You're the only one.... Still, you shouldn't be touching me like this," she whispered. "Not because of your father. Because it's making me crazy."

"Me, too." He swallowed.

Shaking her head, she tried to push free. "What are we doing?"

"Maybe I just need to hold somebody who feels as bad as I do."

This time when he urged her closer, she nestled her warm, wet cheek against his throat.

"You have to talk to me," he whispered in a low, choked tone.

"I'm so scared." She clung, not minding anymore that he held her so tightly. Ever since Caleb's death she'd needed to share her grief. But nobody had wanted to have anything to do with her except Roque.

"They wouldn't let me go to his funeral," she said.

"I know." He ran his hand along her cheek, picked up a lock of her golden hair and spooled it around his thumb. "What happened to those thick glasses—"

"Contacts. You can see them...if you look real close...."

Feasting his emerald gaze on her eyes, he leaned into her. When his warm breath brushed her cheek, she began to tremble.

"Cold?" he whispered.

"No."

"You're shaking."

"When you're this close, I feel...all funny...."

"Dios," he muttered. "So do I."

His heavy hands fell away. He stepped back abruptly. He pushed his fingers through his hair, but the heavy ebony silk flopped over his dark brow again.

He popped his knuckles. Then he stared up at the branches above her head. Jumping up restlessly, he grabbed at the leaves. Breaking off a branch, he flung it as far as he could. He jumped again, broke off another and flung it even farther.

"Dios mio." He sank down beside the mound of flowers.

"It's getting dark," she said. "I'd better go."

He nodded. "That's right. You'd better."

Suddenly everything that had felt right, felt wrong. Dazed and a little sad, she managed to flutter her stiff fingertips, waving goodbye.

He turned his back and ignored her.

"Roque—"

"Go," he growled. "Just go."

For a minute longer she stood watching his broad shoulders. Then the tension grew unbearable, and she ran stumbling through the darkening gloom for home.

13

Ritz came awake the next morning to thin rays of winter sunlight streaming into her bedroom shutters. Her hair was wet; her skin hot. Her body seemed to be humming.

Roque—she'd been dreaming of Roque. Dozens of Roques all dancing around her.

Blushing at the things she'd let them do, she sprang out of her bed and pulled on an old pair of faded jeans.

She buttoned her shirt all the way up her neck and ran a brush through her hair, tying it back demurely in a pony-tail. Why couldn't she stop thinking about him? She'd skipped supper to avoid her parents, fearing that they might read her thoughts.

Josh! She had to call him first thing. Maybe if they made up, she'd be able to forget Roque.

It wasn't even seven, and Josh slept late. Still afraid her parents would see through her, she tiptoed down the stairs and ran out to the barn.

Tails swaying, the big orange cat and his black sidekick strolled up to her and began to weave around her legs. Quickly she scattered a few crumbles of cat food into their bowls, not so many to get them as fat as Molly, the spoiled house cat, but enough so that she could muck Buttercup's stall in peace.

When she'd rolled a wheelbarrow full of horse dung out to her mother's compost heap, she returned and scooped sweet feed out of a dusty bin. Holding it to her face, she let it fall with a tinny sound into a bucket. Then she carried the bucket into Buttercup's stall and hung it on the wall.

As Buttercup greedily gobbled, Ritz stroked her neck.

"How are you feeling, girl?"

Buttercup's ears pricked forward.

"Just listen to the clatter of those palms. It's real windy. And you should see the sunlight sparkling in the peach trees."

The smell of leather and saddle soap and even Buttercup's noisy munching were comforts to Ritz. She stared deeply into the mare's thoughtful dark eyes. "How come the only person I can talk to right now besides you is…is Roque Blackstone. You remember him don't you, girl? You fell in love with him the first day you met him."

When Buttercup blew oats at her as if she did, Ritz jumped back laughing.

"I—I hate him, and he hates me."

Buttercup snorted.

"I do. Only he doesn't blame me for Caleb. And…and he even said I was pretty. Not that I believe—"

An hour later, Ritz had worked up such an appetite, she returned to the kitchen. She flung cupboards open, pulled out her bowl, a packet of oatmeal, and a spoon.

With any luck her father and his cowboys were off working some distant pasture and wouldn't be back until dark. Her mother had left a note saying she was at the hospital.

The house was too cold. When Ritz's teeth began to chatter, she realized her mother must have pulled her usual trick and left the windows open after she'd aired the house.

Normally Daddy closed them. The fact that he hadn't was an indication of how upset he was with her over Steve.

Mother was always airing the house and hanging sheets on the line so that they smelled of sunshine. She set home-made apple pies on windowsills to cool. Ritz was running about slamming windows when she heard a man's heavy boots on the porch stairs outside.

Her father stuck his white head inside. "You're up early."

"Daddy!" She pushed a strand of golden hair out of her eyes and tried to look innocent. "I—I couldn't sleep."

"Guilty conscience?"

An image from her dream of Roque's mouth between her legs rose up to haunt her.

"No, Daddy!" But her fingers slipped when she ripped the packet of oatmeal open. Half of the cereal flew into the bowl; the other half spilled all over the counter and floor.

He swung the door wider. His brows narrowed on her shaking hands. "Where were you yesterday?"

Would he even care if she told him a man had shot at her? "What are you doing home so early?" she asked.

"Irish got sick." He paused. "Your mother and I looked everywhere for you yesterday."

Ritz swallowed. "I—I took the truck into town, remember?" She poured water over her oatmeal and slammed the bowl into the microwave, not caring when her oatmeal sloshed over the sides. "To get that old tire fixed. And I moved Buttercup to the barn. Then I drove her around some. I was afraid she had colic again."

"You weren't at the barn during the funeral."

She turned her back on him. "I was feeling lousy," she whispered.

"Where?"

"I—I took a long walk—" She kept her eyes glued to the bowl revolving behind the dark glass in the microwave.

"You missed supper, too. Which was mighty grim, by the way. Then the hospital called, and your mother left without finishing her dinner—"

Ritz's heart twisted.

"I hear Moya's back."

She didn't answer.

"Made a spectacle of himself at the funeral, too. Upset his daddy. In front of the governor. Stole his brother's horse. Rode toward our land. Blackstone called me last night, wanted to know if I knew— As if I would know—"

She flushed.

His voice took on a new edge. "You wouldn't know anything about this, would you?"

When the microwave timer beeped, she rushed to get her oatmeal.

"I haven't the slightest idea…where he is."

"He's no damn good, I tell you."

She opened the door and set her oatmeal on the counter.

"You've already made this family the subject of scandal and gossip."

She whirled. "What are you accusing me of?"

"What's going on?"

She dipped her spoon into her oatmeal and then let it fall. "I'm not as hungry as I thought." She pitched her oatmeal down the sink.

"Stay away from him, girl."

"All right!" She flounced out of the kitchen and stomped upstairs where she locked herself in her bedroom. Once inside, she flung herself on her bed and buried her face in her pillow. Then she pounded her pillow.

Her tears were falling so fast her beloved horse posters seemed to swim. All her horse statues, her red and blue ribbons she'd won for her riding, even her flashy tiara blurred.

Wiping at her eyes, she got up and put on her rodeo queen tiara. The batteries had long since run down, and as an exercise in humility and maybe sanity, she hadn't replaced them. Used to, she'd sit for hours in front of her mirror fussing with her hair while she wore the flashy crown.

She had won—against great odds. She'd been the youngest contestant, and Buttercup the most unpredictable mount. But Buttercup had risen to the occasion, performing every event with flying colors. In the arena, the mare had behaved like a perfect lady too—even when Roxanne's jealous horse had nipped her in the withers, she'd stayed calm.

Ritz's miserable, gray face in no way resembled the radiant creature in the gilt-framed photo above her bed. In that picture, she was standing on Buttercup, flying around the rodeo arena, her arms outstretched while the crowd roared with applause, her ear-to-ear smile brighter than the electric tiara.

Caleb had been so proud. "You flew for all of them...just like you did with Roque and me."

Steve had been proud, too.

Steve. And Josh. Jet... They'd had so many good times together. Were those all over? Because of one night?

Ritz made a fist.

No...

Slowly she removed the tiara and set it beside her favorite palomino statue.

"I'll go see Steve. At least I can still drive and ride and still walk around. I'll call Josh. And Jet. Maybe we can make up and get over this if we try hard enough."

Josh's machine answered, so she dialed Jet.

Irish made the usual excuses. "Jet's not feeling too good."

His kindly tone made Ritz feel worse. "Jet if you're listening—"

Silence.

"Mr. Taylor, please tell—"

"Hi," Jet broke in, her voice flat and sullen.

"Hi."

Silence.

"Jet, hey, okay. I don't blame you for…for… Please, just don't hang up. I'm really sorry. I didn't dance with him to make you jealous or to flirt. You know I didn't. You were with Steve…."

"But you knew about me and Caleb…"

Ritz chewed her lip as she remembered running away from what she'd seen at the beach house. "Just like you knew Caleb and I were just friends."

"Still, I didn't like you dancing with him…in front of everybody."

"I'm sorry," Ritz said. "I—I called because I thought maybe Josh and you and me could go see Steve today."

"Josh? Is he even talking to you?"

"I'm going to call him."

Jet hesitated. "Give me ten. I was writing something. I've gotta do something to my hair. It's like all greasy. Maybe I'll braid it. Pick me up at the pasture gate."

Josh's machine picked up two more times, and she left messages, apologizing. She was walking out her door when he called.

"It's me," he said awkwardly.

"Hey."

"Why'd you call?" he demanded.

"I was wondering if you were going to stay mad forever?"

"I was wondering the same…. I—I was a jerk. All you

did was dance. One lousy dance. I shouldn't have freaked just 'cause Steve got mad.''

She digested his apology. "Okay. So, Jet and me... I mean Jet and I—we're going to see Steve right now. You want to come?''

"I've got a mile long list of chores.'' She heard the sound of paper shredding. He laughed. "What the hell?''

Josh had a six-pack of beer under his arm and smelled like a brewery when they picked him up. He was popping the top off a second bottle as he climbed into the back seat.

"Josh!''

"Since I'll get grounded, might as well go for broke. Want a beer?''

The girls shook their heads.

"Okay,'' Jet began, "I was telling Ritz I've been making a list. So, I want to know what you think.''

"What kind of list?'' Ritz asked as she hit the gas.

"About my perfect man list.''

Josh laughed uneasily. "This I gotta hear.''

"Jet's Mr. Ten,'' Jet read.

"Ten inches?'' Josh queried through bursts of laughter.

"No, that's my title.'' Jet began to read, "Genius level mind. Reads only the best literature. Never talks about it though, or bores you with how much he knows.''

"I've got news for you. Cool guys don't read literature,'' Josh scoffed.

"Handsome...but not in a showy artificial way.''

"Crap.''

"Knows how to dress...but indifferent to his appearance.''

"Bull.''

"A natural athlete...but he stays in shape without working out or anything. Doesn't go to gym or anything.''

"Did you get this out of a book?'' Ritz asked.

"I'm not done. He has to like animals...but outside. He's a man of action. He won't sit around watching TV or using a computer. So, what do you think—"

Josh snorted and took a pull from his bottle.

"The only advice my mother ever gave me about marriage," Ritz began, "was to marry a man who'll dance."

Unbidden came the memory of flickering firelight. She could almost smell the salt in the air, almost feel the snap of the sea breeze in her hair, almost feel the grit of sand between her toes. But the most dazzling image was Roque's muscular body swaying to the music, filling her with some primitive need she'd never known before.

"But your daddy doesn't dance," Jet said. "He's so strict and stern."

Not like Roque, who was wild and hot, who made her ache and feel passions perfect princesses should never feel.

Nobody said much for a while. Then Josh told them both to keep it simple. "Go for the ten inches."

"No, my mother's got it right," Ritz said, feeling both thrilled and scared when Jet studied her too intently.

Josh kept drinking. By the time they got to the hospital, Josh was so mellow, he almost fell out of the truck when they opened the door.

"And another thing," Jet said. "My perfect man can hold his liquor."

Josh got to his knees and said, "Wace, er, Race you!"

Laughing, the three of them chased each other past a huge pile of debris stacked near the construction ramp that led up to the front doors. Twice Josh fell into the yellow tape that separated the construction area from the parking lot.

Inside, Josh streaked past the information booth. The girls skidded after him and up the stairs two at a time.

Dr. Wanner's beaky nose tightened when Josh sped around a corner so fast he nearly knocked a nurse over.

Still, the doctor kept his eyes glued to Steve's thick chart and continued speaking to Fiona. "He's got a long road ahead of him. Months of rehab. If he works at it, he'll make a full recovery. But it won't be easy."

"Can we see him?" Ritz asked.

Dr. Wanner frowned. "Not a good idea. Your brother has a lot of anger."

Josh fell against Steve's door. "Rithz," he slurred. "Ova here."

Dr. Wanner shook his head. "He shouldn't go in there."

When Josh pushed the door open, Ritz saw Steve strung up like a slab of meat.

"Poor Steve..." Forgetting Dr. Wanner, Ritz raced to her brother's side and put her hand on his.

"Steve...it's me...."

Steve's eyes slitted.

"The doctor says you'll make a full recovery."

"Crap!" Steve pulled his hand from hers. "Get the hell out of here, Ritz."

"But..."

"Josh can stay. You get the hell out of here."

"I'll be just outside," Ritz whispered brokenly. "In case you change..."

His eyes locked on hers with deep malignant hatred. "Like hell!"

Restlessness driving him, Roque's lips were narrow and his eyes hard as he shouldered his way through the heavy hospital doors. Halfway inside the gold band on his left hand caught his eyes. Angrily he yanked it off and stuffed it into his jeans.

What had he done? *¡Dios!* Why had he listened to Chainsaw like he was some expert on immigration law?

Híjole!

Was it noon already? The bright day was still too chilly

to suit Roque, but it was beautiful, none the less. Perfect day to race his bike and forget Chainsaw and Rosita if only he hadn't buried Caleb yesterday. If only he didn't have a score to settle with Steve Keller.

Roque's boots clicked so noisily on the slick, glossy floors, everybody turned to stare. Heat suffused his face. He let go of the ring in his pocket and forced himself to amble up to the information desk in his black leather jacket where he whispered the name, "Keller," as nonchalantly as if he had every right to be here.

Stunned, the blue-haired volunteer gazed up at him in disbelief. "Aren't you that Blackstone boy up from Mexico?"

"Roque Moya," he purred. "At your service." With an excessive flourish of old country courtesy, he bowed low.

Her hands fluttered against her skinny chest. Then she whispered nervously to her friend, who merely smiled vaguely, gave him the room number, and wished him a charming day.

The hospital floors were so clean, his boots squeaked. Even that was enough to ignite his temper. Did everything always have to be better north of the border?

He felt edgy. Conflicting emotions tore at him. He was crushed over Caleb, obsessed about a girl who despised him, homesick and guilty about leaving Mexico, furious at his father—not to mention scared as hell at the thought of raiding the Keller camp. And Rosita…

Had Steve Keller killed Caleb? Or caused his death?

No, the sheriff had assured him earlier in between dusting doughnut crumbs off his uniform.

When Roque reached the fifth floor, he cracked the metal, stairwell door. The sight of Ritz in a fringed denim dress at the end of the hall gave his heart a kick-start.

She sat between Jet and Mrs. Keller. A surly, redheaded

youth with meaty shoulders paced back and forth, watching Ritz so possessively Roque burned.

Willow slim, she was prettier than ever. She swung her leg and made denim fringe dance. His gaze moved to her lips, her throat, her breasts, and back to that shapely leg that wouldn't stop swinging. For a minute or two he watched tassels of fringe bounce against her sun-kissed legs. Then he sucked in a harsh breath and let the door fall shut only to open it again.

All that hair. Her glorious silken, flyaway curls fell in wild tangles about her shoulders. Her eyes were the same shade of violet-blue they'd been yesterday when she'd been afraid. She kept an eye on Steve's door, her lips trembling.

There was fresh pain in her face this morning. And more guilt. Even surrounded by her family, she looked miserable.

He could identify with her.

He let the door fall shut. Knotting his fist, he stared down the stairwell. The urge to run from her nearly overwhelmed him.

When he cracked the door again, her father and two big cowboys were storming out of the elevator.

Again he shut the door. But for Caleb, he would have raced down the concrete steps.

Roque waited a good ten minutes before opening the door again. Keller now had his arms around his wife and was suggesting lunch in the cafeteria.

Five minutes later when the Kellers were gone, Roque rushed down the hall and went into Steve's shadowy room.

Machines hissed. Tubes gurgled. Steve's eyes were closed. Cables were attached to every limb, even his head. The guy was helpless.

Roque went to the bed. "Did you kill Caleb?"

When Steve's eyelids flickered, an acute sense of unease

swamped Roque. That was before the toilet flushed right behind him and somebody zipped his fly.

The bathroom door banged against the wall.

Steve's eyes bulged with fear and hate.

"What the hell are you doing here, Blackstone?" snarled a voice behind him.

Roque whirled.

The redheaded boy blocked his escape.

"Which one of you bastards killed my brother?" Roque demanded.

"Both of us! Now it's your turn to die! Get him, Josh!"

14

"What's the matter with you all? This is good news!"

All eyes were on Ritz's father; all ears tuned to his deep male voice.

"I've got this nursing agency lined up! All the fanciest— What the hell do you call it? State of the art stuff! Equipment! Wanner says we can bring Steve home for Christmas."

"In just three days?" Fiona whispered. "Do you really think he's ready? He's so depressed."

"And angry," Ritz murmured. "Whew!"

"Wouldn't a hospital that specializes in rehabilitation be better?" Fiona persisted.

"The best therapy is being home with you...with his sister."

"How can you be so sure, Daddy?" Ritz's stomach fluttered every time she remembered Steve's hate-filled glare. "He hates me."

Her father gave her a quelling glance and then ignored her completely. Ritz clamped her lips together.

What was the use? Nobody ever listened to her. Defiantly she sagged back in her vinyl chair. She picked up her paper cup and crushed it between her fingers. Then she began to pound it on the Formica-topped table until it was a thick white disc.

Her father grabbed it and sent it skittering down the long table toward the trash can.

"Where's Josh?" Jet whispered under her breath.

"This is lame. Sorry I got you two into this." Ritz jammed her hands in the pocket of her dress and got up and went to the window.

Where's Josh?

Josh was outside with Buck and Hank, Daddy's two meanest cowboys. Hank liked nothing better than to sic his Doberman on the steers when the blood was still wet on their legs right after they'd been castrated.

Josh and the two cowboys were beating up Roque Moya.

Three against one! If somebody didn't stop them and fast, they'd pulverize Roque for sure.

This isn't your fight! He's a Blackstone!

Gut level instinct that had to do with fairness and decency won out over self-interest and common sense. Suddenly she was running, banging into tables, sending cups flying, hardly knowing what she did.

"Where the hell are you going, girl?"

"Nowhere, Daddy."

Then she was outside in the cold brisk air, running straight toward the tussling foursome.

Hank was holding Roque, so Buck and Josh could punch him.

"Can I have a turn?" she screamed.

They turned and grinned so encouragingly, she grinned back and then kicked Josh in the shin.

"What the hell—"

"Stop it, you bullies!"

"Butt out, Ritz!" Josh yelled. Even though he was hopping on one boot, he still rammed a fist into Roque's jaw. Smack. Blinding pain had to go with a blow like that.

Reeling backward as if she'd been struck, she picked up a rock and hit Josh's back so hard, she tore his shirt. He staggered backward.

Josh's face was a mask of fury. "First Caleb! And now his brother!" Head lowered, he bore down on her like a bull.

"Don't you dare touch me. Or...or I'll call the sheriff."

"You'd choose a Blackstone over me again—I don't believe you!"

"Get her!" Hank said. "Hold her, so Buck and I can finish Blackstone—"

"Over my dead body—"

She spun around, her boots slipping in the loose gravel as she ran from Josh. When she reached her truck, she jumped inside and punched the automatic door locks. As she dug in her purse for her keys, Josh caught up and pounded on her window.

Still, digging with one hand, she began honking her horn. He cursed her and raced off to the construction site where she'd found her rock and grabbed a two by four.

Oh, dear...

She turned her purse upside down. Junk sprayed onto the passenger seat—tampons, lipstick, loose change, and her ID's.

She grabbed her keys, started her truck and slammed it in Reverse. Then he ran around the rear and held up the two-by-four to make a human blockade. Honking, she backed steadily. When he didn't budge, she rolled down her window.

"Get out of my way or...or...I'll run over you!"

"Pussy! You don't have the guts—"

At that she stomped on the accelerator, and he shot to one side, dropping the board. Yelping, he hopped up and down on one custom-made boot.

"My toe! My goddamned toe! You ran over my toe!"

"Maybe next time when your girlfriend asks you to move…"

"You're not my girlfriend! Not anymore!"

"Oh, did we break up again—"

When he began to curse, she gunned the truck, raced down a line of cars until she found Buck's Bronco. She straightened her truck, getting just the right angle. Then she started honking again.

"Hey, Buck!" she hollered. "I'm gonna ram this junk heap of yours, if you two don't let him go!"

Buck slugged Roque.

She rammed the Bronco.

Buck let go of Roque and shot her the finger. In the confusion Roque broke free and took off hobbling.

"Get her!" Buck yelled. "Before she rams my brand-new truck again!"

Buck raced toward her while Hank headed for Roque's bike.

"Roque," she called, catching up to him and gunning her engine as he stumbled off the curb. He was limping and looked as disoriented as a drunk. She stuck her head out her window. "Over here. Get in."

When he didn't even look her way, she honked again. Finally he lifted his black defiant head, his green eyes burning her so fiercely she started to shake.

Gently she said, "Get in!"

He sprang clumsily onto her running board and held on. Buck was in his Bronco, revving the engine.

"Hold on!" she warned as she hit the accelerator.

"Those crazies are chasing us!" Roque yelled.

"Get in!"

"That's not so easy! With the door shut and you driving like a maniac—"

"Pussy!" Where had that word come from? Ritz Keller never used words like that.

He glared. She glared back.

"P-u-s-s-y!" She spelled it silently. Aloud she said. "I'm not going to take no for an answer."

"My kind of girl," he quipped.

Swallowing hard, he flung himself through her window into her lap just as she swerved to avoid a red Honda turning into the parking lot.

"Watch where you're going," Roque said.

"It's kinda hard with your cute butt in my face."

"So you like my butt? That's the first nice thing anybody's said to me all day."

"Don't get a big head about it."

"Big head?"

"Conceited. Move over—quick—so I can drive," she told him.

"I thought I was on a suicidal roller coaster."

With difficulty he squirmed toward the passenger side of the truck. Every wriggle of his hard, lean body touched hers in sensitive ways too embarrassing and thrilling to describe. Once he made it to the passenger's side of the cab, he leaned back in the seat and finger-combed dirt and gravel out of his hair.

"Buckle up," she ordered.

He moaned.

She stole a sideways glance at him just as he was pitching two of her tampons onto the floorboard.

They both blushed and glanced away from each other too quickly.

"You look awful," she said, concentrating on the center stripe. Adjusting her rearview mirror, she gasped when she saw the Bronco growing larger.

"You look awful," she repeated.

"You said I had a cute butt."

"The rest of you needs a whole lot of work. You can start with the attitude and your smart mouth."

"Ditto." He swallowed hard and ran the back of his hand across a skinned place on his forehead. Those megawatt green eyes of his were staring holes into her.

Cute, wild boys never looked at her like that. This was how they looked at Jet.

"Well, you look great," he whispered. "And I told myself I was going to stay away from you…"

"I gave myself the same lecture. My daddy gave me that lecture, too."

"So, how come you helped me?"

"I can't believe I did it."

"Killer Keller."

"Don't."

"Sorry," he said.

"Those very same words were burned into a patch of grass. So were the words, it's your turn to die. Then a man shot at me." She began to laugh. Once she started she couldn't stop. She had Roque Blackstone, the sexiest young thug in the universe, in her speeding truck and her boyfriend and two of her own cowboys were chasing her. And she couldn't stop laughing.

Amendment: Josh was not her boyfriend anymore.

"What's so funny?"

"Nothing. Everything. I—I thought the night I was crowned rodeo queen would be the most exciting moment of my life."

"Until you tangled with me."

"We're not tangling…understand!"

"Too bad," he whispered.

"We hate each other."

"Right." He smiled, and she melted.

"Oh, God. I've gotta get you out of my truck."

"Thanks," he whispered, his tone low and raw. "For saving me."

"It was three against one. What is it with you? Do you

like to get beat up or something? What did you do to get them so mad?''

"I went to see your brother."

A horn blasted behind her. His face darkening, Roque whirled and looked over his shoulder. "You Kellers don't give up, do you?"

Ritz hit the accelerator. "I'll lose them—then you get out. And we go our separate ways."

He was silent. Then he said very softly. "I've got a better idea."

"Look, as soon as I lose these crazies, I want you out of my life—for good."

"Not only are you cute, you can prioritize."

"That's a big word for a guy who was born in Mexico and flunked a grade...."

"I went to an American high school. I read all the time."

"I thought—"

"That I was stupid—"

"No."

"I've got dyslexia. But I study. Just not the things I'm supposed to sometimes. I stay up a lot reading books. Books Caleb sends me." A shadow fell across his face. He paused and drew in a rough breath. "Sent me."

"He used to tell me about the books, and I'd tell him you wouldn't read them, that you were probably out hitting on girls."

"'Cause of my Mexican blood?" His voice had darkened.

No! 'Cause you're so hot. Obviously she couldn't say that. "What is this racism crap? Is that your excuse for every problem you've got in the whole world, Mr. Roque Moya?"

He slumped against his door. Then he turned around and peered over his shoulder again. "Enough conversation.

Just drive. Your friend Buck is way too determined to catch us."

"Well, he won't catch us. Daddy gave me this truck for my birthday. It has a huge engine. Huge. It's not a truck at all. It's a jet without wings. We're gonna burn 'em!"

The road was straight. There wasn't much traffic. Soon the Bronco was just a speck in her rearview mirror. When Buck vanished completely, she turned off onto a back ranch road, made several turns onto smaller roads and then pulled over under a clump of oak trees to wait for Buck to give up and drive home.

"What do we do now?" Roque asked.

"We park." She cut the engine. "We amuse ourselves while we wait."

She froze. *Oh, God! I can't believe I just said that! To him!*

"How do you suppose we do that," he murmured suggestively.

"Oh…" She blushed. Drawing herself up into a tense ball, she huddled against her door. "I—I didn't realize how that would sound…to you."

"To me? Like you think I have a dirty mind? Me?"

"Maybe. When it comes to girls." She slanted a long-lashed glance at his cut lip. "How many girls have you kissed anyway?"

"Not enough. Do you want to be next?"

"No!"

"Mentirosa."

All of a sudden she was staring at his wide, sensual mouth and wondering what it would feel like on hers.

"Then?" he whispered, staring holes through her. "How will we amuse ourselves while we…park?"

She forced her gaze from his lips." We…we can sit here for a while and simmer down."

"Simmer? What's this simmer?"

"We'll calm down."

"How?"

"We'll talk...or something." Embarrassed, she picked at the fringe on the bottom of her dress. Just being with him like this sent a dart of excitement through her.

He was sinful and bad; she knew that. That's probably why he got into so many fights and into trouble with girls.

"What did you think you were doing...coming to the hospital like that to see Steve?"

"Maybe I didn't think...any more than you thought when you rammed that Bronco."

"Well, we'd both better start."

"Good idea."

She dropped the strand of fringe and wrung her hands. "I'm going to be in so much trouble. Which means— you've got to get out now."

"You were in trouble...long before I showed up," he said.

"Too true. But when Hank and Buck tell Daddy I rammed—"

"Your father will pay for the damages."

"Then he'll come after me."

"My father says yours is friends with the sheriff. And that's why the sheriff won't do anything to you or Steve about Caleb. So, is your daddy friends with the sheriff?"

"Since they were kids. They used to go hunting together."

"So, what are you so worried about?"

"You don't know my daddy. This is between him and me. He's already mad about the wreck. He told me to stay away from you."

"Looks to me like you're in so much trouble, what's a little more?"

"What?"

"We could spend the day together."

"That's crazy! You've gotta get out! Right now!"

"Why don't you stay with me?" he coaxed.

"Are you out of your mind? Get out now! This minute! I saved you! That's enough!"

"Not for me."

"No!" Even as she said it, she could almost feel her resolve faltering.

"You sure about that?" he whispered. He twisted the key and punched on the radio. His fingers tapped on the dash to a salsa beat. "We could get out and dance."

"Here?"

His hand brushed her cheek. Electricity sparked through her.

She shook her head and he laughed. "Why not?"

The shade of the big live oaks seemed to wrap them in darkness. Beyond his chiseled profile the world was bright, the grasses high and brown, the sky cobalt-blue. And yet being in the darkness with him held more mystery and appeal than anything else she could think of.

She studied the lean, carved lines of his tense face. For days people had blamed her for Caleb. A man had even tried to shoot her. Now Roque Moya was being nice to her.

What was happening to her? She couldn't look at him. Not for one second, without the bottom falling out of her stomach, not without feeling cold and shivery even though it was warm inside the cab.

"You have to get out," she whispered, but softer this time.

He leaned across the seat. "Only if you'll dance." Reaching across her lap, he took her hand in his, startling her.

"You really do have to go."

"You are so pretty," he whispered in a velvet, low tone that was as fascinatingly beautiful as the rest of him.

Why did he have to be so extraordinarily handsome? That blue-black hair? Those smoldering green eyes that lit her up somehow?

"Like I said. We're already in so much trouble, we don't have anything to lose, *gringa*."

She tried to pull her hand away. "I don't understand."

The music was wild. She wanted to get out, to fling herself in his arms, to feel her body move against his.

"*Sí, chica, comprendes.*" His eyes grew intense. A small vein throbbed near his temple.

Little shivers raced up and down her spine. She understood one thing, all right. Being alone with him, knowing he wanted to be with her was way more thrilling than being rodeo queen ever hoped to be. More exciting than ramming Buck's Bronco, too.

Roque brought her hand to his lips. When he kissed her fingers, one by one, unfolding them, she burned and ached all over.

"Such pretty hands, too," he whispered, his warm breath caressing each pink tipped fingernail. He looked up, black hair falling over his brow, and captivated her with a dazzling grin.

"Have you ever done exactly what you wanted for one day, *chica*? Without asking Daddy?"

Her toes curled. "Why no." She could barely breathe. "Have you?"

"Lots of times. But not with you."

His deep voice and that white grin were wreaking havoc with her good intentions and laying bricks in her own personal yellow brick road to hell.

"So," he continued, "I say let's spend the day together, what's left of it. Let's enjoy being outlaws together."

He cut the radio off, and somehow the silence was even more sensual than the throbbing beats had been. He kissed her fingertips again, his lips oozing molten heat.

Her breath caught. "I have to be good. And...and you have to quit...quit grinning like that and kissing my fingers.... Oh, quit. Oh...oh..." She shivered, relenting. "Don't ever stop."

He laughed. Again that vein near his temple was throbbing. His eyes burned hers.

"You've got to get out," she begged.

"You saved my life. You were Caleb's friend. I'm injured. What kind of girl throws a wounded man out on the side of the road miles from home? Why...I could have internal injuries...bleed to death..."

"You're just saying that so I'll feel sorry for you...."

"And do you feel sorry for me?"

She nodded shyly.

"You have a tender heart. And you're so pretty." He was staring at her mouth again. As she was staring at his.

"You're a nice girl."

"Not unless I go home now."

"Stay. Please." He drew a deep breath. "Stay because...because somehow you're special to me. With you...I feel better, saner. I'm different somehow around you than I have ever been with anybody else."

"But I barely know you. Our fathers hate—"

"To hell with their stupid feud. You danced with Caleb to end it. Why can't you stay with me for the same reason? Tonight we'll go dancing...."

With an effort she tried to bring herself back under control. He was bad. She should go home. But that mouth, that wide, bitter mouth and the pain in his eyes drew her to him.

She licked her lips and threw back her head. "Oh, God."

He laughed wickedly.

"You're making me crazy," she said.

"I haven't even begun."

That vein was pulsing, and his mouth edged closer.

She said a silent prayer. Oh, God.... God...please help me....

A lifetime of careful rearing exploded. Easily he shattered all that she'd ever been taught to be or believe.

"Kiss me," he whispered throatily, "and then decide."

"I really don't think that's a good idea...."

A slow insolent grin lit his carved features as he edged closer. Blood rushed through her veins.

Chemistry.

He hadn't even touched her, and already she was on fire.

His grin widened cockily.

"You're not a nice boy. No nice boy..."

"You don't want a nice boy. You haven't since *that* night. And you won't ever again. Not if I can help it."

"You don't know anything."

"You were a little kitten in heat...prowling around in the dark.... I caught your scent, too."

"Marry a man who will dance," she whispered.

"What?"

"Nothing—"

When his mouth touched hers briefly, lightly, and ever so tenderly, she moaned in anguish and delight.

His hands moved through her hair, caressing her, loving her. He tasted faintly of cigarettes, but she didn't mind.

When he slowly withdrew his lips, his eyes locked on hers. Then he put his arms around her and held her close. "Where have you been all my life?" he whispered.

"Why me?"

"Only you, *chica.*"

"Is that some Latin line you use on all your girls?"

Quickly she sealed his lips with a fingertip. "No! I don't want to know!"

He pulled at a silver chain beneath his black T-shirt and shook out her St. Jude medal, causing it to flash.

She gasped. ''You still wear my—''

''Why you? I don't know why. Why not you? You tell me. You show me.''

''But I'm scared,'' she whispered touching the medal that burned from touching his heated body.

''We'll go slow. Just be with me for now. Just for to-day.''

She knew not to trust that, but his lips claimed hers again. When his tongue touched the tip of her tongue, her nipples tightened.

He was murmuring to her in torrid whispers as he slid her downward in the seat. Then he was on top of her, and the wickedness felt so delicious and right as it had that night she'd watched him dance by the fire.

He put his hands in her hair, and all the time his mouth was on hers, hot and wet, his tongue darting in and out, while his heavy body pressed her down, down. She opened her mouth to tell him no, only to sigh and arch her pelvis against his, yielding everything.

This was what she'd wanted *that* night. This. This. Yes. Yes.

''You're so beautiful.'' Deftly he unzipped the back of her dress. Then his rough palms slid against her soft warm skin.

She shuddered, gasping in delight when he undid her bra. Then suddenly he tensed and pushed her away.

Through her lashes she looked at him. His chest heaved; each breath seemed to rasp in his throat. His face was flushed, and the dark fire in his burning eyes told her that he desired her.

''Zip your dress up! Drive,'' he ordered, his voice hoarse.

Tears sprang to her eyes. Confusion and hurt filled her heart.

"Sit up! Now! Here! I'll help you—"

He grabbed her hands and roughly yanked her into a sitting position. When he tugged at her zipper, it caught.

"Ouch! I'll do it!"

Finally she had her dress refastened, only to realize he was staring gloomily out his window, his dark hands fisted under his carved chin.

God, he was beautiful. "Don't you like me?" she whispered.

"I like you." His voice rumbled darkly.

"Then—" She placed a hand on his arm. Instantly he tensed.

"Don't touch me! Don't touch any part of me! Understand?"

"No! I don't." she cried.

His chest rose and fell. "Start the truck, why don't you?"

She brushed her hair out of her eyes. With awkward fingers she turned the key.

"Drive," he said, still in that same sharp tone. Roque closed his eyes and took a deep breath.

"This is crazy." She was still near tears. "I don't want to spend the day with you. Not when you're like this."

"Just drive. I'll be okay in a second. Just don't kiss me again, all right? I liked it too much."

All of a sudden she understood. A shy, thrilled smile played at the corner of her mouth. Then she pulled out onto the road.

"So, where to?" she whispered.

"Matamoros, Mexico."

She slammed on the brakes, killing the engine.

He grabbed the dash. "Are you crazy?"

She laughed.

"I swear we'll just hang out," he said. "I won't kiss or touch you again! I won't ask you to take your clothes off or anything. I swear."

"Okay. I believe you."

His hands had felt good inside her dress. The mere thought of him stripping her caused a dangerous thrill to course through her.

"Well, we'd better be good or my daddy won't just kill me. He'll kill you, too."

15

Shortly after they hit the city limits of Brownsville, Ritz swerved so abruptly into the parking lot of a convenience store, Roque's head cracked against his door.

"Whoa! What are you doing?" He righted himself and ran a hand through his hair.

"Sorry," she smiled. "We need gas. Do you want a cola or something? You said you had to call your friend with the hacienda—"

"Porfirio?"

"I've got to call somebody, too—"

"Second thoughts?" He cocked a sexy black eyebrow. "About crossing the border...with me?"

Try second, third, ten thousand thoughts!

He winked.

She shook her head too vigorously. "No!"

He reached in his pocket and skinned a silver wrapper off a stick of gum. "Then?"

"I don't want my family to worry. I have to call somebody just to make sure they don't completely freak—"

He offered the pack to her, but she shook her head.

"I'll pump the gas," he said, getting out.

She marched to the pay phone, dug around the bottom

of her purse for quarters. Her hands shook when she dialed information for the sheriff's number. Johnson picked up as soon as she said who she was and started talking so fast and so loud, she had to shout over him.

"Mr. Johnson, I called just in case my daddy calls—"

"He's gone plum insane—"

"Tell him hi...."

"*Hi?*"

"I'm taking a little break to figure some stuff out about how I feel about Caleb...Steve...and the feud...and just everything...me...I'm all mixed up, Mr. Johnson."

"Shit! So am I."

"Maybe you should take a day off, too."

"You'd better not be with that Blackstone punk— Tell me you're not with—"

She watched Roque pump gas with carefully guarded fascination.

"Uh, no... No—"

When her guilty voice trailed off into nothing, the sheriff swore. She bit her lips and twirled the metal telephone cord.

"Blackstone's old man's all over my case, too. You kids gotta come back before your fathers forget they hate each other and kill me instead. They're using me for their punching bag—"

She slammed the phone down just as Roque swaggered up to her.

"How did it go?"

"Great." She attempted a saucy grin. Swaying her hips, she sashayed toward the store. She was so keenly aware that he watched her the whole way, her skin burned. When she got back to the truck, Roque was slumped behind the wheel in the driver's seat smoking. He shot to attention when he saw her, leaned across, and opened her door.

She climbed inside, grabbed his cigarette and pitched it out.

When it landed near the gas pumps, he slung his door open and raced to retrieve it. "What do you think you're doing?" Stomping it out, he pitched it in the trash and walked slowly back to the truck.

"This is a gas station!" he grumbled, sliding behind the wheel.

"Wrong seat."

"I'm driving now," he said.

"Why?"

He gripped the steering wheel. "Guys are supposed to drive."

"Not in America. Haven't you heard women have rights up here, too?"

"Is that why they're all in therapy? You got a shrink?"

"Not me."

"Not yet. You're gonna be as frustrated as the next girl unless you learn something *muy importante, chica.*

"What's that, Mr. Macho?"

"What women really want is to be around real men. No real man is gonna let a woman boss him all the time."

"And sitting behind a steering wheel is all it takes to make you think you're—"

"Not all." His gaze slid to her breasts and he grinned. "Just being around you—"

"Stop." She knew she wasn't hot looking like Jet.

"Right. We're talking about driving, so let me finish. When men are men, women are women, and everybody's happy."

"You mean the men are happy."

"If the man is happy, his woman will be happy."

"You can't really believe something that sappy?"

He grinned again. "It's one of my favorite fantasies. Thought I'd test it out on you."

"Well, you and your fantasy get a great big red *F*."

"I'll add it to my collection." His mouth quirked. "Mexican guys. They all say *gringas* are easy."

Remembering that she'd melted when he'd kissed her and he'd had to break off the kiss, she blushed and began to fidget with her fringe again, which drew those hot eyes of his to her legs.

"Easy to get in bed," he continued. "Not so easy to live with. Mexican men prefer Mexican wives."

"Okay, you win. Just drive."

"You know I'm right."

"No!"

"Then how come you saved me from your *gringo* boyfriend? How come you're running off with me?"

She crossed her arms. "It's against all my principles."

"Mine, too, *chica*. What do you say we go wild and enjoy ourselves?"

Later, guilt would prevent Ritz from really remembering the afternoon and night she spent in Matamoros with Roque. Still, even when she was most determined, she couldn't quite extinguish it from her consciousness. The memories that haunted her were washed in a magical glow that made those twenty-four hours seem like a golden dream.

Not that they did anything out of the ordinary. It was simply being with him, doing the ordinary things that seemed so extraordinary. They shopped, danced, swam, talked.

At first they parked on a dusty side street where children played soccer on a hard-packed dirt schoolyard. Then they wandered the crowded main street of Matamoros, fending off tourists with cameras as well as old men selling edible yucca blossoms and street kids selling gum.

The sidewalk was a zoo. Kiosks overflowed with baskets

of fresh chilies. On sidewalk tables, vendors peddled Mexican videos and rock CD's as well as counterfeit watches.

At ease in this chaos, Roque bought tacos and *queso fresco,* a crumbly white cheese. Ritz bought tortillas. These they handed out to the endless parade of begging mothers and children.

When their stores were gone, Roque ushered her into the curio shops where aggressive salesmen hawked leather, pottery, and silver jewelry. Finally, in the last store, he strode up to a glass case and had a salesman pull out a tray of religious medals. He picked out an exquisite St. Jude medal.

"¿Te gusta? You like?"

She nodded as he put it around her neck. "But why—"

"I have yours."

"Give it back—"

He shook his head. "I'd rather give you something to remember me by."

When he pulled out his wallet, a gold ring flew out of his pocket to the floor.

"What's that?"

His face darkened as she dove for it under a table of leather backpacks and purses.

"I'll get it," he growled, trying to pull her to her feet.

She fell to her hands and knees, digging through dust balls and cobwebs. Just as her fingers closed around the ring, and it was a ring, a gold band, he grabbed her waist to pull her up.

"Is this yours?" She held it up. In the sunlight it glinted red.

"Hell no!" He seized it and pitched it into a trash can.

"But, if it isn't yours, it has to belong to somebody."

"Forget it."

"What's wrong?"

"Don't make such a big deal about nothing."

He grabbed a sombrero off the table and tried it on. He forced a grin. "How do I look?"

She was still curious about the ring, but he didn't want to talk about it. So, she made a deliberate effort to forget their silly quarrel and laughed.

"You look ridiculous. Wonderful. Like a dangerous *bandido*."

His frown eased, and soon he was eyeing her tenderly again.

"A *bandido* abducting a *princesa. Señor, por favor,* I want the medal and the sombrero."

While Ritz wandered about the store, the salesman and Roque dickered heatedly for nearly ten minutes before they settled on a final price.

She said she was hungry, and he picked out a bustling taqueria with a booming jukebox. There they sat on high stools at a counter and made a lunch of flautas, tacos, mildly spicy salsas, rice and refried beans.

She couldn't finished hers. "I'm stuffed."

"We have eaten. We have shopped." He folded her hand in his. "What do you want to do next, my lovely *señorita?*"

"I'm tired."

He laughed. "So am I. Let's go to Porfirio's...."

He drove south. Pavement gave way to winding, dirt roads with open sewers. They were ten miles out of town when he stopped before high white walls and tall, carved gates. Political graffiti had been spray-painted on the walls. There was no grass, just bare dirt and blowing plastic sacks and cola bottles everywhere. When he rang the bell, a stooped brown woman soon appeared.

Behind the walls, the restored colonial hacienda seemed like paradise. Lavender impatiens burst from every shady corner in the courtyard. Red bougainvillea tumbled from hand-laid brick walls.

Peacocks strutted across lush green lawns, spreading their tails. Fountains sparkled in the sun. Palms lined a winding drive that led to a swimming pool.

"It's like a dream," Ritz whispered

"The rich live differently in my country than the poor."

"Everywhere it is the same."

"In your country at least you try to give everybody a chance."

"My country? You're an American, too."

"Am I?"

The maid ran before the truck. When they reached the mansion, the housekeeper opened the door and embraced Roque as if he were a long lost son. Trailing behind Roque and the maid, Ritz was led upstairs to a suite of guest rooms.

Ritz's bedroom contained a tall antique, curtained bed and a twelve-foot-high armoire of jacaranda wood. When she flung the doors of the armoire open, it bulged with exquisite clothes for female guests of various sizes. She fingered the bikinis, the one-piece bathing suits, sarongs, and towels.

Ancient, faded tapestries depicting Mexico's violent history decorated the thick, stucco walls.

"Who is this Porfirio?"

"We go to college together."

"Why isn't he here?"

"They have five houses. Porfirio and his family spend Christmas in Cuernavaca."

"What does his father do for a living?"

Roque frowned. "He's a businessman."

"A very successful businessman."

"Enough about them," he said. "Let's go swimming."

She chose the skimpiest bikini in the closet...a little black number that was mostly black strings and made her look sleek and slim.

She went down to the pool. Expecting to wow him, she took off her cover-up. Roque glanced at her and then jumped up, dived into the water, and swam as far from her as he could get.

She ran to him and leaned over the edge of the pool. "Is it cold?"

"Not cold enough." He swam to the other end. When she ran to that end, he raced to the opposite again, keeping a length of pool between them at all times. She gave up trying to be friendly.

The pool was heated, its temperature perfect. She stayed in the shallow end and kicked languidly. It felt good to relax, not to think about Caleb or Steve or the accident…or her father. Or the man who'd tried to shoot her. For the first time in days, she felt guilt free.

Finally Roque got out and threw himself down on a chaise longue. She climbed the ladder and wrapped herself in a towel and lay in the sun beside him.

He was staring at the sky, not at her. "Are you ever going to tell me what really happened to Caleb—"

She put her hands over her eyes.

"Maybe talking would help."

"I don't think so."

Instead, she just stared at him and soon fell asleep. When she woke up, he was gone. The sky was lavender and a sliver of moon winked down at her. The air was a little chilly, so he'd covered her with a blanket.

She found him in the kitchen about to raid the refrigerator.

"I'm starved," he said. "You ready to drive back to town to eat?"

Over dinner they talked, really talked. Why had she thought he was bad? When really he was so vulnerable, so sensitive? He asked her about her childhood and she told him how perfect it had been even though her father had really wanted a second son.

"My parents didn't want me at all."

He told her about his jealous mother and his sisters and his macho uncles, who expected him to make a conquest of every girl he met.

"And do you?"

"You haven't eaten a single bite of your dinner," he said quietly.

Because getting to know him had been so much more fun.

After dinner he took her to a nightclub. When he asked her to dance and held out his hand, she hesitated, remembering the night she'd watched him dance by firelight on the beach.

Two years. She'd ached for this moment for two whole years. Slowly, oh, so slowly, she let her fingertips touch his. Her palm slid warm against his. Then he wrapped her in his arms on that crowded, smoky dance floor, and she flowed into his body as if it were the most natural thing to do.

"Marry a man who will dance," she whispered in a tone so low he didn't hear her. What had her mother meant?

Then the music started.

"I'm not much at the salsa," she said aloud.

"Relax. All you have to do is follow me."

"That might prove dangerous."

"Not on the dance floor."

He was a wonderful dancer and could lead so well, she could follow even the trickiest, Latin rhythms. They swirled around the floor as if they were made for each other. Again, she remembered her mother's advice about choosing a husband.

His voice was at her ear. "What else are you naturally talented at?"

Her heart began to pound.

"Why did you pick that particular bikini—"

She couldn't answer.

"To excite me?"

"No!"

"Yes! Underneath your innocent facade lurks a..."

She blushed.

He stopped, but his eyes said more.

"You're wrong."

"Am I?"

"Yes!"

"No wonder your father doesn't like you leaving the house."

The beat speeded up. Faces caught in throbbing flashes of laser lit and then darkened eerily. Roque spun her and then let her go, so that they could dance separately while staring into each other's eyes.

"Am I wrong?" he repeated.

The dazzling bursts of light followed by utter darkness burned his undulating image into her retina, so that even if she kept her eyes closed, she saw him swaying to the music still. Like *that* first night when he'd caught her in his spell.

He grabbed her hand, pulled her close again. "Am I?"

One instant they were dancing. In the next, he was pressing her against a wall in a dark corner. His mouth closed over hers. His lips, which were hot and wet, parted hers. His kiss was so hungry, she went weak at the knees. One quick kiss and he lit an unquenchable fire deep in a secret part of her heart nobody else had ever reached.

Her fingers reached around his neck, and she pulled him so close she almost felt as if her mouth and body melted into his. Their bodies pulsed to the music, pulsed to each other.

What was happening to her?

A long time later he let her go and said in a low, breathy tone, "Am I wrong?"

Roque was steering with one hand through that tangled maze of black roads that led back to the hacienda as if he knew them by heart.

She had to make him take her home! Now! Because somehow something unimaginable had happened.

It was both horrible and terrifying.

But wonderful, too.

She was in love with Roque Moya Blackstone.

It was after one in the morning. In the dark it couldn't have been easy to navigate the truck around potholes and stray donkeys and chickens.

His arm was around her shoulders. Snugged against him, she was barely conscious of the oil drums, squatty shacks, wrecked cars, clumps of prickly pear, or the occasional white cross draped with plastic flowers that loomed before them along the sides of the road in the headlights.

Finally they were back at the hacienda. The maid opened the tall, carved gates, and Ritz brushed at her hair and reluctantly slid across the seat to the passenger side.

Fool. How could you come to Mexico? With Roque Moya?

When she stared across the seat at his sleek, dark profile, he cocked his black head toward her, equally wary.

"Ritz," he asked softly. "Are you okay?"

The concern in that gravelly voice put her emotions into even more tumult.

"We can't stay here together tonight," she began shakily.

"Why not?"

"I want to go home," she insisted in a panic.

"Then we'll go." But his voice was abrupt.

She swallowed. "Now?"

"Why are you so afraid of me all of a sudden?"

"I'm not."

He reached across the seat, put his arm around her again and drew her close. "Why?"

"It's the situation."

"Didn't you have fun dancing?"

"Too much."

"I shouldn't have kissed you. It just happened."

"I know."

"And you're afraid it'll happen again."

She nodded.

"Well, it won't. I swear."

"Just take me home."

"All right."

"You don't want to, though—"

He shook his head. "The long trip up to the States on my bike...then my bike broke down...then the funeral...the fight this morning...and other stuff, worse stuff I can't talk about. On top of that...after those two beers at the nightclub. We'd both be better off if we spent the night here. You need a good night's rest as much as I do— before you face your father."

"You're right, of course."

"Don't be afraid. Not of me, *querida*."

The maid, her hands on her hips, stood in the dark waiting.

He kissed her brow. Slowly his fingers curved under her chin and slid along her jawline in a light caress. "It'll be okay. We'll leave first thing in the morning."

Strangely enough when they got upstairs, Ritz didn't want him to go. "We never talked about Caleb tonight," she said.

Instead of following Ritz into her lavish bedroom, Roque slouched in her doorway. "You saw him a lot. He wrote about you."

"You read his diaries?"

"Every word," he replied. "Did you sleep with him?"

Her chin went up a notch. A little angrily, she flung open the armoire and shook out a sheer nightgown. Before she realized what it was, she was staring at him through the flimsy pink gauze that floated between them.

"Is that what you think?" she whispered.

His face darkened.

"If it is, just go." Quickly Ritz stuffed the bit of fluff back inside the armoire and slammed the doors.

"Why are you so nervous about him then?"

"Because he's dead and everybody blames me."

"It was an accident."

She nodded. "But he was your brother."

"So—"

"So, there's no way we can be anything to each other."

"Right." Now he was angry.

"Go! Good night!"

Without a word he strode out of the room and slammed the door.

Roque sat, stiff and taut, his muscular body hunched forward in the huge leather chair by the stone fireplace as he bolted shots of tequila straight from the bottle until the bottle was empty. And all the time, he was acutely conscious of the slightest sound from her bedroom. When he heard water splashing in her blue-tiled, sunken tub, he imagined her pink nipples peeking above foaming suds. When he heard the springs of her mattress creak, he thought of her alone in that big canopied bed.

He got so hard, he couldn't breathe. His hand squeezed the neck of the tequila bottle to take another pull. But it was empty. He licked the top of the bottle, his blood on fire.

Then he thought of Rosita and Elena and Chainsaw and

got so furious he flung the bottle at the stone mantel above the fireplace.

Glittering shards pelted him from the hearth.

"¡Hijole!"

He jumped up, crunching through the broken glass. Then he kicked the balcony doors open, and stormed outside.

No sooner was Ritz asleep than she had a nightmare. Caleb was in his burning sports car, screaming her name. Flames wreathed his face. She hurled herself against his window. His fingers were splayed against the glass. She was stretching her hand toward his when glass shattered against the wall behind her.

She cried out and threw off her covers.

Something moved outside on her balcony. Clutching her throat, she made a strangling sound.

"Caleb?" Leaping to her feet, she rushed out onto the balcony. "Caleb…Caleb…"

The moon bathed her slim body in silver.

"Ritz."

She whirled. "Caleb?" Her dazed, unfocused eyes widened when a tall black giant stepped from the shadows. She stumbled toward him, forgetting that all she wore was the pink, gauzy nightgown.

"It's me," Roque said in a grim low tone.

The moon bleached his dark face of all color. Glittering green eyes swept her from head to toe.

She knew she should run, and yet she felt that strange, crazy pull toward him.

"Caleb and I had this stupid notion of ending the feud."

"No, not stupid… Did you love Caleb?" Roque whispered, his voice strange and unsteady.

"He was wonderful."

"Not like me."

"You're not as bad as you lead everybody to think."

"I'm worse. My life's a mess. You don't know…"

"Then tell me…"

"I shouldn't be with you at all."

Her knees were shaky. Being so near him had her stomach in knots. Without thinking she caught her lower lip in her teeth.

"You smell all funny," she whispered.

"Tequila."

She leaned into his dark face. "Are you drunk?"

"Yes. And you're half-naked. That's a dangerous combination, *querida.*"

"Hold me," she begged.

"Go back inside," he muttered fiercely.

Blindly she reached for him. "I had a nightmare about Caleb. I miss him. Hold me…. Just till I feel safe again."

He stepped backward into the shadows, but she chased after him. When his broad back slammed into the wall, she slid her hands on either side of his muscular shoulders.

"We can't be together. This morning Chainsaw talked me into doing something crazy."

"I can't believe I'm doing this, either!" she said.

"Go back to your room!"

"I'm not your slave." She began to whisper against his ear, confiding her dream to him in broken little nibbles and horrible fragments and images. "Caleb was on fire.…"

"*Dios.*" Roque drew her closer and began to stroke her hair. "Poor baby," he began soothingly, kissing her brow, fingering the curls at her neck in such a way that little shivers darted down her spine. He lifted the medal he'd given her and kissed it. "It was an accident."

"I know." She buried her face against his wide chest. When she brushed her lips against his skin, a tremor shook him.

"You're made of solid bone and hard, warm muscle. And, oh my, you taste delicious."

"And you kiss delicious." He gasped after a talented twirl of her tongue. "You'd better stop," he whispered.

"Relax," she murmured.

"You asked for it." On a groan he lifted her against his body. "All right, *querida*. Hold me. Love me."

His hands played in her long golden hair, wrapping heavy curls around his fingers. Tilting her head back, his mouth slid from her lips down the length of her neck to tongue the pulsebeat at the base of her throat. The next thing she knew, he lifted her into his arms and strode with her into his room. With the heel of his boot, he kicked the door shut.

Then she was on his bed, and he was ripping his clothes off before pulling her nightgown over her shoulders. He fell on top of her, and his mouth came down on hers. "You are gorgeous. *Hermosa*," he breathed.

"Your body's nice, too," she said shyly.

"Nice? Is that all?"

He put his hands between her legs and stroked her and still she didn't feel the least bit shy. Not like *that* night when she'd been afraid even to take his hand.

It was as if Caleb's death and her own fear of dying had heightened her senses and made her want to feel alive in this most basic way. Even when he aligned his naked body to hers and began to push and met resistance, she didn't cry out.

Still, he knew. Then he tried to pull away, but she clasped his shoulders.

"You're a virgin," he whispered.

"No big deal."

"To me it is." His caressing hands fell away. "You're not what I thought you were...."

"An easy *gringa*."

"Dios." His one word was low and thick.

"I want you to be my first," she said.

"I have no right..."

"I love you. *I love you.* Maybe since that night I watched you on the beach."

His arms came around her. "Maybe I love you, too." Again she felt the unbearable pressure, but this time he gently pushed until finally he broke through.

She cried out, but slowly the discomfort dissolved into pleasure. He began to kiss her damp eyelids, her nose and her mouth, while his pelvis rocked back and forth. She grew accustomed to him and clung. Soon he was thrusting and she was arching to meet him.

"Ritz." On a violent shudder, he clasped her to him.

His eyes were emerald green, as wide-open as hers, burning hot, and wild.

"You're mine, Ritz Keller," he muttered.

"But are you mine?"

He didn't answer.

When it was over, she wept uncontrollably.

Roque wrapped her in his arms. "It'll be all right," he whispered as she fell asleep.

Ritz rubbed her lovely eyes and yawned. Dreamily she focused on the sunlight flickering behind the drawn curtains in dazzling, ever-changing shapes of flashing light.

Only slowly did she feel the dead weight of Roque's arm stretched across her shoulders and the faint stirrings in her hair from his steady breaths.

Roque. He was naked in the bed beside her, asleep.

She didn't have a stitch on, either!

Last night she'd been so eager to let him explore every inch of her body.

She stared at the glittering shards of his tequila bottle

on the hearth. Then her gaze drifted to her wadded pink nightgown tangled in his jeans and shirt.

I won't ask you to take your clothes off or anything.

He'd been drunk. She'd been fast.

Unable to face him, she lifted his arm and wriggled out from under it. Then she tiptoed softly to her own room.

The naked girl in her bathroom mirror with the smudged makeup and the tangles of sleep-flattened, yellow hair made her feel even shakier. "Oh, dear." A dark bruise marred her silky white throat.

She took a quick bath, scrubbing herself vigorously as if to wash what she'd done away. When the wet cloth passed over embarrassing soft folds of flesh that still burned, she blushed. Dressing quickly, she wound her hair into a tight knot at her nape in a futile attempt to look prim and proper.

No makeup today. Not even her usual pale pink lipstick. Not daring to look at her reflection or that awful hickey again, she scurried down to the courtyard and sank down on a long teak bench by the fountain and covered her face with her hands.

Birds chirped. Peacocks spread their tail feathers.

Even as she wondered how she could ever face Roque, memories of his lips on her nipples and of her own hands shyly stroking him made her blush. She got redder when he joined her at the fountain, two cups of steaming coffee in his hands.

"Ritz."

He stood like a statue at the edge of the garden, his dark gaze glued to the mark he'd made on her throat.

She looked up and tried to smile. His carved, white face was set in harsh lines.

He cut his way through the plump ferns sloshing coffee over the sides of the cups he carried. When he finally reached her, he held out a steaming cup.

She took it.

"About last night," he began, unable to look at her.

"Last night?" she echoed, her saucer tipping precariously, spilling still more coffee, burning her hand. "Ouch!"

He grabbed her cup. "Are you okay?"

"I'm fine."

"Did I hurt you?" His low voice was rough.

A wild hot tear brimmed against her lashes. "I said I'm fine, and I'm fine." she whispered.

"Fine? With that bruise on your throat? Fine? When you won't even talk to me? Or look at me? What's wrong?"

His angry tone shredded her. She slammed the cup and saucer down on the teak bench with a clatter. "Just leave me alone."

"I didn't mean for it to happen."

"I guess that's what happens when you spend the night with one of your easy *gringas*."

"You were scared. I took advantage—"

She closed her eyes. "Can we not talk about this? Can we just go home?"

"Fine," he said, using her word. His face went bleak and cold. He flung his cup down beside hers. "Get your stuff. Meet me at the truck."

"Fine."

"So—even Daddy looks good after a night with me."

"You said it would be okay. You lied."

"You said you loved me. You lied."

"Yes, I did! I hate you! I hate you!"

With a little cry, she put a hand over her heart, and rushed past him.

16

❧❧❧❧❧

Roque drove Ritz to the international bridge in tense silence. It was slow going. School hadn't started yet. Hordes of ragged children played in the streets. Donkeys pulling rickety carts jostled for position with ancient cars and trucks and eighteen wheelers belching black exhaust.

"How're you doing?" Roque asked her at one point.

"I thought we said we wouldn't talk."

He slammed a fist against the steering wheel. "Fine."

He'd made a mess of everything. Why the hell had he snuck into Steve Keller's room? Or trashed his future with those four *F*'s? Rosita? Ritz? He should never have gotten himself smashed on tequila. Or made love to her. Why the hell did he do any of the crazy things he did? His chest felt tight.

But she'd felt so damn good. Every time he looked at her, he got hard all over again. Last night her beautiful eyes had glittered with passion. Such passion.

Híjole. How she'd clung to him. Now, this morning her lovely eyes were shadowed with pain and uncertainty again. And that awful mark on her throat.

Sex with him had done that to her. How would she ever explain that mark to her father?

What if she learned about Rosita? He had to explain that mistake before someone else told her. *Hijo.* What had he let Chainsaw, Chainsaw, the know-it-all, jailhouse lawyer, talk him into?

Dios. How had his life gotten so damn complicated?

He owed Rosita nothing.

He'd had unprotected sex with Ritz. He'd been so horny he hadn't thought. Was that why she was so mad?

Never had he had such powerful feelings about a girl before.

He'd had sex before, of course. Lots of times. But not as often as everybody thought or his Moya uncles would have liked. But enough to know how special last night with Ritz had been.

She'd said she loved him.

She was a Keller.

A Keller, damn it.

Was it possible to fall in love in twenty-four hours? Or had it started long before? He'd felt her so powerfully that night on the beach when she watched him from the dark.

His empty stomach tightened. Her silence was getting to him. He stared at the congested traffic. When she sighed, every muscle in his body tensed. What if she got pregnant? What the hell would she tell her daddy then? He thought of his own father who hated everything Keller.

What about himself? He'd just flunked college. He had no way to make a living. And Rosita loomed over his future like a huge black cloud.

When they finally got to the bridge, every lane was jammed. Ritz began to sob in earnest. "We're never going to get home."

"Sure we will."

She clawed the window.

"What's the matter now?" he asked.

"I just feel so bad. You think I'm low and wicked."

"Is that what you think I think? No, Ritz. I told you I think I'm a bastard for taking advantage of you."

"You—"

"I had no right—"

A Mexican officer stepped up to the truck and asked him a couple of routine questions and then tersely waved them across.

When they were on the other side waiting for a red or green light to determine if they would be searched, Roque made another attempt at conversation.

"We'll go to breakfast. We'll both feel better after we've eaten. We'll talk before we go home."

"Do you even like me?"

His dark head snapped toward hers. "Hell. *Querida,* I'm crazy about you—"

The green light flashed. His toe had barely hit the accelerator when five Border Patrol agents in dark green uniforms charged them and surrounded the truck.

Roque slammed on the brakes and rolled down his window.

"This your vehicle, mister?"

Ritz leaned across his lap. "It's mine, officer."

"You Miss Maritza Keller?"

She nodded.

"And you, sir? Are you Mr. Roque Moya Blackstone?"

The man's tone was hard; his eyes were blue ice chips. "I'm talking to you, Moya."

Roque nodded grimly, staring straight ahead.

"Would you please step out of the truck, Mr. Blackstone?"

Roque's lips thinned, but he knew better than to argue.

"Oh, Roque—" She seized his arm.

"Little lady, we've got a report that he forcefully abducted you. And your vehicle."

"No! No! It was my idea! I invited him—"

"Did he hurt you in any way?"

"No."

Roque's door was yanked open. When he didn't jump out, a hard hand grasped his arm and hauled him out so fast he fell.

"Ritz!"

"Roque—"

She jumped out of the truck and would have run around the hood to him, but two of the men caught her by the arms.

"Ritz!" Roque was kicking at the shins of the three men who held him as they dragged him toward the buildings.

"Just a few routine questions, sir."

"Don't you dare hurt her—"

"Call my daddy!" she yelled.

"Not possible! Both your fathers are in jail…on assault charges."

"What?" Ritz whispered.

"Sheriff Johnson is sending a deputy to drive you home, Miss Keller."

"Roque can drive me—" She was struggling to break free of the two officers who held her. "He didn't do anything!"

"Mr. Blackstone, you're under arrest."

"Miss Keller, did you know that Mr. Blackstone married a Rosita Sanchez yesterday morning? We believe he helped her enter the United States illegally."

"That's a lie," Roque hissed.

"We believe he married her to help her remain in this country. Then he ran off with you. Your father wanted me to tell you that."

Ritz's face jerked toward Roque. He was unaware that his handsome face was a mask of regret. She looked numb. Her lips trembled, but she couldn't utter a word.

"No," she moaned. "No…no…"

Unshed tears glistened on the tips of her lashes. Her face paled.

"I'm sorry," Roque said. "For what's it worth…I love you."

"It's not true," she babbled frantically. "Tell them it's not true. Tell me it's not true." She was on the verge of hysteria. "You love me. You can't be married to Rosita."

"I'm sorry," he repeated dully to Ritz. "Damn you all to hell," he growled at the men who held him.

Her face crumpled.

"So, it's true?" she whispered raggedly.

"Yes and no."

The light went out of her incredible violet eyes. She turned away from him, her tears falling now, all her pride and belief in him gone.

"I love you," he murmured.

"Don't lie to me! Don't you dare lie to me!"

The devilish turn at the end of the long gravel driveway was a challenge for any biker, even at a reasonable speed. Skidding to a flying stop, rocks spraying in all directions, Roque nearly rolled into the sagging fence that was nothing more than strands of barbed wire.

The sky was a dismal, leaden gray. The weather had turned crisp and cold for Christmas.

His father had let him rot in jail for two whole weeks—to punish him. Fourteen days, he'd spent being interrogated and badgered by cops and I.N.S. officers. Two weeks of bad food and worse company. His cellmates had been tattooed criminals with mile-wide chips on their shoulders. He'd had a fight or two.

When Roque swung his leg off the bike, he limped around the side of the trailer past the old washing machines and cars on concrete blocks.

Everything was the same.

Nothing was.

After being constantly on guard, he just wanted to be left the hell alone. Suddenly a low growl of feline rage and the violent chink of chain link stopped him cold.

"Greetings," he muttered to the Bengal tiger. "And Merry Christmas for what it's worth."

The beast snarled, claws raking chain link.

"I know how you feel. Your Christmas turkey late? Where's your know-it-all jailer?"

The trailer door banged open.

"Right the hell here," Chainsaw hollered. "So, they let you loose?"

"For Christmas."

"It's an old American custom."

"My father bribed them. He fixed my bike and got it to me too."

"It's called bail."

"He said he did it on the condition that I go back to Mexico for good."

"What about Rosita?"

"This whole marriage farce was your idea. You shouldn't have meddled."

"Hey, don't blame me for that. You did it."

"Because of you! Why'd you have to go and read law in prison?"

"To sue the bastards. To stay out of jail. To right the wrongs for the little people who get framed."

"Damn it, I'm in as much trouble as she is now."

"Not if you stay married to her."

"You don't know anything."

"You said yourself if she goes back, she and Elena don't have a prayer."

"Okay." Roque rubbed his brow. "How's Long John?"

"He doesn't like the big cat, so I've got him in the south pasture. But he's okay."

"Thanks."

Rosita, looking plumper and prettier than ever in a red dress with her hair braided, appeared at the door.

If only she were Ritz.

"*Feliz Navidad,*" Rosita whispered, her eyes shining almost as brightly as her wedding band. Like a happy child, she scampered down the stairs past Chainsaw and threw her arms around Roque.

Roque endured her shy smiles and her embrace briefly before shrugging free.

"Did you find your father?"

She shook her head and would have hugged him again, only he moved out of range.

"*Dios. Hombre,* she thinks it's a real marriage."

"She put up a real Christmas tree, too, when she heard you were getting out of jail," Chainsaw said. "Natasha has never done anything like that for me. Did you tell *La Migra* where she is?"

"Take her inside. I can't deal with her right now. Or with you, either."

When he was alone again, Roque sank down on the front steps and stared gloomily at the streaky gray clouds and straggly trees.

Christmas.

He should call his mother and his sisters, but the person he wanted to talk to was Ritz. The mere thought of her tear-streaked face brought a sharp stab of loneliness.

"Ritz," he muttered. "Ritz." He didn't blame her for hating him. Hell. He hated himself.

Roque stood up slowly, trudged up the two steps and opened the door. Rosita was holding Elena on her hip as she strung popcorn on her little Christmas tree. When she saw him, she smiled.

She wasn't his wife. Hardly knowing what he did, he slammed the door and bolted down the stairs to the grav-

el drive. She opened the door as he swung a leg over
his bike.

He started the engine and roared away.

Not that he knew where to go.

When he reached the caliche road to the pond, he took
it. At the edge of the water, he sat on his bike, facing west,
watching the startled geese spin higher and higher above
the water.

He remembered the day he'd first met Ritz, remembered
flying. At the thought, he touched the silver medal at his
throat.

It was Christmas. He ached to see her.

He was leaning down to restart his bike when he saw a
slender girl running toward him from the brush.

"Ritz—" He stood up, staring at her intently.

Her long black hair danced in the wind. Her large
breasts jiggled.

"Jet—"

"Hi," she said, her red smile hot and wet, her voice
low and sultry.

"Hi, yourself," he murmured without emotion.

Breathlessly she ran a hand along his chrome handlebar,
her scarlet-tipped fingers stopping just short of his thumb.
"You caused quite a stir—running off with our Ritz."

Every muscle in his body flexed.

"But then you always do," she purred.

His eyes narrowed. How could he have ever thought her
prettier than Ritz?

"How's she doing?"

"She's won't talk about you. Not even to me." Black
lashes dipped against her cheeks like flirty fans. She gave
him a naughty look. "Why?"

"Can you get a message to her?"

She shook her black head a little too saucily. "I don't
think so."

He refused to be baited by her sexual charms. "You're supposed to be her friend."

"I'd rather be yours."

An insolent expression twisted his mouth. "What's that supposed to mean?"

She flushed. "I stole your clothes once, remember?"

"That was silly kid's play years ago."

"I'm not a kid anymore." Her voice was husky. "Maybe I still want the same thing."

"Will you take her a message."

She shook her head and sighed. "I don't care if you're married."

"You've gotta help me."

"No, I don't gotta," she purred.

When he stared at her without a trace of fascination, she faltered. "Okay. But don't tell anybody you saw me."

He nodded.

"She's in the barn nearly all the time right now. Some nights she sleeps there. Buttercup's about to foal, and she doesn't want to miss it."

Ritz smoothed back a damp blond tendril off her feverish brow and tried to rise from the toilet, but the moment she did, awful nausea swamped her and hot bile bubbled up her throat gagging her.

"I'm not pregnant!" she whispered to the pasty-faced reflection in her bathroom mirror when she finally managed to stand up.

Buttercup was due to foal any moment. Ritz needed to be at the barn, but the stall smells had gotten to her, and she'd had to come into the house for a while.

On impulse she opened a drawer and pulled out one of the little white boxes she'd hidden there.

"I want my life back!" Near panic, she ripped into the little box and read the pregnancy test instructions.

Her eyes opened wide when she held up the little cup for her specimen. The directions said first thing in the morning. Oh, well… She blushed as she studied the plastic negative/positive stick.

Losing her nerve, she stuffed everything back into the box.

It was nearly midnight. Downstairs, the house was eerily hushed after having been filled with relatives and cowboys and their families all day. Grandma Keller and her cousins, Kate and Carol, were down from San Antonio. They had gone to bed early. Despite their company and the forced Christmas cheer, it had been the most depressing Christmas Day Ritz could remember.

Steve was home, but he was angry that he was so helpless. He said it was even worse than the hospital because he needed a nurse to help him do everything. He was confined to his room and balcony, and if Ritz or their cousins went anywhere near him, he either barked at them or sulked.

Ritz had been busy today—with Buttercup, with the Christmas tree, with the formal turkey dinner, and with kitchen duties both before and after dinner. So, she'd had plenty of excuses for not taking the test. Again, just reading about the intimate requirements of the test made her mouth go as dry as cotton.

She was hungry, too. Using this as an excuse, she took a deep breath and slipped stealthily out into the hall.

Downstairs, the kitchen was so redolent with the odors of turkey and dressing and squash that she was soon gulping deep breaths and clasping her stomach again.

Shakily she opened the refrigerator and poured herself a glass of cola. After a few sips, she felt well enough to head back to her room. As always, she paused in the main gallery beneath the ancestral portraits of her great-grandmothers. Not that Ritz found solace in their portraits tonight.

Maybe it was her own guilt-stricken mood, but her great-great-grandmother, Eugenia Keller and her great-grandmother, Alice, seemed to stare down at her with stern disapproval.

"But you married young," Ritz whispered to Eugenia. "You eloped when you were fifteen. You had the first of your eleven children when you were barely sixteen."

Eugenia had fought Confederate stragglers and wild Indians. After a bandit had shot and injured her husband, she'd run the ranch single-handedly, nursed him back to health, and taken care of two babies.

"Then there's you—Alice." Ritz eyed the other rigid, white face. "You helped your brother run the ranch after Eugenia's death. You married, had your son, and were a good wife until your husband ran off."

After that Alice had dressed like a man, camped out and had gone on cattle drives. In short, she'd lived like a man and had done exactly what she wanted. She'd bred horses and cattle and had been considered the most talented rancher in Texas in her day.

Ritz swallowed. All her life she'd dreamed of her own picture, her face stolid and sure in middle age, hanging in the gallery beside theirs. She'd dreamed of glorious deeds being attributed to her, too.

If she were pregnant by Roque, she'd be the scandal of the family. On that thought, she fled the gallery for her room.

At least Ritz's parents hadn't pestered her about Roque as much as usual today. However, they had monitored her calls and conversations and observed the slightest changes in her normal habits.

"You didn't touch your gravy," her mother had accused during dinner. "Or your squash."

The gravy had had too much pepper for her delicate stomach. The mere thought of squash bubbling in those bright red tomatoes had made her gulp queasily.

"Or your pecan pie," Grandma Keller had pursed her narrow lips petulantly. "My pecan pie's your favorite."

The sight of whipped cream on those crusty pecans had made the dining room and all their worried faces spin.

Her father had been hacking white meat off the breastbones. "You're pale and drawn, girl. You sick?"

"No, Daddy."

As soon as she could, she'd escaped to the barn and thrown up.

"I'm not pregnant," she said aloud, locking her bedroom door.

For days her father had badgered her about Mexico. Why had she run off with Roque? What had happened between them? Did she know that all a boy like that, especially one with a drop of Mexican blood, wanted was one thing—to get in a girl's pants?

He started off in that vein every morning at breakfast. "Once he's had a girl, he's done with her."

"Daddy!"

"Art!"

"Well, somebody's got to talk some sense into her."

"It's Christmas, Art!"

"You're not to see him ever again!" her father would roar.

"As if I want to! He's married!"

"You should have thought about that before—"

"How could I? He didn't tell me."

"I told you so, didn't I?"

After Ritz forced herself to dig the little box out from its hiding place again, her blood really began to beat. She marched into the bathroom with the cup, produced the specimen, and inserted the stick.

When two vivid red lines appeared in less than a minute, an invisible fist closed over her windpipe.

Shakily she tore open a second box and repeated the test.

Two more little red lines confirmed the first test.

The fist tightened. She couldn't breath. She felt hot. The bathroom was so airless, she loosened her collar. Still, she was burning up. "No... No..."

Flinging both cups into the trash and covering them up with a wad of toilet paper, she leaned her hot forehead against the wall.

She got sick so fast, she didn't make it to the toilet.

Daddy was going to kill her.

Composing herself as best she could, she fled to the barn. At the doors, the barn cats ran up to her, crying and rubbing her legs. When she knelt to pet them, she realized Buttercup had stopped pacing on her crunchy straw.

"Oh, dear." Ritz raced to the stall only to hesitate at the door when she saw Buttercup was licking an inert shadowy form in the furthermost corner.

"Oh, Buttercup, I watched you for two whole weeks."

Ritz had spent the last few nights on a narrow cot just outside her stall because she had known that like most mares, Buttercup had a private nature and preferred to be alone when she gave birth.

An hour ago, Buttercup had stopped pacing, and Ritz had crept over to watch. Only Buttercup had jumped back on her feet and urinated, and Ritz had gotten so nauseated she'd run to the house.

Why wasn't the foal responding to Buttercup?

Turning on the light, Ritz let out a little cry. When she rushed to the foal, she discovered that the small dark head was still wrapped in its amniotic sack. Fear screamed through Ritz as she tore the sack from its mouth and nose.

The body was still warm. So warm. But she was too late.

Clutching the foal to her breast as if it were her own baby, Ritz sank to the ground and rocked it back and forth.

"Ritz," purred a velvet male voice from the stall door. She whirled.

Looking incredibly handsome in a long-sleeved white shirt and jeans, Roque stepped out of the shadows.

"It's dead," she whispered brokenly. "I killed it.... Just like I killed Caleb."

"Don't say that." He knelt beside her, his carved face blank and bleached of all color. After a long time, he spoke. "I could bury it for you."

Her eyes were dazed and unfocused as she clung to the warm, little body. She hardly knew what she said to him. "The ground's softer by the edge of Mother's garden."

He got up. "Where are the tools?"

She told him.

He left her with the foal, but she got up and carried the little animal outside to watch him work with the pickax and shovel. The ground was hard-packed after all. He had to break it up with the pickax and then scoop out little shovelfuls. But he worked as furiously as a madman, rarely stopping to catch his breath.

She watched the network of muscles under his white shirt bulge across his back and shoulders and down his arms. It made her stomach feel funny, but not in a bad way. She knew she shouldn't watch him so hungrily after that. He was married. But she couldn't stop herself.

After flinging the last few shovelfuls, he knelt on the ground beside the mound of dirt, exhausted. "I'll dig some more in a minute."

"Maybe it's deep enough," she replied. With a convulsive shudder, she sank to her knees and laid the little animal in the hole.

He leaned across her and folded the legs so they would fit. In the lengthening quiet, she stroked its muzzle and they huddled over the little grave. He touched a velvet ear.

"Don't watch this part," he ordered gently.

He took her hands and helped her to her feet. His warm, light touch, his strength, but most of all his quiet, sympathetic tone were a comfort even when she shuddered at every dirt clod falling on that lifeless body. When the grave was finally covered, he threw the shovel down and got up.

"Thank you," she whispered, stepping away from him.

"Ritz." A minute passed. "I want to explain about Rosita."

"What's there to explain? She's your wife, and she was even before we went to Mexico. What happened between us is second to your marriage."

"No! I love you."

She drew a sharp little breath.

"It wasn't a real marriage," he said. "It was a stupid mistake...on top of a lot of other stupid mistakes."

"Please," she muttered.

"Have you ever been in the wrong place at the wrong time?"

She shook her head. "Don't. Just don't..."

"What about the night Caleb had died? Wrong place. Wrong time."

She kicked a little clod toward the grave. "That ring that fell out of your pocket...the shop in Matamoros...that was yours, wasn't it?"

"I married her because Chainsaw said that if I did, she and Elena could stay in this country. After what she went through... You didn't see her. You don't know. I cleaned her up. She told me things...." He paused. "Now it turns out Chainsaw doesn't know anything about immigration law."

"If you'd told me the truth then, I wouldn't have slept with you."

"Then I wouldn't be in love with you."

"I don't want your love. And I'll never forgive you."

"I love you."

"Well, it was too late for us...even before we went to Mexico."

When he just stood there, she crossed her arms over her breasts. "What do I have to say to make you go?"

Instead of answering, he lingered like some stricken, dumb animal.

She could've run, but like him she felt paralyzed. Thus, they stood there, bound to each other, neither knowing what to say or do to break the invisible ties.

It was a strange moment, filled with confusion and torment and powerful need. They were too young to love and hate with such depth. Too young to face the realities. Too young to trust enough, to completely confide.

"I'm sorry I made such a mess of everything," he muttered.

"Me, too."

"Oh, hell. You drive me crazy."

His green eyes flamed. Before she could twist away, he seized her and kissed her. One taste and she flung her arms around his neck. Her lips opened to his. Her foolish heart raced. Hunger filled her.

When he let her go, they gazed at each other in shock.

"I've never kissed Rosita, never made love to her. I never will. It's you I want."

She began to shake.

A door slammed somewhere. A flashlight bobbed over the grave. Then her father plunged around the side of the barn.

His yellow cone of light arced violently, capturing Roque and her like two deer in a high beam.

"Moya!"

Releasing her, Roque braced himself to confront the older man.

Her father's sleep-mussed hair stuck out like white spikes and made him look fierce. "I should have known you'd sneak out to meet him, girl, first chance you got."

Roque swallowed. "I was burying Buttercup's foal."

Wielding his flashlight like a club, Art advanced toward Roque. "Get the hell off my place, you lying sonuva—"

"Just go, Roque," Ritz pleaded. "Don't fight with my father."

Roque's gaze fell on her. "All right. But I'll be back. Next time you won't be able to get rid of me so easily."

"Why won't you believe it's over?" she whispered.

"Because I love you."

The next morning when Ritz awaked, she saw her father sitting at the foot of her bed. He used to come into her room when she was a little girl and sit in that very spot and watch her until she woke up. Back then she'd been his perfect little princess.

Today, the sight of him there made her heart feel heavy.

"Daddy," she whispered, sitting up, reaching for him. Oh, how she yearned to feel his arms around her. Oh, how she ached for him to make her feel safe as he had in the past.

But his expression remained so hard, his mouth so tight with animosity that she sank back into her sheets.

"You're pregnant," he said flatly.

She opened her mouth and then shut it.

He closed his eyes and rubbed his brow wearily. "I found the pregnancy tests when I was burning the trash.

Her blood was pounding. "Daddy—"

He got up. "You're not having his baby."

"What else can I do?"

"There are ways. Doctors..."

"You don't believe in abortion."

"In this case, it's the only thing to do."

"But Daddy—"

"If you don't do as I say, you're out of this family for good."

"I won't—"

"Haven't you done enough damage? Your brother's got a broken neck."

"That's not my fault!"

"Nobody knows if he'll walk or ever be himself again. My only son..."

"Daddy—"

"If you give birth to this...this...monster...I'll disown you! And so will your mother. You won't be a Keller and neither will your Blackstone bastard!"

The door slammed. Even when she heard her parents quarreling, she felt too weak to get out of bed. A long time later her mother came in.

"It's a choice, dear," Fiona said. "In time you'll forget and go on."

"Do you really believe it's that simple?"

"Your father and I just want to protect you."

"*Protect?*" The word jarred.

That night when she heard them quarreling over how to "protect" her, she knew what she had to do.

"Protect," she whispered, grateful to have found the answer.

Book 3

Dance as if no one is watching.
Sing as if no one is listening.
Love as if you've never been hurt.

—Unknown

17

Ten years later
Corpus Christi, Texas

Ritz Keller Evans, you smug little lying, do-goody hypo-crite, you're going to pay! Roque thought, fisting his right hand.

The speakerphone was on, and the senator wouldn't quit blabbing. Yawning, Roque eyed the immense sum of money at the bottom of the last page for the hundredth time.

He reached for his lighter and then slammed it onto the mahogany so hard he grooved it. He tore the unlit cigarette clamped between his gritted teeth and flung it at the trash.

You stopped smoking, remember.

Fuming, he slumped over his immense desk in the darkest corner of the vast, twelfth-floor offices in Shoreline Plaza from which he ran his real estate development business and ranching empire. When the senator kept going, Roque raked a hand through his hair.

His Corpus Christi office was meant to impress with its endless plush white carpet, black and chrome leather couches, and sweeping views of the sparkling azure bay.

When the senator bellowed ever more pompously, Roque, who wore faded jeans and boots, loosened his tie, his one concession to a business dress code. Unknotting it, he yanked it through the collar of his crisp, white, long-sleeved shirt. Then he began to wind the strip of blue silk around his hand.

It was all he could do to hold onto his temper as the senator drowned them both with more verbiage than it took to write a genre novel.

Finally in exasperation, Roque wadded the tie and threw it on his desk. "Surely there's something a man in your position can do about *her. Hijo.* She's only a volunteer nurse."

Sputtering, the senator launched into another maddening filibuster. Roque's bored gaze drifted to the outrageous amount of money the state said he owed in fines, interest, and penalties—because of *her!*

When the senator wouldn't shut up, Roque stuck another cigarette between his lips and bit down hard. With his gold pen, he thumped the stack of legal documents meant to ruin him.

"Senator, what you're saying then is that Moya Real Estate has to pay the ten million, that there's nothing you can do—"

"She's a Keller. She pulled strings. Had all those environmentalists out there. Real radicals like Kate Wilhelmie... You've got a canal and a dump that's endangering a salamander nobody ever heard of. Favors owed to her powerful father..."

"But not to *her.* Art Keller doesn't even speak to her. Hasn't even let her on his ranch these past ten years."

Roque remembered the one time he'd seen her a few years back. She'd been tearing away from her grandmother's funeral in Josh's Jaguar because her father hadn't allowed her to come to the gathering at the Keller home afterward. Roque had been riding Long John. The stallion had car issues and had reared, throwing him.

To her credit she'd stopped and got out. As he'd soothed Long John, he'd noted how lithe and sensuous her slim body had been in black.

"Black's definitely your color," he'd whispered. "Maybe that's fitting. You've got a lot to be sorry for."

Her violet eyes had grown huge and wet.

Then Josh had come up and put his arms around her protectively.

"She's still a Keller," the senator droned. "She's out to get you, boy. Maybe you should lay some of your famous charm on her. Get her to call off the big dogs—"

Roque swore.

"What's she got against you?"

Roque thought about the little white cross in Campo Santo with no name or date.

"You've got it backward," he said.

"You're a rancher. Mend your fences. If there's anything else I can do, don't hesitate to call."

Roque slammed down the receiver.

Ten million dollars! In fines! Moya Real Estate was bankrupt! Of course, the corporation stood between that business and his personal fortune as well as his numerous other companies. Still, if he didn't act fast, she'd strike somewhere else. He had to stop her.

It was his fault, of course. He'd known the minute Ritz started taking her damn fool nurses out to his *colonias* and stirring up trouble with those young mothers and their babies about trash and contaminated water wells that he should have stopped her. He'd even tried, but the women had loved her too much. She'd vaccinated their children, brought them antibiotics. What galled him was they'd told him how loving and caring she was to their children.

Bull. She'd played him for a sucker again. How could

he have been so stupid as to fall for her do-goody, hypocritical little nursing act? The only reason Ritz had ever wanted to help poor Mexican women to a better life was to ruin him.

She'd damn near done it, too.

You're going to pay, Ritz Keller. You're going to pay.

With a single movement of his arm, he swept the state documents to the floor. Then he heaved himself out of his chair and began to pace before his floor-to-ceiling windows. His hair was still blue-black and his olive complexion as swarthy as ever from working cattle under the murderous south Texas sun.

He wasn't just a cattleman. He'd made his money, his serious money in more lucrative enterprises. He was a builder, not a pirate. Still, there were people who accused him of being more like his old man than he wanted to acknowledge.

Money was power and prestige. Especially up here in *el norte*. He sent his mother enough so she'd stop complaining about how rarely he visited her in Cuernavaca. She and his sisters came up to see him now.

Money made people who used to despise him respect him. He'd even turned the tables on his father, who'd degenerated into a bad alcoholic after Caleb's death. Blackstone Ranch was now Roque's. He let Pamela and her daughters live in the main house while he kept his drunken father in a trailer on a remote division of his ranch. Only rarely did he see his father, which was good because his father still hated him and still made occasional threats to kill him.

Beneath him, Corpus Christi Bay glittered like rumpled green foil. Not that Roque ever noted the pretty view that included miles of seawall, the marina, the yacht club where he kept his own sailing yacht, *Black Victory,* the pink granite jetty, or the impressive ship channel. Views didn't do much for him since he was color blind. To him, it all looked gray.

Ritz.

He stomped back to his leather armchair and buzzed Marisol.

"Get Mrs. Ritz Evans on the phone. Make that Mrs. Josh Evans. She lives in Houston. River Oaks.

Josh answered on the first ring.

What the hell was a CEO doing home in the middle of the day?

"She doesn't live here," Josh said.

Josh had always hated Roque—Mexican blood maybe. Or jealousy. Roque's software company had beaten Josh's firm in Texas markets.

Roque waited.

"Ritz and I divorced...."

"I didn't realize—"

"As of yesterday..." Josh sounded sad, depressed.

"Congratulations."

Josh went silent for a minute. "Your wife left you, too. Read about the big settlement she took you for. Impressive—"

Roque's mouth thinned. "Does Ritz have a new number?"

"She's not my wife, but I'm damned if I'll give *you* her unlisted number."

Roque slammed the phone down as if it had bitten him.

So, she was divorced, too. He couldn't care less that she was free. He picked up a pencil to jot a note but pressed down too hard and broke it. Staring at the two yellow halves, he remembered Ritz's face when he'd taught her to fly.

So...she was divorced.

He buzzed Marisol again. "Call Esther at Moya Real Estate. Get her to talk to the residents in the *colonias*. I want to know the second Mrs. Evans visits one of my *colonias.*''

''I'll get right on it. Oh, and Pablo called. He wants to know when you're going to decide about leasing land in east Texas— And your mother called. She needs her check a little early…plus she needs a little advance against next month.''

''Write it.''

The worst drought in several years gripped south Texas. It was barely April, way too early for highs in the nineties, way too early for the pastures to be dead and brown. Roque tapped his gold pen. He'd wait a week. If it didn't rain by then, he'd cull cattle and lease enough land to save the best of his stock.

Stacking his hands behind his black head, he sank back in his leather chair. So, Ritz was free again.

Rosita had taken him to the cleaners. But even she hadn't cost him ten million dollars.

Ritz.

Why couldn't he drive her out of his mind? Just thinking about her set his right temple to pounding, so he reached for the cigarette pack he always kept in his pocket.

Only it wasn't there.

Dios. He'd stopped smoking. Seven hellish days ago.

He tore a drawer open. His bottle of aspirin lay on top of a silver chain and her St. Jude medal.

When his hand closed around the medal briefly, a tingle went through him. Instantly he saw a skinny, blond girl in dirty sneakers and cutoffs, her long hair blowing against his face as they flew together on horseback.

Ritz.

He dropped the medal as if it had burned him, and slammed the drawer and forgot to take an aspirin.

She had to pay.

He turned off the lights and sat in the gloom. It was

easier to think in the dark, easier to deal with… He let the thought die.

His calendar lay open on his desk. The sight of tomorrow's date circled in red gave him such a jolt he flipped the page. Not that doing so enabled him to exorcise the pain of this particular anniversary.

Ritz. She was to blame for that torment, too.

All of a sudden he couldn't tear his thoughts from the twisted oaks and the little grave at Campo Santo.

Ritz always hoped for cool weather when she and her medical team visited *Colonia Las Moyas*. Today she'd been almost hopeful. The weather forecast had predicted a thirty percent chance of rain. Now there were darkening clouds to the south.

Oh, dear, how south Texas needed rain. The pastures around the *colonia* that should have been lush green and gilded with red and yellow and blue wildflowers were parched brown.

Despite the improved efforts at garbage pickup, dust and flies blew through the open windows of Magda's ovenlike trailer. Not that Ritz or any of her volunteer staff, who visited the poor *colonias* were about to surrender to the stifling heat.

Ritz had set up three oscillating fans in the tiny living room. Even so, the faces of her poor young Hispanic mothers and their toddlers were flushed and damp as they huddled at her feet on the ancient shag carpet to hear "The Three Bears" in Spanish. Everybody had drunk gallons of ice tea with their *pan dulce*.

Petite and sturdy, Magda, the feisty, self-appointed mayor of *Colonia Las Moyas* was the storyteller today. Like the other women, she was poor but proud and clean. So was her trailer. Maybe the floors were crooked, the shag carpeting old, and the walls decorated with pictures ripped out of magazines, but the trailer was both a home and a community center.

All the young women wore pressed cutoffs and T-shirts faded from many washings. Their long, thick hair hung in gleaming braids or ponytails.

Ritz was holding Magda's adorable newborn, so she wasn't really listening to the story. All the mothers said that whenever Ritz had a baby in her arms, she was in her own world.

Josh had paged her three times, and she still hadn't called him back because Carlos was sucking too greedily at the plastic nipple. When her pager went off for the fourth time, the women laughed when Ritz shut it off again, propped the bottle of formula and smiled fondly at the tiny, brown boy in immaculate white.

At each gurgle and at each kick of his skinny legs against her abdomen, her empty womb contracted. It was April…the cruelest month. And today…the cruelest day.

She stopped those dangerous memories by stroking the little velvet cheek.

Would she ever have another baby? Could she? She had tried so hard to get pregnant.

She was twenty-six. The biological clock was ticking. Josh had left her. The fertility doctors had given up on her, saying even at her realtively young age it would take a miracle for her to conceive.

At least she had Carlitos today and all her other precious borrowed babies to comfort and love. Her work was her salvation. Which was wonderful, since her real life was so empty.

Divorced and financially broke after living so high with Josh for so long and estranged from her family, she had nothing to go home to.

Her beeper went off again, but milk bubbles were forming at Carlos's darling mouth, so she still couldn't do anything about it. When he began to spit up, she gently lifted him to her shoulder and patted his back. He curled his feet up, nestled his small black head against her throat and cooed. She began to rock him, and he was soon fast asleep.

She heard a roar outside, followed by shouts, but the baby had her full attention. She dismissed the ruckus thinking that it was the teenager from next door returning home from school. Then Magda stumbled on a long word and lifted her book to Ritz. Since her eyes remained closed because she was rocking the baby, Juanita, who was three, jumped up and tugged at the white skirt of Ritz's uniform.

Then the trailer door banged open and a giant stepped into the rectangle of light. "Where the hell is she?" a male voice thundered.

Ritz began to read again in lilting Spanish. But the women and children weren't listening.

They were on their feet clapping. *"Buenas tardes,* Señor Moya."

Moya.

Roque's name buzzed through Ritz like an alarm bell and yet didn't quite register.

Even when the children threw their arms around the intruder's long, denim-clad legs and climbed, begging him for candy, which he quickly dispensed, she kept reading.

"Hello, Ritz," came a slow, huskily-pitched, male voice.

Roque.

Ritz's tongue tangled the last syllables of the long Spanish word. Her hand froze on the page.

She looked up, her eyes widening. But with the baby tucked against her neck and all the women watching her, Ritz couldn't jump up and tear past him out the door. Neither could she shout at him or scream.

"What are you doing here, Mr. Blackstone?" she whispered mildly, sitting up a little straighter.

"Maybe I should ask you the same question—Miss Keller. This is my *colonia*."

"*Mrs. Evans! Mrs. Joshua Evans!*" Ritz corrected.

Roque was lean and hard. His green eyes glared as if he wasn't too pleased with her. She tried to remind herself she hated him, too. For no reason at all, she felt the strangest urge to touch him.

To squelch that idiotic desire, she squinched her eyes shut and resumed placidly rocking Carlitos.

"*Mrs.?*" He purred, measuring the word nastily for maximum sarcastic emphasis. "I called you in Houston. Got Josh."

"So, he told you that he left me for his nineteen-year-old secretary?"

"He spared me the grisly details."

What was Roque doing here? Today of all days? Her thoughts in turmoil, Ritz shut her eyes again and willed him to vanish.

Instead he crossed his arms across his massive chest, spread his legs wide, and planted himself in front of the door like a tree sending down a taproot, cutting off her escape.

"Evans did you a favor. I can't imagine why you married him."

"I do not want to discuss my marriage with you."

"Really? And I came here to have a very intimate discussion with you."

Her heartbeats accelerated. In rapid-fire Spanish, Roque told Magda he had to talk to Ritz alone.

"No…" Ritz whispered. "I don't want to talk to him— alone."

He laughed. "Then I'll just have to use my charm to persuade you."

Magda and he exchanged meaningful winks and smiles. Then she held out her arms for Carlitos. Unhappily Ritz realized there was nothing she could do but pass the sleeping baby into his mother's waiting arms.

Only when Magda and the children were filing out of the trailer, did Ritz realize she hadn't rescheduled her next visit. "Magda, I'll be back next Friday to see how you're doing with the garbage collection."

"She will not be back—ever," Roque thundered.

"But the new truck she bought arrives Wednesday," Magda said.

"I'm so proud of all of you," Ritz persisted, ignoring him.

Beaming, Magda bounced Carlos on her hip. "Did you see how clean the *colonia* is, Señor Moya?"

He grimaced. "I got the bill for it."

"Our Magda's a one-woman crusade," Ritz said.

"This place was a dump," Josefina said.

"And its future marginal," Ritz put in.

"So, Señora Evans organized us to change the conditions in our *colonia*," Magda added.

"Oh, she did?" Roque's smile was forced.

"Our men didn't care," Josefina said.

"Neither does your greedy developer here," Ritz added, deliberately throwing Roque to the wolves.

"Greedy?" Roque bristled like a porcupine on a rampage. "Who else would have sold them land? Who else—"

"He's right," Magda admitted. "We were paying hundreds of dollars in rent for terrible apartments. The banks, they wouldn't lend us a penny. But Mr. Moya, he took our cash, even if it was in pennies.... Every month he counted our pennies for us and took what little we had."

"He took every penny you had!" Ritz blurted.

"Did I pressure any of you to pay when you came up short?"

They shook their shiny black heads and smiled at him.

"Adios," Roque murmured, ending the conversation by herding the women toward the door. When the last of the women had scampered down the stairs, he slammed the door and pivoted to face her.

"How could you be so horribly rude to them?" Ritz whispered.

His blazing green eyes pierced her. "You! You've abused my patience and my hospitality. You are to stay out of my *colonias!* I don't want you on this property ever again!"

She flew to the window and flung back the threadbare curtains and pointed an accusing finger at the cinder block shelters and the plywood lean-tos that had only dirt floors. Only vaguely was she aware of the darkening sky and humid breeze that brought the smell of rain.

"Somebody had to do something about this!"

Unfazed, he stared out the window at the dogs and cats and chickens roaming the dusty, dead-end, unpaved streets.

"Not a single house has electricity," she continued.

"These people had nothing in Mexico. Nothing! I sold them lots. Not houses. Not electricity. *Lots!* For twenty-five dollars or less down. They chose to build these houses. Blame *them* for building shacks, why don't you? Blame the world because millions more are even poorer, *princesa.* Some of these people never paid me a dime more than their first twenty-five dollars. Did I kick them out? Or bull-doze their houses? Which is what would have happened to them in Mexico. The border is jammed with thousands, who would give anything to be here."

She stared at him.

"I know a helluva lot more about poverty and what they've been through than you do. I grew up with them. I married one, remember? I got in trouble with the law for that, too. I helped raise her daughter, Elena. I understand these people and what they go through to get even this much—too damned well.''

''Then why don't you do something?''

''Like you? What are you doing here anyway? Holding brown babies? Pretending you care about babies…when you…couldn't possibly…''

She paled. ''Pretending?''

''Does slumming help you with the guilt you feel because you were born a *princesa?* Or because—'' He bit off the rest of his sentence.

''You don't know anything about me.''

He stepped toward her, cornering her. ''Don't I?''

Something in his voice made her blood run cold. Nevertheless, she squared her shoulders and tilted her chin up.

''You stuck my company for ten million dollars in fines,'' he whispered. ''Why?''

''To get your attention.''

''Well, you've got it, *princesa.*''

''The fines are a pittance.''

''Maybe to you. You stay the hell out of my *colonias.* You leave me alone. You call off your dogs in Austin or—''

She shook her head. ''Not unless you promise to see that these women and their babies get medical attention…and…and…''

''And anything else you dream up when you're bored and sitting around in your fancy mansion with nothing to do other than to figure out how to make my life a living hell! Something you're proven to be an expert at, by the way! How come you and Josh never had any children? Maybe if you'd had children, you wouldn't have the time to—''

''What?'' She felt her heart thudding.

With the swiftness of a predator, he seized her hand and

pulled her closer. "I'm a land developer. Not Santa Claus."

"And as their developer, you should have provided trash collection, water and sewers."

Wrenching at his arm, she tried to pull her hand from his grip. But he held on tight.

"They're getting those things...in their own good time."

"Contaminated wells!"

"A few maybe... Because they didn't drill deep enough."

"If their septic tanks had been put in properly *by their developer*..."

His grip crushed her bones and made her too aware of how primitively male and dangerous he was.

"Which is their fault! Not mine!" His sensual mouth curled. "Like I told you," he continued, holding her captured wrist. "I sold them lots. Period."

"Period! How did you get so hard and bitter?"

"I have you to thank."

"Me? I've only seen you all of what...once...in ten years...."

"In the cemetery, I believe." His eyes were ice chips.

Shuddering, she sought a safer topic and relaunched her attack. "You sold them lots—*period?* How can you say that? If you developed land the way you would for your richer clients, you would have put in water."

"Water?" Again, his gorgeous mouth quirked cynically as he let himself be led back to their quarrel. "These people couldn't afford premium properties with utilities. Some of them never paid anything but their down payment. What the hell am I doing? It's no use talking to you."

"Ditto!" she whispered. "We have nothing to say to each other."

"That's where you're wrong."

"I can't imagine…"

"I have today's date circled in red on my calendar. Do you?"

She stared at him for an endless, agonized moment.

"No…"

He released her wrist.

Her eyes, wide and violet, lifted to his, which were savage.

He knew.

Buying time, she slowly went over to the littered children's table and began to stack their storybooks.

His voice was flat and cold. "You could have told me you were pregnant."

She straightened to face him. "You were married, remember?"

"Like hell. If you'd listened to me at all, you would have understood I was a dumb kid with a big, stupid heart. I thought I had to marry her to save her life and Elena's. That marriage wasn't real. Ask Chainsaw. I was stupid enough to listen to his legal advice." His gaze studied her unwaveringly. "But that doesn't matter now. You don't matter. But what you did ten years ago does."

She gasped.

"Why did you get rid of our baby?"

The words seemed to repeat themselves in the silence, drumming in time with her frantic heartbeats.

"Don't say that…."

"Do you ever visit that little grave under the great big oak tree at Campo Santo?"

"No…. I can't bear…"

"What do you say we go to that tiny, forgotten grave and pay our respects to our dead baby—together?"

The trailer fell utterly silent. When he grabbed her arm, she nearly fainted.

"You're going with me, *princesa*. Just once. I don't think that's asking too much."

Lightning crashed outside.

"Oh, dear," she whispered. "The sky to the north is pitch-black. If it's going to rain, I really do need to get on the road. I—I can't go. Not today."

He went to the window and stared at the dark horizon. He didn't move for a long time. When he turned back to face her, the lines in his carved face weren't quite so deeply drawn.

"You're right about the storm. If we're going to beat it, we'd better get on the road." His hand gripped her elbow.

Her lips opened to protest his manhandling of her, but no sound came out.

"Isn't it time, Ritz, that we faced our demons together? They've haunted me for years and years. Haven't they haunted you, too?"

She swallowed. Old hurts rushed back. Always, she'd been afraid he'd find out. Always she'd wondered what he'd do.

"I can't.... I can't," she whispered.

18

Roque's Harley skidded to a stop beneath the purple shade of the oak mott that edged Campo Santo. With fluid grace he stuck out a long leg, set the kickstand, and stood up. Then he stretched his tall, lean frame like a huge cat. Tearing off his black helmet and dark aviator glasses, he strode toward her.

As he came around the front of her gold Honda, Ritz's hands began to shake.

She couldn't do this! The sky was darkening fast. She could even smell rain.

He opened her door.

"I shouldn't be here," she began. "Not with you!"

"Shh," he soothed.

"You're twisting everything around. Accusing me. When you're...when you're guilty."

"Be quiet and just listen. Let yourself feel..."

When he pulled her out beside him, the trees soared above them like a natural cathedral. Quiet and woodsy scents washed over her. Leaves murmured overhead. Birds twittered. Brown leaves rustled at her feet. The breeze smelled of salt and the sea; of home. Of peace.

Houston with its concrete and congestion seemed so

sterile compared to the ranch. While she got her bearings, he knelt and picked a bouquet of pink primroses.

"Ready?" he murmured at last.

When she nodded, he headed through the twisting oaks that arched above them. The branches bent so low that at times they had to stoop to get under them.

As a girl she'd thought these twisted trees were frozen dancers caught in a witch's spell. How she'd loved to scamper after her father through these trees.

"They're only trees," he had explained. "Not magical trees. Just trees sculpted by our prevailing southeasterly winds that blow from the gulf."

Her father. The mere thought of him made her heart ache. He wouldn't speak to her now, not even when she'd come to the hospital to see how he was after his last heart attack. He'd been so gray-faced and thin, so fragile. Even so, he'd turned purple and had ordered her out of his room.

Back then he'd loved explaining natural phenomena like these trees to her. Because then she'd been his perfect little girl, his little girl who'd believed he knew everything, his little girl who'd had big dreams of being the greatest Keller ranch lady who'd ever lived. Once she'd dreamed of ending the feud between the Kellers and the Blackstones.

And now Benny Blackstone was out of the picture. Yet everyone said his son was worse—even more ruthless than his father. But Roque had forced Benny to drop the lawsuit against the Kellers.

Roque's moody silence and his brisk, crunching footsteps reminded her of how profoundly she disliked him for making her come here.

When he reached the clearing, he stared across the meadow with its sweeping late-afternoon shadows, frowning, as if he, too, dreaded this visit. Their baby's grave was nestled beneath the largest of the live oak trees across the meadow. Was he waiting for her or hesitating as the bright little flickers of golden sunlight played across his gleaming, black hair and his tall frame? When she got nearer, a fist seemed to grip her heart as his brown hand tightened around the pink bouquet. He was so handsome, more handsome than he'd been at twenty.

Oh, dear...

When she caught up to him, she was a little breathless, and he couldn't meet her eyes any more than she could meet his.

"What sex was it?" he whispered.

Her stomach turned over. His voice sounded so hollow and sad. He seemed so vulnerable, and all too human. It became difficult to remember that after ten years they were practically strangers.

"A baby girl," she managed to say brokenly.

His mouth thinned. "I would have raised her."

She remembered that still tiny body in her arms, the perfect little hands, the long fingers, the exquisite little fingernails.

She notched her chin higher and resisted the temptation to defend herself. "Don't make me do this."

"I shouldn't have to."

When he turned on his heel, she ran lightly after him. His steps slowed the closer he got to that small white cross beneath the drooping branches of the immense live oak.

She'd grown up with cowboys. He looked good in his jeans, too good. His tight black T-shirt showed off his muscular torso and powerful, brown arms. She looked away, wondering how she could notice such things, here of all places.

Then he knelt at the grave and laid the pink flowers at the base of the little white cross. The blank date on the cross hit her like a blow. Not that he noticed. He was busily separating the pink blossoms and laying them in a straight row.

She sank to her knees beside him. ''Why are you doing that?''

She met his eyes nervously, and he quit. But he didn't answer. It came to her that he was as scared as she was. She picked up one of his flowers and sniffed it. ''My baby. My sweet precious baby girl.''

''Our baby,'' he said gently.

Our. The word engraved itself on her heart.

''You don't know how I grieved....''

''You could tell me.''

Her cheeks heated. ''I don't think so.''

Instead she remembered the pressure she'd put on Josh trying to get pregnant. All those charts and pills and thermometers. All those endless visits to fertility doctors. And the forced sex that had felt deader and deader. The operations had been worst of all.

When the primroses began to blow off the grave, she bit her lips, swallowing back tears. Leaning forward, she picked his flowers up and laid them one by one around the white cross. But they blew away again. When she started to crawl after them, he placed a hand on her shoulders.

''What color was her hair?'' he whispered.

The pink flowers and the white cross blurred. ''Black. Thick like yours,'' she said, brushing at her wet eyes.

''A real little Mexican,'' he murmured with pride. ''Why didn't you ever tell me about her?''

''I couldn't talk about her to anybody. I'm sorry she died. I was then, and I still am.''

''And Josh?''

''He left. It's over.''

''Rosita divorced me, too.''

She swiped at her eyes. ''I guess our lives didn't work out the way we planned.''

"It was for the best. I never should have married her. My life was crazy back then. I felt trapped, furious, brokenhearted. You ran away. I blamed her. And I always wanted to know why you left and what happened to you. Then I found out about the baby." He clipped off that last.

"How?"

"I ran into Jet at the cemetery. I forced it out of her. So—where did you go? How did you live?"

"I went to Austin and then to Florida. Worked for horse trainers in barns. After I lost the baby, my grandmother gave me enough money to get my nursing degree."

"So you could save the world."

"Funny how people who want to save the world sometimes can't even save themselves."

"Me—I just wanted to make money. So I could even the score with my father."

"And you did."

"He scuttled his own ship." His dark face was grim. "Would it surprise you if I had other nobler goals?"

"Definitely."

"You think I exploit the poor."

She stared at the tiny white cross that seemed to shimmer. "There are lots of ways to rationalize, I suppose."

"For what it's worth, I saw people with nothing. No homes at all. In Mexico, they were squatters with no clear title. At least here, they have clear title."

She wasn't up to a debate. But maybe he did have reasons for what he'd done just as she had.

"Compared to Mexico, *Colonia Las Moyas* looked clean to me. I guess I didn't see it with your eyes."

"It's so much easier to hate you than believe you," she whispered even as she wondered if the tiny white cross and the sacred setting were working a miracle in her heart. "I wanted our little girl. I wanted her so badly. But I was young and foolish and all alone. Working with horses was too hard.''

His eyes measured her.

''Sometimes I wonder if I'll ever be able to forgive myself…for what I did…and for what I didn't do. Knowing now that you wanted her, too, and that maybe you would have helped me just makes me feel worse.''

Oh, God. He made her feel all mixed up. Well, it was too late to change any of it. Their baby was dead. They came from two different worlds. They'd hurt each other enough.

''I never forgot you, never got over you,'' he said.

''Don't start— We'd only make each other miserable—''

''Feeling anything for me threatens you, doesn't it?''

''We got into so much trouble before. Maybe we bring out the worst in each other.''

''And your life is so perfect—''

What could she say? She was still paying for running away and losing their child. To save her baby, she'd run away and taken minimum wage jobs in horse barns. She hadn't been able to afford prenatal care. She'd been so ignorant, she'd ignored dangerous symptoms.

Sensing her pain, he stared at her for an endless moment. But when he reached for her hand, she wanted to let him take it.

Instead, she stepped farther away. Had her dead marriage created a vacuum? Was that why he gave her this dangerous buzz?

''My life is lonely as hell,'' he said. ''Why don't we have dinner tonight?''

She didn't answer.

Roque opened her to her grief, but he brought a dangerous comfort, too. Still, what good was their lingering attraction? What good were regrets?

When he began scooping up the primroses and massing them at the base of the cross with gentle expertise, she knew she had to get away from him. Fast.

Hardly knowing what she did, she took a slow step backward followed by another and then another. He was still arranging the flowers when she was all the way across the meadow and almost hidden in the oaks and mesquite.

Then she stepped on a twig wrong and startled a baby javelina. Next the mother squealed and charged her from a clump of palmettos. Ritz screamed.

When Roque shouted at her to come back, she raced away from him through the darkening trees, not stopping even when prickly pear tore her uniform. He kept calling to her. Then she heard him crashing behind her through the woods.

When she reached her Honda, she threw herself behind the wheel and frantically twisted the keys in the ignition. The engine purred, and she gunned it. Whipping the little car onto the ranch road, she hit the gas and dashed for the main highway.

When he didn't appear in her rearview mirror, she still kept a heavy foot on the accelerator. Trees, deer, and cattle passed in a blur. Soon the red blinking light at the highway intersection loomed ahead.

Just as she flipped her turn signal on, his black Harley burst out of the pasture to her right. He leaned over the handlebars, soared over the barbed wire fence, and hit the pavement directly in front of her, whirling to a stop so fast, she had to stomp on her brakes. Her tires squealed. His bike flipped. The next thing she knew he was sprawled on the ground as still as death.

Screaming his name, she threw her door open and raced to him, her white skirt flying. Flinging herself down beside him, she gripped his hand, feeling for his pulse.

"My turn to feel you up," he whispered jauntily, yanking her wrist so hard she tumbled down on top of him.

"Faker!"

Heat radiated from his skin to hers through his black T-shirt.

"Don't you dare try to start anything with me, Roque Blackstone."

"We got started when you were barely fourteen." His hand slid around her shoulders. "Maybe it's time we finished it."

"It's over."

"You sure about that?"

"We've caused each other way too much pain."

"Maybe it's time we had some fun."

He sat up, removed his helmet, and shook dust out of his longish black hair. A fresh cut on his dark cheek was crusted with blood.

"Why'd you run at the cemetery?" he murmured, studying her way too intently.

"Why'd you chase me?" she hedged

"I think you know."

He was very pale. The motorcycle stunt had been more of a shock than he was going to admit.

She touched his bruised cheek, but he jumped back as if she'd stung him.

"Did that hurt?"

He sucked air through gritted teeth. "Do we have a date?"

"We'd only hurt each other."

"You might be right."

"What would people think?"

"I don't care nearly as much about that as I do about seeing you."

"I don't think so. It's late, and I-I'm in a hurry to get home to Houston."

"I got the impression you don't spend much time there anymore."

"Usually I—I do stay at my little apartment in Harlingen."

"Then?"

"Well, with the divorce final, I need to collect the last of my things and talk to my realtor. And…and then…there's… Oh, dear! I almost forgot Josh. He's been paging me, and he never does that."

"Your life with Josh in Houston is over. Whatever he wants can wait. Stay here—with me."

"No."

"You nearly killed me a while ago. You're a nurse. You owe it to me to observe me, don't you think?"

She didn't answer.

"Just to make sure I'm okay."

"Roque, we can't start over again."

"I'm just asking you to dinner. Period."

"I don't know if I want to hang out with someone as crazy as you."

"Meaning?"

"That was a crazy thing to do—jumping that fence. You could have been killed." Her voice was gentle.

He hung his head, apologizing silently. "I guess I was showing off."

"Why?"

"For you. Something stupid and crazy makes me show off for you. Like when we flew. Like the night I felt you in the dark watching me dance."

"You put on quite a show."

"We were kids."

"Maybe I chased you for the same reason you ran at the cemetery. I don't hate you any more than you hate me. I hate how you make me feel. How you always get inside me and…"

The blood rushed from her head.

"The baby's dying wasn't your fault. You didn't hurt anybody but yourself," he said. "And maybe me."

The brittle shell that had encased her heart shattered.

"I have so much to make up to you for," he said. "Let me start tonight."

The way he always made her pain his own touched her heart more than it should have.

"No…"

"Poor Rosita," he said. "She tried so hard to pull herself up in the world…to please me. Just like I've fought to pull myself up to please…"

Even though he didn't complete the sentence, Ritz blushed. Her old feelings for him were as strong as ever. What he wanted charged the air, charged her, too.

Why couldn't she have dinner with him? She was a divorced woman. She was free.

He read her face like a book. "Steaks at your beach house? Since you left, nobody goes there."

Not the beach house. Not her special, secret hideaway. "It's too remote," she argued.

"Which means nobody will catch us there."

"No," she whispered. "Not there. Besides, I really do have to get to Houston!"

Then the sky blackened, and a gust of wind rushed across the grasses, causing her to shiver.

"No," she repeated.

Raindrops began to pelt them like machine gun bullets.

"You nearly killed me, *princesa*. You owe me—big time. Steaks! Your beach house!"

"Don't you ever listen?"

"I'm listening to your heart. It's thrumming as crazily as mine is."

"Listen to the rain instead! We're getting drenched!"

He got up, and they raced to her Honda.

19

Why did I agree to this insane dinner?

Roque was in the kitchen; Ritz was hiding out on the front porch, trying to concentrate on the wind sweeping across the bay and blowing the sand on the beach.

Why did he have to be more dangerously attractive than she remembered? Why did she get as nervous as a cat every time he came near?

No sooner had Roque grilled the steaks on the wood-stove in the rustic kitchen of the beach house and set the platter on the cedar table on the front screened porch, than the storm broke.

A bolt of yellow fire crashed, and the whole house shook. Ritz screamed and jumped into Roque's arms.

He pulled her close. "Hey. I thought we'd eat and drink a little wine first...but if the storm has you in the mood, I've got sheets and blankets—"

"Would you quit?"

Just as she placed her hands against his broad chest to push him away, another bolt rattled the shutters. With a little cry she grabbed hold of his shoulders again. He was sleek, lean muscle. And, oh, dear...even his cologne and musky male scent smelled sexy.

"Good thing I just set that platter down." His heated gaze warmed her.

He was too damn intuitive when it came to her.

"I used to jump in my parents' bed every time it thundered," she said, hoping to throw him off. "Meaning—it's not you, it's the storm."

"Whose bed do you jump into now?"

She blushed. "I'm going to let that one slide."

"I'd really like to know."

"It's really none of your business."

"Touché. So…are you all right?" his deep voice rumbled against her earlobe when she continued to cling.

Earlier he'd showered and changed into a crisp, white cotton shirt and skintight jeans. He smelled so clean. Their bodies fit too perfectly.

Lightning crashed again, this time directly in front of the house. Hardly knowing what she did, she grabbed the front of his shirt and held on tight. She remembered the children climbing on him earlier today. Maybe he felt solid and warm, but he was way more lethal than the storm. So, why did he make her feel so safe?

"I'm not all right!" she forced herself to say. "Just look out there! I can't drive in this! I'm stuck with you. This…this is all your fault! You knew this would happen! That's why you invited me here."

With a laugh he hugged her closer. "If I'd thought trapping you here would bring rain like this, I would've hogtied you in that trailer, slung you over my shoulder and carried you straight here like King Kong. Hey, I kinda like that kinky fantasy. Bondage and a rain goddess and a beach house. It's too bad my crystal ball isn't that reliable."

"Very funny."

"So, relax. We've got a roof over our heads. Since

we're stuck with each other, let's enjoy dinner and each other's company.''

"Impossible."

Why couldn't she make herself budge from his arms?

The storm quickly worsened. While their steaks cooled, she clung to him in the middle of the shadowy porch while rain slashed the screened walls and torrents streamed from the gutters.

"I'll bet the caliche road is as gummy as glue," Ritz said, her tone dismal.

"Soupy quicksand," he agreed cheerily. Since he was a rancher, rain brightened his mood. "So, isn't it better to be here with me…than stuck somewhere up to your hub-caps in white glue?"

"You're too conceited."

"Hey, I'm used to being chased by women."

She didn't want to admit, not even to herself, that he might have a slight point about the road. Nor was she ready to confess that with his arms deliciously wrapped around her, she was almost enjoying the wild flashes of white and the constant drumroll of thunder. The winds whipped the bay into angry black froth. Even the waves slamming against the bluff beneath the beach house were pretty.

"I hope Black Victory's okay," he said, watching the explosions of sea spray.

"We're trapped…maybe for the whole night…and you're worrying about your yacht."

"A line could break. It's in more danger than we are. After all, we have each other."

Each other. His deep voice made her shudder.

Careful, girl. You're still paying for that one night of wild sex with him that made you pregnant.

"Hey, we need the rain. As a rancher's daughter, you ought to know how desperate we've all been down here.

Yes. I'm very happy about it. And if we have to spend the night here together, we'll sleep in different rooms.''

"You said that the last time."

"You seduced me, *recuérdate?*"

The hope in his low tone made her flush.

He pressed her fingers. "What do you say we light the kerosene lamp and have dinner?"

She nodded, and let him lead her to the table.

"So, tell me about this beach house of yours," he said, "that you and Caleb used to come to when you were kids."

"It was probably quite grand and properly furnished when my great-great-grandmother Eugenia built it."

"No doubt. The Keller Ranch was like a feudal kingdom back then."

"She painted sea birds for a hobby. This house is a replica of the Caribbean cottage where she spent her tenth wedding anniversary painting."

"It's amazing how remote it is."

"Too remote," she whispered.

Although it was divided in half, the Keller Ranch was still so vast no other houses or lights were visible. Glancing at his dark face, she shivered. It was as if the two of them were all alone, cut off from the rest of the world.

Despite her misgivings and much to her surprise, she soon found herself enjoying the thick, rare beef, the tomatoes he'd sliced, and the ears of corn he'd grilled along with the steaks.

He'd selected a very fine Merlot, too. Every time she sipped her wine, he refilled her glass. Not that she noticed, until she was dangerously light-headed.

With the rain and the wind and the simple meal that melted in her mouth, he became too easy to confide in. She had to force herself to remember who he was and why she couldn't trust him.

But he asked all the right questions, and she soon found herself telling him about running away and even about losing the baby.

"My father told me I had to have an abortion. He said he was protecting me. He really thought he was. So, I ran away.

"How did you take care of yourself?"

"I didn't have much money. I worked in those barns at minimum wage jobs. When my blood pressure started going up, I didn't know it. I had other symptoms, but I was so ignorant I didn't realize the danger until it was too late. I was very sick when I broke down and called Grandma Keller. She flew out to Miami. But the baby was already dead. I ended up with some female problems, too. I nearly died. She wanted me to come home. But I felt bitter...toward my family."

"Toward me, too, I imagine?"

She nodded. "She gave me the money to go to school."

"So, you became a nurse?"

"To try to prevent ignorant, scared young women like me from doing without prenatal care."

"To save babies."

"So that's why you visit my *colonias*."

He was so understanding. He said all the right things. Before she knew it, she'd told him more about her unhappy marriage to Josh than she'd ever told anybody.

"So, you see it was my fault, not Josh's, that we couldn't get pregnant."

"Endometriosis, you said?" He tipped the bottle of Merlot into her glass. "That's not anybody's fault. It's an act of God."

"You're very fatalistic."

"I'm a Mexican. We believe in destiny. You Anglos think you can control everything."

She raised the ruby-red wine to her lips. "It's a pretty

common condition. But I felt terrible when he left me for a younger woman.''

Roque's hand reached across the table to covers hers. The soothing warmth of his fingers was electric.

''I'm sorry,'' he whispered. ''You've been through a lot. But you've got to put it behind you and go on.''

''That's what my mother says. It's not so easy.''

''You were wonderful with Magda's baby.''

Because every time I hold a baby I imagine it's ours.

The wind howled around the eaves of the house. Tendrils of gold blew against her cheek. Before she thought, she squeezed his fingers.

''Ritz—''

Fringed with those incredibly long black lashes, his green eyes were too sexy for words. He was staring at her with a smoldering intensity that made her know he was every bit as vulnerable as she was. The effect of his raw humanity coupled with his virile sexuality was devastating.

''I couldn't love Rosita...because of you. She worked so hard to pull herself up in the world...for me...but it was no use. I came to admire her, but it wasn't enough.''

''I'm sorry,'' she said.

When he slowly pushed his chair back, her heart lilted.

She knew what he wanted. She wanted him, too. But she wanted so much more.

She hadn't been able to conceive with Josh. But Roque had gotten her pregnant once. Could it happen again?

Suddenly she realized how desperately she still wanted a baby. Even though she was only twenty-six, she'd all but given up....

Until tonight.

Until him.

And she'd called him wild and crazy.

He was so tall and dark and handsome. Cliché handsome. Cheekbones a model would stab for. Oh, and that carved jaw and long, chiseled nose.

Was it the wine? Or this crazy, all-consuming wish for his baby? Or was he really the best-looking man she'd ever known?

He was all wrong. But most of his failings weren't genetic.

Tipsily aquiver, she got up to meet him and melted in his arms.

"I haven't seen a storm like this in more than a year," he said as he traced the softness of her eyebrow and the satin wetness of her lips with his thumb.

A shutter began to bang on the south side of the beach house. When he bent his black head to nuzzle her hair, she snuggled into him.

"Somebody ought to do something about that shutter," she whispered as his mouth heated her nape.

"Yes, they certainly should," he muttered dryly between fervent nibbles that made her blood pulse.

His hand slid down her throat to wind a length of gold around his fist. He let it fall against her shoulder. "You have such beautiful hair. Sometimes it looks white, as white as an angel's hair. And it feels like silk."

Her gaze fell to the mat of dark, curly hair on his chest beneath the V of his collar. "It's yellow with a few red highlights."

"All I know is it's beautiful. And you're beautiful. So damn beautiful, it's hard to stay mad at you. Ten million dollars, you cost me. If this keeps up, you'll be worth every penny."

"Thank you," she said agreeably.

"But no more fines—please. From now on, we work together to improve the *colonias*."

"You would work with me?" The thought filled her with so much joy, it flustered her.

''Why you?'' he murmured. ''Why has it always been you? All these years.... Only you?''

The deep passion in his low tone made her nerves skitter. He was going too fast. But she was, too. Only she wasn't being as honest.

''I wish our baby had lived,'' he whispered. ''I loved you. Impossible as it sounds, I loved you.''

''I loved you, too,'' she admitted, wishing, praying that magic would strike tonight and she'd get pregnant.

''But you ran away.''

''To protect our baby.''

''*Dios.* I should have protected you both. Will you ever forgive me?''

If I get pregnant, I'll forgive you everything.

What if she did? What would he do if she ran away again and he somehow found out?

She cupped his face and drew him to her. She meant to kiss him softly but at the first brush of her lips, his lips became hard and demanding. Soon she, too, was lost in the wave of emotion that swept over them.

It was the wine, she told herself. And the storm. And the secret hope that he might make her pregnant again that made her feel so hot and excited. *Not him.*

''Even when I was with other women, your ghost haunted me,'' he said.

''Well, you didn't haunt me exactly,'' she lied, not ready to admit that he might be the real reason Josh had never stood a chance, not her inability to conceive, that maybe Roque was the reason Josh had looked for love elsewhere. ''But you were unforgettable.''

''Unforgettable. Now there's a word, *querida.*''

When Roque's mouth closed over hers again, she opened her lips, wanting his tongue inside her again, wanting to taste him. Wanting? Wanting? Aching for him...

Not for him.

For a baby.

He picked her up and shoved her against the wall, raining kisses first on her mouth and throat. Only when he'd had his fill, did his head move lower. Her blood was pounding when he buried his face between her breasts and pushed her up against the wood planking.

"Your heart's beating way faster than mine, *querida*."

"I know. I'm rusty at this. Josh and I...we didn't..."

"We can still stop," he whispered raggedly. "I swore I wouldn't let this happen."

"Why do you always make me seduce you? That's a lot of responsibility to put on a girl."

He laughed and looked up at her, his beautiful eyes shining with blind adoration.

The stab of wonder in his gaze bothered her. She was leading him in too deep. But, oh, a baby...

She felt young and alive. Again she was a teenage girl. And it was like the first time. All the years in between dissolved like smoke. Even the pain let go of her heart.

There was only him. Only this moment.

Only him.

If she did get pregnant, she would be so careful this time, take such good care of herself. Again, his tenderness and honesty toward her worried her.

She couldn't be honest. They had too much history and too much baggage for a real relationship. She would give him one night of sex. And if she got pregnant, if...

She'd run away. Maybe to California. There was such a nursing shortage, she could get a job anywhere.

She kissed his brows, his eyelids, cupped his carved face in her hands.

"You're incredible," she whispered.

His dazzling green eyes so close to hers now, held that terrifying vulnerability he no longer tried to hide.

"I love you," he said.

"Don't go there."

"I love you. You don't have to love me back. Not yet anyway…"

But he wanted her to. He expected her to. And she felt… As always with him she felt too much.

Even before he lifted her into his arms to carry her to bed, she began to shake.

In the bedroom, while he stripped, she stood paralyzed, her conscience waging a silent war.

Use his body. Pleasure him.

But he loves you. Be honest.

Men will say anything to get sex.

I believe him.

If you get pregnant, and he finds out—

He won't!

You can't hide a child forever.

Dear God…

Completely naked, he stepped toward her out of the darkness.

"You look even better than a puma," she whispered, remembering Jet's long-ago taunt.

"Thanks."

His hands began unbuttoning the bodice of her white uniform, pausing when he got to her breasts, his fingers burning hot when he cupped them.

"Only you," he murmured. "There's only you. Promise you won't ever run away again—"

She swallowed hard, but the knot wouldn't go down. Gently she began to trace the new abrasion that ran across his cheek to his jaw.

"You took quite a fall. I'm glad you weren't badly hurt."

"You're sweet."

His lips brushed hers reverently.

Tell him.

His hands, so gentle, so expert, drifted lower, peeling off the white cotton uniform as if her body were a precious gift, as if loving her meant so much he couldn't rush it.

The sweetness and depth of his touch made her unspoken lie lodge like a stone in her heart.

This is wrong.

Use his body. Use him.

She thought of all the surgeries and fertility procedures she'd endured attempting to get pregnant with Josh.

She didn't want to hurt Roque.

But maybe he was her last chance.

20

The bedroom windows were open, so they could hear the storm. Occasionally Ritz felt cool misty raindrops tingle when they hit her burning skin. Not so many really because Roque was on top of her, his hand between her legs stroking. Gasping at every slight movement of his incredibly talented fingers, she finally had to bury her face against his neck to prevent more embarrassing screams.

Was he ever going to do it? She was so ready. When arching her body to meet his had no effect, she laced her fingers in his dark hair and drew his mouth to hers. Their tongues met. She licked, sighed. When he shuddered and tightened his grip around her waist, she thought she had him.

But he let her go abruptly and stood up.

"Don't stop," she whispered.

Above the roar of the wind and waves, she heard the telltale crinkle of plastic followed by a curse low in Spanish.

"What are you doing?" she asked, startled.

"They should make tanks out of this stuff."

He had a condom.

"Oh, dear, er, we don't need…one of those."

"I have to protect you."

"But I can't get pregnant."

"There. I've got it on...just to be on the safe side."

He lay down beside her and tried to pull her back in his arms.

She pushed him away, stiffening.

"What?"

"I want to feel you," she said.

"What about safe sex?"

"Let me love you." She found his mouth in the dark and began to tease him with her lips as her hands raced down the ropy muscles of his body to peel the offending condom off his erection.

"Ouch!"

He went still, watching her too intently as she flipped the condom on the floor. "I don't get it."

"Do you get this?" She rolled over and straddled him.

Lightning whitened their faces, and in that stark flash, his gaze was so intense, she was afraid he'd read her intentions.

"What do you really want from this?" he whispered.

"A night of wild unforgettable sex."

"We had that before. Look where it got us."

"Most macho Mexicans would like my answer."

"I'm a failure in the macho Mexican department," he replied almost gloomily. "But don't tell my supermacho Moya uncles when you meet them. They're very proud of me."

"Why?"

"Sometimes I brag...just a little."

"You lie about women...."

"Just to make my uncles happy."

"We're getting off track," she whispered, leaning over him to nibble at his ear as her hands began to roam.

"I want more than one night. Way more."

"S-so do I," she stammered.

"Why don't I believe you?"

"I don't know. Why don't you?"

When he continued as if he were puzzled, she grew afraid. She had to finish this...before he caught on.

Deliberately she rocked her hips back and forth against his. Luckily that was enough to send him over the edge. His breathing roughened and speeded up. Fully roused, his callused, brown hands clamped around her waist. Crushing her to him, he pulled her down hard, thrusting deep and sure.

"Ritz...Ritz."

She returned his kisses wantonly, opening her body for his pleasure. For his seed.

And then he came.

She didn't. But his explosion fused her body and soul to his and made her feel that she belonged to him, that she'd come home and wanted to stay with him forever.

Which was impossible.

Afterward, he was spent and shaking. Stroking his back, she caressed him, weeping a little as she listened to the rain.

How many days and nights had she spent here as a young girl? But never had she felt so content. The smell of wet grass and salt air, and the utter darkness as she lay beside him made her feel cut off from the city and people. Tonight made her know how she'd pined for this place. For him, too. Deep down she was a rancher, as he was, not a city girl no matter how hard she'd tried to pretend these past ten years of exile.

Abruptly she rolled back over onto her back and drew her legs up to her breasts, wrapping her arms around her, assuming the position that the fertility doctors had told her would help her to get pregnant.

"What are you doing now?" There was a keen edge of suspicion in his voice.

"It was just so incredible. The sex, I mean. You. *Us.*"

"Then marry me."

"What?"

"I've built a house on the ranch. Pam still lives in the main house. My house is like Porfirio's Mexican hacienda. You'll love it. You can stomp anywhere in boots. It's quiet, too. There are oaks around it. It's on a knoll, so you can see for miles."

It sounded so beautiful, it scared her. "I'm barely divorced."

"We've lost ten years...and a daughter. Not to mention each other."

She couldn't let him get started. "We've never been good for each other. And...you'll probably feel differently in the morning."

"Is that what you really think?" He reached for her.

"What? Again—"

"You didn't come. I owe you."

"I—I..."

"You're not too good at faking." His voice went deadly. "Or lying, *querida.* After what we've shared today, we should have nothing to hide." His gaze traveled the length of her body and returned to her face.

She laughed nervously. "So—you're more of a macho Mexican than you want to admit. You can't stand it that you didn't make me come."

"I just want to make you happy."

They did it again, and again. When he was done with her third time, she was dizzy and near fainting from too many orgasms. He'd been incredible...tender, adorable, sweet. Too sweet.

How could she leave him? How could she lie to him? How could she not?

* * *

Roque lay in the dark beside her, listening. She wasn't asleep. She was pretending. Why?

He hated mysteries. When she was involved, mysteries spelled trouble. So, he lay in the dark after the best sex with the only woman he'd ever loved and wondered what the hell was wrong. No use to ask her.

Lightning flashed. His gaze drifted across her still shapely form to the wooden floor where the discarded condom lay.

Ten million dollars in fines she'd cost him. Not to mention a daughter and ten angry years.

He had to get to the bottom of this. He couldn't afford to underestimate her.

But she'd been wonderful in bed, almost completely his, almost completely loving. *Almost.* That was the catch. Sleepy and satiated as he was, he couldn't shake off his uneasiness even as he wrapped her in his arms and she nestled against his warmth.

She couldn't fall asleep, either.

Why?

He woke up to dabbles of dazzling sunshine all over the unpainted walls, to a placid bay that gleamed like a silver mirror. But when he reached for her, she was gone.

He shot out of bed and ran out to the caliche driveway. There were deep grooves where her Honda had backed out.

He didn't even have her phone number.

She'd call, he told himself. He went to the bedroom and pulled on his jeans. Barefoot he began to pace the breezeways that wrapped her great-great-grandmother Eugenia's house and connected the various rooms, these screened breezeways cooling the old-fashioned house almost as well as air-conditioning.

She'd call.

But she didn't.

* * *

Ritz barged through her front door without turning on any lights and almost fell into Josh's awful, red leather recliner and his wide screen TV. As always they jarred with her antiques.

Her antiques! They were back! Even the Aubusson rugs and the paintings Grandma Keller had left her had come home! Everything was arranged just as it had been when she'd been married to Josh Evans, and he'd been the richest and most arrogant dot.com king in Houston.

She dropped her bags, blinked twice, just to make sure the furniture wasn't part of a postcoital hallucination.

Then she stepped into the kitchen, and Josh got up from the table and said, "Rough night? Why don't I make you breakfast?"

Her temple began to pound so hard she was afraid she might have a stroke. "Josh!"

"Hello, darling." His boyish grin was wide and sheepish.

"What are you doing here?"

"I'm your husband, remember?"

"Am I missing a page? We haven't spoken for four months. Except when you publicly accused me of taking lovers."

He turned pink. "I was a cad. Forgive me?" He hesitated. "I paged you five times yesterday."

"I'm sorry." The minute she apologized, she hated herself. "No I'm not sorry! You left! You deliberately destroyed my reputation. I'm mad."

"I'll spend the rest of my life making it up to you."

"Did I fall through a keyhole or something?"

"You'll feel better after I make you an omelet."

Her legs were still rubbery from her night with Roque. She needed a bath and to lie down.

"You're not my husband. I'm not hungry. And I haven't forgiven you."

Her stomach growled.

"See, you love my omelets."

"You never listen."

"Husbands aren't supposed to listen to their wives. You need a good breakfast, and I need to talk to you."

Here we go. She arched an eyebrow. "What do you really want?"

"You look like hell."

She flushed. Then she spoke without thinking. "So do you." As soon as she said it, genuine concern filled her as her nurse's eyes studied his pale, gaunt face. "You don't look well."

He was prematurely gray, but that wasn't it. His hair was as thick as it had been when he'd been eighteen. Always athletic, he suddenly seemed pathetically thin. His broad shoulders sagged. There were shadows under his eyes. His suit hung on him like he was a clothes hanger.

He was wasting away. His eyes were haunted.

"I got stuck in the storm," she said quietly.

"Naturally I was worried."

"What about Pat?"

He blushed. "She's out of the picture."

"Oh, dear."

"I'll tell you all about it while I cook your breakfast."

The night of sex had drained her. Which was exactly why she let him cook.

She sat down at the table. From the way he flung the cupboards open, she realized he still knew his way around. Within minutes, he set an omelet just the way she liked it in front of her.

"Mushrooms. Tomatoes. Green peppers," he said proudly.

"You remembered."

"See, I do, too, listen."

"Only when it comes to food."

"And sex?" he began with a smile.

Men were so hopeful. Her fork dropped through her fingers with a clatter. "No way."

"Vegetables. No cheese." He beamed down at her.

"You went grocery shopping."

"A man can't live on mold. Everything you had was rotten."

"I've been living in the valley most of the time."

He opened the refrigerator door, and she saw that he'd cleaned it out, too.

This was bad. She was too afraid to pick her fork up and eat. "What are you doing here?"

"I—I was wrong."

"What?"

"About everything." His voice softened. "About us."

"What about Pat? What about me being over the hill?"

"I was having a mental crisis. Hell, Pat's a teenager. She stays up to all hours listening to rock."

"What about her great body...and all those perfect eggs in her uterus?"

"She doesn't want a baby. She *is* the baby. I don't want a baby, either." A dark, tragic note had crept into his voice. "It's too late for that anyway."

"Josh?"

"I want you back. You're my wife."

"I want you to go. I've found somebody else."

He stared at her, stricken.

"Josh, what's really wrong?"

He didn't answer, but she could tell his mind was racing.

"You're sick, aren't you, really sick?" she whispered.

"I can't ever lie to you."

"Not true."

The melodramatic contortions of his face were too easy to read—fear, fury, impotence, but most of all neediness.

"It's a brain tumor."

"Pat left you, didn't she? Because you're sick?"

"Her mother died of cancer. She's young and wants to have fun. You're such a good nurse…and…. Oh, Ritz, I don't want to die alone."

"So, you chose me."

"You're dependable."

"I—I don't know, Josh. A lot's happened since you left."

He was about to argue, but the phone rang. To her surprise, he slammed his fist on the kitchen table so hard her omelet jumped. "If it's Blackstone calling you again…"

"Roque—"

This was bad.

Her mind raced. Maybe Josh was her solution.

"A-answer the phone. Tell him…tell him…I'm home…and that I've decided to give you another chance."

"You mean it?"

The phone stopped ringing only to start all over again.

"Do you mean it?"

"Tell him."

"Darling…"

"Don't overplay your hand. It's not that good. I'll be your nurse. But that's all."

The phone stopped ringing only to commence again. He picked it up. After a brief conversation, he laid the receiver down. His eyes narrowed on her tangled hair and bruised lips.

Heat crawled up her throat.

"Did you see him or something?"

"That's none of your business."

"You slept with him."

Wearily she got up from the table and headed for the

stairs. "Take the guest suite downstairs. Don't even think about following me upstairs."

"Ritz, how could you—"

She turned. "How could you—"

That night when she came down for supper, they ate at opposite ends of their long, gleaming dining room table. She'd set a splashily colored, huge silk floral arrangement between them, so her view was of red and yellow pansies, and not of him.

Their meal was silent, as so many of their meals had been when she'd tried to believe they had a solid marriage. Now she saw she'd hadn't ever been in love with him, not even when she'd married him. She'd needed someone. She'd convinced herself they could build on all that they'd had in common. But without love, she hadn't been able to reach him. When she hadn't conceived, and he'd lost his business, they'd been unable to comfort each other.

They'd never really had a marriage. She shouldn't fault Josh because he'd had the courage to leave.

For years, even during her marriage, she'd been alone.

She still was.

Unless...

Unless she got pregnant.

Ritz's heels made hollow sounds as she tripped up the single flight of concrete stairs to her second floor Harlingen apartment. The rattle of the palm fronds around the pool beneath in the courtyard gladdened her heart. The warm wind off the distant gulf sent whorls of dust and the sweet scent of ripening oranges and grapefruit and tangerines up from the orchards that fringed her apartment complex.

She was here to collect a few necessities since she might be in Houston for months. Only a week had passed, but Josh was getting sicker fast. Head down, she was digging so hard in her purse for her apartment keys, she didn't pay attention to the dark shape sprawled in front of her door. Suddenly her foot hit something that shouldn't have been there. She nearly missed a step and pitched forward.

As she fell, she saw a man's long legs. Some filthy, dark-skinned vagrant in black leather with greasy black hair had been sleeping on her balcony.

"Careful, Ritz." Roque barely woke up in time to catch her.

"Roque...." Despair coiled around her heart as she dropped to her knees and stared at his bleak, unshaven face. "How long have you been here?"

"I was waiting for you," he muttered groggily as he straightened.

Very gently, as if she were infinitely precious to him, he brushed a strand of hair from her eyes with the back of his hand. "I was a fool. I forgot to ask you for this phone number. I didn't know any other way to reach you. Your nursing agency said you'd taken an indefinite leave of absence due to a family illness. I kept calling Josh, only to get his machine." He sounded so terribly concerned about her it broke her heart.

"But you talked to Josh," she whispered, shivering as she jerked away from his touch which was so gentle and dear.

Sensing rejection, confusion warred with his anger and wounded pride. "I thought he was lying, so I decided to camp here till you came home. I had to see you, Ritz."

"How long—"

"Josh told me the craziest thing the morning after we..."

"He told you the truth. I was there...with him. I told him what to say."

"You love him? Not me?" He laughed derisively. "You really expect me to believe that?"

She stood up and leaned back against the wall. "He's my husband."

"Your ex-husband."

He rose to his full height, so that he towered over her. "What was I?" He yanked out her silver St. Jude medal and held it in front of her face. "Some sort of Mexican stud you used to make him jealous to get him back?"

"A mistake," she whispered.

"I don't buy it!"

He grabbed her and kissed her hard. Instantly hot needy desire melted her bones and turned her knees to rubber. How she'd longed… Her hands slid up his arms and almost went around his neck. But she forced them down to his chest and began to shove at him frantically.

Still, his mouth ravaged hers. Somehow she steeled herself. She fought him desperately, and when she didn't respond after several more angry kisses, he finally let her go.

"A mistake? So the hell were you, *princesa*."

His injured voice was so dark and proud it tore her heart. When her St. Jude medal flashed, it almost drew her out of her numb shell.

But not quite.

Her period was late. She had to end it. Now.

"Just go," she whispered even as the wild anguish in his eyes made her ache all over.

"What are you hiding?"

Her knees became jelly. "N-nothing. It's over. That's all."

"Maybe for you."

"Yes, for me, yes," she agreed wildly, making her voice forbidding.

"Damn you. If I ever find out you were hiding something that night from me, you'll be sorry."

For a long moment her tongue seemed frozen to the roof

of her mouth. Then she got it loose. "H-he's my husband. You're not. I—I finally realize I love Josh. That's all."

"That had better be the truth—"

"Don't you dare threaten me!"

His green eyes pierced her. "Don't lie to me!"

Tell him, said a silent voice.

He waited, his incredible eyes burning her face, giving her one final chance. When she looked away, he turned and slammed down the stairs. Frozen, she watched his wide, retreating back until he was gone.

The next morning when she woke up in Houston, she opened her window and got queasy when she smelled the last of her sweet peas.

"Tell him," said that contrary voice in the back of her mind. *"Or you'll be sorry."*

She went so far as to lay a hand on her telephone.

But no further.

Her hand was still resting on the phone; she was still staring at her brightly colored sweet peas when Josh buzzed her for breakfast a half hour later.

21

Roque was late for the gathering after Josh's funeral. Even though cars were lined up for several blocks, he found a spot for his bike right in front of the mansion.

He loped up the walkway to the door and rang the bell. As he waited for somebody to let him in, he heard voices and laughter inside. For at least five minutes he stared at the funereal black ribbons on the front door, trying to work up enough nerve to punch the bell again.

Ritz. When had she first learned Josh was dying? Had she known when she'd slept with him two months ago? He didn't think so. So, why the hell had she gone back to a husband, who'd left her? Who'd maligned her to the press?

Had Josh told her the next day he was ill? Had she felt sorry for him?

Roque had to know the truth.

Roque rubbed his stubbled jaw. Then he jammed his fist on the doorbell again.

Plump, old Socorro cracked the front door and would have shut it, if he hadn't pushed against it.

"You saw me through the peephole and were hoping I'd give up."

Her flat black eyes gave her away.

"It's okay," he said. "I forgive you." Then in Spanish, he whispered, "How is she?"

She tried to shut the door again, but he stuck a sharkskin boot against the jam.

"Ouch!"

Socorro paled. "You're not a friend of Señor Joshua."

With the flats of his hands, he shoved at the door until it gave. Then he strode past Socorro into a mansion with high-ceilings, immense rooms, paneled walls. The house was too fussy and stuffed with sissy antiques and carpets a cowboy could neither sit on nor walk on.

Their long noses in the air, at least a dozen aristocratic ladies stopped sipping from paper-thin teacups to devour him in his tight jeans and black leather.

His gaze skimmed their frozen faces for *hers*. It took a minute before he found her huddled all by herself in a corner window. Black damn sure was her color. Even pale and drawn, she looked too good to him.

She'd left his arms and returned to Josh. Jealousy clawed him as he strode toward her.

"Ritz…"

She blanched. Then she looked wildly for a means to escape just as a white-coated waiter with a silver tray offered her canapés of salmon and lobster.

Perspiration beaded her forehead. She brought a shaky hand to her lips. Her violet eyes widened. Even before she bent double, he knew she was going to throw up.

He remembered the condom she'd deliberately flung on the beach house floor. She'd rolled over after sex and insisted on lying on her back for quite a while. Her actions had struck him as odd then.

She'd said all she'd wanted from him was one night of wild sex. As he raced across the opulent room and quickly knelt beside her, his mind was making crazy connections. When he placed a hand on her waist, it was thicker.

Her cup and saucer smashed to the floor. "Don't touch me!"

When she'd tried to spin free of him, his hand locked on her arm. He ripped off his bandanna and used it to wipe her mouth.

"Are you going to have my baby?"

Dios. Where had that come from?

Even before he felt her quiver, her eyes locked on his face. For a timeless moment, nobody else in the house existed. She shook her head even as the outlandish truth blazed in her luminous eyes.

"So, that's why you went to bed with me," he whispered, "when you despised me. You want my baby."

Desperately she tried to yank free. "No." Her voice was strange, unsteady.

"You owe me the truth—this time!"

Agony and fury mushroomed inside him like a poisonous gas. Her eyes hated him with equal passion.

When his grip tightened in an effort to force an answer out of her, she began to kick and scream so hard and so loud, he couldn't hold her. She fell, and he almost died inside when he saw her blood oozing from her arm onto chips of white china.

Her eyes clung to his a minute longer as he knelt to help her. Then everybody was pushing him aside. Josh's mother and Irish began to fuss. Jet joined in.

Feeling lost and absurdly wounded, but furious, too, he heard voices behind him. The neighbors were gossiping about Ritz's alleged infidelities with immense relish and wondering where he fit in.

At the divorce trial, Josh had told everyone she'd been unfaithful. Because of the Keller name, his accusations had made the papers. Why had she reconciled with him?

Suddenly it made sense.

Josh had found out he was ill.

She'd hoped she might become pregnant.

Roque's mind clicked. She hadn't been able to get pregnant by her fancy husband or the high-class lovers she'd replaced him with. Had she seen the night at the beach house as her last chance?

She'd used him as a stud.

Damn her to hell.

How many other men had she tried first?

He thought of that little grave at Campo Santo so near Caleb's. No matter how many men there had been, he had to marry her.

He could not give up his child...again.

Jet had Ritz on her feet. When they headed for the stairs, he barged through the crowd and blocked their path.

"No...not that way," Ritz pleaded weakly, staring into his eyes.

But when Jet met his gaze, she lost some of her boldness and stepped aside. Roque led the trembling Ritz and pressed the towel to her arm as they climbed the swirl of marble together.

From the upstairs windows, he saw the sweep of green lawn and his bike at the curb.

Dios. He wished he could just ride away and be free of this tangle. But he couldn't risk another grave in Campo Santo. Pushing Ritz inside her bedroom door, he shot the bolt.

Never as long as she lived would Ritz forget this tense drive from Houston to Blackstone Ranch. She'd buried a husband and been abducted by a madman, who was forcing her to marry him.

Not that he'd paid her the least bit of attention now that he had her. No, he'd made a dozen calls on his cell phone, some of them business, some of them personal. Pretending not to listen, she'd kept her face pressed against her window and her hands fisted.

But the personal calls to his family had been too much. He'd set their wedding date for next Saturday. Although his mother had screamed so loudly, even Ritz could hear her, Blanca was planning to come and run the show.

Ritz couldn't have moved if she'd wanted to. Both the back seat and trunk of her Honda were jammed with suitcases and plastic sacks. Beneath her feet, her favorite books and albums were wedged so tightly she wondered how they'd ever get them out.

When she'd refused to pack, he'd done it for her—grabbing garments and shoes out of her closets and drawers and books off her shelves, and stuffing them all into the suitcases and sacks willy-nilly. He'd packed the car the same way.

"Gotta go," Roque said, ending his lengthy call to Pablo.

"Punch off," he snapped, tossing the phone in her lap. Next thing she knew, he was whipping past an eighteen-wheeler and then easing back into the right lane.

Fence posts flew past. Whirling to watch the eighteen-wheeler on their bumper, Ritz drew a long, shuddering breath. "You drive like a maniac."

"I have you to inspire me."

"You can't be serious about this...this wedding. Next week?"

"Pablo and Marisol are making the arrangements for the ceremony and reception as we speak."

"We can't get married. You hate me."

He frowned at the racing highway. "That's beside the point."

"And I hate you, too."

He clenched the wheel. "At least we agree about something."

"What kind of marriage could we possibly have?"

"Look on the bright side. Fifty percent of marriages end in divorce. At least we won't have to deal with disillusionment about ours."

"You're marrying me—intending to divorce me?" Strangely the thought of divorce hurt even more than the thought of a forced marriage.

"How do you see this ending, *princesa?*"

"Marriage is supposed to be forever."

"Then what happened to you and Josh?"

"We thought we could love each other and make our marriage work."

When Roque saw a gas station ahead, he put on his blinker and slowed to make the turn.

"What are you doing now?"

"I need a cigarette." His voice was stiff.

"You quit."

He swerved into the parking lot. "Today I seem to be resuming several bad habits—the worst being my relationship with you."

"If you smoke in the car, you might hurt the baby."

"As if you care."

The car snarled to an abrupt stop. "Do you want anything?" He yanked her keys out of the ignition and got out.

"I'll get it myself."

They stomped inside together, but shopped separately. However, he waited at the counter to pay for her diet cola. When he came outside, he opened the pack and shook out a cigarette. He took a single drag and met her eyes.

"Damn it," he said. "I can't smoke with you glaring at me."

"Good."

Pitching his cigarette on the ground, he snuffed it out with the toe of his boot and then threw the rest of the pack in the trash.

She drew a sharp, triumphant, little breath, almost smiling at him before she remembered she hated him. "I'm glad you did that."

"Why don't you try not talking to me for a while?"

"Fine."

They got in and slammed their doors. He drove in silence for maybe the longest half hour of her life because the whole time, since he'd told her they couldn't talk, that's all she wanted to do. She kept turning toward him, only to remember. Maybe it was being closed inside the car, maybe it was his hostility, but never had she been more keenly aware of any man.

She hoped he was suffering even more than she, and there were signs he was. He couldn't sit still. His every action was a careful insult. He snapped the radio on and drove her mad flipping stations. When she began to hum along with her favorite song, he snapped it off.

And his driving! Either he speeded recklessly or he tailgated. He played with the air-conditioning like a woman suffering with hot flashes. It was either too hot or too cold. She in turn shot her vents either at him or away from him.

When she sucked the last of her diet cola a little too noisily, his mouth thinned.

"What kind of marriage can two people who hate each other possibly have?" she finally demanded in a goaded undertone.

When she saw trees edging the road up ahead and realized it was a rest stop, she blurted, "I have to go to the bathroom."

"You should have gone when we stopped before."

"I didn't have to until I drank that cola. If you're going

to be married to a pregnant lady, you need to know, they go to the bathroom a lot.''

His face turned red, but he put on the blinker. Soon the Honda rolled to a stop beside a picnic table and outdoor grill.

''When you're done, I'll tell you what kind of marriage.''

He reached into his pocket for a cigarette only to scowl at her when he came up empty-handed.

''It's not my fault you threw the pack away!''

''You don't have to look so damn smug about it.''

''Smoking is bad for your health.''

''You don't give a damn whether I live or die.''

''My concern is strictly professional. I'm a nurse.''

''Don't remind me!''

He walked her to the ladies' room, went inside and made sure it was safe. Then he left her there.

When she came out, he was sitting on a picnic table. He didn't look up when she climbed onto the table beside him. For a long moment they sat together, watching the constant rush of big trucks on the NAFTA corridor. He flexed his fingers and unflexed them as if he felt as awkward as she did.

''Look,'' she began, ''you don't want to marry me. I don't want to marry you. We don't have to do this, you know.''

He scowled and said nothing, but she could feel his hostility as he fought to get enough control to speak.

She looked away from him, seeking a more pleasant view. The sky was big and blue. There weren't many trees other than those that had been planted and watered just to shade them. She began to count the cactus plants and then the trash bags blowing loosely against the bleak fence line.

Growing bored with that, she decided to get their little

show on the road. "You were going to tell me what sort of marriage you have in mind."

Still, Roque said nothing.

"Well?" she prodded.

"You took a leave of absence from your nursing to take care of Josh. You don't go back until our baby's born."

"That's impossible."

"We will live together. In my house. Until our baby is born, and I know it's okay."

Our. The word lingered. "What about Buttercup? I'm boarding her at a barn in Houston."

"I'll send Pablo back with a trailer."

"Thank you."

"After the baby's born, you can divorce me and we'll work out the custody arrangements."

"And sex?" she said.

"No way will I be so stupid as to let you seduce me again."

"Me seduce you? Dream on, cowboy."

"You have to admit, it's been a bad habit of yours in the past."

"Separate bedrooms?" she demanded edgily.

"Except when my family visits."

"Oh, so, you'll sleep with me only for appearances sake?"

"The marriage has to look real."

"Why is that so all-fired important?"

"Because of our baby."

"Our baby." Why did that little word, *our,* have to imprint itself on her heart every time he said it.

"Okay," she said, her voice softer. "You've got a deal. One more thing. About the wedding. We have to have a small wedding."

"Big," he growled.

"No. Getting married is bad enough. I can't stand the idea of a spectacle."

He set his jaw. "Huge. I'm a Mexican, remember?"

22

Even on such short notice, the wedding was indeed huge. It seemed even bigger because the Moyas had such big personalities. Better put: Roque's family was loud.

Thus, the historic ranch chapel was filled to overflowing with roses and exuberant Moyas. Hundreds of guests, many employees from Roque's various businesses, and his family from Mexico, stood outside the church. Dark-eyed Moya nephews and nieces were held up to the windows by their enthusiastic parents so they could see the ceremony and chatter and gush to their parents about what was going on inside.

On the surface the affair was gay and happy, but Roque's smiles were even more forced than her own. Except for Aunt Pam and her daughters, Kate and Carol, no Keller had come. Only Ritz, Jet, Socorro, and Irish were there from her side. Because her father had spurned his invitation, Irish had to give her away.

As Ritz stood beside Roque at the altar in a floor-length gown of creme-colored silk, holding a bouquet of orchids, she felt frozen inside and so spiritually remote, it was as if some vital part of herself had fled to a safer place.

What could the ceremony mean, if she couldn't forget

the past with all its hurt any more than she could forget her husband was planning to divorce her as soon as possible?

Then it was over, and the pastor said, "You may kiss the bride."

Before she could instinctively step back, Roque's arms were around her, his lips grazing hers, possessively lingering a split-second too long, which brought grins to his uncles' dark faces.

The reception was even more difficult to get through than the ceremony itself. The food was Mexican. Blanca had come early and dealt with the caterers. She'd hired the bands of Mariachis that strolled about strumming guitars and singing folksongs in Spanish.

There were so many Moyas running around the courtyard and in and out of the house, Ritz couldn't keep them all straight. Roque had at least a dozen beautiful, feminine Moya cousins, who buzzed around him, laughing and batting their long black eyelashes. It wasn't long before they had him grinning like a conceited fool. Even Jet, who was free because Steve hadn't come, spent an inordinate time either dancing or in rapt conversation with her new husband.

"You're going to have to watch him," *Tío* Eduardo advised with a salacious wink.

"The ladies love him, and he loves the ladies." This from *Tío* Marco.

"But then you're his wife. He will have to come home to you," *Tío* Eduardo said.

Have to. Ritz nodded miserably, wondering why it hurt that he was friendly toward every beautiful woman except her. She should be glad for the reprieve. For he'd kept a too vigilant eye on her this past week.

"I hope Blackstone realizes how lucky he is," Irish said, lifting a champagne flute in a toast to her.

Ritz smiled weakly.

"Last week a funeral…"

"Don't, Irish."

Blanca and Roque's sisters were next.

"I was shocked when Roque called and said he was getting married again," Blanca said, her red-tipped fingers curling around the stem of her champagne flute as she sipped.

"No more shocked than I was." Ritz's forced laugh was brittle. "It all happened so fast."

"Too fast," Blanca murmured, studying her with bright eyes. "Why isn't your mother here?"

Before she had to answer, Roque's favorite nephew, a handsome young man named Juanito, bowed low and asked his *Tía* Blanca to dance, and she whirled away in his arms.

"Don't worry about her," plump Carmela said.

"She's always been possessive of Roque," Ana agreed. "She wanted him to marry a Mexican and return to Mexico."

The next time Ritz's gaze chanced on Roque, he was laughing with Rosita, who looked too stunning in black lace. Elena, his adopted daughter, a real little beauty herself, was clinging tightly to his waist.

They look like a real family, Ritz thought, and she felt more like an outsider than ever.

Just as Roque's uncles decided it was time to toast the bride and groom, Roque joined her and took her hand in his, smiling down at her, but not nearly so warmly as he'd laughed with Rosita.

"Spare me," she whispered through gritted teeth.

"Smile. Look happy," he commanded.

Blanca made a lengthy, overly emotional toast that got all the Moyas crying. Everybody was wiping their eyes with hankies when *Tío* Marco lifted his champagne flute.

Before he could speak, the doors were thrown open, and a short, dark stranger with green glittering eyes burst into the room. He was unshaven; his clothes were dirty. He stank.

Everybody gasped.

Even when he pointed at her and she felt the full force of his malevolence focused on her, Ritz wouldn't have known who he was if Aunt Pamela hadn't stepped between then and whispered, "Benny...no...please...no. Go home...."

Blackstone stumbled drunkenly past her, grabbed a champagne flute, and raised it to Ritz with a shaking fist. "You killed my good son! Now you marry this...this thief!"

Blanca began to scream at him to leave.

"May you both rot in hell!" Benny said. "A curse on you and yours! If it's the last thing I do, I'll see you dead. Where's my gun? Somebody...Pamela, get me my gun!"

He would have said more, but Pablo, the cowboys, and the Moya uncles seized him and dragged him outside. When he continued to rant obscenities about Roque having swindled him out of the ranch, Roque ordered the bands to play. Blanca was so furious she wanted to run out and attack Benny. Roque had to hold her and calm her. Then he persuaded his sisters to stay with her until she was herself again. He sent Pamela home with Benny to make sure he settled down. When the crisis was past, he led a shaken Ritz onto the portable dance floor that had been erected beneath the oak trees behind the house.

"Your father hates us so," she whispered.

"Some things never change."

He held out his hand as he had *that* first night. This time she took it.

"He threatened to kill us," she whispered when he drew her close.

"Not now," he said gently.

"How did you make so much money? How did you end up with his ranch? Why did he and Aunt Pamela divorce?"

"Long story, and much of it doesn't reflect well on him. But his downfall started with Caleb's death."

"How did he get through the ranch gates?"

"He lives here. In a trailer. On a remote division. I take care of him. Usually he behaves himself...if I keep him in booze."

"In booze?"

"He's a blithering alcoholic."

"That's not a very nice way to put it."

"It's not a very nice reality. But hush. No more talk about him. Not a pleasant subject for either of us, I imagine. Smile at me. Dance with me. Pretend you love me. After all, this is our wedding day. Didn't your mother once advise you to marry—"

"Don't mock me...or her."

When they began to dance, everybody else circled them. Her dress floated around her slim legs.

A woman said, "Don't they look wonderful together?"

The following morning, Ritz woke up alone in Roque's vast bed. She stretched sleepily and felt almost happy until she heard voices in Spanish downstairs, and remembered she was Mrs. Roque Moya Blackstone.

All the Moyas were staying with Roque. Oh, dear. For a week, during this incredibly difficult time, she'd had them underfoot.

Today she was simply too tired to face her lively in-laws. Suddenly she wanted to stay in bed forever, or at least until her interfering mother-in-law and Roque's beautiful sisters and cousins went home to Mexico.

Since the reception had been at the house, the guests

had stayed nearly all night. Not that she'd been able to party as long as they.

The moment she'd begun to fade, Roque had noticed and had lifted her into his arms and carried her upstairs and over the threshold of his bedroom. She knew his thoughtfulness had nothing to do with her and everything to do with appearances and their baby. Still, when they were behind the door and no one could see, he kissed her on the cheek and returned to the reception.

She had gotten undressed and slipped into bed alone, wondering when he'd come up, only to fall asleep before he did.

Suddenly she heard footsteps outside the door. She closed her eyes. When Roque came in, she recognized him by his cologne. He stepped over to the bed. She felt him watching her.

"Still determined to fake everything."

Her eyes snapped open.

"I made breakfast," he said. "Come down when you feel like it."

He didn't wait for her answer. After he shut the door, she got up and showered, savoring the feel of the warm suds running down her belly and thighs. If this were a real marriage, he probably wouldn't have wanted his entire family in the house on their wedding night or had them here this morning.

She would have awakened in his arms…after a night of wild, wanton sex…. Perhaps he would be in the shower with her right now. At the thought her breath quickened. She closed her eyes with a sigh.

"You don't want that. Don't even think about it."

But she couldn't stop herself.

He'd been so wild and yet so vulnerable at the beach house. Such an incredible lover. These last couple of months, memories of him while she'd dealt with Josh had made her ache for him all over again. Dancing with him last night had made her know how much she loved being in his arms.

No sooner had she stepped out of the shower and toweled off than she heard the door open and heavy footsteps from the bedroom.

Roque.

Deliberately she let her towel drop.

When he stepped into the bathroom doorway looking fierce and dark, she wanted him so badly, she didn't dare meet his eyes.

He drew a sharp breath and said, "Sorry. I—I didn't realize you weren't dressed. I came up to see what was taking so long."

Desire for him raced through her veins. "The warm water felt so good...."

Did she only imagine that he flushed?

"I'll be downstairs," he said abruptly

Then he left her.

She was so mortified by his deliberate indifference, it took her a while to summon the courage to pick up her towel and dress. When she did come down the stairs, he jumped up from the table and acted like an adoring bridegroom, rushing across the den to take her hand.

"He cooked a special breakfast for you," her mother-in-law said, her voice low and jealous. "It's in the oven."

"No chilies for you," *Tío* Eduardo said, winking at her knowingly.

Ritz blushed. He'd told them. She could tell by how her mother-in-law's black eyes watched her with such intense interest. Ritz was so mad she wanted to snatch him baldheaded. He had no right to tell them without asking her. She was his wife. His first allegiance should be to her.

The more pleasant and chatty he was with his family, the more she boiled. She could barely swallow her eggs and toast without strangling him.

After breakfast there was an hour or two of confusion as the Moyas began to pack suitcases and cars. They'd spread their things all over the house, so they kept picking shirts and books and electronic games up and asking everybody whose they were. The process took hours. Thus, it was almost noon when she and Roque were holding hands in the driveway, waving goodbye to them.

"You told them about the baby," she said as they watched the last van drive away.

"It's a reality."

She yanked her hand out of his. "I feel betrayed."

"Then you might have a glimmer of understanding as to how I feel."

"The baby's the only reason you married me."

"Do you want there to be another reason?"

Something dark in his deep voice tugged at her heartstrings. Conflicting emotions struggled within her.

"No. No. Of course not."

"Good. Neither do I."

And yet… It had felt wonderful to dance with him.

He strode off toward the barn. Soon he had Long John in the round pen and was working him with long lines. More than anything she wanted to watch. But, of course, that was the last thing she would let herself do. She didn't care what he did, or how he did it.

Suddenly realizing that she was alone with him in his house and that she was his wife, had her feeling self-conscious and ill at ease around him.

Did he have to be so tall and dark? Did he have to make her ache and her heart beat faster every time they were in the same room?

* * *

She went inside wondering how to spend the first day of her marriage, when the man she was married to was a stranger who wanted to avoid her at all costs.

When Roque trooped into the kitchen to get a cup of coffee and then locked himself in his office to go back to work as usual, loneliness washed over her. Not knowing what else to do, she went out to the barn to check on Buttercup.

Long John stood in the door with a seventy-five-pound sack of feed in his mouth. While she watched, he slung the sack against the wall so hard, the bag shredded and feed flew everywhere. Then he lowered his black head and began to nibble feed off the concrete floor as docilely as a lamb.

She grabbed the feed sack. "Quit making a mess! How did you get out anyway?"

She seized his halter and led him back to his stall. Then she got a broom and began to sweep. When that was done, she went into the stalls and one by one led each horse to the wash rack where she used a big puffy sponge and a bottle of water to wash their heads. She squeezed the sponge and let the water run down their noses. An hour later, the barn was tidy, and she felt better.

When she got back to the house, Roque was still on the phone in his office; obviously he preferred to talk to any one but her. To take her mind off him, she plunged into picking up the house, doing laundry and making plans to cook supper. She put on some music to make the work time pass more pleasantly and was soon singing as she broiled and baked.

He slammed his door. When it was time for dinner, she rang the dinner bell in the courtyard. To her surprise, Roque came.

"Looks good," he said as he sat down to a gleaming table decorated with vases of freshly gathered wildflowers.

"It's just pot roast and a few vegetables."

He stared at her as if he was amazed she'd gone to any trouble on his account. "You don't have to worry about flowers...or feeding me."

"It wasn't just for you. It's for me, too. And for the...*our*...baby." Why had she chosen that word that so shocked her? She jumped up, to cover her nervousness, and ran lightly into the kitchen, calling back to him. "Oops. I forgot the bread."

He didn't start eating until she sat down and lifted her fork.

"You don't have to wait for me," she whispered.

They ate with very little conversation. But the food melted in their mouths and brought the comfort that a good meal in pleasant surroundings can bring. The dining room had tall glass windows that looked out across the ranch. Pink oleander and red bougainvillea bloomed in profusion near the house. The grasses stretched to far horizons.

They ate slowly, lingering over every bite, as if to stretch this time they were forced to share. Then he helped her carry the dishes into the kitchen and even offered to wash them, but she wouldn't let him, saying she had to do something.

So, he left her and went into the den to watch a movie on television. It must have been a comedy because she could hear him laughing.

When she was done in the kitchen, she went upstairs alone to the smaller bedroom across from his. She got undressed and climbed into bed with a book. But when she tried to read, all she could think of was Roque downstairs laughing...without her.

Finally she heard his footsteps on the stairs, heard him hesitate before her door. Why did he stand there so long?

She held her breath. When the knob turned, her heart began to pound.

Then his footsteps retreated. His door opened and closed.

He was keeping to their agreement. It was what he wanted. What she wanted. Why did she feel so lonely all of a sudden?

She felt like such a fool for anticipating…for even thinking that he might… For wanting…

Wanting…

She passed a restless night. It must have been dawn before she fell asleep, hoping that he was every bit as miserable as she.

He was.

Dios. He lay in bed, his hand under his black head.

The last two days and nights had been absolute hell. First, there had been the wedding and the reception to get through. Afraid to share her bed, he hadn't dared to trudge upstairs during the reception until he was sure she was asleep and equally sure he was too exhausted to do anything except pass out beside her in bed.

Even so, the lines of her body beneath the sheet had been pure poetry. Her yellow hair had flowed around her face in the moonlight, and she'd looked so innocent and smelled so sweet, it had been hard to hate her for deceiving him.

She ached for their lost baby just as he had. He knew that. She still wasn't over that tragedy. He understood why she'd wanted a baby so badly, why she'd done what she'd done. If only she wanted him too.

Dios. Why was it so damned hard to hate her?

This morning, surprising her when she stepped out of the shower had nearly undone him. The image of her body had seared itself into his brain. He hadn't been able to look at her without the torture of remembering how flushed and lovely she'd been with bath water dripping off her skin.

Then tonight he'd mounted the stairs, half hoping he'd find her door open, half hoping she'd invite him to her bed just like she'd invited him to dinner. He'd even stood in front of her bedroom door like a lovesick dog, waiting, his heart pounding, hoping she'd hear and come. Hell, he was such a fool. All she'd ever wanted from him was his stud services.

He closed his eyes and clenched his fists. She wasn't worth his anger. His breath came in short rasps.

He spent a sleepless night tossing and turning.

Ritz awoke the next morning and felt better. She made breakfast. He joined her. Again the meal was pleasant and only a little strained around the edges. She found that she wanted to talk to him, wanted to ask him how he planned to spend his day. But every time she almost opened her mouth, she stopped herself.

When he drove off with Pablo without even telling her when he'd be back, she felt desolate. She had to remind herself this wasn't a real marriage and that she should be glad he was gone and that she wasn't the least bit interested where he was going. She didn't want to be with him. She didn't.

Nothing relaxed her more than being with horses. So, she put on her jeans and went out to work with them. Again, Long John was out. Since she'd locked the feed room yesterday, he was busily chewing the seat off Roque's John Deere Gator.

"You are bad," she whispered, leading him outside. Then she turned everybody else out of their stalls, too, so that she could brush their manes and tails and spray them with fly spray. When she was done, she let them graze and went back inside to clean their stalls.

She forgot to shut the barn door, so the ever mischievous and inquisitive Long John followed her everywhere.

"You like being brushed, don't you, fella?"

He pricked his ears toward her.

She hadn't ridden in so long. Maybe she should put him through his paces. "I'm about done. How about a short ride? Just me and you?"

She went into the tack room and found a saddle and a bridle. Once she had him saddled, she headed for the pond. He felt stiff this morning. Even so she was soon enjoying the wide open pasture and the blue sky so much, she didn't really notice how far they'd gone until they were nearly to the ranch road between the Keller Ranch and Blackstone Ranch. In the past ten years, the fence line along the ranch road had become so overgrown with brush, the road was barely visible. So, when her parents' truck raced by, its tires whistling and whirring on the hot road, she was as surprised as Long John.

She waved a little shyly.

The truck slowed, but they didn't wave back.

Suddenly Long John decided the tires were making a really scary sound.

Terror struck. He reared in panic, but she managed to hold on. Her parents braked. Her father got out to scream orders.

"Keep his head up," he yelled when the stallion lowered his head to run.

Ritz knew that if she let him run, he'd go faster and faster.

"Whoa," she said, afraid suddenly for her unborn baby.

If he threw her, she could hit her head on a rock or fall into a bed of cacti.

She held tight with her knees. "It's okay. See the truck is stopped. It's just Daddy."

Unconvinced, Long John pranced and snorted. When

she pulled on the reins lightly and patted his neck, he reared again, jerking his head. He became so increasingly agitated, she couldn't make him be still.

"Let him go in circles," her daddy hollered. He'd climbed under the fence and was walking toward her.

"We know what to do, don't we, boy," she said to the stallion, stroking his neck. Somehow she guided him into making small circles. Only soon he was going so fast, he stumbled on a rock and almost fell down.

She kept stroking his neck and trying to talk him out of his terror, but she was getting scared too.

Suddenly Roque's truck stopped behind her father's. He jumped the fence and raced past the older man. He began talking to her and to Long John, his deep voice low and soothing and yet firm and commanding, too.

Soon Long John slowed. Finally he stopped altogether and let Roque take the reins. She dismounted.

"Thank you," she whispered gratefully as she slid out of the saddle and dropped to the ground without using a stirrup.

Roque's face was as hard as granite. "Drive the truck back to the house for me, would you?" It wasn't a question. He tossed her the keys.

Her mother was running toward her. Roque would have turned his back on all of them and led Long John to the barn except her father was too upset to let him off that easy.

"What are you trying to do, Blackstone?" her father demanded. "Why'd you put her on that dangerous stallion? Are you trying to kill her?"

Roque stopped.

"Letting me? Daddy, it was my idea. Long John just got a little spooked that's all."

"You nearly got your damn neck broken, girl."

"I'm sort of surprised you care."

"He married you to get back at me, you little fool. He's tried everything he can think of these past ten years to ruin me."

"I—I thought he dropped the lawsuit."

"Don't you dare defend him."

"I married her because I had to," Roque said, his voice cold. "She's pregnant. You're still her father even if you haven't acted like it in a spell. Anything you can do to keep her off that horse would be much appreciated."

"Pregnant?" Her father glared at them both in utter disgust. "So, that's why you married him— Because you had to!"

"You're pregnant," Fiona gushed. "When can we expect our grandchild?"

"Get in the truck, Fiona."

"But, Daddy—"

Without another word, her father turned to go. His shoulders sagged. He looked so thin and frail. So old. Would he be set against her for the rest of his life?

"Daddy... The baby will be your first grandchild."

The sound of her voice only spurred his long thin legs to move faster.

When she got back to the house, Roque's dark face reddened every time their eyes met. But he remained stonily silent the rest of the afternoon whenever she was near.

In this tense atmosphere, she roasted chicken and made bread for their supper. When she rang the bell, he joined her, but the silence tonight was thicker and more hostile.

He poured himself a tall glass of Merlot, the same label they'd drunk *that* night at the beach house.

"Want some?" he invited acidly, lifting the bottle.

She shook her head.

Instead of eating what she'd cooked, he drank. Several tall ruby-red glasses.

"Why don't you eat something?" she whispered.

"Because I need courage more than food."

"Courage?"

His dark face seemed carved with deep lines of pain and contempt. "To get through one more day and night with you."

His voice cut like a dagger. Her mouth went dry as dust. After that she couldn't possibly swallow another bite, so she set her fork down and stared out the window at the blue sky on the far horizon.

"It looks so bleak. Like our future. I feel so trapped," she whispered.

"Ditto."

"I can't live like this," she finally said.

"Maybe neither the hell can I."

"What do you mean?"

"I thought you were a responsible adult."

"What did I do?"

"As if you don't know," he said, his tone deadly. "You got on that stallion."

"But he has a sweet temperament."

"Don't deliberately endanger another baby of mine."

"I didn't."

His green eyes sparked.

"And while we're at it, do you have to tell everybody I'm pregnant?" she whispered.

"I told my family and your parents."

"It's embarrassing."

"Because it's mine?" He slammed the half-empty wine bottle down. "Don't ride Long John again…or…or else."

"Or else what?" She leaned forward, wanting to push him. Better this hot anger than his cold silence and their unendurable marriage. "Or you'll shoot him…like your father wanted to."

"I'll do what I have to do to keep you off him."

"Even shoot him?"

He lifted the bottle and poured more wine. "If you ride him again, I will."

"Why?"

"To protect *our* child."

"Not me though," she murmured. "Not me... Is Daddy right? Do you hate me so much? Roque... Oh, Roque... I—I never meant to hurt you...."

"Like hell!"

"Would you prefer me dead then—"

When he merely glowered at her coldly, she got up from the table. "I can't stick this out! I can't!"

"You have to."

"No..." She whirled and ran.

23

Roque tore through the house looking for her. But she wasn't in her bedroom or the kitchen or anywhere. When he ran out to the garage and found her Honda, he took off for the barn, running with clenched fists.

He was enraged, tormented, driven to the brink. First she'd crawled into bed with him. Like a fool, he'd fallen in love with her all over again.

All she'd wanted was his stud services. Even Rosita, dear Rosita, who'd started life as a whore in Mexico, had wanted more.

Ritz couldn't stick it out! Well, neither the hell could he!

Ten days trapped in this house with her had him insane. He craved her sexually all the time even as he loathed her for what she'd done.

He flung the barn door open and stormed inside, his savage heart bent on destruction. Then he heard her crying. Fool that he was, his anger melted instantly.

Soundlessly he made his way to Buttercup's stall. She was inside, pressing her face into Buttercup's neck. How slim and lovely she was in her jeans with those loose tendrils of gold falling like a shower of moonlight about her

shoulders and her breasts heaving with every shuddering sob.

Buttercup stared at him reproachfully as if to say,
"She's crying because of you."

"Ritz?"

She fingered Buttercup's mane. Ritz's stomach was
tight, the tears hot as they slipped down her cheeks. When
she heard Roque's voice in the barn, she swiped a shaky
hand across her cheeks.

"Go away," she sobbed. "Just leave us alone."

"Ritz?" His deep voice was soft and tender the way it
had been *that* night in the beach house. "Are you okay?"

"As if you care."

Buttercup's stall door creaked open. "Can I come in?"
Again his voice was so gentle, it got through her de-
fenses.

"Why would you want to? W-when you hate me?"

"I don't hate you."

"You don't?" she breathed, letting go of Buttercup in
confusion and turning to meet his warm gaze, reading the
wild dark emotion burning inside him. He held out his
hand.

"Roque," she whispered. "Oh, Roque—" Then she
was across the stall and in his arms, her face buried against
his wide chest. "Hold your nose. I smell like horse."

"My favorite perfume," he whispered, stroking her hair.

"Oh, Roque," she murmured, clinging with all her
might. "I do love your cologne. Sometimes I think you
wear it to drive me mad."

"I know the feeling, *querida*."

She felt his lips against her brow. Instantly she wanted
more. When his hands slid up and down her back, she
thought surely he would kiss her on the mouth, on her
throat, everywhere.

But he didn't. He just held her until she quieted.

It felt so good, so perfect being in his arms. Why had she married him? Was this what she really wanted? Had wanted for years? Even though the circumstances weren't exactly the best? Even though her family hated him? She'd seen him dancing one night. Ever since she'd wanted him. It was simple really.

Surely she couldn't feel like this otherwise. Just being in his arms soon had desire for him flaming inside her with that familiar, all-consuming need.

She'd wanted to be his from the first moment she'd watched him dance, from the first moment they'd flown on Buttercup. Only she'd never believed she could have him. Even when she'd fallen in love with him, she hadn't believed in him or her own feelings enough to fight his family and hers for their love.

"What's happening to us…to me?" she whispered.

"What always happens when we get around each other," he replied. "I wonder why."

"What are you saying?"

"You're going to seduce me again," he suggested hopefully.

"Oh, you think so, do you?"

"The sooner the better. I can hardly wait."

"But our deal…"

"Was lousy," he growled. "We want each other. We always have."

"Whose bedroom then?"

"You choose."

"Yours," she whispered. "I like the shower better."

"This is good."

"Carry me."

"All the way back to the house?"

She threw her arms around his neck, and he lifted her into his arms. "Definitely. We're going all the way."

* * *

The second they were over the threshold of his bedroom, he began to kiss her, his passion wilder than she'd ever known. She slid her arms around his neck and kissed him back.

I'm his wife. He doesn't hate me. He's never hated me. It's not just our baby.... It's me, too. He wants me, too.

She put on a CD. The bedroom pulsed with music. She began to sway as he had before the fire on the beach. "Get naked!" he whispered. "Fast!" He stood back, his eyes devouring her. "I want to watch!"

"All right," she purred, peeling off her blouse so slowly, he had to grit his teeth. Then she twirled it around her head and threw it at him.

He laughed and snatched it from the air. "More."

"You're hot." She threw her bra at him.

"And getting hotter."

"Your turn," she whispered when she was naked and dancing to the wild drumbeats.

He tore his clothes off while dancing. Then he carried her to bed. When they made love, with the moonlight streaming over them, it was more exciting than it had ever been before. She wondered if the intensity of her passion had to do with her marriage and her pregnancy.

She was married. She loved him.

"There's never been anybody except you for me," she whispered. "You have to believe me. I'm sorry...so sorry for causing you pain."

They made love a second time. When it was over, she began to weep.

He held her close, his big brown hands smoothing her hair. "Why are you crying?"

"Because it was so wonderful and because I'm so happy. Because I'm afraid it'll all go away...like before...."

"This time it's forever."

She fell asleep in his arms.

Some time during the night, she woke up and was startled to find him gone.

A boozy, unwashed, old man's smell filled the airless trailer. Not that Benny gave a damn as he took a final pull from his whiskey bottle and flung it against the trailer wall.

"I own it. I can break it."

He swiped the back of his hand across his wet mouth. Then he scratched at his crotch. He was unshaven, uncouth, and he didn't give a damn. Not anymore. His murdering son had stolen everything and turned him into a two-bit wino dependent on him for liquor and the slop those bastard cowboys brought him to eat. Pamela had left him, for cheating on her, she'd said. But that wasn't the reason. She hadn't loved him. She followed the money. Roque had the money. Roque supported her now.

Was he fucking her, too? Did he make her crawl?

"Roque, you've got to die!" he yelled into the dark, hot night. "Do you hear me? And that bitch murderess wife of yours is going to die, too...for killing Caleb! For everything!"

There was a sound outside, but he ignored it, his scrawny arm reaching under the bed in search of a fresh whiskey bottle.

His fingers closed around the neck of the bottle. Then his door swung open, and a tall dark figure strode heavily inside.

"Roque? That you?"

"Yeah. It's your turn to die."

Benny broke into a cackle of evil laughter just as Roque's gun spit fire, just as he felt his flesh tear open and his guts spill all over his filthy bed.

"I—I can't die. I—I've still got to kill that murdering bitch you married!"

Another bullet smashed through his skull.

"Don't worry. She's next."

The next morning when Ritz woke up, Roque made love to her again. When they recovered, he took her on a drive to show off all the improvements he'd made.

"You won't know the place," he said, grinning at her like a young boy in love as he drove her to the pond.

"You built a dam. Why it's beautiful. You cleared out some of the brush, and the oaks have spread out. It looks like a park."

"It was always a favorite spot of mine.".

"It's where we really met," she said. "Where we flew."

He took her hand and led her back to the truck. "When exactly did you learn Josh was dying?"

"The morning after we made love. When I got home to Houston he'd moved my furniture back into the house."

"Why didn't you tell me the truth then?"

"I'm not sure."

"If we're going to make our relationship work, we have to be honest."

"Blaze new trails. Like your pond." She laughed lightly. "For some of us that's not so easy."

"Try."

"I—I don't know. I was mixed up. For years I'd grieved because I'd lost our baby. I had a lot of bad feelings for you, too. I didn't trust you or me."

"But you trusted Josh."

"I used his illness to do what I wanted to do…to buy time…to see…."

"If you were pregnant…"

She nodded guiltily.

"I can deal with all that…if you can. It may take some time."

"Rosita's so beautiful. I saw you talking to her at the wedding."

"We're friends. She has an incredible story that I can't tell anybody without her permission. She's come a long way. If she can change her life for the better, so can we."

"You don't love her?"

"Not like you mean." He put his arm around her shoulder. "I couldn't love her because I never got over you."

"Can we ask my parents to dinner tonight?"

"You can ask them, but they won't come. Your father is pretty dead set against me."

"We have to start somewhere."

"There's not a man in all of God's Kingdom as stubborn as you are, Art Keller!"

Fiona had flung those words at her husband when he'd refused supper with their daughter last night and breakfast this morning.

She still felt torn as she drove Art's truck up to Roque Blackstone's red-tiled mansion. Then Ritz came running out, her face soft and pretty while Roque stood in the door, watching his wife with the sheepish look of a bridegroom who was embarrassed to be so head over his heels in love.

Fiona's heart softened toward him. There had to be more to this boy than Art claimed. As she got out of the car and ran to her daughter, she remembered the quarrel she had last night with Art.

"He breaks up our ranch…" Art was so stern. So strict.

"Not ours any longer. Your saintly brother saw to that."

"Sells out to *those* people!"

"You're talking about *Colonia Sonia?*"

"Damn right! Lots! No bigger than postage stamps! His *colonias* are all instant slums!"

"I'm sure it's all they can afford."

"Whose side are you on?"

"I just want my family together again."

"I was taught to hold this ranch together. Five generations of Kellers preached that. Then Blackstone..."

"No, your precious Buster—"

At that point Art had turned purple, and she'd had to ask if he'd taken his blood pressure pill.

Ritz embraced Fiona. "I'm so glad you came, Mother."

"I'll regret to my dying day that I didn't stand up to your father and come to your wedding. I had the prettiest pink dress that would have been perfect."

"He can be a hard man to stand up to."

"Tell me about it."

They both laughed.

"You're such a beautiful couple," Fiona said, grinning almost flirtatiously at her son-in-law.

"He dances," Ritz whispered.

"That doesn't surprise me." Fiona laughed.

Roque held up dirt encrusted hands and apologized. "I was repairing the hot tub." He pointed to the kitchen. "That way."

"I guess I'm used to a little dirt."

She assessed him with a rancher's wife's eye for good breeding stock. Tall and dark, he was, and so handsome. Needed some darkness to the skin down here with such a hot sun. Good teeth, too. The baby was bound to be beautiful.

Moya had made a fortune in a short time. That meant there were brains somewhere. Maybe from his mother.

Genes were everything.

"You're going to love Roque when you get to know him," Ritz said.

"I'm sure."

They sat down to a feast of pancakes, eggs, ham and biscuits.

"Your father's favorite breakfast," Fiona said. "I'll have to tell him. He had cold cereal."

Roque went to his office, so she and her mother could catch up. After all, it had been years since they'd really talked.

"I've missed you," Fiona said. "We haven't been close to Steve or Jet, either. Your father can be so…"

"So bossy and such a know-it-all."

"But I'm glad, darling that, at least, you've come home."

"*Home. At last.* Oh, me too, Mother. Me, too."

"When's the baby due?"

"Six and a half months."

Roque and she were stretched out on quilts under the oaks by the pond. Wrapped in Roque's strong brown arms, Ritz lay quietly crying as she watched the clouds sail across blue sky.

"Why do you always cry after we make love?"

"I tell you every time. Because I'm so happy."

He hugged her close. "What's for supper?"

"Oh, you!" She sat up and winked at him. "You're beginning to sound very much like a real husband."

"Which is exactly what I am, *querida*."

"In this liberated age, I might throw that question right back at you."

"And I've got the perfect answer. Elena called. We've got an invitation for barbecue at *Colonia Sonia* tonight. That's where she lives. So, how about it?" Roque asked.

Ritz lay back and closed her eyes. "Elena means Rosita."

"Elena means Elena," he said. "But being the greedy developer, I built the *Colonia*. They're my slaves. To further exploit them I force them to give me a free meal every…''

''Don't…''

''I want you to meet them.''

''All right then. Roque, you never did tell me how you got so rich.''

''All the Blackstones have made money. It's in the genes. It's what we do.''

''But your father lost his to you.''

''He broke the rules.''

''What rules?''

''The law. I was there to pick up the pieces.''

Two different roads at the intersection led to *Colonia Sonia*. When Roque signaled to make a left, Ritz placed a gentle hand on his sleeve.

''I never go that way….''

He nodded and turned right.

''Dead Man's Curve,'' she whispered, reminding him.

''Sometimes I go that way on purpose. I keep a little shrine there to Caleb, so people don't forget him.''

''I've never been that way again.''

The other route took them past the cutoff that led to Irish's double-wide. Irish was on a tractor, mowing the shoulder.

She waved and was a little surprised when he didn't wave back. Probably the sun was in his eyes or something.

''He doesn't have to do that,'' she said when they zoomed past him. ''The county will mow it.''

''Not often enough to suit him. He's a real stickler for perfection,'' Roque said admiringly.

Like *Colonia Las Moyas*, *Colonia Sonia* was a ramshackle collection of trailers, cinder block shacks, and plywood lean-tos at the end of a caliche road. No wonder her father was outraged that what once had been pristine Keller ranch land had been turned into such deplorable development.

And yet when the crowd of dark, smiling Hispanics rushed out to greet Roque, their shouts warm and friendly as they embraced him, she could see the place through his eyes, too.

After years of wandering and yearning to be Americans, these people had homes they could call their own in the United States. Roque had helped them gain this fragile toehold.

''Roque! *Aqui!*'' someone shouted.

''Rosita and Elena. They've been looking for you,'' said a woman with huge breasts and a nose nearly as big for trouble. She eyed Ritz too knowingly.

''This is Ritz. She's my wife now, Lupe. So behave. Rosita came to the wedding and gave us her blessing just as I will give her my blessing when she remarries that border guard she's dating.''

Roque kept his hand at Ritz's waist and introduced her to everybody. At first they were shy and wary of her. But after a few beers and bags of tostados washed down with spicy salsa, they became almost too friendly.

Then Rosita and Elena drove up. When they got out with paper shopping bags, the women sitting beside Ritz at the picnic tables and the barbecue pit got real quiet.

Dark haired, black eyed, Rosita was so beautiful. When she smiled at Roque, Ritz's heart beat nervously. But Rosita turned the same dazzling smile on Ritz, even taking her hand, and saying she was glad she'd come.

''Roque gave me money to shop for Elena. We bought some beautiful things. Wait till you see them.''

Elena began ripping dresses out of the sacks and holding them up to her body. The women oohed and aahed. The men leaned back in their chairs again and began to laugh and tell Roque their latest dirty jokes.

They were halfway through the first slab of burned brisket when a shiny new red truck rolled up so fast, stirring clouds of dust. When the men got up and shouted at him, the driver hit Reverse and backed a safe distance waay from the picnic tables.

"Chainsaw!" everybody yelled to the fat bald man in the neon-green hula shirt who got out.

"You never come," Roque said, when his old friend grabbed the chair next to his.

"Sorry I missed the wedding."

Chainsaw was twice as big as Ritz remembered, or at least the bright shirt made it appear that way. His bald head and face were toasted a permanent purple.

"Didn't ever think you two would get back together," Chainsaw said to Ritz as Elena came up and began twirling in front of Roque to show him a new skirt. "This ain't your kind of crowd, is it?"

"Roque wanted to come."

"Meaning you didn't."

"Meaning we're married, and I want to make him happy."

"It's about time." Chainsaw took a noisy pull from his bottle.

"Where's Natasha?"

"Gone. Got me a new retread wife, too."

"You don't like me, do you?"

"If you stick around, I'll like you fine."

"So, what are you doing these days? Still keeping tigers?"

"I'm an immigration lawyer. And a sometime member of the Blackstone legal staff."

"I don't believe you. You went to prison."

"I was framed. I got a pardon. I've always been interested in law. Went back to school... You need a degree or two to know what you're doing. Hell, girl, these people here helped me get my real start. See that skinny old man with only one front tooth over there.''

Ritz nodded.

''He came to me and told me Benny Blackstone offered him money when he was on a jury.''

''And you and Roque blackmailed...''

''Let's just say that when the dust settled, Roque's daddy couldn't buy himself out of trouble. He deeded everything to Roque. Roque took over his father's massive debts, too. Roque takes care of him as well as his ex-wife.''

''I didn't realize.''

''Roque was grateful. To me. And to these people. He gave them this land.''

''Gave it to them...''

''He doesn't exploit these people the way you think.''

''So that's why they all love him.''

''And because he's never stopped giving. He's like family. Roque's father hung out with the governor. Roque hangs out with all kinds.''

''Including you.''

''And you.''

Elena rushed back in the house to change.

''If he hadn't married Rosita, Elena would probably be dead.''

Ritz didn't know how to reply.

When Roque sat down by them, Chainsaw stood up. ''Gotta go, *hombre*.''

''What were you telling her—''

''Not much, *hombre*. Not much. Sorry I missed the wedding. Next time...''

''There won't be a next time,'' Roque whispered. ''This is for keeps.'' Then he kissed Ritz full on the lips.

It was dark when they headed home wrapped in each other's arms.

"See, I can, too, make supper," he said.

"Yes. Which means we're going to be so happy," she whispered sleepily, hugging Roque more tightly. "Forever and ever."

She put her head against his chest.

A split second later somebody shot at her.

The bullet shattered the windshield and shredded the upholstery beside her right shoulder. She jumped as more bullets zinged into her side of the truck.

With one hand, Roque spun the wheel to the left. With the other, he ripped off her seat belt. "Get down. On the floorboard! Now! Close your eyes! I'm going to knock a bigger hole in the windshield so I can drive!"

He swiped his hand through the webbed glass, sending a shower of sparkling glass into his lap. When he slammed his boot down hard on the accelerator, the truck leaped forward.

Ritz tried to make sense of her scrambled thoughts. "Who was shooting at you?"

"At you!"

"Who shoots at people around here."

"One guess. Who hates us both?"

"Your father?"

"He's shot at me before. He can go really really nuts."

"And like you tolerate this?"

"I thought we had him under control. We took his wheels away. We take his food out to him."

"But he's a lunatic."

"Don't worry. He's never going to do it again. I'll take care of him. Tonight."

"Why don't you just call the sheriff?"

"He's my father. I'll take care of this my way."

"And you said you weren't macho."

She tried to get up, but he had a death grip on her curls and forced her head to stay down. "Not till we get home—'' He released his grip as he skidded to a stop in front of the garage, missing the trash can by an inch.

''Show-off.''

''I wanted you to see that.''

He pulled her into his arms and held her close. Then they got out, and she stuck her fingers into the holes in her door.

''Big holes,'' she said.

''Big bullets.'' He frowned.

''Impressive,'' she said. ''Neat line.''

''He was a helluva shot in his prime.''

''Not bad for someone so drunk.''

Roque didn't say anything. He was staring at the bullet holes, a puzzled look on his dark face.

24

"I don't want you to go," Ritz said, clinging to him.

"Believe me, *querida,* I'd rather stay."

He'd been standing at the door for five whole minutes, holding her, stroking her, trying to calm her down. But the more he talked, the more tightly she clung.

"The sooner I go see about him, the sooner I get back."

"What if we're wrong? What if it wasn't him?"

"Who the hell else could it be?"

"I don't know. But we didn't see him. We're guessing. I really think we should call the sheriff."

"He's done it before. So, lock all the doors. Keep the shades down. And I'll be back before you know it. I'll call Pablo to check on you—"

"Leave your cell phone on, so I can call—"

He kissed her hard.

"Wait!"

"When I get back, I want to taste every inch of you."

She smiled. "I love you so much."

Then he was already racing out the door.

Benny's trailer wasn't that far if you knew the back roads.

The moon went behind a cloud. When it came out,

Roque was roaring up his father's driveway on his bike. By day, huge oaks shaded the trailer. By night the shadows were so dark that despite his extraordinary night vision, Roque could barely see.

Even before he climbed the concrete stairs and rattled the doorknob, the silence that wrapped the house felt sinister. No night bugs sang.

It was too quiet. Deathly still.

All of a sudden, Roque felt the presence of evil. Even before he pushed on the door, he was sure somebody was watching him.

Then the smell hit him. He reeled backward engulfed by flies and the rotting stench of flesh decomposing.

His father was dead.

"What the hell—" he murmured in horror. His nemesis was gone—but what new evil lurked in the shadows. Or maybe it was not new...maybe it had always been there.

"It wasn't him. It was me," said a familiar voice behind him.

Roque didn't even feel the blow. He was falling, and his cell phone was ringing.

"Ritz—"

"You can't save her," said the horrible voice.

Roque didn't feel the second blow that sent him spinning into darkness.

He closed his eyes, and everything went still.

"Ritz!"

Ritz was staring at the clock on the mantel, frantically punching in Roque's cell phone number for the third time, when the lights went out.

"Ohhhh!"

The furniture and drapes took on weird ghostly shapes. Her hands began to shake so badly, she dropped the phone. Sinking to her knees, she groped along the edge of the bed, gasping with relief when her fingers closed around the cool plastic receiver.

She jabbed at the button, but there wasn't a dial tone.

Dread filled her. She'd called Roque three times and gotten his voice mail. Which meant either he or somebody else had turned off his cell phone.

The phone fell through her fingers to the carpet.

What if the shooter wasn't Benny? What if Roque was wrong? What if whoever it was…was…

She heard a sound outside and went wild with panic.

Get a grip. It's probably nothing. Just your imagination working overtime.

A bullet through her windshield and five big bullet holes in her door weren't nothing.

"Where's my cell phone?"

"Downstairs. In my purse," she whispered, answering her own question.

"Can't go down there!"

"Have to go down there!"

What if the shooter had Roque?

Her heart was racing as she moved stealthily down the long hall and then down the stairs. It was all she could do to tamp down her fear when somebody threw a patio chair through the glass door.

Glass shattered. Grabbing her purse off the back of a chair, she flew out the front door and raced for the garage only to find all four of the tires of her Honda slashed.

In a panic she ran toward the barn, fumbling in her purse for her cell phone the whole way. When she found it, she tried to remember Pablo's number.

Somebody had let the horses out. As always Long John was into mischief. He stood under the light in the door, waving something that looked like a snake. When she got closer, she saw that it was the hose from the submersible pump Roque had used to repair the hot tub when her mother had visited.

"How did you get that? Where's Buttercup, you big rascal?"

Long John munched plastic hose while batting it back and forth.

"Come on, boy..."

She had to get to Pablo or to the road and get help. Buttercup and the other horses were nowhere to be seen. She had to ride him.

Remembering Roque's threat to shoot him if she did so, she stared into Long John's sweet, dark eyes and then gently pulled the hose away and patted him.

"Nobody's going to shoot you. Nobody..."

Did anything in the whole world shine like a black horse? He was so beautiful. She couldn't bear the thought of him dying. "I have to ride you, you sweet devil."

Pungent and foul smelling, the barn was really a mess. Long John had torn the grain buckets off the wall, stepped on everybody's salt blocks, and defecated in the tack room.

Ignoring these crimes, she grabbed a red saddle blanket and a tooled Western saddle. Curious as always, Long John clomped inside behind her.

"Get back! I have to get away, and you, you big rascal, you're the only means of transportation."

Quickly she had the stallion saddled. No sooner was she out of the barn than she hit a trot and headed for Pablo's house, which was a mile down by the break to the west. Only when she got there, his house was dark, his doors locked, and his truck gone.

She'd wasted precious time. Her only hope now was the road.

And her cell phone. She dialed 9-1-1. The girl on the switchboard wanted to keep her talking, but she couldn't ride and talk, so she gave her the essential information, her location, and the fact that somebody, *no! she wasn't sure who,* was trying to kill her. Then she called her parents but got their machine.

After her daddy's gruff message, she left one of her own. "Daddy, oh, Daddy, somebody's trying to kill me. Roque thought his father had gone nuts again and went down to deal with him...but somebody came to the house...slashed my tires—" The recorder beeped, cutting her off.

Feeling panicky, she slipped the phone back inside the pocket of her jeans.

She was on her own.

As if sensing her desperation, Long John put his head down and ran like the wind until they got to that place on the edge of the brush that was steep and rocky. She pulled back on the reins, and they picked their way up to the road. At the gate, she headed down the road for her parents' house.

She trotted at least a mile without a single car passing. Not that that was strange, considering the private road served only the two ranches and their ranch hands. Just as she approached the turnoff to the Keller Ranch, headlights loomed behind her. She tried to get Long John as far off the road as she could, but he was in no mood for headlights or the scary sound of whistling tires.

He began to buck, and she fought to keep his head up. Holding both reins in her left hand, she reached up and tried to grab hold of the headstall. He kept rearing, and every time, he hit the ground so hard, her teeth rattled. Suddenly she looked down, and it was like she was riding a horse with his head cut off. She pulled, both hands on the reins, but it was no use. He bucked again, lunging forward in to black space. Another forward jump and she was flying over his head.

She came down in soft sand and sticker burrs. As she

stood up, she saw the last of his shiny black tail as he streaked back to Blackstone Ranch.

Then Irish said, "Sorry about that. Wouldn't have come up on you so fast if I'd known you were out for a midnight ride."

He stuck a hand that was as rough as saddle leather down and pulled her to her feet. That was the luckiest fall she'd ever had. The baby was fine. She was sure. Just as she was sure she'd never been so glad in all her life to see anybody.

"Oh, Irish!" She threw herself into his strong arms. "Irish, you've got to take me to Mother and Daddy's. We've got to get the sheriff. Somebody's trying to kill me."

He stared at her in wonder.

"Everything's going to be just fine. Don't you worry." His craggy face hardened, but his deep voice was as soothing as always.

She felt safe with him. So safe.

For the first time in hours.

Until he kept going at her parents' turnoff.

"Irish, where are we going—"

When he didn't reply, she stared at him.

His craggy profile was the same as ever. And yet...

"Irish—"

He sped up.

And then she knew.

"It's not Benny Blackstone," she whispered. "Irish? Why? Why Irish?"

Roque roared up to his dark house and yelled her name. From the shadows a black horse nickered to him. Then Long John danced toward him. He was saddled and dragging long leather reins. The sweaty stallion was chewing his bit, drooling. He'd been ridden hard.

"Dios."

He pulled his pistol out of his waistband and took aim at the beautiful black head.

Long John, his dark eyes trusting him completely, stared straight at the gun.

Roque pulled the trigger.

Irish was weaving erratically, his truck gathering speed.

"Irish, where are you going? What are you doing? Slow down!"

When he got to the intersection, she yanked at her door handle. He grabbed her by the hair and pulled with maniacal strength.

"Don't even think about it," he muttered as he veered to the left.

"Not Dead Man's Curve," she whispered, shaken even after he let her go. "What are you doing? Speak to me, Irish. Speak!"

"My name isn't Irish. I was a doctor. A surgeon. Dr. R. D. Meyer. In Houston."

"Of R.D. Meyer Heart Institute?"

He nodded. "Your father-in-law took that life away by telling lies in a courtroom. He twisted the law and defiled my reputation and me. Afterward, my hands started to shake. I had what used to be called a nervous breakdown. I couldn't operate. I was trained to save lives, not to take them. He destroyed me, so I came here years ago to destroy him and everything that is his."

"But I'm not him. He hated me...."

"I was there the night Caleb died. I watched you dance with him in the school gym. I saw how jealous Jet was because she'd slept with Caleb. So, I chased Caleb from the school. I wanted to kill him because he slept with her, but I lacked the nerve then. I wanted him to die...because of Jet. I saw him use her one night in your beach house.

Even so, when it came down to it, I was too big a wimp to kill him. But I watched him die.''

''You saved Steve. You're not a killer. You're not.''

He laughed. The back wheels slid onto the shoulder and popped gravel.

''Oh, you're wrong. I've got blood on my hands now. I shot your father-in-law. Finally. It felt good. He stinks worse than a dead pig, too.''

She gasped.

The truck weaved all the way off the road, thumping through rocks and tall grass. Her heart began to pound. ''And you shot at me?''

''Because you're pregnant.''

Her mind raced frantically. ''Who told—''

''Fiona. Silly fool! She's thrilled. She doesn't seem to realize about breeding. Bad blood will out.''

She risked a quick glance at the speedometer. He was doing ninety.

''It's not too late to stop this crazy...''

''Shut up! First he got Buster, then me. Buster and I were in medical school together. I loved him like a brother. Revenge has been a long time coming. For all his guts and cussed stubbornness, your father couldn't do what needed doing, and for a long time, neither could I. Until now. I guess as you get older, you have less to lose. I don't know.''

''This is some sort of weird suicide mission, isn't it?''

''They'll think it's an accident. With any luck Roque will get stuck for murdering his father.''

The truck skidded out of control.

''Oh, God...''

Her hand inadvertently touched the bulge in her pocket.

''When you came down those stairs after Josh's funeral and Blackstone said he was marrying you—a Keller, defiling you— When I realized you were pregnant—again— Something snapped.''

Slipping her fingers around her cell phone and punching it on, she tried to talk to him calmly.

''I'm a Keller. Surely you don't want to kill Buster's niece, Art's daughter. Art's only grandchild.'' Blindly she stabbed at the numbers, hoping to get Roque.

''If she's pregnant by a lousy Blackstone, I do. Caleb's death destroyed Benny. So, even though I didn't murder the boy, I was fairly content until I saw you with Blackstone at the beach house a couple of months back.

''You saw us?''

''If you hadn't gotten pregnant, you wouldn't have to die.''

''And Roque?''

''I hope he rots from the inside out with grief for you and the baby just like his father rotted after Caleb died. I know what that's like...dying by bitter inches. My wife left me because of Blackstone.''

Yellow highway signs that warned traffic to slow down streamed past in a frightening blur. When she lifted the cell phone, they were hurtling toward Dead Man's Curve at suicidal speed.

''Roque!'' she screamed. ''Dead Man's Curve... Irish... Help...''

Then she lunged for the keys and tried to pull them out of the ignition. She grabbed for the gearshift just as they catapulted around the hairpin curve.

Irish seized the buckle of her seat belt. He was unlatching it so she'd die.

Her only chance was to make him crash before he succeeded.

She grabbed the wheel and sent the truck flying toward a fringe of trees to the right. They bounced over rocks, skidded wildly. The truck tipped onto its side, and she screamed. Then they rolled.

Afterward the world was white and still. She was on Buttercup, her arms outstretched. Roque held her, and Caleb was running behind.

She was flying.

She was free.

She was dead.

The Harley roared into the night. Roque leaned forward when he saw the eerie orange glow on the other side of Dead Man's Curve.

His mind froze.

She was already dead. And so was their baby.

He was too late.

In the split second before he made the turn he remembered the feel of her eyes burning him from the darkness that first night. He remembered flying with Caleb and her. They were dancing in Matamoros. Again they were at their baby's grave. She was sick at Josh's funeral. He had hated her and loved her, but most of all he had loved her.

Dios. He slowed when he saw the warning signs.

Then he saw the flames.

25

She opened her eyes. She was lying in the grass on the side of the road beside a small wooden cross. The next thing she saw was Roque.

"How did I get here?" she whispered.

"Be still, the ambulance is on its way."

"*Our* baby…"

"Everything's going to be all right."

"Hold me."

"Always, always," he said.

"Only you," she whispered.

"Only you," he agreed. "I love you. When I found Long John—"

The anguish in his eyes terrified her all over again. "You didn't shoot him…."

"I thought about it."

"Oh, God—"

"But I couldn't."

"I do love you." Suddenly she felt very tired. "I—I crawled through the window. I—I smelled gasoline. I—I didn't even try to get Irish out. It was just like Caleb."

"It wasn't your fault…either time."

"I couldn't help him. I was too afraid...for the baby...."

"*Our* baby," he whispered gently.

"Say it again."

"*Ours,*" he repeated, tears in his voice. "*Ours.*"

His voice washed over her and she lost consciousness in his arms.

When she next opened her eyes, she was in a hospital bed, her arm attached to an IV. Dr. Wanner's white-coated back was to her. Her father's voice boomed from the hall.

"If she needs blood, I'll donate. So will her brother, Steve."

"Roque—"

"Right here, *querida.*" Roque came forward. Leaning over his wife, he pressed her hand between his strong brown fingers.

"And Mother and Daddy?"

"It's a regular party out there," Dr. Wanner said with a grin.

When her father pushed the door open, Roque got up to go.

"Stay," Ritz pleaded.

"But your parents have been waiting out there for hours. They need some time...alone with just you."

"Daddy...please tell him...you want him to stay. Please...for my sake. For *your* grandchild's sake."

An interminable moment seemed to pass as Art stuffed his hands into his pockets and said, "Stay, Blackstone," in the sort of gruff undertone he might use with a dog. Then a sheepish smile flashed across his thin white face. His voice lost its usual edge. "Please... Blackstone."

"Roque," Ritz corrected.

"But—I don't belong...."

"Hell, you're family," Art said. "If you don't belong, who the hell does?" And that seemed to settle it.

Ritz took Roque's hand and held on tight.

"Everything that happened tonight was my fault," Art said.

"No, Daddy…"

"But I knew about Irish. Gave him the job after his breakdown because Blackstone ruined him and he wanted to start over doing something else. He grew up on a ranch, you see. He was as good a foreman as he was a doctor."

"It wasn't your fault. It was his," Roque said.

"What about our baby?"

"The baby is going to be fine…if you take it easy…and spend a lot of time in bed," Dr. Wanner said.

At the word, bed, Roque squeezed her hand and winked. "Does that mean no riding black stallions?" he asked, his voice wicked and soft.

"Definitely," agreed Dr. Wanner.

"I can come over and help out any time you need me during the day," Fiona said.

"So can I," Art added.

"That leaves me with the night duty." Roque squeezed her hand and winked enthusiastically again.

"When can I go home?" Ritz murmured.

Irish and Benny were buried the same brilliant day in Campo Santo. For the first time since Buster had died, Blackstones and Kellers mourned together beneath the purple shade of the oaks.

While Roque and Ritz held Jet, Art gave a moving eulogy for Irish. He focused on Irish's life as a heart surgeon and then on his second life as a splendid ranch foreman. When both funerals were over, Fiona had everybody in the county to the Keller ranch house.

Ritz wore a short, tight black dress that showed off her

hips and legs. Roque hadn't touched her since he'd brought her home from the hospital, and it was driving her crazy.

She wanted to stir him up a bit.

The dress was working, too. Roque couldn't take his eyes off her dark mesh stockings.

"Why'd you wear that?" he whispered in a low agonized tone. He'd come up behind her so he could cup her buttocks without anybody seeing.

"Behave. We're at a funeral," she teased.

"If you'd wanted me to behave, you wouldn't have worn that hot little black number."

"Do you really think I'm hot?"

"As a pistol."

"Dr. Wanner said we could…if we're careful."

"*Dios.* I can't wait to take over my night duties."

"How about an afternoon preview…now."

"With everybody watching?"

"We're newlyweds. We can get away with a lot."

So, he kissed her in front of everybody, and when he was done, people were smiling. Even her father.

"Looks like the feud is over," Roque whispered, his breath warm against her lips. "Thanks to you."

"Good thing, too. I'm in the mood for love, Blackstone."

"What do you say we go home early."

"I say this pregnant lady needs a nap."

"Not by herself, I hope?"

In answer, she kissed him again, and so enthusiastically, all doubt about her intentions fled his mind.

Epilogue

On with the dance! Let joy be unconfined;
No sleep till morn, when Youth and Pleasure meet
To chase the glowing Hours with flying feet.

—George Gordon, Lord Byron
—Childe Harold's Pilgrimage, III.22

Epilogue

Bodies never lie. At least theirs hadn't. Always, always they had wanted each other.

Roque and Ritz were dancing. Christmas Eve was gray and misty, but the Keller ranch house was cheerily ablaze. Fires burned in all the downstairs fireplaces. Its red lights twinkling, the spruce Christmas tree in the parlor dwarfed all the other furnishings and filled the house with its fragrant smell.

Laughter and music and gaiety were the order of the evening. After all, the house was stuffed to overflowing with Blackstones, Kellers and Moyas.

"Your family's loud," Ritz whispered to Roque as he whirled her in his arms. "Have I ever told you that?"

"Oh, no. Never...not even once."

They laughed as they danced.

"And your father's bossy," he whispered against her earlobe. "Not to mention your brother, Steve." Steve had recovered fully from his injuries, and had his own career and life, but was still very vocal when it came to family business.

"He lets you run both ranches, doesn't he?"

"With a lot of advice from the sideline."

"Helpful advice, I'm sure."

"Very."

"Good thing Izzy has them all distracted in the nursery," Ritz said. "We don't get much time to dance anymore."

Izzy, short for Isadora, had been born early, and it was a good thing because she was a large, mature baby. A good baby, too, who slept most nights through. Not that either of her parents minded when she woke them up to nurse. They would both run to see about her together.

Now that the Moyas were here for their Christmas visit, every feeding at night was a regular midnight party. When Ritz sat down with Izzy in the rocker, sometimes as many as thirty Moyas, of various ages, surrounded her. Elena was so crazy about her little sister, she came over every day.

"*Mamacita* is so wild about Izzy, she is thinking she might retire in Texas on the ranch," Roque told Ritz.

"She says she wants to baby-sit," Ritz said, "so I can get back to my nursing."

"She wants to run our lives. That's what she wants."

"She loves you."

"I'm so lucky," he whispered. "She loves you, too."

"She's mellowed since Izzy."

"There's nothing like a baby to bring love into a house," he said.

"*Our* baby. Even when you hated me, I loved it when you said *our* baby."

"*Querida.*" They stopped dancing, and he kissed her. "I never hated you. Never for a single minute."

Art banged on the table in the gallery. "Attention, everybody! I've got a surprise."

Everybody ran to see what it was. Ritz lingered in her husband's arms, so she was one of the last to enter the gallery. When she did she gasped. For between the paintings of her great-grandmothers, there was a new painting of her in her bridal gown.

"Daddy?"

He smiled at her just like he used to when she'd been his perfect daughter.

"What's my picture, er, my painting doing there...on the wall reserved for great Keller heroines?"

"Don't you know?"

She shook her bright head, staring at Roque in confusion.

"You taught us that to love was more powerful than to hate. You ended the feud between the Kellers and the Blackstones. Because of you, the ranch is whole again."

Was that a tear glistening in her daddy's eye? She would never know because his thin, tired face began to swim. Her own eyes were full of joyous tears.

Then Roque's arms came around her, and he said, "Elena says Izzy's hungry."

"Oh, darling...darling..."

"Why are you crying, *querida?*"

"Because I'm so happy we're all together."

"I love you, *querida.*"

Hand in hand, they mounted the stairs together. Then he shooed Elena and the throng of black-haired Moyas out of the nursery and lifted their black-haired daughter from the cradle he'd carved by hand.

"Just this once, on Christmas Eve, I want to be alone with my wife and daughter."

Ritz and he looked into each other's eyes for the space of three heartbeats. And then she unbuttoned her bodice, and they concentrated on their hungry daughter.

When the baby began to suckle at her breast, Ritz closed her eyes. She'd waited so long for love, so long for this child. So long for Roque.

"I love you both," he whispered.

"I love you more," she replied.

"Ditto."

She sighed. It was so wonderful to belong to each other, to this place, to have their own home, to have their families united behind them.

"Only you," she said.

"Only you," he repeated.

He held his hand out to her. She took it and drew him near.

Love was a risk.

But it was worth taking.

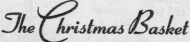

ANN MAJOR

66623 WILD ENOUGH ___ $5.99 U.S. ___ $6.99 CAN.
FOR WILLA
66548 INSEPARABLE ___ $5.99 U.S. ___ $6.99 CAN.

(limited quantities available)

TOTAL AMOUNT $_____
POSTAGE & HANDLING $_____
($1.00 for one book; 50¢ for each additional)
APPLICABLE TAXES* $_____
TOTAL PAYABLE $_____
(check or money order—please do not send cash)

To order, complete this form and send it, along with a check
or money order for the total above, payable to MIRA Books®,
to: **In the U.S.:** 3010 Walden Avenue, P.O. Box 9077, Buffalo,
NY 14269-9077; **In Canada:** P.O. Box 636, Fort Erie, Ontario,
L2A 5X3.

Name:_____
Address:_____ City:_____
State/Prov.:_____ Zip/Postal Code:_____
Account Number (if applicable):_____
075 CSAS

*New York residents remit applicable sales taxes.
Canadian residents remit applicable GST and provincial taxes.

MIRA®

Visit us at www.mirabooks.com MAM1002BL